Just a Bunch of Bluebells

Maureen J Bell

Mindblowing Books Ltd © 2019

MINDBLOWING
BOOKS LTD

Foreword

The book you're about to read has been on quite a journey. It began way back, just over a decade ago in the mind of my late Mum, Maureen Josephine Bell. Late in 2008, Mum started writing down her events from her childhood. Events that happened in World War II. Over time, Mum built up a picture of an exciting story. *Just a Bunch of Bluebells* can best be described as semi-autobiographical. With dramatic license accounted for, most of the occurrences happened. It is a breath-taking story founded on extraordinary true events, that even after some sixty-six years, had remained as vivid in my Mum's mind as when she'd lived through them as a child in the war.

Mum's stunning memory supported by her painstaking hours of underpinning research enabled the creation of this book. It may not seem like a great feat. Many people write books these days. However, consider this. Mum started this book when she was seventy-three. She enrolled in a local college to learn how to use word processing software on a pc and then typed the book. Mum continued writing, revising and editing this book even after she was diagnosed with Vascular Dementia just four years later. Recalling the past and writing it down helped Mum push against the devastating effects of Dementia.

This book gave her focus. She literally lived to write. She told everyone about her book, and it gave her something to be proud about at a time when Dementia was starting to whittle away the person she was.

In the first year of her Dementia, she still gripped hold of her ability to write. By the second year, that wonderful ability had been ripped from her. She'd pick up a pen and stare at it. Deep inside her the words were still there, but the capacity to put them down had gone. Two years later she lost the battle completely and passed away.

Her pride and joy was left unfinished.

This was not what Mum would have wanted. I knew that, and I was determined to do something about it. Between my Editor, Ceri Savage and I, we re-edited and finished the story; all the time staying loyal to Mum's words. These were her experiences, her life. I didn't want to change what she'd written. Just make it complete, as she would have wanted.

In a world where notions of hope and faith are a scarcity, and heart is nothing more than an emoji, this book shows the true meaning of having a strong heart, faith and hope. Much of the book is seen through the eyes of a young child who had to grow up very fast. It shows the indomitable power of the human spirit and the courage, when we're tested, that exists within us all.

My regret is that Mum passed away before she saw this book in print. But as I'm typing this now, I feel somewhere, she is watching, and she knows that I have taken her dream and made it a reality. Her guiding hand has manifested itself in many ways, not least in the cover art, provided by Sam Nash, who depicted a scene from the book exactly, somehow capturing my Mum as a child with her Mother (my Grandma), without reading the book.

If Mum hadn't been struck down by Dementia, she would have finished her manuscript. I can only think about the many people who have been denied the opportunity of doing something they love, and never get to see the end result. Dementia is a wicked disease, and I care passionately about finding a cure. It is for that reason that half of the royalties of every sale of *Just a Bunch of Bluebells* will be donated to two Dementia-based Charities: Dementia UK and Alzheimer's Society.

Thank you for buying this book, and for helping to create the day when Dementia is eradicated forever.

I'll get off my soapbox now and let Mum take you on a journey of the incredible.

Michelle Medhat, 2019

Prologue

June 2009

Rain splattered on the windscreen. Mary drove anxiously. She detested driving alone at night. It had been a long, tiring day and she had anticipated making an early start but unfortunately her sister, Jo, thought otherwise. It was always the same whenever they were together, all the chitter chatter, impossible to get away.

She had driven non-stop from Derbyshire and now she was beginning to feel the strain. Mary decided to turn off the motorway and onto an A road where she could find a place to stay for the night. On the smaller road, without the illumination of other cars, Mary found it difficult to see and even more troubling to focus. The rain poured down delivering more gray to an already gloomy autumn evening.

Then, quite suddenly, the roar of an engine shattered through Mary's concentration. The car made an appearance from a small side country lane. The car came in close, skirting her own vehicle by a few inches and almost clipping her mirror. Mary knew the driver must be high and out for kicks. Four young lads leant out the window as their car came close, and they screamed obscenities at her, laughing. They shot in front of her into middle of the road. The boys skidded their car around in a circle and raced forward, loud music blasting out the windows.

Mary looked over her shoulder, shivering, and heard them grind to a halt behind her. Then they revved up and sped ahead, skirting close to her driver's side, virtually touching her tires. Then, in a clearing further up the road, they swerved again, revving up hard.

Mary couldn't see anyone else around. Her solitary position had made her their target. She had to get away. She had to get somewhere crowded. But, to do that, she had to get past them.

Panic flooded through her tired body, but she knew she had to keep a cool head. With no other cars on the road, their recklessness increased by the second. Mary gritted her teeth with determination, slammed on the accelerator, and forced her mini down the road at a speed she doubted the little car could take.

Fueled by a lack of witnesses, they spun their back wheels, kicking up dust, and turned around to face her car hurtling towards them. Their engine screamed as they floored the accelerator. Mary knew they still had their handbrake on. Headlights flashed like demonic eyes in the dark.

Oh God, thought Mary, they're playing a game of chicken.

Instinctively, she pulled off the accelerator. But as she did it, she rationalized her position. *If I stop, they'll get out and attack me. If I continue I may be crushed to pieces.* Mary had a split second to decide on the lesser of those two evils.

Mary swallowed. She could see their headlights blazing.

Frantically, her brain worked like lightning. She was plunging down towards the joy riders at fifty-five miles per hour. To do a normal U turn, she'd have to stop and turn in the road. By that time, they would have caught up with her or collided with her car. Breathing deeply, she remembered what her son-in-law, Sam, had taught her.

Mary lifted her foot off the accelerator. Immediately, the weight transferred to the front of the car, reducing the load on the back tires. In parallel, Mary spun the steering wheel into a tight lock to the right and pressed down on the clutch. She tugged up the handbrake and pressed in the release button, and then dropped it down as the back of the car swung in a tight radius at speed. Mary let the steering wheel feed through her hands quickly as the car took up position in the opposite direction. She gunned the accelerator, released the clutch up smoothly, and zoomed off in the opposite direction.

Mary dared to glance in the rear mirror and saw no one following. She breathed out. Her speed had gone to seventy-five miles per hour. But she didn't care about the speed limit. She just wanted to get somewhere safe and away from those dreadful thugs.

Back on the A27 again, Mary didn't know where she was going. The rain was heavier and she couldn't see a few feet in front of the car. Her body felt like she had avoided certain death. Mary started to sweat. The intensity of the situation fell upon her as she drove. The steering wheel slipped through her wet hands as she tried desperately to think positively.

Suddenly, from out of the cold, gray sheet of rain, lights came into view on her left-hand side. Mary slowed down. She could just make out a town sign that read 'Bursledon'.

The lights belonged to a pub: The Coach and Horses.

Thank heavens for civilization at last, thought Mary.

The pub was situated on the corner of a lane and enshrouded by trees and foliage.

Mary turned into the car park and checked for places. But it wasn't full. She stepped out of the car then reached in the back and grabbed her weekender, just as the heavens opened and soaked her completely. Whilst she pressed the lock, another car pulled in, loud music blasting.

Mary swept a glance behind her. But the interior lights were off and the rain pelted down to obscure any clear picture of who was in the car. Mary swallowed hard. She ran across the driveway, her weekender and handbag slipping down into the crook of her arm to eventually dangle from her wrist.

Mary thought she heard something drop to the ground. But she didn't stop to find out. She wanted to get into the pub as quickly as possible.

There were only a few people in The Coach and Horses. A couple sat on high stools at the bar, and a small group were seated at candle lit tables that extended the full length of the windows. The large, bright windows were the reason Mary could see the pub so easily from the road. She hastily made her way to the bar. The barman clocked her and came promptly to her assistance.

"Good evening," he said cheerfully. "What can I get you?"

Mary forced a smile. "Good evening. A large cognac, please." Mary held a beat, and then added, "Oh, no, on second thoughts, better make that a black coffee. I'm driving."

"One coffee it will be then," said the elderly barman, smiling at her.

His questioning eyes searched Mary's, clearly asking 'Is something wrong?' but Mary deigned not to invite discussion. The barman shrugged, turned, and made his way to the other end of the bar where he kept the coffee percolator.

Loud music at the entrance caught Mary's attention. She gulped, fearing the worst, but breathed out with relief when a middle-aged man and woman entered, followed by two teenage girls.

"I'd like a G and T please, Mum," stated one of the girls, giggling.

"No. Definitely not," said the man. "And you can turn off that racket." He pointed to his daughter's phone. "Otherwise I'll take you both straight home!"

Good heavens, just an ordinary family. You fool, Mary, old girl. This won't do. You've got to pull yourself together.

She glanced down the bar to where the barman was approaching with her coffee and noticed a card placed on the counter; it read B&B.

That's it, I'm staying, thought Mary. I'm in no fit state to drive home tonight.

"There you are. That'll be two pounds to you." The elderly barman smiled. "Bad night to be out driving," he said. "I wouldn't put a dog out in this."

"I agree. It wasn't by choice. I've driven down from Derbyshire. I'm afraid I've left it rather late to drive all the way home, especially in this weather. I see you are a B&B. Do you happen to have a room for tonight?"

"Yes, I have a couple of rooms. But I'm afraid they're rather cold. My wife's away for the weekend, and silly old me forgot to put on the heating. If you care to step this way, I'll show you both of the rooms. When you've decided, I'll find you some kind of heater."

"Oh, that's quite all right. Please don't bother," said Mary anxiously. "I'll take either one."

The barman nodded, grinning. "This is a large house and I'm not given to allowing my guests to catch a cold. Keep an eye on the bar, Rita. I'm just popping upstairs to show this lady around."

"Okay, Bill," echoed Rita, the barmaid.

Bill led the way up the eighteenth-century staircase that was crying out for a bit of care and attention. The whole ambience of the place filled Mary with warmth, despite the implied lack of heating. The barman looked quizzically at Mary as she chewed her bottom lip. She was still deeply agitated by her traumatic experience that night. Mary knew, sooner or later, he was going to ask her if she was okay. But despite wanting to regale the events of the evening, in a strange way, Mary was embarrassed. She just wanted to forget the whole thing ever happened.

"Here we are then," said the barman, beaming from cheek to cheek. "This is the smaller of the two. The larger one is across the landing."

Mary walked into the room. "Oh, this will be fine. It's a delightful little room. To tell you the truth, I'm so tired I could sleep anywhere tonight."

"Yes, I can see you've had a long journey. You must be exhausted. I'll just go and get the heater." He turned, and then paused, and looked back. "By the way, the name's William Howard, but everyone calls me Bill. Are you hungry?"

Mary nodded.

"Well, we have bar food. It's not a great selection as the misses is away and she's usually in the kitchen. But it should keep the hunger pangs at bay."

"Thanks, Bill. And I'm Mary, Mary Busher Mackenzie."

"Good to meet you, Mary. I'll just get that heater and warm up this place for you."

Once alone, Mary walked across the little bedroom to draw the pretty, check curtains that matched the carpet and duvet quilt.

She stood for a moment looking out at the dreadful, stormy night. Rain hit against the window and the dark trees swayed as the wind issued its mournful cry. Yet, through the dim, beneath the pub's sign, Mary could see the name of the town again. Bursledon. Something about that name seemed to Mary to be synonymous with dreadful weather.

Something echoed from her past. A hazy blur of memories long since forgotten.

Yet how could it possibly be? She had never been here before in her life. Or did she live here in some kind of past life? Or was it all a nightmare and she was slowly going out of her mind?

Mary walked over to the bed and sat down holding her head in her hands. Those crazy thugs had terrified her much more than she had realized.

A knock came at the door and Mary jumped, her nerves fried and on edge. Cautiously, Mary pulled the door open. She found Bill standing in the hallway cradling an electric radiator.

"There we are. This will keep you nice and warm. Sorry I've been so long. It took me quite a while to find it. I never know where my wife puts things." He glanced at her, that questioning look flaring in his eyes. Mary knew he was going to ask her. "Why, my dear, are you all right?"

"Yes, I'm quite all right. But, you know, I told you, I hate driving alone at night."

"Indeed you did. I keep telling my wife not to drive late at night. That's why I advised her to stay the night with her sister. You never know what to expect on the roads these days."

Mary paused, looking away from Bill, and shuddered.

"No…No, you don't, Bill."

She could feel his stare burning into her and she couldn't hold back. Mary launched into an account of what had happened and the narrow escape she'd had that night.

"Good heavens," said Bill in astonishment as Mary finished. "I'll get on to the local police right away. What bastards! Oh, please excuse my language, Mary. But I get so infuriated when I hear of anything like this. Why on earth didn't you tell me this before? I had a feeling something wasn't right the second I saw you."

Mary looked at Bill, at his soft, chubby features and kind, blue eyes, and she couldn't answer. Why on earth hadn't she said something? Maybe she was annoyed with herself for leaving it so late before she'd departed from her sister's house. She'd just not had the heart to tell Jo to shut up and let her leave. Perhaps she was angry for her inherent weakness of being too kind.

What did her dad used to say? "If you're too good, you're good for nothing!"

Certainly, if she'd cut short the many gossiping avenues her sister had lead her down, she'd be home right now, and she wouldn't have had to face off a pack of thugs trying to ram her off the road.

Bill, seeing Mary was lost for words, changed the subject.

"Anyway," he said in a kind manner, "you have a rest now and come down whenever you're ready. Or I can arrange to have something sent up? Whatever you wish, my dear."

"Why that's awfully kind of you, Bill. Thank you. But I really must come down and ring my family. It got so late and I had to leave my sister's in a rush, I rather stupidly left my mobile there. You do still have a public phone?"

"Yes, of course. It's just outside in the lobby." He glanced at his wristwatch. "I'm afraid I'm going to have to dash off now. It'll soon be closing time."

"Yes, and thank you so much for everything."

"Don't mention it. My pleasure." Bill opened the door to leave. Holding his hand on the knob, he turned. "I'm pleased you confided in me. Now don't you worry about anything. I'll get it all sorted."

Mary smiled. "You're more than kind, Bill. Thank you."

Mary was surprised by Bill's politeness. It was something of a rarity in these days of selfishness and self-obsession.

His mannerism took her mind back in time once again. Had she been there before? Wistfully, Mary glanced at herself in the dressing table mirror and grimaced on seeing her appearance.

My word, Mary old girl. You look an utter mess. You need a decent wash and brush up.

She'd always been proud of her looks and taken great pains to make herself youthful. Heading for sixty-five on her next birthday, she didn't look a day over fifty, and on a really good day, maybe forty-six.

Mary had always looked amazingly young for her age. But tonight had taken its toll. In the mirror, someone haggard and drawn stared back.

"Oh, well never mind," she said. "At least I'm still alive."

A sharp tap sounded on the door. Mary opened it. Rita the barmaid stood holding a tray of biscuits and a glass of cognac.

"Bill asked me to bring this up for you."

"Thank you. Pop it down there," said Mary, indicating to the small table by the window.

"Is there anything else I can get you, Mrs. Mackenzie, before I go home?"

"No, thank you. I shall be down in a few minutes. But this is going to go down a treat."

Rita smiled. "Great. Well, good night, Mrs. Mackenzie."

Mary sipped at her cognac and sat back in the chair beside the window. She was amazed at the kind hospitality she'd found at The Coach and Horses. She seriously doubted if one would receive such attention even in a five-star hotel.

She looked out the window into the blackness and shuddered. If she'd pulled off that handbrake turn incorrectly or just carried on driving, she'd have been dead. No question about it.

It felt to Mary that she'd had a taste of her own mortality that night. She picked up the glass and knocked back the cognac in one gulp. Not used to such a move, Mary made a face, but she could feel the warm liquid immediately soothing her fractured nerves. She stood up, lay down on the bed, and closed her eyes. She was finally feeling more relaxed.

With her eyes shut, everything seemed a little clearer. It was like pieces she never knew existed came together in a puzzle she knew she was destined to solve.

Her thoughts wandered into memories. Those of her parents. If only they were here on this mortal coil, they would have the answers, she realized sadly.

Such a very long time ago now and so much since had happened.

She'd married Andrew Mackenzie and moved to Scotland, where she had one daughter, Nina. Andrew had been an engineer. Now retired, they lived in the small village of Topsham in Devon.

Mary was unfamiliar with Hampshire and Dorset. She was born in Kent where she'd lived as a child. As far as she could recall, she'd never been to Bursledon. But something about the name called to her from a place in her mind she'd forgotten.

She remembered the small hamlet of Ebford in Devon where her parents had rented a small cottage, close to where they were now living in Topsham.

As a small child, Mary loved the peace and quiet of the Devonshire countryside.

Maybe that's why I pushed Andy to retire there, thought Mary, smiling.

Mary got up, saw the town sign again, and pushed herself hard to remember. Something was beginning to take shape. Now the scary haze had lifted from her eyes, she could see clearer.

Glancing at her wristwatch, Mary realized she'd been daydreaming.

My word, it's getting late. I'd better go down and have something to eat before Bill closes. And I need to ring home.

Mary looked at herself in the mirror once again. She ran her brush through her blonde hair, which was gradually turning gray. She applied some lipstick and mascara, and pouted in the mirror, and then nodded, satisfied with what she saw.

Mary had always been dress conscious. Despite the years floating by, she'd kept her trim figure, and her clothes displayed well on her tall, shapely form. She wore a sienna brown Karen Millen trouser suit with matching ankle boots. The jacket, finely cut, fell just over her waistline, and the trousers shaped around her, boosting and accentuating her already lovely figure.

She walked down the old, rustic staircase with an air of inherent elegance.

The bar was now empty except for Rita, who was just leaving with her boyfriend.

She glanced up at Mary admiringly. "Good night, Mrs. Mackenzie."

Mary spoke in a soft voice. "Oh, good night, Rita."

Bill smiled warmly as she approached the bar. "There you are, Mary. I think this could possibly be yours. It was handed in by the young girl who was here earlier with her parents. She said you dropped it in the driveway."

"Good gracious. I'd have been upset if I'd lost that," exclaimed Mary. "It was a gift from my daughter."

"It's a beautiful bracelet."

"Does that family come in here a lot?"

"Never seen them before," replied Bill, shaking his head.

"That's a pity. I'd like to have given her some kind of reward."

"I shouldn't worry about it, Mary. I doubt she'd have handed it in without a little encouragement from her parents. Kids these days, they're all the same."

Mary smiled. "Yes. Some of them. Anyway, I'm very pleased to have it. Well, if you'll excuse me, Bill, I'll just ring my family."

"Okay. Whilst you're doing that, I'll make some fresh sandwiches. What would you prefer, chicken or beef?"

"Oh, chicken. Thanks, Bill."

"By the way, Mary, you can use my mobile if you wish."

Mary realized Bill had been more than helpful already and had no wish to press his hospitality further.

"Thanks, Bill. But really, it's no problem for me. I'll head outside."

Mary walked leisurely out into the hall lobby to the phone booth. She dialed the number and glanced up at the double-glassed windows. With the dark shadows and swaying trees, it all looked terribly sinister outside.

Mary could see her reflection against the dark world that lay beyond the glass. She shivered and hurriedly swiped her credit card to use the phone. Her eyes fixed on the abyss of nothing outside. Inside, she dearly wished she'd taken up Bill's offer to use his mobile.

On the other end, a voice came on the line.

"Hello? Mary, is that you? We've been worried sick about you." Mary recognized the powerful, deep tone of her son-in-law, Sam. "Nina, it's your mother," he called.

Mary could see, in her mind, her daughter: a tall, blonde-haired woman in her mid-thirties with eyes of sparkling blue-gray.

"Mummy, where on earth are you?"

Mary was about to respond to her daughter when she glanced up to see two hideous-looking thugs wearing masks over their heads, peering in through the window in front of her.

"I must go now, Nina. I'll speak to you later."

"Mummy, what's wrong?"

Mary could hear the worried ring in her daughter's voice but she had to leave. Mary dashed out. The receiver was left dangling with Nina's voice echoing, "Mummy? Mummy, what's happening?"

Breathless, Mary ran into the bar.

"Bill!" she screamed.

"What is it, Mary?"

Mary swallowed, forcing herself to get the words out of her mouth. She turned and pointed to the double door.

"You've got thugs trying to break in."

"What?" said Bill.

Then he whistled and two German shepherds came scampering out of their cubbyhole.

"Mary, stay here. Leave this to me."

Mary knew she should have stayed where she was. But she couldn't. Ever the brave one, and feeling that Bill needed back up, she slowly followed and watched. In the lobby, Bill issued a word of command to the two dogs, who he called Eddy and Bobby.

Instantly, the dogs obeyed their master. They growled, baring their fangs, and started to bark ferociously. Mary watched as the two thugs, who'd been lurking outside, took one look at the snarling, fierce animals and fled.

Mary grinned, feeling victorious as Bill stood shaking his fists in the air.

"And don't come back here again or you'll know what you'll get."

Bill locked up and entered the bar with the dogs, patting them gently on their heads.

"Good boys. Better than a security alarm, these two. I'll get onto the old bill once again. This'll keep them on their toes for the rest of the night," said Bill. "Here you are, Mary. Have another one." Bill handed Mary another cognac to quell her shaking nerves. "My word, you've had your fill of scares for one day."

Mary sighed. "I sure have, Bill."

The police arrived within a few minutes. Mary handled their questions.

"Do you think the joy riders and those thugs trying to break in were connected, officer?" she asked.

The officer shrugged. "Could be. Not impossible." He turned to Bill "You did a great job with your dogs tonight but you gotta be careful and not take unnecessary risks. Especially at your age, grandad!"

When the police departed, Bill sneered. "Did you hear that young bobby, Mary? 'Don't take any risks, grandad.'" Bill sighed. "If we don't try and protect ourselves these days, who will?"

Mary sipped her cognac and nodded in agreement.

"What a night, eh?" continued Bill. "Anyway, never mind. How about those sandwiches, Mary? Do you still fancy them?"

"Yes please, Bill"

"That's the ticket, girl. It'll take more than a couple of thugs to scare you, eh, Mary?"

"Actually, Bill, I sensed something when I went out there."

"Really? Yet you still preferred to go out there rather than use my mobile. Why?"

"Well, you've been very kind and I had no wish to impose upon you. I can't quite describe it. I just had an awful feeling. But I knew I had to contain my fear. It's the way I was brought up. You understand?"

"You're very courageous, Mary."

Mary didn't answer. She looked at Bill and a slow smile took her over.

"Anyway, it's been quite a night," said Bill. "I just wonder sometimes what's going to be done about the crime in this country. Dammed thugs. They should bring back conscription or put them all in jail and throw away the key."

"I agree entirely. They have it all too easy these days. A little discipline never hurt anyone."

"Oh, how right you are, Mary. They wouldn't have had the chance to get away with it in my day. I was in the Second World War. A Royal Navy serving in the North Atlantic. I was only eighteen." Bill paused. "I'll never forget it. But listen to me going on. You don't want to hear about that after your ordeal tonight."

"Oh, yes I do, Bill. Please continue."

"No, sorry. It's too painful, even now as I speak of it."

He stopped talking and poured himself a tot of rum.

Mary, deep in thought, sat munching her sandwiches. She also seemed far away.

"Bill, I wonder whether you can tell me. Was there ever a Royal Marine Commando camp here during the war?"

"My word, I should think so. Just down the lane from here."

Mary looked, wide-eyed, at Bill, and whispered, "I somehow thought so."

"Yes. The whole area was a restricted zone to anyone who lived outside the village," continued Bill.

"I know," said Mary.

"You know? Well, I suppose you've read all about it in your school history books. Or seen it on TV. Most people have," said Bill.

"Yes. Most people have. I agree. But I was *actually here*. I was here a day before they embarked for Normandy."

"What? But I thought you told me that you had never been here before in your life?"

"Yes. That was before I started to piece things together. It was the wind and rain, you understand, Bill. It brought it all back to me."

"Well," said Bill, looking completely mystified, "you don't look the type to spin a yarn, and you've only had a couple of drinks. Anyway, there would be no point. However, I can scarcely believe it."

Mary's grin merged into a little laugh. "I really was here, Bill."

Bill shook his head, staring at Mary, disbelief erupting in his eyes as he took in her shapely, young form.

"How could you possibly have been here? Even if you were old enough, which I very much doubt, no one was allowed anywhere near the place."

"No mistake, Bill. I assure you I was there at the Royal Marines camp. I remember everything now as though it were yesterday, talking to the marines and so on. They were so kind and friendly. I'll tell you about it. If you're interested? However, I'm quite sure that you have more knowledge of the war then me and can give a better account of it. After all, I was just a child."

"Yes, you're quite right, Mary. I can remember so much. Too much, in fact. And most of it, I'd rather forget. I'm still curious to know what a little kid was doing in a Royal Marine Commando camp on the day before D-Day."

"It's quite amazing really. I thought I was going out of my mind a little while ago. I struggled to remember where I had seen this place before. I do have a vivid memory of the war years, but it was a long time ago, and so much was going on at the time. It all began when my father received his conscription papers..."

Chapter 1

March 1941

Terence Busher sat, forlorn and staring into space. His calling-up papers lay sprawled out on the table in front of him.

"I have known about this for some time now. I just didn't know quite how to tell you. It's the Royal Marines Portsmouth division."

His wife, Joanna, stared at him, unable to believe her ears.

"But surely there must be some mistake. I naturally assumed you'd be exempt at your age. I can't believe it, Terry."

"No mistake, darling. Older men than me are in the firing line, and thirty-five is no age."

She looked stunned. "What about your work with the MOD? Surely that's more important."

"I thought so but they need warm bodies."

"Oh, Terry, this is dreadful!"

Joanna Busher was a petite woman in her late twenties. Light, blonde hair fell to her shoulders and her deep, brown eyes sparkled even through the infiltrating pain.

"It's not the end of the world, darling."

Terry stood up from the table. He was tall and blond-haired with high cheek bones, a squared jawline, and emotion-packed eyes of blue-gray. He had more than enough charisma and charm to rival any film star from the silver screen, and his blonde hair was unusual for a man of his age.

"Try not to worry, my sweetheart. I hate to see you looking this way."

Joanna looked straight into his eyes and moved towards him. "Why you, Terry?"

"Why indeed? I'm afraid I have no idea. All I know is that I have to go. I suppose, with a little persuasion, they may have considered my work.

However, that's a big maybe. And you know me, Jo, the very thought of such an idea, well, it leaves a nasty taste in my mouth. I'm no shirker to my duty. You know that trying to get out of it would be inconceivable to me."

"I understand, Terry," she whispered dispiritedly.

Joanna knew him better than anyone. He'd never run away from what was expected of him. That was the problem. He was all about integrity. Doing one's duty. Uploading the right way. Her brown eyes swam like dark pools as she gazed up into his. Then, unable to stand, she melted into her husband's arms.

"What am I going to do without you?"

Terry had been the only son of Royal Naval officer Terrance Michael Busher. His mother had died following complications at his birth. His father, devastated by the loss of his precious wife, Mary, to whom he was devoted, took retribution on his son. He somehow came to the conclusion that his son, Terry, had been responsible for the death of his wife. Terrance came to hate his son. He completely disregarded his welfare and washed his hands of overseeing Terry's future progression.

Terry's father shut himself down and focused on a life in the military. He dedicated his entire life to serving his country. But he did not serve his son for one second of that time. Terry's formative years came and went, and his father showed no interest in the slightest. Had it not been for Terrance's brother, Thomas, taking pity on him and bringing him into the fold of the family, Terry's life would have been a complete disaster.

Thomas made up for his vengeful sibling and showered Terry with love and compassion, rearing Terry as if he were his own son. After Terry's father was killed in action at the battle of Jutland in World War One, Thomas and his wife, Maude, formerly adopted Terry as their own.

Thomas and Maude Busher were a loving couple, and the two had aspired to have many children. However, fate dealt Maude a poor hand and, despite continued attempts, Maude never conceived. Terry's arrival was greeted with joy. It was as if an angel had answered the prayers Maude had whispered before slumber every night and on waking every morning. Her strong faith finally delivered the son she had so longed for.

Throughout Terry's development, Maude cared for him in the best possible way she could, though, as she was never a mother herself, some of her instincts lacked the inherent maternal touch. Her relationship had elements of big sister rather than mother.

But Thomas compensated for any of his wife's shortfalls. He gave Terry a good education and applauded him when he won a scholarship to grammar school and a bursary enabling him to enter university. Thomas was a great believer in personal accomplishment through education; he himself had graduated from university, taken a pupillage, and eventually sat the Bar to become a barrister like his father before him. With such a background steeped in following the legal profession, Thomas expected Terry, upon graduation, to uphold the family's traditions, to enter the Bar, and become a barrister.

Terry, meanwhile, had other plans. A year before graduation, he dropped out of university and commenced an apprenticeship in engineering. Thomas, although deeply disappointed, had to respect Terry's independence and personal integrity to chart his own path in life. After a short while, Terry realized that, despite enjoying engineering work (he was natural designer and problem-solver), the remuneration was far from satisfactory.

When a position in the banking sector arose, he grasped the opportunity and set to work. Terry wanted to secure his future and repay his Uncle Thomas. He was indebted to him and wanted to reward him for all his kindness.

With Terry's astute brain, he learned quickly. He was a risk-taker who could see a good business opportunity. Investment banking was an immediate magnet for him. So he set up and brokered large deals, and ran a successful portfolio. Within a short time, he mastered his field and became accomplished and respected.

Life was going well.

Then the depression hit. Terry's business investments took a dive. His risky bets were too risky and the portfolio he'd built up suffered a rapid down turn.

Banking was suddenly not a good business to be in.

Looking for pastures new, Terry signed up and joined the Merchant Navy. He had always wanted to travel the world and life had shown him a way to feed his desire. In true seaman's tradition, every port became his home. He turned his restlessness to an advantage. He sought out and forged new friendships in new and exotic places.

Though a lucid talker, in his heart of hearts, Terry remained very much a loner. He talked more out of a need to not feel lonely. At night, whilst alone, his insecure beginnings he had as a child manifested and nightmares prevailed.

Terry was aware, despite being able to turn his hand to anything and be successful at it, something in life still evaded him.

He hadn't found that something that would him feel whole. His insecurities bubbled beneath him like an insidious undercurrent, questioning his abilities and pouring scorn on his right to be successful.

Until he met Joanna.

She turned his life around. Like the odd-shaped piece fitting so neatly into the jigsaw puzzle, she made him whole.

Within three months of meeting, they were married on 21st February, 1933. A year later, Joanna gave birth to a beautiful baby girl. They chose the name Mary in honor of Terry's birth mother who gave her life so he could live.

On Mary's emergence, Terry's life took on a whole new meaning. It was now blissful and complete. For six years, their life was exceptionally happy. Terry left the Merchant Navy, having noticed that banking had become prosperous once more. He bought a spacious family house in the small village of Greenhithe in Kent near the River Thames. With enough room to increase the family four-fold, Jo and Terry both laughed when signing the sales documents. Their dream home was now a reality.

The perfect place to bring up a young family.

Then, in 1935, trouble began to brew in Europe. Talk of conflict and patriotism influenced Terry to work with the Ministry of Defense. Through his high-level contacts made in banking, he took a senior engineering position in advanced weapons development.

The prescient wave Terry had caught in 1935 became all-out war in 1939, and their idyllic world was carved up like a scythe sweeping through wheat. Hopes of more children were dashed. With the awesome threat of a Nazi invasion looming from across the Channel, neither Terry nor Joanna wanted to bring children into a world of uncertainty and torment.

In 1935, no one really considered that the conflict would descend into a world war that would eat away six years and leave a trail of utter destruction, death, and suffering.

The majority believed it would all be over by Christmas.

Oh, how wrong they were.

Chapter 2

The following day, Joanna reconciled herself to the fact that Terry was going, and there was little she could do to prevent it. Although, still in a state of shock, she continued to voice her opinion.

"I just can't believe it. I wish you'd told me earlier. Why didn't you give me more warning?"

Terry responded, looking at her forlorn face, "Jo, darling, I had full intentions of telling you sooner. However, I knew what your reaction would be. I just wanted to spend what little time we have together in peace and quiet without any arguments. It had to happen sooner or later. It was just a matter of time. Surely you knew that, my sweetheart. Anyway, it will soon be over."

"Oh, Terry, how can *you*, above all people, say that when you know we've spent more time in the past three months in the shelter than anywhere else. How can you stand there and say it will soon be over?"

"It'll be over when chaps like me get off their backsides and start doing something about that madman. You don't really think I want to go, do you?"

"Well…I'm not quite sure, Terry."

"Jo, listen to me. I'm going because I have to. If we all sat around and twiddled our thumbs, he'd take over the whole world. He has to be stopped."

"So you think you're going to be the one to stop him?"

"Yes…No. Oh, Joanna, don't be such a tease. You know perfectly well what I mean. We all have to stand together and fight that little corporal." He looked at Joanna's twinkling eyes and smiled.

"That's good. The way you were speaking, I thought you were going to take on the entire German Wehrmacht single handed."

They both laughed and hugged each other. A calm period before the storm.

"Jo, I've been thinking. It may be a good idea, what with my leaving and everything else, for you to get as far away from London as possible. These air raids are not going to let up. You know that, darling. I would suggest maybe up north, or even the midlands, where I think you will be reasonably safe." He nodded his head in a positive manner. "Mary needs peace and quiet if she is going to recover completely from her accident. The disruption of these dammed air raids will play havoc with her nerves. She's only a child. She needs some kind of stability. Bless her."

Joanna pulled away from Terry, reflecting on his words. Evacuate up north? That had never been the plan. However, her husband going to war had not been the plan either.

"Terry, how on earth can I leave? Think about Mum and Dad. And Mary loves her school here. It would be dreadful to take her away from St Joseph's, especially now she is progressing so well." Joanna looked questioningly at her husband. "Also think about my work with the Red Cross. They need all the help they can get. This is our home, Terry, and I am certainly not leaving."

Her bottom lip trembled but her stance was adamant.

"Jo, for God's sake, the Red Cross can survive without you. Mary is our main concern. This environment is doing her no good. She'll settle into a new school. You know how adaptable she is, especially if she isn't disrupted night after night by these insufferable bombs and sleeping rough in the tunnel."

Joanna was already shaking her head in anger as he spoke. "No. No, I have made those bunk beds very comfortable."

Terry silenced her with his answer. "Comfort, Joanna, has nothing to do with it. You know very well what I mean. You must think I'm stupid. Why do you keep trying to evade the subject?"

What had started as a little discussion was now merging into a heated argument.

"I know you're not stupid, Terry. I never said that you were. However, I do think going north would be a mistake."

"Why? Give me one good reason. Or perhaps it's just your weird premonitions working overtime again?"

"Terry, don't be ridiculous. It's Mother and Father, of course. We just can't up and go, leaving them alone here."

"Oh, I see now we're getting somewhere. Your parents!"

Joanna glared at him, clearly interpreting the significance of his words. Her parents were always the problem.

"Joanna, for heaven's sake, listen to me. I have spoken to your father and he most certainly approves of your leaving. However, it's your mother who is against the idea, the selfish old goat. She would like to keep you here by her side regardless of the consequences. She rules the roost." Terry continued, nodding his head in annoyance. "Your poor father is completely under her thumb. Her word is his command. Poor old chap. I feel heartily sorry for him."

Joanna was fuming. She knew Terry spoke the truth, but she would never concede defeat.

"Don't speak about my mother in such a way. She is my mother and therefore deserving of a little respect from you."

"I do respect her. But look, face facts. You know as well as I do what your mother is like. It's no good trying to play the dignified daughter act, Joanna. The other day, I asked your father why they never come down to the tunnel with us. 'Oh that's out of the question, my boy. She won't even go outside to the Anderson shelter, let alone go down the tunnel. She says they are filthy places fit for animals and little else. That's why I built the Morrison in the spare room at the back of the bungalow. But don't you worry about us, my dear boy. We'll be fine'. I'm sorry to say this, Joanna, but she doesn't deserve him, your father. He's such a gentleman. But your mother is so high and mighty, it's quite unbelievable. Her life is at stake yet she will not compromise her values for her own safety, let alone your father's."

"That's not true," said Joanna, feeling she had lost the argument before it had begun.

"Oh, no? You remember the other evening when we suffered that terrible raid that lasted all night?"

Joanna nodded. She opened her mouth as if to speak then closed it, remembering the occurrence to which Terry was referring. She realized that at this point it would be fruitless to continue with any counter measure.

"Your father tried to get her into the Anderson shelter. She stood there on the steps of their veranda, immobile and resistant to his insistent pleas for her to move. She stated, quite emphatically, that nothing would induce her to go into that dirty, old shelter fit only for rats. Stick bombs were raining down, the heavens alit with artillery, ack ack guns blasting away, and she didn't blink an eyelid." Terry shook his head. "What do you do with a woman like that?"

"Exactly," said Joanna, feeling that her side of the argument had regained life. "That's why I can't leave. I have never understood my mother, and I know Dad has resigned himself to dealing with her whims of fancy. Nevertheless, Terry, if I leave, he will be alone. He will have no one."

"Listen to me, Joanna. I understand how you feel. But there is nothing you can do to help them. If they choose to stay and take their chances, it's entirely up to them. My only concern is for you and Mary. Please, Jo, do try it. At least then I would be happy in the knowledge that you are safe and out of harm's way. Then I will be able to get on with whatever has to be done with a clearer mind."

Joanna suddenly saw the sense in his argument. She would go. If only to give him peace of mind.

"All right. If that's what you wish and it will make you happy then we'll go. However, I will only leave after I have seen you on your train."

"You promise?"

Joanna grinned. "I promise."

On realizing she had relented to his wishes, Terry thought it safe to add, "Of course, if you don't like it up there then you can always come home."

Joanna smiled. She knew he would never have conceded to her wishes if she had not agreed to go. She kissed him gently on the lips.

Later the same evening, Terry had an idea.

"Jo, it has just occurred to me. Do you remember the name of the woman we stayed with back in '38 when I was on that special contract?"

"Yes. I remember. A Mrs. Cox. She lived in a little village just outside Derby. Charming woman. Only she never stopped talking about her nephew. She went on and on about him every evening."

"That's the woman." Terry laughed. "Mary loved it up there, didn't she?"

"Yes," whispered Joanna. "That was when she could speak."

Terry stood in front of the writing bureau, busy going through phone numbers, and didn't appear to have heard her remark. She watched him standing there with his back turned to her making plans, taking the lead as he always did. Oh God, she wondered, how on earth was she going to endure life without him?

He turned around slowly, almost as if telepathic to her thoughts. She looked sideways, trying desperately to avoid his gaze and her inner emotions. Then she opened her handbag and produced a black, leather notepad, opened it, and checked the telephone numbers.

In a direct tone she stated, "I've found it."

Joanna made her way quickly to the hall telephone. After a brief conversation with Mrs. Cox, who admitted that she would be delighted to help them in their hour of need, Joanna replaced the receiver and glanced at Terry who was standing in the hall doorway.

"Now everything has been set. We leave a day after tomorrow," she said in a matter of fact voice.

Terry looked at her straight. "Darling, what's the matter? I intended on making all the arrangements. I didn't want you worrying your pretty head over anything."

She looked at him pleadingly. "Oh, Terry, can't you understand? I have to do these things. I'm not a child."

She spoke with a sob in her voice and turned her head towards the wall.

Terry walked over to her. Joanna still had her hand placed on the receiver.

"It's all right, Jo," he whispered, laying his hand upon hers. "You know you are doing the right thing."

He gently turned her head around to meet his and cupped her face in his hands.

"Don't worry, my precious darling. Everything is going to be fine, and Mary will speak again one day when all this is over."

Chapter 3

It was a crisp, sunny, spring morning in early March when the train pulled into the little railway station in Greenhithe. It had been dead on time, which was unusual, considering it was normally late.

So there had been no chance to snatch a few extra moments with Terry before he left.

It felt to Joanna as if even the train was running by some kind of military command, all in order to whisk Terry away from her.

Mary stood clutching the bundle of sandwiches that Joanna had made for her father. Her forlorn little face told the story in her silent world of what she could not say.

In the spring of 1939, Mary had been involved in a road accident whilst visiting her grandparents with her cousin, Elizabeth. They had taken the bus. Unthinking and excited at the prospect of visiting her grandparents, she had crossed the road behind the bus, straight into the path of an oncoming lorry. The impact threw her one hundred yards down the road and she was knocked unconscious.

Doctors feared brain damage, but Mary proved them wrong. A day later, she regained consciousness. All her faculties fell back into place. Except speech.

Her parents consulted numerous London consultants to find a cure for Mary's sudden loss of speech. Unfortunately, as it was not connected to a definite brain defect, nothing could be done.

"It is all psychological. Mary will have to come out of it herself."

That had been almost two years ago, and there was still no sign of Mary regaining her vocal abilities.

Two lonely figures stood, watching and waving, as the train accelerated and gradually disappeared around the bend of the tiny rail track. Terry's head vanished from sight. All that could be seen was his waving hand, quickly becoming smaller and smaller.

Mary looked down at her father's sandwiches, which she was still holding. In all the activity of saying goodbye, they'd been forgotten. When she realized this, it broke her brave look of courage and the tears fell in torrents as she held the sandwiches up to her mother.

Joanna bent down to comfort her daughter.

"There, there, Mary, my love. Don't cry. We will see Daddy again very soon."

She placed her hand in Mary's and they began their walk away from the station.

"We'll go home and make a nice cup of tea, and then you can help Mummy pack the case for our exciting journey tomorrow. We'll go to Gravesend and do some shopping. Then we can visit Nanny and Grandad and have tea with them. Then we shall come home and get ready early for the shelter tonight, and you can play with Marianne. That'll be nice. Don't you think?"

Joanna, forcing a smile, let her words tumble out almost incoherently. However, she knew she must preoccupy Mary's mind from the anguish of her father leaving.

Mary almost knew the game her mother was playing. So she smiled wryly and nodded in recognition of Joanna's words.

The shelter was a disused railway tunnel built into solid chalk. This type of chalk was plenteous in this part of the country and extended for miles, eventually emerging into the quarry pits. The tunnel was the best place anyone could possibly be during an air raid. At least it insured some kind of safety. Although nothing was a hundred per cent.

It was well organized. The sanitation was quite adequate given the limitations. Comfort was something that could only be acquired by individual occupants. Regular ablutions were undertaken in the best possible way. ARP wardens and caretakers worked hard to ensure cleanliness was kept a priority.

Every occupant in the shelter had their own bunk bed and blankets. If some occupants required a little privacy then they were asked to bring a curtain that was placed onto a wire rod and assembled around the bunk. This had been much appreciated by all.

No animals were allowed inside the tunnel for sanitation reasons. So the familiar sound of a child calling out for their pet could often be heard during the night.

The tunnels were also jolly places. People would sing and have musical evenings. They would play cards, and generally make the most of what little they had. Mary could recall the first time she entered the shelter. The chatter of people, the cries of children, and the bemoaning discussions relating to the war all came together like one opus that played each night.

The one aspect of the tunnel that meant more to Mary than anything else was the smell.

The dank, mildew aroma, mingled with that of the paraffin lamps, would remain forever in her memory, representing a place of safety rather than hardship.

The countryside surrounding the tunnel consisted mainly of orchards and hop gardens. The tunnel was completely enshrouded by trees and foliage. A footpath led down from the main London road through the woods and across the old railway cutting.

It was a beautiful, peaceful spot where one could almost forget that a war was raging, reflected Joanna, as she emerged from the tunnel the next morning.

Joanna always liked this walk. She had played here with her friends when she was just a child, no older than Mary.

Poor Mary. How was she going to stand being uprooted like this?

She had always run to her father for protection. If they had been accidentally caught out before the siren sounded, he would carry her piggyback style on his shoulders down this very footpath.

The blackout never really bothered Joanna. She realized now that she would have to be the protector, and coming down here could be a life or death exercise. There were no motorways with brilliant overhead lighting in those days. The only source of light was from torches, which had to be pointed to the ground at all times every night.

That was why the British summer timetable never changed during the war; it gave people a little more light.

Those in the unfortunate situation that their battery ran out stood the chance of falling down a hole or taking the wrong turning and stumbling into the path of an oncoming train. Many hazards prevailed in the blackout, which was why carrying a torch was just as important as carrying a gas mask.

Hours later on a northbound train, Joanna sat forlornly and looked at the countryside rumbling past. She hadn't even had time to say goodbye to her friend, Nina, and her three children, John, Michael, and Marianne, who shared the bunk beds opposite them in the tunnel.

Nina and her family hadn't slept in the tunnel last night, even though the air raid had been horrendous. It was totally out of character as Nina had always been a loving mother and made sure her children were safe in the shelter.

Joanna made a mental note to write to Nina when they had settled into their new abode.

She turned her head from the window and looked at her daughter, who was quietly reading her Beano and Dandy comics. Feeling content in the fact that they would not have to suffer any more air raids for a while, Joanna laid her head back and closed her eyes in an attempt to catch up on some much needed sleep.

Chapter 4

At that precise moment, Nina was franticly rummaging through her cupboards in a state of absolute despair. She was looking for something to cook for her husband, Joshua, when he returned home from his night shift. Josh had avoided call-up due to a supposed wound in his leg from shrapnel. He paid off a doctor in a shady part of East London to pass him unfit for drafting, and then he secured through his other nefarious contacts a position as factory shop foreman in an ammunition factory, a protected industry that prevented workers from conscription.

After turning over food stuffs and containers, Nina eventually managed to find half a tin of dried egg.

Then she suddenly froze with horror.

Nina realized that she didn't have any bread to accompany the egg. She had given the last to John and Michael before they went to school.

"My God," she whispered. "What am I going to do?"

She quickly dressed three-year-old Marianne and ran like the wind down the road, with the little child in her pushchair, to the local bakers.

Nina was once a beautiful woman who had been ravaged by the passing years. Life had not been kind to Nina. She was a tall woman, almost bone thin, and frail in build. Her eyes were hazel, large, and glassy, and she had long, chestnut hair, now tied back with an old piece of elastic. Her skin was tightly drawn over the bone structure of her face, displaying her unusual and delicate features. Nina was just twenty-nine. Yet she bore the face of someone much older.

On returning with the bread, Nina realized that Joshua was home.

"Where the 'ell 'ave you been then?" he roared.

Nina timidly held out the bread as though offering it as a sacrifice in some weird ritual.

"I ran out of bread," she ventured. "I'm sorry…I-"

Her words were cut mid-sentence by Joshua's bellowing anger.

"Why the 'ell can't you get enough food in the bloody 'ouse?"

Joshua was of medium height and stoutly built with sinister, dark eyes and heavy brows that were constantly creased in the delivery of wrath, usually to his poor, long-suffering wife, Nina.

"Because food is on ration, Josh, and the children eat so much. They are growing, after all."

"Let 'em starve. Little sods. Won't 'urt 'em for a bit. Didn't 'urt me."

"Oh, Josh, no. They need something inside them before they go to school. You must understand that," she muttered, and then stopped any further response.

"In future, you save the food for me, woman. I'm the worker, ain't I? Anyway, no more arguing. Get me food, and quick about it, otherwise you'll get what you got last night. And I'm not joking."

"Yes, Josh. Of course. I'm sorry, Josh."

"Don't stand there fiddling, woman. Get on with it."

He pointed to the kitchen door.

Nina instantly did as she was told. In her haste, she overcooked the fried bread a little. But everything else had been tastefully cooked. She had even managed to find half an onion to mix with the powdered egg. The meal was good given the circumstances. She laid it on the table before Joshua and returned to the kitchen.

Soon after, Joshua stood up from the living room table and marched into the kitchen. He stood behind Nina as she faced the sink, drew up close to her, and then shouted in her face.

"What the 'ell do you call this?"

Joshua strode across the sparsely furnished kitchen and flung open the kitchen door. Then he threw the plate with its entire contents out into the garden.

He turned back to Nina, who was cowering like a frightened child, her eyes accepting the reward that she would receive for her hurried efforts.

"That's what I fink of your cooking," Joshua yelled. "And this is what I fink of you."

He finished his sentence with a blow to her face, his fist heading deep into her cheekbone.

Nina tried to turn. But Joshua dealt a further blow to her cheek. Then another blow to the other side. She tried desperately to defend herself by holding both hands up to her face.

Screaming, she cried out, "No. No more please!"

Josh's fist made an alternate direction. Nina screamed in agonizing pain as he pummeled into her stomach.

Marianne stood, watching and crying, as her mother, unable to stand the pain any longer, slumped into a heap down onto the stone floor.

And all was dark.

Chapter 5

On reaching their destination, Joanna felt a little troubled as she gazed up at the antiquated house. It was built of gray stone and sat back off the main Derby road, making it completely invisible to passersby. Concealed by overgrown trees and shrubbery, it gave the place a dark and ominous feel.

The surrounding countryside made an impressive picture with the Dales in the background and small, slate rock walls dissecting the landscape. Lovely on a sunny day but not very comforting when the clouds hung low and lifeless, and the whole scene took on an eerie ambience.

They received a warm welcome from Mrs. Cox, who resembled the epitome of the country bumpkin. Amply proportioned with a homely North Country accent, she overwhelmed them with her hospitality.

Betty looked at Mary and exclaimed, "My lass, you've grown! Now I expect you'll both be wanting to freshen up." She led the way up an old staircase. "Did you have a good journey?"

"Well, if you don't mind crowded trains, it wasn't too bad," said Joanna. "Actually we were very lucky to get a seat. Do you know what travelling is like these days, Betty?"

"I do indeed."

Joanna followed Betty to the first bedroom.

"Well, this is the double and over there is the single, just right for the wee one," said Betty, glancing at Mary who was hopping from one foot to the other. "Oh, my wee lass, that's the room you'll be wanting." Betty pointed to a door down the hallway.

Mary made a frantic dash for the bathroom. Once her daughter was out of earshot, Joanna explained about Mary's accident. Betty was shocked. But she agreed that Joanna had made the right decision in coming north away from the blitz.

"She'll do wonders at school with no bombs to worry about. I suppose her schooling has suffered? Poor little thing," said Betty.

Her tone of voice, although sympathetic, was also slightly patronizing.

"Yes, quite," retorted Joanna, her pride bristling forth. "Of course, you know, under such circumstances, Mary was progressing very well at school. I felt a little reluctant in taking her away."

Mary emerged from the bathroom relaxed and happier than before.

Both Joanna and Betty knew that their conversation could not be pursued.

Betty announced cheerfully, "I have prepared a meal of toad in the hole. I hope you both like it."

Joanna, not wishing to appear ungracious, replied, "Why, how kind. That happens to be Mary's favorite dish."

Betty chuckled. "Is it? That's good. Come down and I'll dish it out."

With that, Betty descended the stairs in a flurry.

Mary could only communicate through pencil and paper. Joanna always made sure that she had a notepad with her at all times. To Mary, her pad and pencil were vital to her standard of living.

That night, Joanna crept into her daughter's room to say goodnight before she went to sleep. She found Mary sitting bolt upright in bed writing rapidly and getting frustrated about her spelling. Joanna never criticized Mary's spelling. She only pointed out how the word should be spelt and then wrote it down clearly for her to study. Often Mary would attempt words that were difficult for a child at least three years her senior. But Mary's tenacious perseverance always won.

She quickly handed the pad to her mother. Joanna sat on her bed and read the words out loud.

"Do you think we are going to like it here? I do miss Henry. Mrs. Cox speaks so hard and quick. Do you think she really likes us? I wish we had not come here now. I don't think I am going to like it."

Joanna paused and chose her own words carefully.

"Of course you will, my darling. Mrs. Cox is a nice lady, and look how lovely and quiet it is here. If you were at home now, you would be lying on that hard, old bunk bed in the tunnel, not tucked up warm in a nice, comfortable bed."

In reply, Mary quickly scribbled, "I know, Mummy. I just miss home and Daddy."

Joanna replied, "I know you do, darling. I miss him too. But this war will soon be over, and then we will be together again. Meanwhile, we have to stay here and try to be content, and Henry will be fine with Mrs. Stokes. She loves budgies."

Mary continued to scribble on her pad. "I know she does, Mummy. But I don't think Mrs. Cox will put on the wireless very much. She only listened to the news tonight. I don't think she will put on Itma and Girt and Daisy."

She handed her mother the note, and then continued writing.

Joanna smiled and tried to reassure her. "Oh, I am sure she will if I ask her nicely."

Mary finished writing and gave the pad to her mother. Joanna read the contents of the message. The impact of those fumbling words, written by a child so young, overwhelmed her.

"Mummy, has there always been a war? I don't know anything else, and it won't go away. I just want it to be quiet, and live together with you and Daddy, without any inter…inter…I can't spell what I mean."

Mary's hand stopped writing then she picked up the pencil and continued.

"I wish Daddy was here and we were all at home. I wish there was no war. And I wish I could talk."

Mary looked up at her mother with red, glassy eyes.

"Mary, my darling." Joanna cradled her daughter in her arms, desperately holding back the fears, anxieties, and emotions that plagued her soul. "Listen to me, Mary. There has not always been a war. One day, you will know what it is like to live in peace. The three of us will be together again with no interruption. You will know what it is like to sleep sound in your own bed at night. You will be able to walk down the road without fear of hearing the air raid siren starting up and having to run for your life. You will be able to eat a different type of food whenever you like, anytime you like, sweets and chocolates until your heart is content. You must never stop believing in that dream. That is why Daddy has gone to war. We are all fighting for peace and freedom, my darling. Our very freedom."

All though the words were spoken to a child, they were said with the emphasis fit for a minister addressing the nation. Joanna spoke her words as if the very existence of them brought new hope and a new definition to life.

"Try to like it here, darling, at least for Daddy," Joanna said softly.

Mary wrote on her pad, "I will try. But only for you and Daddy." Raising her face to her mother's, she wrote, "Kiss me."

"Of course I'll kiss you, my darling."

As Joanna left the room, she felt a little apprehensive about them both being in the house with Mrs. Cox. She had been reluctant to leave her home, and only did so to please Terry. Her discussion with Mary proved she was not alone in her suspicions. Joanna could not comprehend Betty's bizarre behavior. The woman had adopted an almost sarcastic way of speaking. She seemed to continuously patronize her and Mary. Joanna felt that the whole situation was very unnerving.

She thought that maybe her imagination was playing tricks. Then she remembered their last stay at the house. Betty was always brusque but there had been benevolence in her mannerism. This, now, was sorely missing.

Chapter 6

Mary started the local school. It was a small establishment, which sat in the foothills of the picturesque setting of Darley Dale. Close to a couple of shops and a post office, the school accommodated no more than fifty pupils. Mary soon settled in and was beginning to like studying without disruption. Unfortunately, disruption of another kind reared its ugly head.

Mary's loss of voice was soon translated into her being the 'silly kid from the city' where a bomb had dropped on her head leaving her stupid. She was soon nicknamed the 'dopey dummy girl from London'. Later she became the victim of intense intimidation. It all started with simple teasing and name-calling, and then led to graver consequences.

When Mary's name reached the ears of big Mazey, the local bully of the third year, Mary's life soon became a living hell. Mazey and her gang would deliver a range of punches to poor Mary during their daily ambushes. Mazey was smart. She made sure that the torture inflicted on Mary never drew any blood.

Joanna, totally oblivious to her daughter's plight, did, however, notice bruises on her arms and legs. She asked her daughter what had happened.

Mary replied using her pen and pad, "I fell over during PE."

Mary felt she could not confide in her mother. She feared big Mazey and her gang would discover she had told on her. Then they would really kill her. She also cared about her mother and had no wish to burden her with more worry. So Mary suffered her intolerable anguish in silence.

After one particular bout of utter sadism, when Mazey and her entourage hid amongst the trees at the foothill behind a clearing then attacked, Mary looked down through the branches to the railway station and contemplated running back to London. But she realized that it was not the answer.

Later the same evening, she went to her mother's room and quickly wrote, "I don't want to go to school anymore. I don't like it there. I want to go home. Please, Mummy. Please. I don't care about the bombs. I just don't want to stay here."

At first, Joanna thought Mary might be having problems settling in. After all, she had only been there two weeks. However, she realized this to be unlike Mary. Her daughter was usually so adaptable and cheerful. Joanna's concerns grew. She looked at her daughter's white, terrified, little face and realized something was definitely wrong.

"Mary, my sweetheart, you must go to school. I will be at the school gate to meet you tomorrow afternoon, and then we'll find out what has been troubling you. There is nothing to be frightened of, my sweetheart. Whatever it is, Mummy will deal with it."

These words of solace helped Mary. She smiled and gave her mother the thumbs up sign in agreement.

The next day, after leaving Mary safely in her class, Joanna made her way to the head mistress' office.

"Oh, I'm sorry, Mrs. Busher. I think Miss Tomlinson is in conference at the moment. However, take a seat, and I'll find out when she is able to see you."

"Thank you," replied Joanna abruptly.

She watched the plump secretary disappear beyond the office door. Joanna had never been pleased with the school's reaction to take Mary. Regarding her lack of speech, they had immediately suggested that Mary should have extra tuition to bring her up to the same standard of her peers. Joanna had been resolute in her assurance that Mary was a gifted child and highly advanced for her age, and certainly needed no further tuition. The fact that Mary had undertaken most of her studies in the air raid shelter never occurred to their country yokel mentality.

Miss Tomlinson appeared in the doorway, all tweeds and brogues and little else. She did not impress Joanna in the slightest. Miss Tomlinson gave Joanna a condescending stare. Joanna, wearing a trim, fitted suit and high-heeled shoes, was regarded by Miss Tomlinson as unsuitably dressed and little more than a tart.

Joanna informed Miss Tomlinson of her concern for her daughter.

Miss Tomlinson replied as if she had been engaged in another conversation entirely.

"Well, Mrs. Busher, I can understand why your daughter is having problems.

She should really be in a special school with children of her own caliber. The fact that she is working with children who are far more advanced than her is going to make her feel unhappy and left out of everything."

Joanna interjected at this point with a curt, "That is not what we are discussing here. And, for your information, my daughter does not need a special school. She is more than capable of carrying out her studies at this level and even higher. The point in question is that my daughter is frightened of something or someone in this school."

"Of what, pray?" said a surprised Miss Tomlinson, suddenly coming alive to the real issue.

"That, I have yet to find out, and when I do, you will be the one who is praying. Good day to you, Miss Tomlinson."

Joanna left abruptly, dismayed and angered by her encounter with the head mistress.

News travelled fast that the stupid dummy girl's mother had seen the head mistress. Mazey and her gang were determined to teach Mary a lesson once and for all.

"She's a little sneak. I'm going to sort her out good and proper," said Mazey viciously.

"We'll strike her when she's on her way back home. She'll probably think everything is okay and won't be worried. We're gonna wait in the woods at the bottom of the hill. What do you say, Billy?"

Billy, a short boy with freckles, looked sheepish. "Well, Mazey, I don't know. I live near there. Me mom might see me and give me a good hiding."

"If yer scared of yer mom, yer a wee chicken. Yer should be scared of me too. Come on, Anna, Jilly, let's beat him up."

Mazey grabbed Billy by the scruff of his neck and yanked his head back.

"If you don't come with us, keep yer mouth shut. Or I'll kick yer head in."

Billy ran off.

With a wicked smile, Anna shouted, "Oh, don't worry about him. We've got work to do. We'll teach that mummy's girl that talking costs lives."

Joanna called in at the local shop, posted a letter to Terry, and then bought some sausages from the butchers. On her way up the hill, she discovered a farm that sold fresh eggs off the ration. Delighted with her find, for such things were a rarity in the south, she continued on her way to her new abode. In her heart, she tried to like this place. But her heart ached for home.

Glancing down through the trees at the railway line, Joanna examined her dilemma. Mary was safer up here in Derbyshire yet undoubtedly happier back home. What was she to do? Joanna had never witnessed such terror in her daughter's eyes before. Even in the midst of an air raid, Mary had not shown so much fear.

Terry had said that if they didn't like it, they could always return home. But that would be defeatist. Joanna knew she had to remain, if only to uncover what was troubling Mary.

When she arrived at the house, all was silent. She stood still. Not even the sound of a bird song could be heard. As she approached the steps to the front door, Joanna looked up briefly at the windows and noticed the curtains were still drawn even though it was mid-morning.

Joanna entered the hall. It suddenly appeared to her rather frightening with the long, dark corridor ahead of her. She called Betty's name. No reply was forthcoming. She ventured further into the house, unsure of what she would find but curious nevertheless.

In the breakfast room, sitting in a corner by the table, she found Betty holding her head in her hands.

"So there you are, Betty. I was worried. Didn't you hear me calling you?"

Betty raised her head. "No. I didn't hear you."

Her eyes were puffy and bloodshot. Her skin had taken on a sallow complexion.

"Oh my God. You look dreadful," said Joanna. "Shall I call a doctor?"

Betty waved her hand to dispel Joanna's concern. "No. No…I'm just tired, Jo. I have this terrible headache. It just won't go. It keeps banging on and on in my head."

Betty seemed exhausted just uttering those few words.

Joanna immediately sat down and took Betty's elbow.

"You poor dear. Sit there quietly and I'll make us a nice cup of tea. Have you anything you can take? Aspirin or something?"

Joanna made the tea and placed the tray down on the table beside her groceries.

"There you are. I'll pour," said Joanna soothingly.

"I appreciate what you have been doing for me, Joanna. Thank you."

"Think nothing of it, Betty. You've helped me tremendously by accommodating us."

Betty gave a weird smile. "I suppose you miss your home and work with the Red Cross?" She spoke in a dazed, languid manner.

"Well, it's a small price to pay for one's safety, Betty," replied Joanna, trying to be cheerful. She changed the subject. "By the way, Betty, I almost forgot to ask you, how is that nephew of yours? Do you see much of him?"

At the mention of her nephew, Betty became unresponsive and failed to recognize anything, staring blankly into space. Joanna knew immediately there was something terribly wrong with Betty.

"Are you all right?"

"I'm fine."

Betty looked menacingly into Joanna's eyes. Then suddenly, she snapped herself out of the trance almost as rapidly as she had entered it.

Her amiable self once again, she acted as though nothing had happened.

"You know, Joanna, there is a rehabilitation hospital on the other side of the village. I did hear they needed helpers. Why don't you pop over there and volunteer?"

"Yes," responded Joanna falteringly, unsure of Betty's sudden change of character. "That sounds interesting. I could go there before I pick Mary up from school."

Betty gave a weird laugh. "Ain't the lass old enough to pick herself up?"

Her voice sounded hostile and cold. With the color rapidly returning to her cheeks, she looked dangerous.

Joanna felt a cold shiver run through her as she answered her question.

"Yes, of course she can. It's just today I promised I would meet her from school, and speaking of which, I think I ought to be leaving now."

Joanna tried in vain to get past Betty, whose entire persona had taken on a baneful posture. She persisted with a frenzied rambling.

"They should be able to look after themselves these days. I had to. I wasn't molly coddled. I had to struggle for my very existence. And for what? *Nothing!* When Hitler comes he's gonna straighten everyone out."

Joanna knew she had to get away from this mad woman.

When she reached the kitchen doorway, Betty screamed, "Hitler will take your Mary away from you like he took mine. Just you wait and see."

These words were too much for Joanna. She realized she was imprisoned with a mad woman. She turned quickly to face Betty who suddenly stood behind her. In her right hand, Betty brandished a kitchen knife high above her head. Her eyes shone like red-hot coals, her face a deep magenta.

"My God, Betty. What is wrong with you? You've gone completely crazy," Joanna could not help but exclaim.

"Crazy! You think I'm crazy?"

Betty screamed, banshee-like, and hurled herself towards Joanna, the knife pointed towards her throat. Joanna dropped the tray she had been holding, sending it crashing to the floor.

The sound disoriented Betty. She plunged off target as Joanna darted sideways into the kitchen. This caused Betty to fall and hit her head on the window ledge. As she collapsed, she grabbed the tablecloth. Consequently, the groceries and china came crashing down around her.

Joanna could see Betty was completely unconscious, and she quickly bent down and picked up the knife lying beside her. Then, realizing there was no phone in the house, Joanna made a frantic dash out the front door to the phone booth down the road. In her desperate state, she accidentally slammed the door shut behind her.

The ambulance arrived swiftly but not swift enough. In the short space of time it had taken Joanna to call the emergency services, Betty had regained consciousness and was walking trance-like around the house.

When Betty heard the attendants breaking a window to get in, she screamed almost incoherently, "You'll not get me too, you bloody Nazis. You won't take me alive."

Betty opened her needlecraft box and took out a pair of dressmaking scissors.

With a final, "You'll not kill me, you bleeding Nazis," she slashed her wrists.

The attendants were quick to respond.

"You'll be all right now, love," they muttered.

They held her down whilst the chloroform took effect, and then they quickly bandaged her flooding wounds.

Joanna stood, still and ghostlike, unable to comprehend what was happening. It was as if she was witnessing the whole scene through some kind of hazy dream, not quite there. Joanna rode with the attendants and nurse to the hospital.

Chapter 7

Upon arrival, the building that was said to be the hospital resembled that of a country mansion, complete with overhanging ivy and lush, green landscape grounds. Marble steps led up to an ancient, huge, oak door flanked by massive stone Corinthian pillars.

Joanna watched, still stunned, as Betty was rushed to a new wing of the building.

The nurse asked her to take a seat in the reception area and offered her a cup of tea. Still feeling cold from her traumatic experience, she eagerly accepted.

After a short wait, a youthful, handsome man with a limp appeared. He was wearing a white coat, had light, brown hair, and was of medium height, walking with a stethoscope around his neck.

He extended his hand as he approached Joanna.

"How do you do? I am Dr. Matthews. I understand that you came here with Mrs. Cox?"

The young doctor gave a broad smile as he shook Joanna's hand. His closeness made her blush slightly.

"Good afternoon. Yes, I came in with Mrs. Cox. Could you tell me how she is please?"

"If you are referring to her self-inflicted wounds, those will heal. Unfortunately, far deeper wounds remain in her brain. Her mental condition is virtually irreparable. Two other doctors will examine her later today but, I am afraid, with a psychiatric case such as this, we do not hold out much hope. She simply is not safe to be amongst people anymore."

Joanna gasped at the bluntness of Dr. Matthews' statement.

She repeated his words. "Not safe to be with? But surely something can be done to help her. Some type of treatment?"

Dr. Matthews continued, "The incident that happened today is a reflection of how unstable she is. You had a narrow squeeze. In her state, she could have killed you and never known what she had done. By the way, are you a relative or a friend, Mrs....?"

"Just a friend. And the name is Mrs. Joanna Busher. We came up here to stay for a short time to get away from the blitz. We live outside London and, as you are aware, most days are intolerable. We came up here for a little peace and quiet. In fact, my husband had insisted that we come for our own safety."

Joanna smiled at the irony of the situation.

Dr. Matthews immediately picked up on the signal. "To be quite honest, you would have been safer with a bombardment of landmines going off around you." He smiled and gave a slight laugh. "Rather than up here with Mrs. Cox." He coughed, trying to sound a little more official. "Now, Mrs. Busher, are you going to take proceedings against Mrs. Cox? I have already informed the police and they are awaiting your instructions."

"Well, frankly, Dr. Matthews, I would firstly like to know what happened to Mrs. Cox to cause such a drastic change in her character."

Joanna gave Dr. Matthews a stony stare that clearly indicated, 'Don't even think of being evasive with me, sonny'.

Dr. Matthews shook his head and glanced down at his shoes.

"She is another victim of this dammed war. Excuse my profanity. But her situation warrants it. Apparently, she had always played a model role in the village. She was well liked and a great enthusiast in the community. Then, suddenly, one morning, she received news that her beloved nephew had been blown up at Dunkirk. Last year. After this, her world literally fell apart. She had a complete nervous breakdown initially, which brought on manic depression. She spent six months in a mental institution. She was only released when her sister confirmed that she would take full responsibility of her. Sadly, Mrs. Cox's sister died a few months ago from pneumonia, leaving her alone. Somehow, in all the muddle of the war, the authorities overlooked Mrs. Cox. She was thus left to her own devices."

"She has never attempted anything like this before," said Joanna. "You understand?"

"I don't suppose an occasion has ever arisen to make her want to do so."

Joanna felt appalled at such a dreadful quirk of fate.

"I really do not know a great deal about her case," added Dr. Matthews. "I'm only here recuperating and lending a much needed helping hand whilst my leg heals. Then I'll return to my squadron in the RAF. But I have an idea what might have triggered her behavior."

Joanna was mystified by Betty's sudden attack and sought more clarification.

Dr. Matthews attempted an answer. "I believe it was you and your daughter."

Joanna looked flabbergasted by his unexpected reply. "Us? For heaven sake, Dr. Matthews, why us?"

"Let me explain my hypothesis. And remember, I am no psychiatrist. However, I believe she saw the happy, domestic picture that you and your daughter presented, and this triggered off the deep psychosis that lay dormant. Your happy family circle reminded her of her own misfortune at not having a family and the deep loss of her beloved nephew, who, as I have already mentioned, was killed last year. I could be completely wrong, of course. But that is my prognosis."

"Oh my God. How dreadful. To think, if we had never come here, all this may never have happened."

"Just a moment. You should not blame yourself. She has been suffering from a mental disorder for over a year now. Something would have sparked her off eventually. Now she will remain in an asylum for the rest of her life. However, that is not your fault."

Joanna looked directly into Dr. Matthews' eyes. "Dr. Matthews, I knew Mrs. Cox years ago before the war. She was more than just a model citizen. I can only describe her as a kind and loving woman, and I will not be pressing charges against her."

He smiled as if expecting the response. "Very well, Mrs. Busher. I shall inform the authorities straight away." He looked down, shaking his head. "As I have already mentioned before, she is but another victim of this insane war."

Joanna sadly nodded her head in agreement.

Dr. Matthews changed the subject to a brighter note. "I suppose now you will be looking for new accommodation under the circumstances?"

"I really don't think so, doctor."

"Please drop the formalities. Call me David. I don't regard myself as a doctor at the moment. Not until this war has been fought and won."

"Well, David, I am not staying here a moment longer. I have a home down south and that is where I'm going. Today. So if you will excuse me, I have to go back and pack my bags."

David looked shunned and awkward as he looked at Joanna, admiring her forceful nature. Yet he knew she had a soft side. Her compassion showed when discussing Mrs. Cox. She was so like Ann, it almost made him gasp. So close. He would have loved to have held her, to have felt her warm, silken skin, and inhaled her delicate perfume.

Snap out of it, David, he told himself briskly.

She's not Ann. Just an acquaintance. Someone you don't even know. Don't do anything you will regret.

But the moment seemed to freeze.

Joanna stared back at David and smiled.

"I apologize," she said. "I did not mean to sound brusque. It's just, after all I have been through, and I don't just mean today, I've had enough of Derbyshire."

"No offence taken, Mrs. Busher," he said formally, watching his place.

"Listen, David, you may call me Joanna."

David's eyes shone with delight. Then, looking at his wristwatch, he declared, "My word, Joanna, it's twelve o'clock already. I wonder, would you care for a lift back to the house in my car?"

"Oh, would you? Thank you so much. That's awfully kind of you, and I can tell you everything on the way."

"Splendid," said David.

The word echoed his feelings.

They both walked to his red sports car that was parked in the upper driveway. When Joanna had explained her reasons for leaving, her suspicions about Mary's school, and her feeling totally out of place in Derbyshire, David conceded to her decision.

"Joanna, my dear, you have made the right decision. It's certainly one I would have taken myself. Shall we collect Mary on the way back to the house? Then we can grab a bite to eat on the way to the station."

"Yes. All right," said Joanna, looking surprised. "But where shall we eat? I don't know anywhere. And have we enough time to eat?"

"Joanna, sit back, relax, and leave everything to me. But please hold onto your hat."

With a cheeky smile and eyes sparkling, he started the engine and his red sports car kicked up the dust behind them.

When they arrived at Derby Central, the 14:15 train to St Pancreas, London, was standing at the platform.

"Well, here we are. I said I would get you here on time and I have with ten minutes to spare." David grinned. "Even though you had to hold onto your seat." He lifted Joanna's cases onto the rack. Then he bent down and kissed Mary goodbye. "Now, if anyone scares you at school, Mary, you just write a letter to me and I'll come after them in my Spitfire."

There was a slight shiver of laughter from the other passengers in the compartment. He then turned and faced Joanna, who was standing outside in the corridor.

She gave him a broad smile. "Thank you so very much, David."

"Don't mention it."

He extended his hand to shake hers when suddenly two sailors hurried by, pushing David close to Joanna. He found the urge to kiss her almost impossible to resist. But David resisted. He realized it would be far too risky and had no wish to spoil a delightful acquaintance. As he looked at her, visions of the past came flooding back to him. She was so like Ann, it was uncanny. He had reminded himself once already that this was not Ann but Joanna, a young woman who was happily married and head over heels in love with her husband.

They just stood and stared at each other for a few seconds. Joanna blushed to the roots of her hair. David stood back quickly.

"Well, goodbye, Joanna, and please take care of yourself. No more life or death situations. And I'm not just referring to the war."

He looked serious.

Joanna smiled, looking more relaxed. "I'll try. And you be careful too, David."

He answered when alighting from the train, looking over his shoulder. "It's not so much a matter of being careful. In my game, it's more the luck of the draw."

Joanna looked solemn as she watched him standing on the platform through the open window in the corridor. He understood her thought pattern and quickly spoke on a more humorous note.

"Oh, I nearly forgot to tell you, Joanna. I'm going to be based down south very shortly. So if you happen to see a Spit flying low over your house, you'll know it's me dropping in for tea."

They both laughed as the train slowly moved away. David waved and blew her a kiss from his hand. Joanna smiled demurely but did not return the compliment. She only replied with a light wave of the hand.

David had married Ann, a lovely, young nurse, just before the war. They met at the same hospital where David had trained to become a doctor. Flying was always a leisure activity that he had grown to love over the years. His uncle taught him to fly at a young age. When the time came for David to make a decision whether to join the RAF or follow in his father's footsteps and become a general practitioner, he chose the latter. But when war was declared in 1939, David joined the RAF. His wife, Ann, wishing to be near him, applied for a transfer to the local hospital situated close to the airfield.

In the summer of 1940, when the Luftwaffe were attacking, bombing, and strafing fighter stations in southern England, Ann, whilst assisting a stretcher-bearer from the ambulance with her patient, had been gunned down by a ME109 enemy aircraft flying low over the hospital in combat with a fighter Spitfire.

Since that day, David had only one thought on his mind: to fight and destroy every enemy aircraft as much as was humanly possible. He used his handsome, debonair charm as a façade. In truth, he had no aspirations for any other woman. For David, now, his greatest pleasure was to fly, and every Nazi he shot down was one scored for Ann.

But Joanna had stirred something in him, a something he thought was dead. She was so warm, so compassionate, and so like Ann. He whispered his thoughts as the train slowly accelerated in motion.

"Goodbye, dear Joanna. Goodbye."

Chapter 8

Joanna and Mary arrived at St Pancreas Station at approximately 18:15. Their train was two hours late, hardly allowing them enough time to make their connection at Charring Cross to catch the slow train to Greenhithe.

Crowds of people were making their way to the underground and already organizing their beds for the night. Joanna grew anxious at the sight of so many people in one place at the same time. She grabbed Mary's hand. Stepping over the crowds, who were stretched out on the platform in front of her, she saw them all: mothers, young children, and women breast feeding their babies and settling them down comfortably before another night of torment began.

Joanna had often thought the conditions in the tunnel to be bad. But it was nothing compared to this.

Hurriedly, she pushed her way up the escalators with her heavy suitcase, anxiously holding Mary's hand at the same time. They finally entered the platform where they boarded the tube for Charring Cross.

The same problem presented itself as they disembarked. Stepping over people this way seemed terrible to Joanna. But she had her own worse fears, those of being trapped in London alone with Mary in the middle of the night during an air raid.

She breathed a sigh of relief when a porter came to her rescue.

"Where are you going?" he asked.

"Greenhithe, the slow train to Chatham," replied Joanna.

"Gawd blimey," came the cockney reply. "You've left it a bit late, haven't you? Jerry'll be overhead in a few seconds. Oh well. Never mind. Just follow me, love. I'll see you okay."

"Thank you so very much."

Joanna felt safe and relaxed once they were settled in their seats within minutes of boarding the train. The siren sounded. Darkness was already beginning to close in on them. The train slowly gathered speed out of Charring Cross Station.

Mary stared at her mother. Joanna knew she must think of something to quell her daughter's fears.

"It's all right, Mary, darling. Don't worry about the air raid. They never bomb trains. They move too fast."

Mary didn't look at all convinced. She rummaged in her bag to find a notepad and pencil.

She quickly wrote, "It's okay, Mummy. I'm not scared."

Joanna smiled proudly at her daughter and they both gave each other the thumbs up sign.

At that moment, a railway inspector entered the compartment. He was checking all the windows to see if the blackout blinds had been properly fastened down. He announced to the passengers that there was no cause for alarm providing all the blinds were securely fixed. Then he stated emphatically that not the slightest glimmer of light must be seen.

"That's why, I'm afraid, I must insist that we travel in complete darkness at least until we are out of the city. Then you will be allowed to have the dimmer lights on. I'm sorry about this, everybody. But if they can't see us then they won't trouble us."

He then left the compartment and made his way along the corridor. There was a ripple of anxiety among the other passengers. Especially when the artillery guns opened fire. It sounded terrifying, as if shrapnel was bouncing off the roof. The train driver continued with his awesome task, courageously battling through all the turmoil out into the open countryside, whilst the Luftwaffe raged above.

That evening, Joanna was pleased to be in her own home once more, even though she felt utterly shattered from the hazardous journey. Quickly, she began to prepare a meal of cheese on toast from the few provisions she had brought home with her.

"Here you are, Mary. Come along and eat this up. Then you must go straight to bed. It's getting very late."

Then it occurred to her.

Bed. What bed? And where do we go if Jerry decides to return? It's far too late to attempt the tunnel.

Joanna began to panic. Then stopped. She told herself not to be so stupid. She was home now and would just have to carry on. Hurriedly, she walked into the hall and tried ringing her friend, Jean, in the house next door. Almost before she dialed the operator, her instincts told her there was no one at home.

She then tried the house on the other side, her friend Dr. Stanley and his wife, only to find the same response. It was obvious to Joanna now. Everyone must be in their shelters. That meant another raid was to be expected.

Joanna walked back into the dining room. Not wishing to alarm Mary, she sat down in the armchair and lit a cigarette. She then switched on the wireless, only to hear the appalling voice of the famous propagandizer, Lord Haw Haw, announcing 'This is Germany calling'.

Joanna quickly switched off the set and turned to Mary, who had already finished her meal and was now looking terribly tired.

"Mary, I'm just going out to see if the Anderson will be okay for tonight. You stay here, darling. I won't be long."

Mary nodded her head in agreement.

Joanna ventured into the darkness of her garden with just a small torchlight. She heard a rumble in the far distance and knew immediately that the Luftwaffe would return on their usual route following the line of the river.

At that moment, she heard a rustle coming from the bushes behind her. She turned around abruptly, as a voice called out, "Who goes there?"

Joanna recognized the voice of old Bob, the local ARP warden.

"Oh, hello, Bob. You gave me quite a scare. I thought you were a prowler."

Bob stepped back, looking surprised. "Why, hello, Joanna. I'm sorry if I startled you. I've been keeping an eye on your place whilst you've been away. That's all. We didn't expect you back so soon."

"I didn't expect to be back so soon, Bob. We only arrived home this evening. I'm checking the Anderson to see if it's okay for tonight. I'm afraid it's too late to go down the tunnel."

"You haven't time to get ready for anything, Jo. We've just been told to expect a third wave, and they will be overhead in a few seconds." There was urgency in Bob's voice as he spoke. "I would advise you to settle down somewhere in the strongest part of the house. I know it's not much of a choice, Jo, but it's all I can suggest at the moment. I only wish I could be of more help. But I haven't finished my rounds yet. I've got to check on old Mrs. Jones up the road and see if she's okay."

As Bob spoke, the siren sounded. They both looked up at the night sky on hearing the awesome drone of the Luftwaffe.

"Now you go in the house and take care, Jo. I'll try and look in on my way back."

"Thank you very much. But please don't worry. We'll be okay. Take care and goodnight, Bob."

"Good night, Jo. I'll see you tomorrow."

He disappeared into the darkness.

Joanna turned on her heel and ran like the wind up the garden path back to the house. Mary had fallen asleep but roused slightly when her mother entered. Joanna hurried up the stairs and hastily collected pillows and blankets from the linen cupboard.

Before she had descended, the Luftwaffe bombers were nearly overhead. Joanna could hear the noise of artillery guns and the whizzing spurts of gunfire from allied forces. Joanna had grown so accustomed to the war that she knew every sound of both allied and enemy planes.

Mary rubbed her eyes as she stood and watched her mother prepare their bed for the night in the cupboard under the stairs. Only then did she realize that they would not be going down the tunnel, and silently, she began to cry.

Joanna quickly took her by the arm. "It's all right, Mary, my darling. Don't worry, sweetheart. We will be quite safe under here. It's not going to be a bad air raid."

By comforting Mary, Joanna found it easier to hide the fears and misgivings that were now rising within her chest. Had she been right to bring Mary back to all this?

Oh God, what have I done wrong? This is a nightmare.

Mary felt settled for a little while by her mother's comforting words. Then, when the noise intensified and the whole house seemed to vibrate from the blasting of falling debris, Mary sobbed. She rolled her hands into a tight fist grip, pulling at her nightdress.

Joanna remained calm whilst her inner turmoil twisted and tore at her very soul.

"It will be all right, my darling. Everything will be all right."

Her serene voice sounded like a divine plea to the heavens asking for forgiveness.

Mary, unable to express her terror by shouting out, held onto her mother's arm, digging her nails into her flesh. Joanna held her daughter tight and realized she would have to divert Mary's attention by doing something different.

"Would you like me to sing you a song, sweetheart?"

Mary nodded.

Joanna began by singing one of Mary's favorites: 'There'll be blue birds over the white cliffs of Dover'. She continued to sing until it was totally impossible, and only then did she stop, when the whole house felt as if it had been shaken to pieces. Joanna sat looking upward and holding Mary in her arms.

Only when the dreadful noise began to subside and the all clear sounded did they try to attempt any sleep.

Chapter 9

Early the next morning, Joanna crept out of the cupboard and expected to find half the house blown away. To her surprise, she only found the French windows in the dining room and kitchen blown in, and the frames still hanging loosely on their hinges. Joanna stood amongst the rubble where the French windows should be. She looked up at the early morning sky and thanked God that yesterday had only been a long day. And not their last.

"Oh, Jo, poor old you. What a turn up for the books. Imagine! Going all the way up there and nearly being murdered," said Nina, as she made her bunk beds the following evening. She smiled. "I'm sorry, Jo. But I just can't help seeing the irony of it all."

"Yes, I suppose it does sound rather humorous. I can hardly believe it myself. It's difficult to realize that it all happened only yesterday. It seems more like a dream now."

"What a blessing you had this...What was his name? Oh, yes, Dr. David, to help you. He sounds a nice sort of chap." Nina looked at Joanna with a curious grin.

"Yes...well." Joanna paused. "As I have already explained, it seems a long time ago now and I'm very pleased to be home again." Joanna spoke in a matter of fact tone. She had no wish to go into details about David and discreetly changed the subject. "You must have given your head a terrible bang when you walked into that lamppost the other night in the blackout, Nina. I've never seen such a dreadful bruise. Your poor face looks terribly painful."

"Yes, it was nasty at the time, Jo. But it's much better now."

"I suppose you went to see your doctor?"

"What? Oh, no, Jo. It wasn't necessary. Anyway, doctors are far too busy these days with urgent cases to worry about me. I wouldn't waste their time with a little thing like this."

Nina looked a little agitated, and then Marianne started crying. Nina turned her full attention to the children.

"John, Michael," she shouted, "stop teasing Marianne and get into your bunks at once."

Her voice sounded tired and strained. Nina never discussed her private life with anyone. She felt acutely embarrassed about her poor, unfortunate marriage, and tried desperately to avoid talking of it whenever possible, especially when in the company of Joanna. They had both become very good friends since coming to the shelter. However, the last thing Nina wanted at the moment was her pity.

Joanna stared at Nina's poor, tired face and sensed that something was definitely amiss. It was obvious she wished to evade the subject. Joanna didn't pursue the question.

Instead, she added, on a more lighthearted note, "It's dreadful when that happens. I've had my torch fail on the odd occasion, but never when I've been coming down here, thank goodness." Joanna laughed. "That poor old lamppost must have wondered what hit it."

With Joanna's cheerful, unbiased attitude, Nina seemed a little happier and began to laugh.

"I have an idea," exclaimed Joanna hastily. "Why don't we make a pact to meet somewhere, maybe at the top of the avenue, and make our way down here together? That would solve both our problems. It's highly unlikely that both our torches will fail at the same time."

Nina smiled warmly. "That sounds a lovely idea, Jo. But I wouldn't want to be a hindrance to you."

Joanna looked a little bewildered. "Hindrance? But-"

Nina interrupted her. "Look, I appreciate your offer. But, you see, Jo..." Nina paused. "Sometimes I'm a little late in leaving. With Josh's dinner to prepare and getting the children ready, sometimes I'm at sixes and sevens, and I wouldn't want to keep you waiting."

"Nevertheless, I shall be waiting for you at the top of the avenue at around eight o'clock starting from tomorrow night. Or maybe you would prefer I call for you?"

"Oh, no, please don't do that, Jo." Nina paused. She looked apprehensive. "I'll try and be there. But I can't promise."

Joanna looked straight into Nina's eyes. Her stance was adamant yet affable. "I want you to promise me you'll be there, Nina. If not for yourself then think about the children. They deserve some kind of safety. Please be there, Nina."

"Okay. You win," said Nina, sighing. "You're impossible. You know that, Jo?"

"Yes. I've been told that quite often." Joanna smiled.

Eager to change the subject, Nina inquired, "Oh, by the way, how are your parents? I haven't seen much of them lately."

It didn't escape Joanna's attention that Nina appeared rather evasive whenever discussing her private life. "They're fine, apart from dad's odd touch of rheumatics."

"It's a great shame your mother is unable to come along with us. I don't suppose it's easy for her with your father being in the Home Guard and so on."

"She's quite able, Nina." Joanna smiled but showed a slight annoyance at the mention of her mother. "Now, she is one person I can never win over. No one can. Believe me. Terry and I have tried to get her into some sort of shelter. But she would rather stay in the house and risk not only her own life but also my father's. Poor Dad. You have no idea how he suffers, Nina."

"I always thought that your mother was an invalid. I thought she was sick or something."

"Sick," uttered Joanna. "She makes me sick."

Nina smiled. She viewed Joanna, at that moment, as a rather comic figure, standing there and waving her arms around indignantly. Joanna, quick to realize this, continued with her monotonous chatter concerning her parents. To anyone else, she may have sounded like a pain in the neck.

"Oh, I'm sorry to be such a bore. What must you think of me, Nina?"

"No, you're not." Nina laughed. "Do continue, Jo. I'm interested. It's nice to hear of other people's troubles." Nina looked happier and more relaxed. "It must be terrible for your poor father to be domineered all the time like that."

"Well, Terry and I have both tried to tell him, but he just takes it all. Some people are like that, Nina. They never give tit for tat. Poor old Dad."

Nina sat on the edge of her bunk bed, deep in thought. "Yes. I suppose so."

Just at that moment, the siren sounded.

"They're early tonight," commented Joanna, as she poured hot coco from her thermos flask. "Here you are, Mary. When you've drunk this, I would like you to put your comics away and then bed down. You scarcely had any sleep at all last night. When you're finished, I'll put cotton wool in your ears. That'll help deafen the noise. I always think that helps to eliminate the pandemonium outside. What do you think, Nina?"

Joanna turned around to find Nina still sitting on her bunk bed. She looked far removed from everything that was going on around her.

"Sorry, Jo. I wasn't listening. What did you say?" Nina spoke in a vague voice.

Joanna, mystified by her sudden mood swing, had no wish to appear intrusive. She just smiled. "Oh, nothing important. Would you care for a cup of coco?"

"Thank you, Jo. I wouldn't say no."

"What about the children?" Joanna offered a cup towards them.

"They're okay, thanks, Jo. They've had their drinks earlier."

Michael ventured in a low voice, peeping from beneath the blankets, "I'd like a cup of coco."

Joanna laughed and eagerly handed him a cup. "John, would you like a cup?"

"Yes please, Mrs. Busher."

"And what about little Marianne?"

"Oh, she's fallen asleep. Bless her. You're very kind, Jo," said Nina, looking more alert. "But you won't have enough left for you, will you?"

Joanna reassured her. "Please, don't worry. I always come prepared."

"Thanks, Mrs. Busher, very much."

Joanna glanced at the two boys hurriedly drinking up the coco.

"I have another flask in my locker. You can finish this one if you wish."

"Cor, thanks, Mrs. Busher," shouted John and Michael.

"Think nothing of it. It's my pleasure." Joanna smiled. "Well, I'm off to bed now. I feel absolutely shattered after yesterday's events and I'm not going to allow Goring to bother me tonight," said Joanna with a little chuckle. "Good night, boys. Good night, Nina. Sleep tight."

Nina and the boys echoed their good nights as Joanna climbed up to the top bunk. She lay there for quite a while before extinguishing the small nightlight in the holder by her bunk that had been casting shadows around the high-circled roof of the tunnel.

As the noise outside grew louder, her thoughts were not of the air raid but of the muffled sobs she heard coming from Nina's bunk bed.

Chapter 10

In the days that followed, hostilities intensified. Joanna found herself increasingly occupied with the Red Cross and helping Dr. Stanley. At this stage in the war, casualties were high in numbers. Joanna hardly gave herself time to think about Terry. Her work became an asset. It gave her a sense of wellbeing.

Only in her waking hours did she allow her mind to wonder. She envisaged Terry lying there beside her. Then she came out of slumber and heard the bemoaning sound of voices in the tunnel.

On one such dismal morning when Joanna was returning home, she was met by Pete the postman. He handed her two letters. Joanna stared, wide-eyed, at the postmark on one letter.

"Are they from who I think?" said Pete with a cheeky grin.

Joanna beamed and nodded her head. "Well one of them is, Pete."

Anxious to get into the house, she bid him good day.

Once home, she read Terry's letter first, caressing it as one would a valued treasure.

Terry was soon to be posted somewhere in the southwest of England, but he didn't know exactly where. He also thought maybe he would soon be having a spot of leave, but he didn't know when.

The second letter was from Uncle Tom informing her that he would be attending the Easter concert. Joanna was delighted that Tom had decided to pay her a visit. Perhaps now she would be able to persuade him to give up his work in London, where he had practiced law all his life, and move out to the suburbs.

Whenever Terry had advised him that it was far too dangerous for a man of seventy-eight to be working in war-torn London, he would totally dismiss the idea by saying, "If everyone ran from the capital, there would be nobody left to defend the heart of the world."

Joanna smiled. They were so alike, Terry and Tom, in character. Joanna was happy, and in her blissfulness, she decided to give Mary her favorite dish of mincemeat greens and potatoes when she came home for midday lunch.

It was rare, at this stage in the war, to have any air raids in the middle of the day. However, there was always the exception to the rule. And today was to be one of them.

Mary delighted at the prospect of seeing her father again. Though she could not speak, it was all there in her eyes.

With excitement, she wrote down, "I am so happy. Please can I have some more castard and that there?" She pointed to the treacle tart.

Joanna found the sentence rather amusing and laughed.

"Of course you can, darling. I know you love treacle tart and custard. Oh, by the way, this is how you spell custard, darling." Joanna wrote, "C-u-s-t-a-r-d." Then she smiled down at her daughter. "Now, I think we'll celebrate and eat it all up together. Then you must hurry up and get ready for school."

Mary quickly wrote, "I am so happy. Can I call for June next door? She always reads what I write."

"No, I'm afraid not, Mary. She has chicken pox, and you wouldn't wish to look like a spotty dick when you see Daddy and Uncle Tom now, would you?"

Mary smiled that slow smile, that certain smile, which always reminded Joanna of Terry.

They both laughed and shook their heads in agreement.

"Now off you go. I'll wave to you from the bedroom window, and then I'll have to hurry up and get ready myself."

Mary ran down the road gleefully kicking up the stones in front of her and looking for pieces of shrapnel to add to her collection. Before she was even half way to school, the siren sounded. Within seconds, the Luftwaffe appeared from nowhere. Or so it had seemed to Mary.

Artillery guns opened fire and all hell let loose. Mary ran like the wind. Then came a massive explosion from a distance away. Yet it was near enough to hurl Mary into the air and fling her headfirst into a hawthorn bush. Mary screamed in terror.

Then, quite suddenly, a soldier appeared on the scene and lifted her out of the bushes. Mary screamed even louder when she saw the blood pouring from her face.

"It's okay, love," said the soldier, who happened to be a sergeant in the Home Guard.

He ran with her in his arms to the nearest shelter. Mary's screams became convulsive.

"There, there. You're okay, love. You're okay now. You're safe."

Joanna, in the middle of changing into her uniform, looked up on hearing the siren.

"Oh my God, Mary," she gasped.

She threw on her skirt and jacket with lightning speed and fled out of the house and down the road. *Ack Ack.* Guns firing. Incendiaries going off all around. The blasting of bombs in the near vicinity. Burning shrapnel bouncing on the pavement beneath her feet. All seemed to heighten Joanna's speed, propelling her forward.

With outstretched arms and her head thrown back, she screamed. "Mary! For God's sake, where are you?" Her voice almost a sob, she stood in the middle of the road at the heart of all the chaos. Between a vegetable field and the hedge-grove, she threw her arms high in the air. With clenched fists, she shouted to the heavens, "Oh, God. Where is my Mary?"

At that precise moment, the Home Guard sergeant jumped into the middle of the road.

When he saw Joanna, he called out, "Are you looking for a little, blonde-haired girl?"

"Yes! Yes!" shouted Joanna nervously.

"She's with us. She's safe, love," said the sergeant. "Just follow me."

He took Joanna's elbow and guided her over the fallen debris into the shelter that was situated between a field and the village shops.

"She's over there with Mrs. Parkinson, the butcher's wife. She's in a terrible state, poor, little love. Mrs. Parkinson is trying to clean up her face. It's a miracle she's still alive. I thought she was a gonner when I first saw her lying there until I heard her terrifying screams. My God, did she scream. I've never heard anything like it. But she's okay now. She'll be pleased to see you. That's all she's been saying. 'I want my mummy'. What bastards, coming over here in the middle of the day, catching us all on the hop."

Mrs. Parkinson, the butcher's wife, shouted out, "Don't swear like that, Mike. There are children present."

"Okay. I'm sorry, Mrs. Parkinson. But it makes me mad. I'd better be off now. Someone else may need help outside."

"Don't be stupid, Mike. It's dangerous out there," called Mrs. Parkinson.

"Oh, I'll be okay. Anyway, I think they're going away now."

Joanna interjected, "Just one moment." Dazed and covered in dirt, she threw back her long, blonde hair from her face. She slowly turned her gaze from Mary to the sergeant. Then she looked directly into his eyes and whispered, "What did you say?"

Mike assumed she'd found him offensive and quickly apologized.

But Joanna was impervious to everything, including his swearing. The only thought that registered in her brain were the words, 'I want my mummy'.

Joanna, in a state of stunned confusion, went to Mary's side. Embracing her daughter and holding her tight, she whispered, "Mary. Mary, my darling."

Mary responded in a soft voice, "I can speak, Mummy."

Joanna thanked God once again for this very hour.

Chapter 11

"Well," said Dr. Stanley later that day, "Mary is a lucky young lady. Her speech has returned on a permanent basis. This happens occasionally in cases of extreme shock. It's triggered off by circumstances similar to the one Mary already suffered a couple of years ago. I do not feel that there is any need for further investigation. Unless you would like a second opinion, Joanna? Then, of course, I will make the necessary arrangements for her too see a London consultant."

"No, I do not think so, John. Not at this stage anyway. I think it may do more harm than good."

"My thoughts entirely, Joanna. Too much probing around may have adverse effects. I think we should allow nature to take its course. Mary had a bad shock and must take each day steadily. As for her facial scars, they will heal in time, especially with your loving care. However, her pronunciation may not always coordinate. If you do have any such problems then we can always arrange a few lessons in phonetics."

Dr. Stanley turned and glanced at Mary, who stood watching the goldfish in a tank under the bay window that had been boarded up.

"She'll probably drive you mad with non-stop chattering now." He smiled with a twinkle in his eyes. "Do you like goldfish, Mary?"

Mary replied, "Yes, sir." She spoke in a crisp, sharp voice, clearly indicating that there was no need for any lessons in phonetics.

"Would you like one, Mary?"

"Oh, yes please, sir. You see, I had a pet budgie called Henry and he died of fright during that dreadful air raid the other night."

Dr. Stanley, charmed and surprised by Mary's little speech, added, "Then you shall have any three you like, my dear child."

"Oh, thank you very much, sir," said Mary, beaming from cheek to cheek. "I will try to love them as much as poor Henry."

"That's very sweet of you, John," said Joanna, smiling.

Dr. Stanley turned his attention to Joanna. "Not at all. It's not every day we have something to celebrate. Joanna, my dear, I wonder, are you going anywhere near the Red Cross center today?"

"Yes. I'm going after lunch. Is there something you'd like me to do?"

"Yes. I wonder whether you would be so kind as to deliver those two boxes of bandages for me."

"Why yes, of course." Joanna smiled.

"It's because of these infernal air raids. They've sent these to me and I suppose they have sent *my* equipment to the Red Cross." He sighed and shook his head. "I do not know where it will all end, Joanna."

Joanna was aware of how tired Dr. Stanley appeared recently. He was a man approaching his seventy-fourth birthday. He worked hard during the day, and more often than not, he was asked to leave his shelter at night and tend to the sick, injured, or dying. He did it all in the name of duty.

Joanna asked him on the odd occasion, "I suppose you will be retiring soon?"

His answer had always been the same. "Only when the bloodshed stops and there are others around to take my place. Then I shall retire."

Dr. Stanley was synonymous with many elderly people during the war who refused to retire, including Terry's Uncle Tom, and her own father.

"Oh, by the way," said Joanna, "I wonder if you and Celia would care to come to the Easter concert at St Joseph's church hall on Saturday afternoon. We are trying to raise funds for the Red Cross and also a little extra cash to help Mike's widow. She was in hospital giving birth to their first baby at the time he was killed. It was so dreadful. Poor Mike."

She remembered how Mike had been so pleased that Mary had spoken her first words again to him in the air shelter. Joanna suddenly paused, a hard lump rising in her throat. Dr. Stanley stood next to Mary looking at the goldfish. He turned his head slightly and raised his hand as if to cut off any further conversation.

"Yes," he muttered wearily. "A dreadful business, that Messerschmitt coming down like that almost on top of him. We're living in terrible times, my dear."

The air was tense for a second.

Then Dr. Stanley spoke on a brighter note.

"Yes. I'll take two tickets for the concert. Especially if you are going to charm us all with that wonderful voice of yours."

Joanna regained herself a little and forced a smile. "Really, John, you are the most dreadful flatterer. But I'm afraid I really must go now. I've so much to do."

"I understand." Dr. Stanley smiled. "Haven't we all?"

"I'll send Mary around with the tickets later on. TTFN, John, and do take care."

"I will. And you do the same, Joanna. Oh, and don't forget your goldfish, Mary."

"No, I won't forget, and thank you very much. Goodbye, sir."

"Goodbye, Mary." Dr. Stanley smiled affectionately.

Chapter 12

"Oh, come on, Mary. It's beginning to get dark now. We've waited long enough for Aunty Nina. She doesn't appear to be coming, and if we wait any longer, Jerry will be overhead."

"Why do we have to wait here anyway? Why can't we go to her house and see if she's there?" asked Mary.

"Because Aunty Nina would prefer that we wait here," said Joanna.

"Why?" Mary looked curious, a tiny pucker forming on her brow.

"I have no idea, Mary. Aunty Nina probably has a very good reason."

"I wonder what it is," said Mary inquisitively in a lingering voice.

Joanna laughed and looked at her daughter's wistful face. "Mary Busher, since you've found your tongue, you're becoming a right little nosy parker. Now let's see if your legs are as fast as your brain. Come on. Hurry up. I'll race you to the tunnel before Jerry joins us for supper."

Bob's wife, Maggie, stood with arms folded leaning against her bunk. She watched them enter the tunnel just as the siren sounded, and then made her way up through the center of the room.

"So she's kept you waiting again, Jo? I don't know why you risk your neck hanging around for her."

"Yes, I must confess, I have taken a few chances. However, it's not going to happen again."

"Good for you, Jo. Of course, I'm not one to tittle-tattle, but whilst you were away up north, there were some nights she didn't bother to come down at all. There's something strange about it all. It's those poor children I feel sorry for, especially little Marianne. She must be terrified, the poor child. That business about Nina walking into a lamppost, I take with a pinch of salt."

Mary stood listening until Joanna gave her a thermos flask to take along to their bunks.

"Well, quite frankly, Maggie, I don't think it's anyone's business, and until such a time comes that Nina wishes to discuss her private life with someone, I think we should all stop this idle chatter and get on with what we are doing. So, if you'll excuse me, Maggie, I have my beds to make up."

Maggie stood with her mouth open, ready to speak, and then closed it again. She was a kind-hearted woman, but whenever there was a speck of scandal to pick up on, she was always the first one to spread the news.

Maggie appeared to be a little rebuffed by Joanna's bluntness. She turned indignantly and made her way up through the tunnel with a hand towel and toiletries bag under her arm, ready to take her usual nightly ablutions in cold water.

Suddenly, John, Michael, and Marianne entered. They pushed past Maggie and ran straight up to Joanna.

Maggie called out, "Oh, you're here at last, are you? Even if you can't be polite enough to say excuse me." Then she mumbled quietly to herself, "Children of today haven't any manners. I don't know what the world is coming too. It wasn't like that in my day. Well, never mind. I'd better hurry up. Otherwise Jerry will catch me with my pants down."

Old Maggie continued on her way out through the small door at the end of the tunnel to her destination: a cold water tap situated on the wall outside. It was now dark. She closed the door behind her and shone the torch downward. Maggie paused. She could hear heavy breathing coming from somewhere nearby.

"Stop. Who goes there?"

Maggie shone her torchlight in the direction of the wall tap. Although it was dark, she could faintly distinguish Nina's outline. Maggie gently moved her torch a little closer and screamed at what she saw in front of her.

Nina stood with her head over the sink and, propped against the tap, her face covered in blood.

"My Lord, what has happened to you?"

Inside, Joanna listened to a hurried story that Michael and John both dreamed up as they spoke. They didn't sound at all convincing. Nina had supposedly tripped on a stone, sending her head first into a tree. In any other situation, their story would have appeared rather comic. However, Joanna believed something was definitely amiss, and she could see the children were agitated.

"Okay, boys. Now don't worry. Take care of Marianne and start getting ready for bed. You too, Mary. I'll be back in a second."

Joanna was soon on Maggie's tail. Once outside, she vaguely distinguished Maggie standing with Nina by the water tap, but she couldn't see properly in the dark.

"What has happened, Maggie?"

"Over here, Jo. Take my torch and shine it this way and you'll find out."

She gasped as she saw Nina's battered and bleeding face.

"My God. What has happened to you?"

Nina tried to mutter a few words through her swollen lips.

At that moment, the dreaded droning of the Luftwaffe could be heard, growing closer.

"I think we ought to get her inside quickly."

"Well, what do you think I'm trying to do?" snapped Maggie, her hurt pride clearly rising to the surface. "If you can hold my torch up, Jo, I'll wrap this towel around her face."

Nina was dazed and near to collapse.

"It looks as if she's had another one of her peculiar accidents," muttered Maggie.

Old Bob emerged from the cutting and shouted, "Put that bloody light out. Are you crazy? They're almost overhead." As he came closer, he recognized his wife. "Gawd blimey! What's happened here?"

By this time, both women had their arms wrapped around Nina, helping her into the tunnel.

Joanna called out, "It's okay, Bob. Nina's just had an accident."

Inside, there were whispers among the other occupants. "Well, I wonder what's happened to her."

Joanna and Maggie soon set about tidying up Nina's wounds.

"Of course, what she really needs is a doctor," said Joanna.

"Name me a doctor that's going to come out in all this," Maggie retorted.

"Dr. Stanley wouldn't mind."

"We're a long way from the nearest phone box. Any more bright ideas, Joanna?"

On realizing that Maggie had taken her words to heart, Joanna gently patted her on the shoulder. "Maggie, you've been marvelous. I really don't know what we'd all do without you and Bob. You both work terribly hard."

The older woman turned slowly to face Joanna and smiled. "Thanks, Jo. That's very nice of you to say so. You've done pretty well yourself. Your nursing experience really came in handy tonight."

"Think nothing of it. Anyway, it's my job."

"You're too modest, Jo. But it was damn lucky you brought your medical kit with you."

"I have to take it everywhere I go now, Maggie."

"Well, it feels good to have someone like you around, Jo."

"Thank you." Joanna smiled.

"I know I'm an old blather at times, but I really am concerned about Nina. What do you think we should do?"

Joanna whispered, "Well, judging from the state of her, you'd think she'd just done ten rounds with Jack Dempsey."

Joanna stopped talking as she glanced at Nina lying on her bunk. She looked at Maggie and put her index finger to her lips. Maggie nodded in response.

Nina muttered something.

"What did you say, dear?" asked Joanna.

"Thank you both. I'm sorry to be a nuisance."

Joanna looked at her tenderly and answered, "You're not a nuisance. Now try and get some sleep, darling."

Nina tried to smile. Then, turning her head, she closed her eyes.

"She'll sleep now. At least we've made her more comfortable until the morning."

"Yes, Jo," whispered Maggie. "But between you and me, I just wonder what the hell's going on."

Joanna looked directly at her friend. "I shudder to think, Maggie."

Chapter 13

Terry had been posted to Lympstone, a delightful spot deep in the heart of the Devonshire countryside near to the River Exe. The encampment, which had existed for approximately twelve months, consisted mainly of huts. The first recruits joined Lympstone in 1940. It had been designed especially for Royal Marine Commando training, enshrouded by high trees and foliage as camouflage against the enemy.

Terry fitted in well with military training, and strange though it may seem, he would have enjoyed it had he not been plagued by thoughts of Joanna and Mary living in the midst of all the bombing. Air raids in this part of the country were rare. The blitz on all major cities in the southwest had not yet begun. The peaceful tranquility seemed almost unreal to Terry and only added to his fears for Joanna and Mary.

However, he realized that life had its compensations. On receiving the news that Mary had regained her speech, he was overjoyed. Nevertheless, he would have preferred to hear the good news under different circumstances.

Terry had befriended an elderly woman who came regularly to the local pub for her nightly jug of stout whilst he and a few lads from the base were enjoying a glass of beer. Mrs. Dent lived alone in a picturesque cottage quite close to the base. Terry always seemed to find time whenever he was off duty to do the odd job or two around the house, chopping firewood, bringing in the coal, or fixing her wireless set.

Mrs. Dent's style of dress matched that of her cottage. She wore a white apron over a long, black dress, and her hair tucked into a tight bun at the back of her neck. She looked like an elderly woman who had just stepped out of a children's storybook from the last century.

Mrs. Dent was eternally grateful to Terry and told him that if there was anything she could possibly do to repay him for his kindness, she would not hesitate to do so. Therefore, on another typical evening, Mrs. Dent decided to give him a lovely surprise.

Terry sat alone in the bar of the George and Dragon sipping a glass of whisky and looking rather dissatisfied with life. He and the rest of his platoon had just been informed that all leave had been postponed until further notice.

"Hello, Terry. What are you doing here all on your own?" said Mrs. Dent, entering the lounge bar.

Terry looked up. "Good evening, Mrs. Dent. Lovely to see you again. Do take a seat. What can I get you to drink?"

"Oh, nothing, dear boy. I've just come for my usual and then I'm off home. You're just the person I wanted to see."

Terry was slightly hesitant, assuming that she had another job for him to do. Not that he minded. He enjoyed it. He just wasn't inclined to discuss odd jobs at the moment.

"Why, what's the matter, my boy? You look rather glum."

Terry explained that he wouldn't be seeing his wife for quite a while.

"Oh, I see. That is depressing news. Actually, I don't know how they expect you boys to carry on without being able to see your families from time to time."

"Well, that's war for you, Mrs. Dent, and there isn't much we can do about it, I'm afraid."

Mrs. Dent's eyes sparkled. "Well, maybe I'll be able to do something about that."

"Oh, really?" said Terry, looking curious.

"Yes. I have a proposition to make. You remember I told you I have a granddaughter living in Cornwall?"

"Yes. I believe you did," said Terry, looking more interested.

Mrs. Dent looked at Terry seriously. "Well, she has a small farm down there, and next week, I'm going to stay with her for at least two or three months. Now, what I suggest is-"

Before Mrs. Dent had chance to finish her sentence, the bar door flung open, and in marched the lads from the base followed by their girlfriends. A few exhibitionists were wearing their blue uniforms to impress the girls. In a matter of seconds, one of the lads came rushing over to Terry.

"Hello, Terry. What'll you have to drink?" The marine looked at Mrs. Dent. "And you too, ma?"

"No thanks, Mick. I'll be leaving soon."

"Okay. One for the road then. By the way, this is my girlfriend, Rose."

Before Terry had chance for any counter argument, Mick was already up at the bar.

Terry turned to the supposed girlfriend. "How do you do, Rose? Please do take a seat while you are able. May I introduce my very good friend, Mrs. Dent?"

The elderly woman smiled and shook the younger woman's hand. "How do you do, my dear?"

Before Terry realized it, the bar was almost full of marines. A few of their girlfriends were in the Land Army, based at one of the local farms outside Topsham.

"Terry, my dear boy, I think I had better depart," said Mrs. Dent. "Yes, it's getting awfully crowded in here."

"I'll walk you home."

"No, Terry. I insist you stay here and have a drink with your friends. However, I would like you to pop in on your way back to camp this evening. I have something I wish to discuss with you."

She smiled and walked with Terry to the door. He had a suspicious grin on his face that broadened into his usual slow smile.

"Gertie Dent, you're a devious but delightful little lady. I promise you, I'll be there."

"Good." Mrs. Dent smiled and left.

Terry eased his way through the crowd and stopped briefly to chat with the lads.

Mick returned to join Rose at the table with the drinks.

"Who's that cracking looking bloke?" whispered Rose.

"Oh, that's my mate, Tel. Eyes off, Rose. He's married. And he never goes anywhere unless it's old ma Dent's house."

"What a smasher," Rose continued. "Such a waste. Pity we can't fix him up."

"Rose, I've said, he's married."

"Well, you see, Mick, I've got this friend who would love a date with a chap like him."

Rose's sentence was suddenly interrupted when Terry appeared.

"I'm sorry about this, everyone, but I'm afraid I won't be able to stay very long. I have some letters to write."

Terry felt slightly uncomfortable in Mick's presence. He knew what his fellow marine got up to, and in no way did he ever want to risk the powerful love he had with Joanna and Mary to engage in frivolous, carnal flights of fancy. He knew only too well Mick was a married man with three children.

"Hey, come on, Terry." Mick spoke in tempting tone.

Terry said in a resolute voice, "No. Really, Mick, I have to go."

"Don't tell me you have a date with old ma Dent."

Mick smirked and then laughed raucously.

"Well, yes. As it happens, I have."

Terry grinned casually then glanced at Rose.

"Goodbye, Rose. It's been a pleasure. Bye, Mick. See you later."

Then Terry left.

Chapter 14

There seemed to be a hush in the tunnel the morning after Nina met with her amazing accident. Joanna and Maggie stood outside the tunnel talking.

"I didn't believe a word of her story. I can't understand her, Jo. We've done everything we possibly can to help her. We even got her boys off to school. Yet she's walking around in there as if nothing happened last night. She even refuses to see a doctor. What do you think of it all, Joanna?"

"Well, she's definitely trying to hide something, in my opinion."

Maggie looked wide-eyed at Joanna. "Yes, and my guess is it's her husband. If that's not a woman who's being beaten up then I'll eat my hat."

Joanna nodded her head. "Yes, I agree, Maggie. In point of fact, Nina's entire persona emanates that of much depravation and obviously male treatment. But, Maggie, if what we assume is true then why hasn't she sought advice?"

"Listen to me, Jo," said the older woman hastily. "I've seen cases like this before. Maybe she's too damned scared."

"You know, Maggie, you could be right. I've often wondered but dared not think."

"Look, Joanna, you're young and quite friendly with her. If she's going to confide in anyone, it'll be you. Find out what you can, Jo. Then maybe someone will be able to help her."

Joanna was touched by Maggie's sincerity, and she patted her on the shoulder.

"Please don't worry, Maggie. I'll do all I can."

"I knew you would. Bye for now. See you later. Take care, Jo."

"You too, Maggie. TTFN."

Joanna returned to the tunnel and tided up the rest of her things. She found Nina folding her heavy blankets and Marianne bouncing up and down on her bunk.

Nina called out lamely and with no definition in her voice, "Stop doing that on Aunty Jo's bunk, Marianne."

The child continued to do so until Joanna called out, "Now, come along, Marianne. You know you mustn't do that."

She spoke in a kind yet firm voice. Marianne jumped down immediately. She looked hesitantly at Joanna with fear in her eyes.

"It's all right, darling. No need to look so frightened. What are you playing?"

"Jumping high into the sky," came a timid reply.

"But there isn't any sky in here, darling," said Joanna tenderly.

For her age, Marianne couldn't speak very well. Her words were incoherent.

"I want to be where the sky is," she mumbled.

"I see." Joanna paused. "Well, we'll soon be outside. Then you can play under the sky. Meanwhile, would you like to draw me a picture of the sky?"

Marianne nodded her head.

"Okay, darling. I have Mary's board and chalks right here. You may keep them if you draw me a pretty picture."

Marianne sat down and began her work of art.

Joanna had noticed, during recent months, that Marianne had grown timid and slightly introverted.

"My God, Jo. You have a way with kids. She wouldn't do that for me," said Nina.

"Yes, she would."

"That's what you think. She's a real little devil at times. Plays me up something shocking. Kids are all the same. You want to thank your lucky stars you only have one."

"Terry and I would love more children. If it hadn't been for the war, we would have. We still may, once it's all over and we've won."

"You're very optimistic, Jo. What makes you think we're going to win?"

Joanna looked serious. "I think we have to be optimistic."

"Well, I wish I shared your opinion, Jo. But it's the kids that worry me."

"That's because you're tired and unwell."

"No, you don't understand, Jo. Anyway, what did you mean by that remark?"

"What remark?"

"You said I was tired and unwell."

"Well, it's obvious, isn't it, Nina?" Joanna stared hard into Nina's eyes, analyzing her poor, tired, and battered face. "Why don't you tell me what really happened last night? And all the other nights?"

"It's nothing to do with you, Jo. I have no wish to discuss my private life with anyone."

"Nina, I thought we were friends"

"Of course we are. But there are some things I cannot divulge."

"Why, Nina? You can trust me."

"Oh, I don't really think so, Jo. If I spoke one word, you would go straight to that gossiping old busybody."

"That's not entirely true, Nina. Maggie is a caring woman. She's worried about you. We both are."

"Then don't interfere. Please, Jo. Nobody can help me."

"I give you my word. I promise you, Nina. No one would hear anything from me."

"Jo, why can't you understand? I have nothing to say. I appreciate how you and Maggie helped me last night. But it's over now. So please go."

Joanna felt shunned. But as she looked into Nina's eyes, she saw terror.

"Very well. If that's what you wish, Nina, I will go and never offer my help again." She made her way to the end of the tunnel, and then called out, "Oh, by the way, Nina, I won't be here to bother you for quite a while. You see, I'm going down to Devon in two weeks to see Terry. Goodbye, Nina."

Joanna opened the door and left.

In the background, she heard Nina's voice echoing, "No. No. Please don't go, Jo. I didn't know what I was saying. You're the only friend I have." She spoke with a sob in her voice.

Joanna walked up through the woods, and then she stopped dead in her tracks. Nina's last words kept going around in her head. *You're the only friend I have.* She turned on her heel and run back to the tunnel. Joanna found Nina sitting on her bunk, her head buried in her hands.

She looked up as Joanna entered.

"Jo, I'm so sorry. I had no right to speak to you like that after all you've done for me. Please forgive me, Jo."

Joanna smiled as she sat down on the bunk beside Nina and gently touched her hand.

"Nina, there is nothing to forgive." There was a heavy silence as they looked at each other. "It's Josh, isn't it?"

Nina nodded as the tears fell. She found herself telling Joanna the whole story.

"My God. He's a monster. You must leave him, Nina."

"I can't, Jo."

"Why, for heaven sake?"

"Because I'm three months pregnant."

Joanna, horrified, whispered, "But why, Nina? I don't understand."

Nina looked directly at Joanna. "Oh, Jo. You are so naïve. It's obvious, isn't it?"

Joanna put her hand to her mouth as she looked at Nina's poor, battered face. Her throat tightened as if a large chestnut had surfaced in her throat.

Nina continued, "He made arrangements for me to see a back street abortionist. I haven't been near her. The last time I had an abortion, she nearly killed me. I'm not going through that again. I think he's rumbled that I'm not going through with it. That's partly the cause of these sudden outbursts of violence. There's nothing anyone can do to help me. I have even been to the police. They said they couldn't interfere in family affairs, especially when they have more important issues to attend to. The war, for example. However, they did suggest the children should be evacuated to somewhere safe. That's why I'm not going to seek their help again. It would please Josh. He hates the children. And me. The whole world, I suppose." Nina spoke in an indifferent tone as if nothing really mattered. Joanna could see her will draining before her eyes.

"How did you meet a man like Josh?"

"He was a regular in a pub where I worked as a barmaid in Putney, South West London. He always had a quick wit and a disarming smile that I found attractive. I guess I was looking for a way out. I was pretty stupid then."

"No, not really. People often have many sides. It's difficult to see them all when you first meet someone."

Nina nodded, her eyes fixed on a point in the past.

"Did he always have a violent side?"

Nina shook her head and grinned a little, recalling again her life gone by. "No. When we first met, it was all dinner dates and roses. He flattered me with compliments. Couldn't do enough for me. He proposed so quickly and I just got caught in the moment."

"So once you were married, what was he like then? Did he show his anger, his aggressive side, straight away?"

"No, not in the first three months of marriage. It wasn't until I became pregnant with John. That's when it all started."

"But why on earth didn't you leave him and go back to your Aunt Bertha?"

"Aunt Bertha. That's a laugh. I'll tell you my life story someday, Jo. It would make a good book. But right now, I have this thumping headache."

"You'll have more than a headache if you continue to live with him." Joanna looked deep into her eyes. "Why not stay with me for a while?"

"What?" gasped Nina. "Do you realize what you are saying, Jo?"

"Yes. Of course I do. Why not try it? At least until you're well. Then we can find somewhere more permanent for you."

"I can't do that."

"Why, Nina? Don't tell me you still love him after how he's treated you."

"Of course not. I've never loved him. I hate the bastard."

"Then, for heaven sake, Nina, go back, pack your bags, and come home with me." Joanna looked at her with a fixed expression. "Nina, leave him today while there is still a chance. I'll look after you and the children. I promise. Dr. Stanley lives next door to me. You can see him for medical treatment. And whilst I'm away, I'll ask my father to keep an eye on you. Also, there's old Bob and Maggie. You have plenty of friends, Nina. We all want to help you. We can inform the police again. You say you've told them once already. Well, this time, we'll make them sit up and take notice."

"No. No, not the police."

"Why not for heaven sake?"

"I've just told you, Jo. Please listen to me. If I told them, they would take the children away from me. And what if there were to be an invasion? I may never see them again."

"That's nonsense, Nina, and you know it."

"Jo, my dear friend, I appreciate everything you and Maggie have done for me. But I can't leave him. You don't understand. I have the children to consider."

Joanna saw real terror in Nina's eyes. She sighed, remembering Maggie's words. *Maybe she's too damned scared.*

"Very well. If I can't convince you now, then maybe you'll think about it. And if you do change your mind, then you can write to me. This is the address of where I'll be staying in Devon. Unfortunately, they're not on the phone."

Joanna quickly wrote it down and handed it to Nina.

She gazed at the address. "Orchard Cottage. Sounds lovely. How long did you say you're staying?"

"I don't know exactly. About two or three months, I would think."

"You'll enjoy yourself there, Jo. I know you will."

Nina smiled, and for a brief moment, she looked almost youthful.

Joanna mindfully gazed at her friend. "I wish you'd allow me to help you before I go."

"I've already explained, Jo. Let's leave it at that."

"Very well. If you wish. But, Nina, I'd like to ask you. What exactly did you mean when you said if there is going to be an invasion?"

"Well, it's obvious, isn't it?"

"No, I'm sorry, Nina. I still don't understand."

"I thought you knew, Jo. Josh is Jewish. Though you'd never believe it. He's not the practicing religious kind. So you see, Jo, I cannot implicate you or anyone else. If we lost the war, then…" Nina paused. "The only thing left for me to do would be to kill my darling children. Then myself. And Josh can go to hell."

Joanna made no comment. The sudden horror of Nina's words were written in her eyes. There was a hush between the two women. Joanna chose her words carefully.

"Well, if it's any consolation to you, we are going to win this war. Even if we have to go through hell and high water to do it, I assure you, we are going to win. I believe what Mr. Churchill said. Otherwise, why would they have taken men like my Terry? Not forgetting the RAF and the rest of the armed forces fighting body and soul. Look, Nina, come and stay with me. Please. Everything is going to be fine. You must have faith, and you don't need that monstrous husband. I'll look after you."

"No, Jo, my dear. I'm sorry. This is my final answer." Nina smiled through her swollen lips. "It's okay, Jo. Please don't worry about me."

"Blimey. Are you still here?" came a voice from the end of the tunnel. It was old Bob. "Anyone would think you haven't a home to go to. You have, by the way. I've just checked. It's a wonder though, after last night. My Gawd, what a strike, eh? I heard poor old London got a right pasting again. And around here, so they tell me. Craylands Lane took some flake."

"Oh my God," said Joanna. She turned to Nina. "I'll see you tonight, dear. Take care and think over my suggestion. I must go now." Joanna looked at old Bob. "My parents live near there. I intended on helping Nina with her bags." She paused.

"That's okay, Jo. You go," said Nina.

"Yes," agreed Bob. "I'll look after Nina. Go and see if your mum and dad are okay."

"Oh, thank you, Bob. See you both later. TTFN."

Joanna dashed out of the tunnel and made her way up through the woods.

She sensed that familiar acrid smell, the remnants of another bad raid, to which she had grown so attuned. She prayed no harm had come to her parents.

Chapter 15

Joanna didn't go straight home. She was anxious to find out if her parents were safe. Instead, she hurried into the nearest phone box and rang Wainrights, the local newsagents who were situated in close proximity of her parents' bungalow.

"Yes, yer mum and dad are okay," came the cockney reply at the end of the line. "Yer dad has not long been in for his morning papers. They only had a few windows blown out, the same as us. All our back windows are blown completely off their hinges. Still, never mind. It'll take more than a few Jerry bombs to put us out of action. What do you say, love?"

"Yes, you're absolutely right," agreed Joanna.

"Problem is," continued the woman, "the sods busted the main water supply. So we're on standby pipes for the moment until they're fixed. I'll deliver yer message to yer mum and dad, so don't worry, and I'll tell them you'll be up shortly."

"Thank you very much, Mrs. Wainright," replied Joanna.

A while later, Joanna was locked in a stubborn conversation with her mother.

"Mother, please come down the tunnel with us tonight. You will be much safer than stuck here."

"Now you know my opinion of those shelters, Joanna. Why must you keep pestering me?"

"Mother, listen to me, please. Why can't you forget your pride just for once and think of Father?"

"How dare you speak to me in such a manner? Go home, Joanna. I have nothing further to say. And that is final."

Her father quickly intervened when he saw the conversation turning into a little more than just an argument. He quietly turned to his wife. "Kathleen, please."

"*You* can keep quiet, Alf," she snapped. "I have nothing more to say. Now will you please go, Joanna? I'm not going to stand here and be insulted by you any longer."

She turned her back and preceded up the steps of their veranda.

Joanna stormed after her. "Yes, I'll go when I'm finished speaking. You're my mother and I'm ashamed of you, of how you treat poor Daddy, and everyone else who you imagine is beneath you. You're a stubborn, stupid, and selfish woman. At this very minute, men and women are sacrificing their lives for people like you. You should be thoroughly ashamed of yourself."

"Oh, I've never been spoken to like this before," screamed her mother.

Kathleen looked at her husband who was anxiously going from one foot to the other.

"Alfred, take her away. I never want to speak to her again."

She went into the house and slammed the door behind her, which eventually fell off its hinges.

"What do you do with a woman like that?" said Joanna in a furious tone. "Why do you tolerate her, Daddy? Why don't you put your foot down? She treats you dreadfully and you just stand there and take it all."

He smiled. "I'm afraid it's too late for that now, Jo, darling."

Alfred led Joanna up the garden path to the gate, through which, on either side, stood a garland of high-standard rose bushes that were not yet in bloom. Instead, there was the fragrant perfume of cherry blossom trees. This was unusual after a heavy air raid. The whole garden had a touch of heavenly splendor, an old world setting toiled by her father's hard-working hands.

"My dear Jo," said her father with so much warmth, "you must not worry about your mother and me. I'm the one who is responsible for her embittered state of mind."

"You, Daddy? Why?"

"All those years I spent at sea when I should have been by her side."

"But you can't blame yourself, Daddy. You were only doing your duty."

Alfred Partridge was a small-built man in his mid-sixties, of medium height with sad, brown eyes and light, gray hair. Alfred had been a Royal Navy man all his life. Now retired, he still contributed to the war effort by continuing to work for a local ship building company. In his spare time, if he had any, he did his bit in the Home Guard, mainly on their river patrol.

His father and grandfather had both been commissioned officers in the

Royal Navy. After his retirement, Alfred's father continued with his work teaching on the royal naval training ships, the Arethusa and the Cutty Sark, until his death. A hard military man, and not the type to be trifled with, his father assumed Alfred would follow in his footsteps and rise to the rank of captain.

Unfortunately, this was not to be. Captain Partridge forced Alfred into nautical collage. Alfred was just thirteen. When he refused to go, his father chained him between the posts of the four-poster bed and whipped Alfred with a rod, an instrument synonymous to that of ancient naval punishment: the cat of nine tails.

Later, Alfred entered the Royal Naval College in Dartmouth to qualify and become an officer. But Alfred failed to make the grade. It was a bitter blow to his father. He now regarded his son with the utmost contempt as the boy who had brought disgrace on the family name. Yet despite the humiliation of his son not being a commissioned officer, he still thought Alfred would work hard and rise through the ranks.

Again, this wasn't to be. Alfred still bore the scar on his back that his father had inflicted as a result of his failure, and even greater scars remained on his emotional character. Alfred had no interest in the pomp and circumstance of being an officer, and was quite content to remain an able seaman. He found solace whilst at sea, and found good friendship in his fellow naval colleagues. In a bid to ease the pain of his father's eventual hate, he lost himself with his colleagues in a little gambling.

Alfred, in his early years, had aspirations of becoming a singer. With the correct training, he may very well have become an opera singer, such was his smooth, tenor voice. But this dream had been thwarted by his father's harsh discipline and the fact that he had expected better from his son. With his father's idealistic view of the Navy, he failed to see his son's full aptitude. Alfred's talents extended far beyond singing. In his excellent landscape paintings and sign writing, many more attributes lay hidden in this most extraordinary man.

Alfred met and fell in love with the lovely, blue-eyed blonde from Ireland, Kathleen, daughter of a wealthy Irish landowner. When Kathleen's father discovered her intention to marry a mere seaman in the Royal Navy, he visualized their family name would be mud, and thus he cut her off without a penny.

Kathleen and Alfred had four children, and this was when their troubles began. Their first two children were Annabelle, now thirty-four, and Joanna, twenty-nine. Their twin boys died of measles at the tender age of two years old. Alfred had been at sea during this difficult period and Kathleen's love had faded into bitterness.

"No, Joanna," continued her father, shaking his head despondently. "I have brought your mother much heartache and given her nothing to be proud of. Except, of course, you and Annabelle. But, you know, even your sister regards me with condemnation."

Joanna smiled. "I wouldn't pay any attention to Bella, Daddy. She can't see the wood for the trees at times."

Her father looked down at his feet, and then shook his head. "I have tried, Joanna. Believe me. I have tried. But…" He paused. "I'm afraid it's too late. I'm a failure and always will be in your mother's eyes, and to your grandparents."

"That's not true, Daddy. You must stop thinking like this. You're a wonderful person. I love you so much. We all do. Terry looks upon you as if you were his own father, and Mary adores you."

Alfred looked at Joanna, and then his lips broadened into the most delightful smile that lit up his entire face. He took her hand in his and gazed into her eyes.

"Joanna, my dear child, Terry is a fine young man."

She smiled, her eyes sparkling. "I know that, Daddy."

"I believe you told me you're going down to Devon next weekend?"

"Yes, that's right."

"Well I'm very pleased to hear it. Very pleased indeed. Joanna, I would like you to listen very carefully to what I have to say. Take a little advice from an old fool like me. We don't know how long this war is going to last." He paused, tilting his head to one side. "What I'm trying to say is, if you have the slightest possible chance of being with Terry, take it and never mind the consequences. Grasp love in your two hands and never let it go, because it doesn't come readily."

Joanna looked into her father's care-worn eyes. "Oh, Daddy, you are so wonderful."

"Nonsense." Her father smiled. "Now that's enough of the dramatics. Let's get down to business. I would like to take Mary for a boat ride this Saturday. That is, of course, if we have no interruption from the Luftwaffe."

"That's a wonderful idea, Daddy. But haven't you forgotten something?"

"Oh, have I indeed? And what is that?"

"The Easter concert. We're both singing in it. You're Peter and I'm Mary Magdalene. Remember?"

"Oh, my word, I nearly forgot about that."

"And Uncle Tom is coming down from London," continued Joanna. "So we must put on a good show, Daddy."

"Yes. We must indeed. Tom's a fine fellow. I must be getting near my dotage, forgetting that, or thick upstairs."

They both laughed. She hugged him tight, and then left.

Eventually, Saturday arrived. The day of the Easter concert.

Women were floating around displaying their Easter bonnets and new clothes, and the men were looking uncomfortable, as if they wanted to be down the pub rather than in St Joseph's church hall.

A stage had been erected with scenery reflecting biblical times and daffodils were festooned around the bottom of the stage and along the sides of the hall. A piano had been freshly tuned and brought in to accompany the singers' voices.

Joanna and her father turned to look at each other and nodded appreciatively at the work the town had put into the proceedings. They quickly headed for the back room to change into their costumes.

With a quick swig of whisky from her father's flask for courage, Joanna entered the stage. She looked out to the audience. People weren't paying any attention. They were gossiping amongst themselves. The pianist began to tinkle the ivories and Joanna moved forward to the front of the stage.

She opened her mouth and began to sing the part of Mary Magdalene.

The audience suddenly stopped gabbling on. Heads turned in Joanna's direction. Her shrill, pitch-perfect soprano voice held them entranced.

Her father stepped forward to pick up the song, delivering his part as Peter. Joanna watched, listening to the music and waiting for her cue. She caught Mary's eye sitting on a front row seat with her grandmother. Mary beamed with pride at Joanna's performance and took a glance around, her face saying, 'That's my mum up there!'

Joanna issued a swift smile, and then counted in to her next cue.

The rafters of the old church hall reverberated with the sound of her sweet voice and the strong, tenor voice of her father. Joanna knew her musical abilities originated from her father and, for that, she would hold an everlasting gratitude.

"Voice of an angel, that one," said someone in the audience, and others whispered similar sentiments.

As Joanna caught the whispers of their praise, she smiled, and her eyes sparkled with happiness, knowing the joy she was giving to others. Joanna felt herself almost shine from inside and her heart seemed to fill to its bursting point with love.

Chapter 16

Joanna and Mary made their way along the crowded, dust-laden platform to reach their train leaving from Paddington bound for Exeter. The station was crowded with not only service men and women but also streams of civilians all heading for trains leaving for the West Country. Joanna's intention to leave at the weekend had to be postponed until Monday due to a violent raid over London. It was the most horrendous and destructive air raids of the entire blitz. It happened on a moonlit night on May 10th 1941. Many civilians were killed and injured.

Joanna and Mary quickly boarded the train and pushed their way along the corridor in search of seats. Two military policeman dashed past them, giving chase to a couple of soldiers who were hurrying out of a compartment at the far end of the corridor. Joanna hastened Mary to the end compartment and into two vacant seats.

When they were comfortably seated, Joanna considered the two soldiers and felt slightly troubled at taking their seats. She wondered who they were and what they had done wrong to cause them to flee from the MPs.

Mary looked at her mother as if predicting her thoughts. "I wonder why those soldiers were running away, Mummy."

"I have no idea, Mary."

A young army officer in the Royal Engineers sat by the door. He smiled, and answered Mary's question. "They probably didn't like the army, dear, and decided to go home." He winked at Mary.

She smiled at him, nodding her head doubtfully.

As the train moved slowly from the station, Joanna managed to glance out the window at the charred city below. The devastation caused by that one air raid on Saturday night had certainly been horrific. The hollow, skeleton-like buildings projected up from the smoke-filled streets, still smoldering from the mighty blow inflicted by the Luftwaffe.

Mary, sitting next to the open window, shouted, "What is that horrible smell, Mummy?"

"It's coming from outside, Mary. Would you like to change places with me?"

"Yes, please."

Joanna stood up to close the window in an attempt to shut out the filthy, acrid stench that slowly wafted in. She asked the other occupants if they had any objection. They all nodded their heads in agreement. There was grief in Joanna's eyes as she gazed down at the London she now hardly recognized.

"That's better," said Mary.

Unable to share her mother's growing concern with the events of war, she settled herself down with her comics, the Dandy and Beano. Joanna sat down feeling a little restless. She had always believed they were going to win the war. Now, however, she had her doubts.

Joanna closed her eyes in an effort to blot out the horrors of war and catch up on some much needed rest. She cast her thoughts back to Terry's last letter. By how he had described Ebford and the cottage, it sounded a delightful and tranquil spot. She knew in her heart that she was going to love it. But, even more, she knew she would love the thrill of seeing her Terry again.

Yet she felt guilty for having left her parents and Nina. Poor Nina. She was beginning to play a major part in Joanna's life now. If only she could do something to help her. Once her holidays were over, she vowed she'd find a way. Somehow.

Just when she was beginning to nod off, Mary shook her arm.

"Mummy? Excuse me, Mummy. Where is the toilet?"

"I don't know, Mary," babbled her mother in a tired voice, yawning and putting her hand to her mouth.

"I think there is one at the end of this corridor, dear," said an elderly woman sitting next to Mary.

"Thank you very much," said Mary. Then she jumped up and made a beeline for the door.

"Mary, come back and sit down at once," exclaimed Joanna. "It's very crowded out there. You'll be pushed around all over the place."

Mary did as she was told and returned to her seat.

Joanna sighed. "I'll go first and see where it is."

She made her way to the door, apologizing to the other passengers. The officer sitting on the end seat smiled and opened the door for her. Joanna pushed her way along the corridor. She found the toilet, and to her surprise, two armed MPs guarding the door.

"I'm sorry, miss. You can't go in there," said one of the officers.

"Why ever not?" questioned Joanna indignantly.

"I'm afraid you'll have to return to your compartment."

"I asked you a question, officer," said Joanna with a stony stare. "Why?"

"Okay, I suppose everyone will have to know sooner or later, seeing that you're the third person who's wanted to use it. There are two dangerous criminals on the run. They've locked themselves in there in the hope of trying to escape."

Joanna made an effort not to smile at these two heavily-built young men with their peak-caps touching their noses. She thought they looked ridiculous. It was obvious they were trying to show off their new brand of authority. They appeared, to her, rather amusing.

Joanna replied, "Well, they're not going to get very far in there, are they? Unless, of course, they pull the handle and flush themselves away."

"This is serious, miss," said the other MP. "We must insist that you return to your compartment immediately."

"Good gracious. Are we in any kind of danger, officer?" said Joanna with a mocking smile.

"Nothing to worry about, I can assure you, miss. Just taking routine precautions."

"So I take it there is no other convenience in this carriage?"

"None whatsoever, I'm afraid, miss. You'll just have to sit it out until we reach Exeter."

Though Joanna found the situation amusing, she did not like their discourteous attitude.

"Very well, gentlemen. I will just have to make alternative arrangements at the next station. I will probably be able to sit it out, as you so bluntly put it. But I doubt very much if my eight-year-old daughter will be able to do so."

Both MPs looked, open-mouthed, at Joanna, and then saluted her.

One of them ventured to speak. He paused, and then muttered, "But we didn't think you were-"

Joanna interjected, "Married and with a daughter, officer? With all due respect, gentlemen, I would be in uniform serving my country if I wasn't, not standing here in idle conversation with two MPs trying to get into a toilet." Joanna threw back her long, blonde hair in her usual haughty yet alluring manner. "Good day to you, gentlemen."

She turned and proceeded back to her compartment.

"Blimey," said the MP who had been speaking most of the time. "That surely is some woman."

"Yes, she certainly put us in our place, snobbish bitch," said the other MP, called Max. "I keep telling you, Ricky, you're far too pushy with the good lookers. Now what'll we do? If she starts shooting her mouth off, we'll be in dead trouble."

"What for?" said Ricky.

"Pasting those two bastards in there of course," said Max.

"No. A classy cow like that probably won't even mention it. She'll be too bothered about what others think."

"I hope you're right."

"Of course I'm right."

"You shouldn't have told her they were dangerous criminals."

"Why not? They're as good as," said Ricky with an insidious smile. "Bloody deserters. You worry too much, Max."

Joanna sat back down beside Mary in the compartment.

"Hello, Mummy. You've been a long time. Can I go now?"

"No, darling. I'm afraid you can't."

Joanna immediately announced to the rest of the occupants of the carriage the experience that she had encountered with the two MPs. The elderly woman sitting next to Mary declared she couldn't possibly wait until they arrived in Exeter. Two pretty wrens who hadn't said a word until now confirmed that they also couldn't wait until they reached their destination before having a wash and a brush up.

The young officer sat listening to the various comments. He then turned to Joanna.

"You say that this is the only convenience in the carriage and they're guarding the door?"

"Yes, that's right," Joanna said in a dissatisfied tone. "Rather strange, I thought."

"Yes. Very strange indeed," agreed the officer.

He then stood up and left the compartment, easing his way along the corridor towards the toilet, where he found two ATS girls arguing with the MPs.

"Now what's going on here? Can I be of any assistance?" said the officer, using an authoritarian voice in accordance with his rank.

The ATS girls stood immediately to attention and saluted him, followed quickly by the two MPs.

The captain spoke to the ATS girls in a discerning tone. "If you two young ladies wouldn't mind returning to your compartment, I'm sure I'll be able to settle this matter for you."

They both replied, "Thank you, sir," and disappeared.

As the captain turned to the two MPs, they both stood to attention. They saluted and said in unison, "Sir."

"All right, men. At ease. Now would one of you kindly explain what you are doing guarding this convenience?"

"Yes, sir. We have two deserters in there. They resisted arrest and did a runner on us. We nearly caught them, but they jumped on this train, ran into the toilet, and bolted the door."

Ricky answered all the questions whilst Max didn't say a word. He stood guarding the door with beads of perspiration rolling down his face. The captain wasn't at all convinced.

"I see. Well then, I suggest one of you go and fetch the inspector."

"Yes, sir. I'll go right away, sir," said Ricky.

"Not you. You stay where you are," uttered the captain. He pointed to the other MP.

The burly-built Max stood rigidly against the door. He had lost his nerve completely.

"I can't go, sir. I've got cramp."

"Don't be so ridiculous," exclaimed the captain. "Now just a moment. Stand to one side, both of you."

He turned the doorknob and out fell two badly beaten-up soldiers.

Mutters of astonishment echoed through the corridor.

"Right. Just as I thought," said the captain, glaring at the two MPs. "You'll both be on a charge for this."

When the situation had been safely resolved, and all the excitement was over, Mary returned from the toilet with her mother. She tucked into her much longed for spam sandwiches, rock cakes, and cherryade. Before they realized it, the train was pulling into Exeter Station. Joanna hardly noticed the time. It seemed to fly by with all the activity.

Boarding the little steam train to Exton, Joanna found an empty compartment.

"Here we are, Mary. This one will be fine. There doesn't seem to be many people getting on. I think we'll have the compartment to ourselves."

"That'll be nice. Not like the other one with those big men with red hats to disturb us. They were horrible, weren't they, Mummy?"

"Yes. I must say, they were not very friendly."

"They reminded me of those dreadful Gestapos I see you reading about in the newspapers."

"When have you seen me reading about them, Mary?"

"Every day when you're reading the newspapers."

Joanna looked at her daughter pensively. "Oh, I see."

Joanna knew Mary could read very well for her age, even if she couldn't understand it all. She had always tried to keep the inner horrors of the war hidden from her daughter. It was beginning to be quite impossible now. However, she would just have to try a little harder in the future.

She changed the subject and pointed to the platform.

"Oh, look, Mary. There are two elderly ladies struggling with their cases and trying to open the door. Come along. We'll help them in. We're not going to be on our own after all."

The little steam train trundled its way out of Exeter city and into the open countryside. Immediately, Joanna observed the scenery taking on a more panoramic view.

Mary announced, "There aren't any toilets on this train, Mummy."

"Oh, it's only going to be a short journey, Mary. I'm sure you won't need to go before we arrive."

"Will Daddy be at the station to meet us?"

"Well, I sincerely hope so, Mary."

The two elderly women sat listening. They both smiled at Mary.

One of them asked, "Are you going to see your daddy, dear?"

Mary smiled and nodded.

"Is he in the Royal Marines?"

Mary quickly looked at her mother. Joanna winked, pressed her lips together, giving her the 'keep mum' sign.

Mary smiled at the two women and answered hastily, "I don't know exactly. I think he's in the Royal Society for Backward Monkeys."

Joanna could hardly keep a straight face. Since Mary recovered her voice, Joanna, who was aware her husband was involved in secret war work, had insisted that her daughter gave no information at all about her father's placement to strangers, even her close friends. However, Mary never ceased to amaze her mother with such comical answers. She often wondered where she found them. Possibly her comics.

Thinking of which, Joanna handed Mary her Film Fun.

"Why not read this, dear? It will keep you occupied. I think that's the only one you haven't read, isn't it?"

"No, thank you, Mummy. I feel a little tired."

She turned her head towards the window and began to nod off.

Her mother touched her gently on the arm. "Mary, we'll be getting off very soon. Try not to fall asleep, dear. I find it so difficult to wake you once you're in a sound sleep."

Mary was grateful her mother woke her when she did, for the sight before her eyes was such that she had never seen before. Delightful scenery appeared in view. Stone, white cottages resembled little dolls houses depicted from a child's fairy story. Mary seemed in a dream world as she gazed out at the rolling landscape. Kent was beautiful, but this was something quite different.

Joanna felt the same sensation. She saw a style of life she had not experienced in a long time. Peace. Complete peace. Yes, that was it.

The train trundled on its way past small railway stations with whitewashed walls and thatched roofs. To Joanna, it seemed like another world far removed from the city they had left behind, where grays and gloomy hues dominated. Joanna laid her head back and closed her eyes in reverie.

When they arrived at Exton Station, Mary was enthralled to see her father. He stood waiting for them by an old, white, wicker gate at the entrance of the tiny railway station. Terry stood beside the fascinating figure of an elderly man who looked tailor made for the setting. He was the station master, porter, and ticket collector all rolled into one. Spring flowers framed the entrance while wild flowers of every description banked the single railway track. On the opposite side of the rails, through high bushes and foliage, ran the beautiful River Exe.

Joanna, surveying the entire visual magnificence of this perfect spot, felt deliriously happy. Breathing in the fresh, scented air, her eyes met Terry's. He smiled and gathered both Joanna and Mary in his arms in a tender embrace. They both closed their eyes. For, at that moment, words did not matter. It was only the action of love that held meaning.

Chapter 17

"So what did Mrs. Lloyd 'ave to say?" asked Josh, as he was about to sit down at the kitchen table and devour his midday lunch of sausage, bacon, eggs, and chips. That included part of the children's ration. He spoke in a phlegmatic tone of voice that sounded menacing.

Nina stood in front of the oven with her back turned to her husband.

She glanced sideways over her shoulder, and whispered, "Nothing can be done. She told me I'm too far gone, and it would be dangerous to attempt anything at this stage."

"What are you talking about?" demanded Josh. "You didn't go to see her, did you?"

"Yes. Of course I did, Josh," Nina answered, without raising her eyes and trembling from head to toe.

"No you bloody well didn't. I can tell by your face. You're a bloody lying cow."

At that moment, he turned, hearing a noise from the living room. John and Michael had just descended the stairs. Marianne was sitting in a tattered armchair playing quietly with a jigsaw puzzle that Mary had given to her the previous evening. Josh stood up from the kitchen table and marched into the living room. He glared at the children.

"What the 'ell are you lot doing in here?" he bellowed, and pointed to the back door. "That's where you should be. Outside. You bloody well know you're not allowed in the 'ouse while I'm 'aving me meals." His voice was now thundering.

John quickly apologized and rushed to take Marianne outside, whilst Michael had already disappeared out the front door. Marianne, reluctant to move, had been completely unaware of the situation, being a child so young.

She cried out, "No. No, go away, John. I don't want to go outside."

John quickly grabbed Marianne by the arm. "Come on, Marianne. Hurry up," he whispered. "Dad's getting angry again." He started to pull her off the chair.

Marianne began to squeal and struggle with him. "No. I don't want to go outside," she screamed.

"Shut that bloody racket," bellowed Josh, glaring at little Marianne.

John stood in front of his little sister, bravely shielding her. He looked up at his father with terrified eyes. "She's only a baby, Dad. She didn't mean to make a noise."

Josh was enraged by John's gallantry and that the boy should even dare to confront him.

"Why, you little bleeder. I won't tolerate this defiance in my own 'ouse. You will stay outside when I'm 'aving me meals. I'll make you do as you're told," he stormed, and delivered John a mighty blow to his head, knocking the boy sideways.

John fell to the floor.

Marianne ran to her mother.

Josh continued cursing and swearing. "I'll teach you a bloody lesson, you little bleeder."

Just as the boy was staggering to his feet, Josh inflicted another blow to John's head.

Nina screamed, "For God's sake! Stop it, Josh."

She pushed Marianne quickly into the kitchen out of harm's way. Nina ran to John's aid and threw herself between her son and her husband just as Josh was about to bring his fist down on John once again. Nina took the impact meant for John. Josh's mighty fist came down on her jaw and hurled her to the floor.

Josh bellowed, "I've told you not to interfere when I'm dealing with the kids."

Then he turned back to John.

Nina, with all the strength she had left, dragged herself up from the floor, and screamed, "No, Josh. No. They're my children too. He's only a boy, for heaven sake. Have you gone completely mad?"

Josh stopped dead in his tracks and slowly turned around to face Nina.

"What did you say to me?"

When Josh was through with Nina, she lay in a crumpled heap on the living room floor.

Chapter 18

Over two hundred miles away in East Devon, the happy trio made their way down the lane, which led from the station and through the tiny picturesque hamlet of Ebford. Orchard fields lay on one side of the lane, and on the other, scattered among the trees, lay fairytale thatched cottages. Wild spring flowers of every description decked the grass verges. Finally, they reached their destination: Orchard Cottage.

Terry turned around to face his wife, and with out-stretched arms, he proudly declared, "Well this is it, my darling." He bowed to Joanna in a jocular fashion. "May I present Orchard Cottage to madam?"

Mary burst out laughing.

Joanna stood back, taking in the entire magnificence of the place. She opened her mouth as if to speak then closed it again. Gazing up at the cottage, she saw garlands of early roses surrounding the front door. The roof was neatly thatched and a crazy-paved pathway led to the garden well. Even the sun shone through behind a cloud of cornflower-blue sky to welcome its visitors.

"Well, do you like it, darling?" asked Terry eagerly.

As Joanna turned to her husband, her laughing, brown eyes answered his question. Amused by his eager expression, she replied with a comical smile, "Well, it's not so bad."

Terry looked at her with a roguish grin. Then he turned to Mary. "I think your mother is in one of her silly moods, Mary. Do you like it, sweetheart?"

"Oh, Daddy, it's wonderful. I think it's like heaven would be if we had died in an air raid and gone to heaven." She paused, tilting her head to one side. "Yes. I suppose it would look like this. I think I'll call it Devon heaven."

"Well..." said Terry, looking a little surprised by his daughter's frank remark, and her insouciant reference to the air raids and death. He rubbed his chin, musing on her words for a brief second, and then, as if searching for an answer, he glanced at Joanna. Their eyes locked and there was a fleeting tenseness in the air.

Mary continued with her childish prattle.

Terry smiled that slow, quiet smile, and clapped his hands. "Well, girls, what are we waiting here for? Let's go inside, shall we?"

The house was equally delightful inside. Chintz curtains adorned the windows with matching window seats. Ornaments stood proudly on antique furniture. Plants displayed a ray of splendor, bursting from copper and brass bowels. Low oak beams crisscrossed through the entire house, expressing warmth and an aura that held one in its adoring embrace.

It was all so far removed from the hostilities of war.

"The only problem is the water. I'm afraid it has to be pumped up from the well. I'm sorry about that, darling. I've filled the tank up in the kitchen. I'll do it whenever I'm here. My sweetheart, I won't allow you to lift anything. I wanted so much for everything to be perfect."

Terry looked a little downcast.

Joanna assumed a straight face. "Well, I suppose, now I'm here, I'll just have to put up with the inconvenience."

Mary stayed outside to explore the entire garden.

On their own at last in this tranquil haven, Terry and Jo were lost in each other's arms in a passionate embrace.

"Oh, Jo, darling, I've waited so long for this moment. I thought it would never come," Terry whispered. "I'm sorry about the water. I do hope you like it here, Jo."

"Like it? I think it's divine. Simply divine. Just how I imagined it to be." She smiled. "Terry, please don't mention the water again, darling. It's a small price to pay for all this. Although there is just one thing."

"Oh? What's that?"

Tilting her head sideways and raising her index finger to her cheek, Joanna replied, "Food. One cannot live in a beautiful country cottage on fresh air and scenery alone, Terry. I've saved a few points to come down here. Now I find we're in the middle of the country miles from anywhere."

She was just about to open her mouth to speak again when Terry came closer, looking down into her crystal, brown eyes, and then closed it with a kiss.

"You're a greedy woman, Joanna Busher," he remarked with a roguish grin.

Just at that moment, the romantic interlude came to an end with, "Daddy! Daddy, come and see what I've found."

He called out, "Just coming, Mary." Then he turned to Joanna, his eyes sparkling. "I believe I'm needed elsewhere at the moment, darling," he whispered. "But I think your fairy godmother has paid you a visit. Enjoy yourself, sweetheart." Then he disappeared out the door.

Joanna stood in the doorway of the low oak-beamed lounge.

"Fairy godmother?" she said, mystified.

She sighed, shrugged her shoulders, and then began making a tour of the entire house. Beginning with the upstairs, she opened the door of their bedroom where Terry had put their cases. Joanna looked at the four-poster bed and smiled, taking stock of the antiquity of this most delightful room.

Hearing laughter coming from the garden, she hastily walked across the room to the window seat. She peered out to find Terry and Mary both playing with a baby rabbit. Joanna realized that Terry was evidently enjoying speaking to Mary after two years of silence. She decided not to join them but to leave father and daughter alone for a while.

Joanna made her way downstairs again and into the quaint, old-fashioned kitchen. Then she opened the larder door and gasped at the sight before her eyes. The larder was filled to the brim with food, rows of homemade jam, and bottled fruit, which stood proudly in front of her, along with various types of farm produce.

But her eyes were focused on a large chicken sitting appetizingly on a stone shelf in front of her. She held her breath before placing one hand hesitantly upon it, almost as if the bird was going to take flight at any second. Joanna gasped.

Good heavens. A real chicken. I can't remember the last time I saw one of these. This is absolutely marvelous.

Joanna had never seen so much food all at one time. It had been a rarity, a thing of the past. She grasped a couple of items then lay them down carefully again as though they were made of porcelain.

This is what he meant by your fairy godmother, but where did it all come from?

Eagerly, she decided what they would have for dinner: eggs, bacon, bottled tomatoes, and crusty bread. That would be easy to prepare. Oh, yes, and some of that delicious looking fruitcake. She cut three large chunks of cake, laid the food to one side to be cooked, and then hurried off into the garden.

"Terry," she demanded, "where on earth did all that food come from?"

"What food?" said Terry, still acting the fool.

"The food in the larder, of course."

"Shoo! You mustn't shout. The little, green goblins at the bottom of the garden will hear you and tell our fairy godmother." Terry grinned.

Mary looked at her mother's straight face, and laughed her head off.

Joanna, with her hands resting on her hips, declared, "Terry, I'm not joking. Where did it come from?"

"Not now, darling. I'll tell you later. Come and join in the fun. We've just found this baby rabbit."

Mary interrupted. "No, Daddy. *I* found him over there by the well."

"Oh, I beg your pardon, your royal highness." Terry laughed.

"Isn't he a darling, Mummy?"

"Yes, he is," said Joanna in a quieter tone. "But you ought to let him go. His mother will probably be looking for him. That is, of course, if he is a he?"

"Yes, it is a boy. Daddy just turned him upside down and looked at his bottom."

"Really?" said Joanna, trying to refrain from laughing.

"Please let me keep him, Mummy. He's so tame. I wanted to put him in a box and keep him until we go home."

"Yes," agreed Terry, laughing. "Fatten him up for Christmas and make a nice meal."

"That's a terrible thing to say, Daddy," declared Mary.

"Don't take any notice of Daddy, darling. He's just being stupid. However, I do think we should let him go and find his mother."

"Yes, your mother is quite right, Mary," agreed Terry, trying to look serious.

The rabbit scampered away when Mary put him down.

"Pity," said Terry, laughing. "Great waste of a delicious Christmas meal."

He stood in the middle of the lawn as if conducting an orchestra.

"Now, altogether, everyone. Run, rabbit, run, rabbit, run, run, run."

Mary joined in with her father whilst Joanna stood giggling. Terry wrapped his arms around both his girls and led them into the cottage singing at the top of their voices.

That evening, he lit a fire in the lounge, which was set deep into an old inglenook fireplace. After they had finished eating a sumptuous evening meal, Mary announced that she was tired and would like to go to bed early. She was anxious to try out her new bed in her pretty, old-world style bedroom. The view from her window was absolutely enchanting, over-looking the orchard fields and, in the far distance, the glorious River Exe.

Mary looked a quaint, little figure as she ascended the large staircase carrying her potty under her arm and wearing a large, white nightie. Terry looked up from stacking logs in the bucket. He thought how well she fitted the surroundings. She peered through the banister rails.

"Daddy, why do I have to have this potty? It's just like being in the tunnel. Don't they have bathrooms in Devon?"

Terry laughed. "No, darling. They haven't been invented down here yet."

Mary yawned. "Oh, I see. Goodnight, Daddy. Goodnight, Mummy."

Terry and Joanna chuckled, echoing, "Goodnight, sweetheart."

"Oh, Terry, I've just remembered something," said Joanna. "Are there any water pitchers in the house?"

"Yes. I'll show you. Follow me."

"Mrs. Dent keeps them all in the cupboard under the sink in the kitchen."

Joanna noticed that Terry appeared to be fully acquainted with everything in the house. He turned around to fill up the water pitcher from the tank.

She smiled. "You've done this quite often, haven't you, Terry?"

He turned around slowly to face her then paused. "Well, yes. I suppose you could say that. Look here, darling. I'm sorry about this inconvenience."

"What inconvenience?"

"Well, the toilet outside in the garden, having to pump water from the well. But don't worry, sweetheart. I'll get everything done whilst I'm here."

Joanna stared at her husband and smiled. He looked like a comic figure standing there, holding the pitcher in front of him with such a somber expression on his face.

"Oh, I'm really worried about all that." She put her hand to her mouth and roared with laughter.

"Joanna Busher, you're a little tease."

The fire was now blazing in the lounge.

"There. What do you think of that?" said Terry proudly, as he poured two drinks of homemade cherry wine.

Joanna comfortably sat in the cozy chintz sofa in front of the fire.

"I feel as though I'm soon going to wake up from a wonderful dream, darling. Nothing seems quite real."

"Do not even consider waking up, my sweetheart. Not yet anyway."

"How long did you say Mrs. Dent would be staying in Cornwall?"

"Oh, a couple of months, I believe. Her granddaughter runs a farm with her younger sister, practically single-handed apart from a few Land Army girls.

She's managed it since 1938. Between them, they have four children, Mrs. Dent's great-grandchildren."

"But where are their parents?"

"Their mother ran off with someone else, and their father, who is Mrs. Dent's son, died a few years ago. The old lady gets awfully lonely here on her own, so the dear old soul has gone down to lend a hand with her great-grandchildren."

"Where is her husband?"

"I hoped you wouldn't ask that. He was one of those poor, unfortunate chaps in the British expeditionary force at Dunkirk."

"I see," whispered Joanna, sipping her wine and gazing into the fire. "They sound like a wonderful family."

"Yes, they are," agreed Terry.

"That's why you do all you can to help her, isn't it?"

Terry nodded and sat down on the sofa beside her.

She drew up close to him. "You know, Terry, this place, the house, it all seems to have a special kind of magic."

"Yes, my darling. That's what I think."

They sat talking until the small hours in each other's arms by the glow of the fire. The romantic scene was such it could have been the setting for a movie.

"I wish we could go on like this forever," whispered Joanna.

They sat gazing into the fire. The dancing flames captured the moment, illuminating their eyes.

"Yes," said Terry, smiling in reverie. "But forever is now."

Suddenly, the flames seemed to diminish, casting shadows over Joanna's face. She shuddered.

"Why, what's the matter, darling?" said Terry.

Joanna stared at him with a tinge of fear in her eyes. "Terry, what is going to happen to us all?" She spoke with uncertainty in her voice.

"What do you mean, sweetheart?"

"Oh, I don't know, Terry. It's everything really. This war, how long it's going to last. I saw it written in your eyes, Terry, when you said forever is now."

"Oh, darling, I was only dreaming."

"That's precisely what I mean, Terry. We're just dreaming. Not wishing to wake up. Being oblivious to what is going on out there. And trying to forget why you are here. That's why you said now is forever. I cannot forget the reality of war and the suffering that is going on all around us in our dear country." Joanna was now choking back the tears. "You hear every day the most dreadful stories of what is happening in Europe. The bombing on London. My God, that poor city." Her voice was almost a sob. "My dear friend Nina whose children are Jewish. What will happen to them, Terry? She told me that if there were to be an invasion, she would kill the children and herself. Dear God. What would we all do? Just stand by and let it happen? The thought is horrifying."

Terry stared at her. He looked surprised by her words. They paused, looking into each other's eyes. Only the flicker of the fire could be heard. He knew Joanna to be a strong woman and not given to her emotions. This was the first time since the war began that he had ever heard her speak of defeat in such a way. He realized this and gathered her in his arms.

"Hush now, my darling," he whispered. "You mustn't speak in such a way. Joanna, listen to me, my sweet. There is not going to be an invasion."

"Yes, Terry, that's what we have always believed. But you haven't seen London recently, have you? So how can you be so sure? I worry about everyone. Uncle Tom. Mother and Father. And now Nina."

Terry spoke on a much clearer level. "You asked me why I'm sure. I'll tell you why. Because he had every opportunity last year at Dunkirk. Anyone with half a brain would have marched straight in. The man's nothing but a fool. And fools do not win wars, Joanna. Goring tried to beat us in the skies. But thanks to our brave lads in the RAF, he didn't succeed. The bombing on London is just another attempt to try and scare the nation into submission. Can't you see that, Jo? I know you are different from the average woman. You're brave. You would never succumb to any kind of Nazi propaganda. Churchill has the right idea. And if that little Hitler ever tried anything stupid, why…" Terry paused. "I really think that every man, woman and even child in this country would fight for their freedom. There is never going to be an invasion, darling. *Never.*"

"Oh, Terry. I'm so sorry. I have no idea what came over me. You must think I'm a dreadful defeatist and coward."

"You, a coward? You're forgetting something, Joanna. I know you. I know you too well, and coward doesn't come into your category, my darling. However, you must try not to worry. If your friend Nina refuses help then I'm afraid there's nothing much you can do." He spoke in a firm tone. "You know, Jo, you concern yourself far too much in other people's problems."

"I can't help it, Terry. That's me."

He looked at her with those loving, blue eyes.

"Yes. I know it's you, my darling. But you must take care."

He held her close, looking down into her clear, brown eyes. They kissed, a long lingering kiss, and Terry smiled.

"Do you know what I think?" he said under his breath. "We've both had too much cherry wine."

Chapter 19

Nina knew she had to swallow her pride and seek refuge with her Aunt Bertha.

Life had become intolerable since Josh learned of her failure to have the child aborted. She now feared not only for her own life but those of the children. By all the laws of nature, Nina and the child she was carrying should be dead.

Aunt Bertha agreed to take Nina and the children until after the baby was born, and then she would have to find alternative accommodation. She stated emphatically that she could not allow the children to stay any longer, owing to her bad health and the effect the air raids had taken on her nerves. Bertha pointed out that Nina and the baby could stay a little longer, if she so wished. However, the children would most definitely have to go back to their father. Or be evacuated like most children around London those days.

Nina totally disagreed with the idea. However, she realized that she would have to compromise until after the baby was born. Then she would think of something. She had been on the point of writing to Joanna on several occasions but refrained from doing so. Nina felt hesitant, and had no desire to encroach on Joanna and Terry. After all, what right had she in thinking Joanna would help her, even if she had offered?

Nina considered that Joanna had offered help out of sheer pity. It was obvious that she wanted to spend as much time with Terry while she was able, before he was sent off to God knows where.

Nina was fully aware that staying with Aunt Bertha wasn't going to be easy. She was patronizing and mean to the children. She was indeed a wretched woman and only content when she was making Nina feel as miserable as herself.

However, Nina realized that this was heaven in contrast to living with

Josh, where he treated her as less than an animal. Nina had considered that if the worst happened, and Aunt Bertha threw her out, she would live in the tunnel rather than go back to Josh. They spent most of their time there anyway. She knew it wasn't much of an alternative. Yet it was better by far than going back to her husband.

Bertha Macdonald had adopted Nina at the age of two from a London orphanage when she'd been approaching her forty-fifth birthday. Still unmarried, Bertha regarded herself as an old maid and a woman left on the shelf. Her thoughts were typical for many women of her age in 1915.

Bertha was the third child of a Scottish coal miner who had died before his time of silicosis of the lungs. He'd left his wife and family with no financial support. Her mother died two years later of hard work and exhaustion, leaving her eldest daughter, Bertha, now sixteen, to bring up her younger brother and sister alone and fend for themselves.

Bertha had been extremely courageous. She worked hard scrubbing and cleaning for the harsh pit owner who lived in the mansion house on the hill. He was regarded by many of his workers as the tyrant lord of the manor.

Bertha brought up her brother and sister well but with a rod of iron. Thus life had left its mark. Only when both her siblings had grown up, married, and immigrated to Canada, did she consider coming south.

She worked as a chambermaid in some lower grade guesthouses and hotels, slowly rising to housekeeper in one of London's leading hotels. It was at this time that Bertha decided to adopt a child to help keep her company in her old age.

With the Great War and the Germans sending their dreadful Zeppelin airplanes over London, she thought it a wonderful act of charity, on her part, to rescue a poor, unfortunate child.

Nina had been born to a titled and wealthy aristocratic family. Her mother, Lady Harriet, already spoken for in an arranged marriage, unfortunately became pregnant as a result of the drunken advances of her father's cousin. Unfortunately, Lady Harriet suffered complications whilst giving birth, and minutes after Nina issued her first cry, she died.

Harriet's parents, distraught over the death of their daughter, wanted nothing to do with their granddaughter, Nina. Not wanting to have scandal brought on the family name, Nina's father never came forward, and he remained anonymous.

Information reached Bertha's ears through the adoption grapevine that a pretty, little two-year-old girl of aristocratic birth had been placed in a

London orphanage. Bertha did her homework well. She discovered that a legacy was to be settled on Nina, formally the Lady Christina, and this would be entrusted to her adopted parents until she reached the age of twenty-one. However, if Nina broke the code of law by an act of dishonor or shame, the inheritance would be passed to her adopted parents.

Bertha had been kind to Nina in her formative years though slightly outmoded in her style of bringing up a young, intelligent girl in her adolescence. Nina surpassed herself at school and Bertha had been troubled by her ability to gain perfection at every turn. If this continued, Bertha knew she would stand to lose all. So she waited for an occasion to arise when she could turn her fortunes. And when it did, she knew she'd act with quick precision.

Meanwhile, back in 1941, Josh had become involved in something far more devious than a little black market activity. He became increasingly annoyed with everything that had transpired between Nina and himself. He was determined to get her back at all costs. She was, after all, his wife. Once he had achieved that, he would make her regret ever having left him.

With this thought in mind, he decided to pay Nina a visit. He was sly enough to know how to act when the time came. Josh walked down the road to Bertha's house with an insidious expression on his face, carrying a box of black market chocolates and a bunch of flowers.

"Hello, Aunt Bertha," said Josh, when she opened the door. He had a stealthy smile on his face. "I just thought I'd pay my family a visit, just to see how they are. Oh yeah, and these are for you."

He handed Bertha the bunch of flowers. She looked surprised.

"Thank you, Josh. Will ye nay come in and have a cup of tea?"

"Ah, thanks, Aunt Bertha."

"Please do take a seat. I'm afraid they're out at the moment. The boys are doown the park playing football, and Nina is away doown the village with the wee one getting the messages. She will nee be long. I'm sorry. I have no sugar until she gets back. Will yee be taking saccharine in yee tea?"

"Yeah, that's fine. How yer keeping these days, Bertha?"

"Oh, not so bad, Josh, me lad. I must admit, I do suffer with the ole back lately, and these dammed air raids don't help my head any."

"That's a shame," said Josh, trying to look sincere. "Why don't yer go down the tunnel with Nina and the kids?"

"No, laddie. I'm better to stay in the Anderson in me own back garden."

"How yer getting along with Nina and the kids?"

"Well…" She paused. "We manage, if yer ken what I mean?"

Bertha turned and twisted her hands in a disgruntled fashion. Josh grasped the opportunity whilst he had it, and using all the gentility he could possibly muster, he began his little scheme to get Nina back where he wanted her.

"Of course, you know, Bertha, I didn't lay a finger on Nina. I wouldn't do such a thing. Now I don't know what she's been telling yer, but I'll tell yer what really happened. If you'd like ter know? She tripped up coming down the stairs and landed a cropper. That's all it was."

"Is that so?" said Bertha, looking dubious.

But by the time Nina came in with the shopping, Josh had worked on Bertha with such dedicated gentle persuasion, she was totally convinced he was speaking the truth.

Chapter 20

The days passed quickly in Devon as spring turned to summer. Country life certainly agreed with Joanna. She looked and felt as fit as a fiddle. Pumping water from the well, gardening, and walking two miles to and from the village of Topsham for groceries didn't bother her at all. She even found the simplest of tasks, such as collecting eggs from the farm whilst still warm, a delight. The entire ambience of living in this captivating spot seemed to amplify her radiance. Joanna knew it couldn't last forever. However, whilst it did, she intended to enjoy every minute of it.

Mary too had never been able to comprehend the true meaning of peace until now. Living in such a delightful spot was absolute heaven. It was something she would never forget. She soon made friends at the local school, which had once been two large cottages and was now charmingly converted. It nestled enchantingly between the cornfields and surrounding countryside. On warm, summer days, the children would learn their lessons and drink milk or apple juice in the shade of a huge, old oak tree. She often dashed home announcing she would like one of her friends to come home for tea. So today was no exception. Joanna was becoming accustomed to Mary's little demands.

"Mary, not today, dear."

"Why?"

"Because Daddy will be home early. He has a weekend pass and we're going to the RM base to see a film show tonight."

Mary looked po-faced. "That'll be boring, and all about the war, I suppose, like the last one."

"No, it will not. Old Mother Riley is being shown."

"Oh, is it really, Mummy?"

"Yes, and you don't want to miss that, do you?"

"No, I don't." Mary pondered on what to say next. "Well…it's rather difficult, Mummy. You see, I've already invited them."

"Them? How many are they, for heaven sake?"

"Only three. Can they come to the film show with us?"

"No, Mary. They cannot. Didn't it cross your mind to ask me first?"

"Yes…Well, no, not really, because you always say yes."

"Well, next time it'll be *no*. You're getting spoilt since we've been here, Mary."

"I see," said Mary, looking glum. "That means I won't be seeing them again. School closes next week for the summer holidays."

"They only live around the corner, Mary."

"No, you don't understand. They're all going down to Cornwall tomorrow. They're going to stay with their aunt who lives in Padstow. They're digging sandbags for air raid shelters. And we're going home in two weeks' time, aren't we, Mummy? I wish we could stay and dig sandbags." Mary sighed mournfully. "But it doesn't matter, Mummy. I'll just pop 'round and tell them they can't come." Mary looked up at her mother. "I'm so sorry I'm spoilt. I don't try to be."

She was on the point of opening the kitchen door when her mother called her back.

"All right, Mary. No need to look at me with those sad, puppy dog eyes. Go and tell them they can come on a picnic if they hurry up. I have shopping to do in Topsham today so we can have our picnic down the strand."

"Oh, wonderful, Mummy. Can we have some more of those delicious strawberry tarts and clotted cream like we had last time?"

Joanna sighed. "We'll see. Now off you go and tell them to hurry up. It's a long walk to Topsham and back. We must be home by seven o'clock. The film show starts at seven forty-five."

Mary ran up the rough, dirt path which led to the dairy farm. She didn't mind the ducks, drakes, and chickens following her now. However, it had been a far different tale a few weeks ago.

Every morning, Mary would fetch the milk for her mother, carrying the empty milk urn. The first morning she attempted this task, she casually looked over her shoulder to find a band of clucking ducks and chickens happily following her. Mary, unaccustomed to seeing large numbers of farm animals gathering around her, naturally assumed they were chasing her. She ran for her life, dropping the milk urns, and fell flat on her face in the mud. Three children sitting on the wall burst out laughing. Mary looked up, spat out the mud, and then joined in the fun.

Since then, Mary, Jane, Mark, and Peter had become the best of pals.

"Well, hello," said Joanna to all three children. "If you're all ready and tickety boo, then we'll go."

"Yes," echoed the giggling four. "We're all ready and tickety-boo to go with you, Mrs. B."

Joanna loved taking the children on picnics, especially to Topsham. They would walk around the quaint, old graveyard by the church of St Margaret's, which led down steep, stone steps onto the most charming promenade and causeway with enchanting views overlooking the River Exe and surrounding woodland. If ever Joanna had been asked where her favorite place on earth was, she would most definitely have said there.

Chapter 21

By the time Josh had made his second visit, Aunt Bertha was making plans for Nina to leave. She insisted that Nina would have to go on the grounds that the children were getting far too much for her. She declared that they were now playing havoc with her nerves.

"Well, Aunt Bertha," said Nina, on hearing Bertha's request, "you may have been a little more frank with me than to use the children as your excuse when you know very well they've been as quiet as little mice. No. You just didn't want me here, did you?"

"Now yer ken, that's not so, Nina."

"Really?" continued Nina. "You still haven't punished me enough, have you, Aunt Bertha?"

"I din' nah ken what yer talking aboot, lass."

"You know very well what I mean. I mean what happened when I was only fifteen years old. You still blame me for it. That's true, isn't it?"

"I'm sure I din'nah ken what you're talking about, Nina, and I canna stand here arguing all day."

"Well, Aunt Bertha," said Nina, looking intense, "never try and see me again. For whatever happens now, I hope it'll be on your conscience for the rest of your life. That is, of course, if you have a conscience."

Bertha screamed, "Why yer low doown little scum of a bastard. I shoulda left yer to rot in that orphanage. After all I've given yee."

Nina, indignant and fuming, answered, "Yes, and you've seen I got everything I deserve, haven't you, Bertha?"

The doorbell rang and Bertha answered it.

"'Ello, Bertha. How are yer then?" Josh marched into the living room. "I 'ope I'm not interrupting anyfink."

"No, you're not interrupting a thing, Josh. I think we'd better go now," said Nina coldly.

Josh sat down in the armchair, ignoring Nina's words.

"You're looking wonderful, Nina, darling," he said with his usual dangerous smile. "Thank yer for looking after them so well, Bertha. They won't give yer anymore trouble."

Nina looked at Josh in utter contempt.

She spoke in an exacting tone of voice, "I said I think we'd better go now, Josh."

He glanced at his wife and noticed the look of defiance mingled with courage in her eyes. Josh pursed his lips, knowing she wouldn't have that expression on her face for very long.

Josh had given Nina an abundance of promises in the presence of Bertha, all of which meant nothing to her. She had no words suitable to describe this thing that everyone regarded as her husband. Nina knew very well the devious motives he had for getting her to go back to him. He took delight in making her his punch ball and his slave, forcing her to submit to anything he wanted to do to her. It gave him a feeling of supremacy.

It would have been lunacy for Nina to consider living entirely in the tunnel at this stage in her pregnancy. She had no other alternative but to go back with Josh at the moment. But leave him, she would. Nina was resolute in that belief.

Slowly, she had acquired an inner spirit to fight back.

She'd had enough of Josh and felt certain there was a better world out there somewhere. Nina didn't care now what he did. She would try and fight back. For she was no longer afraid of this creature that walked beside her.

Nina had walked blindly into her marriage with Josh, accepting the first offer that came her way. In her haste to escape from Bertha and acquire a home of her own, she'd found herself in an even worse dilemma.

Nina, in her formative years, had worked very hard at school and later achieved a certificate to enter secretarial collage to learn short hand and typing. Bertha was proud of her prodigy and boasted about her successes to all and sundry. A quiet girl, Nina had seldom mixed with young people of her own age. She kept in accordance with her strict upbringing. That was until the night before Christmas Eve.

Nina had been invited to the annual college party. Everything was going splendidly until her friend, Sandra, introduced her to a young boy from Gravesend Grammar School. Nina, now only fifteen and not as worldly-wise as Sandra, had mistaken the young boy's totally innocent gestures as sexual advances.

Bertha had always taught her to have nothing to do with boys. She had emphasized emphatically that they only wanted one thing from a girl: 'dirty sex'. With this in mind, Nina decided that she would leave immediately. Her friend Sandra had been taken by surprise.

"You can't leave now. It's getting late. I thought we all agreed to go home together?"

"Yes, we did. But I'm not staying here to be mauled about by your friends."

"Whatever are you talking about? Bob's a lovely boy. He did nothing but want to dance with you. You know your trouble, Nina? You're too damned old fashioned."

Sandra looked moved when she stared into Nina's eyes. She could see her fear and confusion. She added with a touch more understanding, "Look, let's not argue. It's Christmas. I really would like you to stay, but if you must, go. But please do take care, Nina. There are unsavory characters going around at this time of the year."

"I will, and thank you for thinking of me, Sandra. But please don't worry I'll be fine. Have a happy Christmas."

"You too, and please, Nina, do take care," said Sandra, shaking her head.

Nina began her long walk home.

Her decision to leave the party early would be one she'd live to regret.

Before she was even half way home, a sailor from of one of the local ships, and the worse for drink, emerged from a riverside pub. He looked at Nina and smiled, licking his lips with salacious intent. Nina spotted him and ran for her life. But her short legs were no match for the muscular sailor. Despite the drink addling his sense of direction, he caught up with her. He smirked, gripped her shaking frame, dragged her into the bushes, and raped her.

Nina told her aunt what had happened.

Bertha replied, sneering, "Don't be so ridiculous, girl, making up filthy stories like that. Get up to bed."

In the light of what had happened, a few months later, Nina informed her aunt that she was pregnant. She replayed the story of the sailor assaulting her, insisting that it really happened. But Bertha was horrified, thinking she'd led on the assailant, and she didn't believe a word of her story.

"You're a dirty, lying, little whore," she screamed.

Nina stared at this despicable woman, ranting with her outmoded, prudish ideals. She seemed fixed on one thought. That Nina was a dirty slut.

"Well, yer canna stay here, that's for sure. Whatever will people think?"

Bertha emphasized that she would not turn Nina out on the street. However, she would have to go away somewhere until after the child was born. Then it would have to be adopted.

"If you're a good girl and don't get up to any more dirty mischief, you may come home again after," she added scornfully.

Bertha was unequivocal. As Nina had 'got herself into trouble', she was not prepared to pay any more college fees. Nina would have to leave school and work for a living. This, her Aunt emphasized, was part of her punishment for being 'a disobedient, ungrateful, little slut'.

Bertha made arrangements for Nina to enter a home in London run by the Salvation Army who accommodated young, pregnant girls. Bertha assured them that Nina was willing to work hard for her keep.

What Nina endured whilst in the home was incomprehensible to anything she'd ever known. Nina, with other young girls her age, worked from dawn until dusk. She worked for six months in what could only be described as ultimate drudgery, on her knees, scrubbing and cleaning the long stone corridors and staircases that led to their cells. It was as if she had been judged and punished for a crime for which she had been so unjustly accused. The crime of being pregnant. She was treated like a prisoner.

Slowly but surely, she became weaker. The baby was eventually stillborn.

Nina was abhorred by her aunt. Bertha believed if ever there had been a time for Nina to atone for her misdemeanors, it was now. But Nina had no desire to see or speak to Bertha ever again.

Michael, John, and Marianne followed their parents up the road without a spoken word, with careful deliberation, carrying their few possessions in little bags, and wondering what was going to happen next.

Chapter 22

Joanna had just finished packing the last of her two suitcases. Summer in Devon had come to an end all too soon for her. Terry had been given a posting and Mrs. Dent was due to return from Cornwall. Joanna had continually told herself it wasn't going to last forever. Yet when the time came, she found it difficult to accept. She realized that she must pull herself together. After all, she'd had a wonderful time here.

Terry was even taking them to another film show at the base in Lympstone tonight.

Yes, she had no reason to feel downhearted. She could think of a good many people who would gladly change places with her. She would be happy to see her parents again and, of course, poor dear Nina. Joanna grew concerned and wondered why she had only received one letter informing her that Nina was now living with Aunt Bertha.

It had been so long now. She hoped and prayed she hadn't come into any danger.

However, Joanna intended to make her last evening in Devon a memorable one. She lay out her red and white spotted dress on the bed, the one Terry liked so much. She had made it herself before coming down to Devon. It fitted her like a glove, showing off the contours of her slender figure, alluring yet extremely elegant.

She had worn it the first time she gone with Terry to the George and Dragon in Ebford. Joanna smiled cheekily to herself, remembering the occasion.

She had caused quite a stir that night. When she opened the door and walked in, wolf whistles echoed throughout the bar. Most of the men didn't realize Terry had a wife. They stood back, dumbfounded, especially when she walked straight up to him. He introduced her to a few of his close friends then escorted her through the crowd and outside into the lounge bar.

Mick stood with his arm around Rose, staring at Joanna and Terry, totally confused.

"What's the matter, Mick?" said Rose. "Cat got your tongue?"

Mick opened his mouth as if to speak, and then paused.

"You see," continued Rose, "that's why Terry wasn't interested in us Land Army girls."

"Yes," said Mick. "Or anyone else for that matter. I understand now, just by looking at her. She's quite a dish."

"Yes, not bad, if you like that sort."

"I sense a touch of jealousy, Rose?"

"I'm not jealous of her. And if you're going to talk like that, I'm off, Mick. And, for your information, I think you're the one who is jealous."

"Me? Of what?"

"Terry, of course."

"What? Me jealous of Tel? Never. He's one of the best chaps I know. Good luck to him." Mick looked serious. "I often wonder about him though."

"What do you mean?"

"Well, at times, he doesn't seem like one of us. Know what I mean? More the officer type, I'd say. Keeps his own counsel. Keeps everything close. I mean to say, most chaps like to show photos of their wife, especially one like that. But not Tel. He never lets his right hand know what his left is doing."

"Yeah, I understand," said Rose, with a contemptuous grin on her face. "But you don't have to look so miserable. How about getting me another drink?"

"Oh, yeah. Sorry, love. Of course."

Mick made his way to the bar. He had a terrible feeling. Deep inside, he knew Terry wasn't the only one who didn't show photos of his wife. He kept his own tucked away, but not for the same reason as Terry. Just thinking about Terry happy with his lovely wife and young daughter made Mick feel suddenly very guilty.

The next morning, Joanna rose early. She could hear Terry downstairs already making tea. He had been granted a twelve-hour pass. Joanna stood by the open window taking in the view and breathing the fresh, scented air from the honeysuckle bush that framed the window. She plucked a bloom and laid it between the pages of her poetry book.

"Morning, darling." Terry stood in the doorway holding a tray of tea and biscuits. "What's the matter? Having second thoughts about leaving?"

"No…No, not at all. Just having one last look."

"Jo, my sweetheart, if you would like to stay here, there is always Mrs. Fraser up-"

Joanna interjected, "Up the lane. Yes, I know, Terry. You've told me a hundred times. We are going home today, my love."

Her voice sounded as soft as the honeysuckle she had just plucked.

He gazed into her eyes. "Yes, you're quite right. I gave you the wrong advice last time and you were nearly killed."

"No, darling. You had the very best intentions at heart for both of us. You must never hold yourself responsible for what happened in Derbyshire." Joanna spoke in a direct tone, looking straight into his eyes. "Put that silly tray down, Terry, and come over here."

He obediently adhered to her wishes.

"Now, listen to me, sweetheart. If I'm not able to be with you then I must return home where I'm needed by my family and friends, who I love and to whom I feel I have an obligation. We've had a wonderful time here, Terry, but now it's over, and I have to play my small part in trying to win this bloody war, just like you. It may not be very much, but it's better than sitting on my backside here watching the daises grow."

Terry looked into her eyes as if seeing his wife for the first time. This wasn't the young nineteen year old he had married. This was a strong woman of the world.

"You know, Joanna, you're quite an amazing woman. I love you even more now than when we first met. More than I ever realized was humanly possible."

Joanna looked up into those loving, blue eyes as Terry gathered her in his arms.

Chapter 23

Mary looked dispirited as she seated herself in the compartment of the little steam train leaving Exton Station.

"It's not fair, Mummy. I wish we could have stayed longer."

"Yes, I do too, Mary. Never mind, dear. Perhaps one day we'll come back again. Maybe if Daddy is posted back to Lympstone."

"Yes, I know, Mummy. But why did we have to leave so soon? It was such a lovely place."

"Well, Mary, you know Mrs. Dent is returning home with her daughter and family."

"Yes, I know that, Mummy." Mary looked despairingly at her mother. "But I don't want to know it."

Joanna glanced at her daughter and felt terribly remorseful at having to drag Mary back to Kent. However, she had heard the raids were becoming more sporadic now. She hoped it had been true and not another propaganda trick to boost morale.

"Mary, would you have preferred to stay with Mrs. Fraser up the lane?"

"Only if you had stayed, Mummy."

Joanna looked sad. "Well, I couldn't stay, my darling. But Mrs. Fraser is a very nice lady. She has children down from London staying with her."

"No, I wouldn't like to have stayed. Not without you, Mummy. I know those evacuees she has staying with her. They went to our school. I'm pleased I'm coming home with you. It's not the blitz I'm worried about, Mummy. It's not being with Daddy. You understand what I mean, Mummy? The three of us together in that lovely cottage, so peaceful and quiet."

Joanna smiled with a pained expression in her eyes. "I understand, sweetheart. But try and cheer up. When this stupid war is over, we'll be together again, the three of us."

Mary nodded and gave the thumbs up sign.

"That's my girl," said Joanna.

They eventually arrived home after a long and tiring journey. Joanna prepared a quick meal. Then they went straight to the Red Cross unit and ARP office in Cobham Terrace for news on recent developments. Joanna put her head around the door and was greeted by Bob.

"Why, hello, Jo." He gave her a broad smile. "Am I pleased to see your face. We all thought you were gone for the duration."

"I must say, Bob, it was a very tempting idea. Anyway, how is everyone?" Joanna smiled.

"Just about managing to hold the fort. You're looking well, Jo. And you look as fit as a fiddle, young lady." Bob laughed, ruffling Mary's blonde hair.

"So what's been happening in my absence, Bob?"

Bob gave her a full update on the general news. He didn't hesitate to mention his efforts in trying to get her parents into some kind of shelter.

"Did you succeed?" said Joanna, grinning.

"No, I didn't. And, if you don't mind me saying, Jo, I think it's your mother."

"Oh, please don't worry, Bob. She's as stubborn as a mule. I'll be going up to see them shortly. I may stay the night. It's been quite a while since I've seen them."

"I wouldn't do that, Jo."

"Why ever not?"

"I heard Lord Haw Haw on the wireless this morning, and he says they're going to rage hell over the southeast tonight."

"Oh, Bob, really? He loves to frighten us with all that propaganda. I heard on the news before I left Devon this morning that Jerry is having a slight respite."

"All right, Jo. Please yourself. But think of Mary."

Something in Bob's eyes made her change her mind.

"Yes, maybe you're right. I'll leave it until tomorrow. It's getting rather late. Are my bunks still available, Bob?"

"No, but you can have Nina Franklin's."

Joanna looked surprised. "Why? Where is Nina?"

"No one seems to know where she is at the moment."

"What are you saying, Bob? I heard from Nina two months ago informing me that she was living with her aunt."

"Yes, that's right. But since then, no one seems to know much. Maggie tried to find out the other day when she happened to meet Nina's aunt in the village. Nasty woman. She told Maggie to mind her own business. Said she had no wish to discuss it with anyone. Then she walked off with her head in the air. I just don't know what to make of it all, Jo. Some say she was taken to hospital. Others say she's in Scotland with her kids."

Joanna grew agitated. "So what do you think has happened to her?"

"I honestly don't know, Jo."

"Well, Bob, she couldn't have disappeared into thin air."

Bob looked anxious. "Look here, Jo. There's nothing we can do. You're better to let sleeping dogs lie. You know what a so and so that husband of hers is."

"What? How on earth can you stand there and say that, Bob? Let sleeping dogs lie. Never."

"Jo, you must understand. We've been too busy here to worry about one person."

"That's your excuse, Bob. But I'm afraid it's not mine."

Bob sighed. "You can't go interfering in husband and wife squabbles."

"Now, listen to me, Bob. You know as I do it's a little more than that. Well, I'm getting to the bottom of it. I'll find out."

Joanna, now enraged, stormed out, slamming the door behind her. Mary, disappointed at the prospect of not seeing her grandparents, felt irritable and found it difficult to settle down in her bunk bed. She hadn't cherished the idea of coming down the tunnel, having grown accustomed to a better lifestyle in Devon. She could now comprehend what her mother meant when she had spoken to her of what life was like before the war.

Mary felt totally fed up. When the siren sounded, she buried her head in the blankets, not only to shut out the noise, but also to hide her gloom. Joanna handed her a sandwich and hot coco.

"What's the matter, sweetheart?"

"Oh, nothing. I'm just a little bit fed up. Mummy, please can you read me a story from my Hans Christian Anderson book?"

Joanna was tired and had other things on her mind. "I've seen you reading that book quite well yourself, Mary."

"I know, Mummy, but you read so lovely. It helps me sleep and shuts out that dreadful noise outside. Please, Mummy. Just a short one."

Joanna agreed after looking at Mary's forlorn little face. "Very well. Which one would you like me to read?"

"The Little Matchstick Girl."

"Mary, that's so sad. Do you really think it will cheer you up?"

"Please, Mummy. I really love it."

"All right. Pass me your book."

Joanna began reading the story. "It was frightfully cold and the snow was falling. Darkness was closing in. It was New Year's Eve..."

She had nearly concluded the story when they heard an enormous explosion.

Everyone mumbled, "That was a close one."

It seemed to be in close proximity of the tunnel. It was obvious to everyone that all hell had broken loose outside.

Joanna continued to read in her usual calm voice, finishing with the piece where the little match girl saw the vision of her grandmother.

Mary asked, "I wonder why she never saw her grandfather as well?"

"I really have no idea, Mary. I suppose because it's not in the story."

At that moment, an almighty blast vibrated all around the tunnel. Mary gazed up nervously at the circular roof.

"Are we safe here, Mummy? A bomb can't come smashing down through the roof and suffocate us, can it?"

Joanna answered in a comforting voice, "Of course not, silly." Then she laughed, hiding the fact that her daughter's question could very well be true.

"That's good. I'm going to sleep now. Goodnight, Mummy."

"Goodnight, my darling."

Joanna raised her eyes to the roof, reflecting upon Mary's question. The noise was so penetrating tonight, worse than she had ever experienced. Once again, she felt tormented by her mixed emotions. What kind of mother was she to bring Mary back to all of this?

Yet she felt a loyalty to her parents and all those around her who depended on her.

One thing was sure. She knew that she had been right in taking that irritating old man's advice in coming down here tonight.

Chapter 24

Gently, Joanna pushed the gate which hung awkwardly on its hinges and walked briskly up the shabby path leading to an impoverished-looking terraced house close to the railway. Nina had never been very proud of where she lived. Joanna, aware of this, never wished to impose herself. Today, however, was different.

On seeing there wasn't a doorbell, or even a knocker, Joanna knocked on the door with her bare fist. She waited a while. There was no answer. To make absolutely sure that no one was in, she thudded on the door with both fists. Still no answer.

Just as she was about to leave, she heard a muffled voice coming from within. Then suddenly, the door opened, and there stood Josh.

"Who are you," growled Josh, "banging on my door like that?"

Joanna turned abruptly. "Oh, good morning. I've come to see Nina. She is a friend of mine. I am sorry about the noise. But I would very much like to see her."

"Well, you can't. Who the bloody 'ell are yer anyway?"

"I have already told you. I'm a very good friend of your wife, Nina. Can you tell me where she is please?"

Joanna spoke in a quiet voice but her stance was adamant. She was determined not to leave without first finding out where Nina had gone.

Josh wanted to get rid of Joanna as quickly as possible.

He answered in an anxious tone, "She's in Gravesend Hospital. Now clear off."

His entire presence as he stood there could only be described as nothing less than an uncouth brute. He wore a scruffy shirt and filthy trousers that were held up by a thick leather belt, which, it was obvious to Joanna, had alternative uses.

She walked up to him and gave him a long, hard stare, her eyes piecing his. She tolerated the odor exuding from his drunken breath, which seemed to mingle so readily with the acrid stench left from the night raid.

Joanna continued, "Where are the children?"

"Why do yer want ter know? It's none of your sodding business. Who the bloody 'ell are yer?" Josh paused. "Wait a minute...You're that bloody toffee-nosed Joanna Busher, ain't yer? I've heard about you." He grinned menacingly.

Joanna gave him a long, cold stare. "Well then, you can trust me, can't you?"

"You've got a bleeding cheek coming 'round here," bellowed Josh. "Mind your own bloody business."

"I asked you a question," exclaimed Joanna.

Josh relented in a bid to get rid of this adamant woman. "I've evacuated 'em up north where they bloody well belong."

Joanna continued, "Where up north?"

Josh's patience was wearing thin. He bellowed, "None of your bloody business. Now clear off, you nosey, old cow, before I get the police onto yer."

"Thank you and good day," said Joanna.

She ignored his abusive remarks, turned on her heel, and quickly made her exit to the gate where Mary was waiting.

Joanna's intention was to see her parents without delay. But, by a quirk of fate, the Gravesend bus was waiting at the top of the avenue. Quite unaware of what she was doing, she grabbed Mary's hand and jumped on.

It was obvious, on entering the hospital waiting room, that the air raid during the night had raged havoc, judging from the sick and injured lying around being tended to by dutiful hospital staff, whilst more urgent cases were rushed straight inside. There was an aura of urgency all around.

Joanna managed to find the reception area and made inquiries.

"Are you a relation of Mrs. Franklin?" came a hurried reply from the woman behind the desk.

To cut through protocol, Joanna answered instinctively, "Yes. I'm her cousin, Mrs. Joanna Busher."

"I see. Very well. Mrs. Franklin is in ward six." She glanced at Mary. "I'm afraid no children are allowed into the wards. She will have to wait here until you come out."

"Wait here?" exclaimed Joanna, looking indignant.

"It's all right, Mrs. Busher. She'll be quite safe, I can assure you. Please don't worry about all the hassle this morning. We're used to it."

"I know you are. I'm in the same line of work myself. But..." Joanna paused. "It's just, with so many injured lying around..." Joanna seemed lost for words.

"I know," said the woman, as if reading Joanna's mind. "Last night was dreadful. We've been working flat out. We just don't know where to put everyone. The wards are full."

"I'll be fine, Mummy. Please don't worry about me. I can sit over there next to that lady with the baby."

Joanna felt suddenly anxious to everything that was going on around her. She had that strange formidable perception she so often felt in times like these.

"I won't be long, sweetheart. When I've seen Aunty Nina, we'll go straight to see Nanny and Grandad."

"Give my love to Aunty Nina, Mummy."

"I will, darling."

The ward sister stood waiting for Joanna. She spoke quietly before ushering her to Nina's bedside.

"Mrs. Franklin has been terribly ill," whispered the nurse. "She has made a marvelous recovery since her dreadful experience. And, of course, losing her baby the way she did. It was a terrible business."

"What dreadful experience?" echoed Joanna.

"I can't say any more. If you would like more information, see me in my office later."

"Yes, I will, and thank you," said Joanna.

"Well, how do you feel today, Mrs. Franklin? You have a visitor. Your cousin has come to see you."

"Cousin?" repeated Nina, looking up from reading her newspaper.

Joanna scarcely recognized the frail figure propped up against her pillows. Her face looked a ghastly gray, and her lovely, green eyes were now a deathly pale.

"Jo, this is a surprise. What are you doing here?" Her voice sounded drained.

"I'll leave you two together," said the sister. "Now try not to tire yourself out, Mrs. Franklin." She glanced at Joanna. "No longer than fifteen minutes, Mrs. Busher."

Joanna smiled. "I understand, sister."

Joanna bent down and kissed her friend on the forehead.

"Jo, it's wonderful to see you again. Did you have a nice time in Devon?"

"Yes, it was glorious, dear. Now tell me what you are doing in here."

"Not now, Jo, dear. Please. It's a long story. Some other time. I'd much rather hear about you and Terry and what you've been doing down in Devon." Her voice was a mere whisper.

Joanna conceded with Nina's wishes and began giving her a full update on recent events.

When she had finished, Nina said, "It sounds like a beautiful fairy story. It must have been wonderful for you, Jo." She spoke in a broken voice, her eyes nearly closing. "If you'll excuse me, Jo, dear, I think I'll have a little sleep now. Thank you so much for coming to see me, Jo. Please come again."

Joanna whispered, "Of course I will, sweetheart. I'm home now. See you tomorrow. Take care. TTFN."

Joanna walked to the end of the ward where she found the sister waiting. She led her into a small office.

"Do take a seat, Mrs. Busher."

"Thank you. Now what happened to Mrs. Franklin, sister?"

"You mean to say you don't know?"

"I know nothing," said Joanna anxiously. "I've been away for the past three months. I wrote to her several times and only received one letter two months ago."

"I can understand why. She has been in here nearly two months."

Joanna gasped. "What?"

The sister sighed. "Yes. When she was first admitted, we never thought she was going to pull through. She's made a wonderful recovery. However, she's not out of the woods yet."

Joanna looked aghast as to what she would hear next.

"She was attacked one night in the blackout whilst on her way to the air raid shelter. Her husband had been on night duty in the ammunitions factory. She had been assaulted, brutally raped, and..." The sister choked on her words. "The poor soul was then mercilessly beaten up and dumped in her own back garden. If the ARP warden hadn't found her when he did, she would most certainly have died. Her husband is eager to find the culprit who did this monstrous thing. However, I'm most surprised he hasn't informed you."

Joanna looked cautious and did not answer the question. "Have you any idea where her three children are?"

"Oh, they're in Scotland. They were evacuated before all this happened."

"I see," answered Joanna reflectively. "Sister, I would appreciate it if you kept this conversation confidential."

"Yes, of course. But her husband said if anyone asks questions-"

Joanna intercepted, giving her a long, hard stare. "Please. I'm asking you to do this to help Mrs. Franklin."

The sister looked questioningly at Joanna.

"Sister, when I can prove to you and the police that I know who did this-"

At that moment, a hurried knocking on the door interrupted them.

"Yes, come in," said the sister.

A young nurse entered. "Excuse me, sister. But is there a Mrs. Joanna Busher here?"

The sister nodded towards Joanna. "This is Mrs. Busher. What can we do for you, nurse?"

"Dr. Clemance wishes to see Mrs. Busher immediately." The nurse looked at the sister and then at Joanna. "It's terribly urgent."

"I see," said the sister.

"Why?" exclaimed Joanna. "I left my daughter in reception to wait for me."

The nurse interrupted her. "Your daughter is quite safe. Please, follow me, Mrs. Busher. It's very important."

Joanna was mystified. "But why? What's happened?"

The sister knew which ward Dr. Clemance was on and urged her to go quickly.

"Please, don't worry, my dear. We can continue our little chat another time."

The nurse escorted Joanna into a room at the end of the corridor where Dr. Clemance sat at his desk reading some documents. He looked up when the nurse announced Joanna.

"Ah, thank you, nurse. You may leave us now."

He stood up and drew out a chair for Joanna.

Dr. Clemance was a man of medium height with light-gray hair and eyes that were lukewarm. Yet when he smiled at Joanna, they held so much compassion.

"Please do take a seat, Mrs. Busher."

"No, thank you. I'd rather stand." She looked puzzled. "What is wrong, doctor? Why do you wish to see me?"

Dr. Clemance went back to his desk, sighed nonchalantly, and sat down. He picked up a document.

"You are Mrs. Joanna Busher? Daughter of Mr. and Mrs. Partridge of Weeping Willows, the bungalow on Craylands Lane?"

"Yes, I am," answered Joanna dubiously.

The doctor spoke hurriedly. "My colleagues have been desperately trying to contact their next of kin all this morning without any luck. It was just fortunate for us that you happened to be here." Dr. Clemance looked directly at Joanna. "I'll come straight to the point, Mrs. Busher. I'm afraid I have bad news. I'm terribly sorry to have to tell you, but your parents' property suffered a direct hit last night. Your mother only just escaped with her life. But, I'm afraid, your father wasn't so lucky. He was in the house at the time and was killed instantly."

Joanna gasped. "No…No," she cried. "It can't be true. Not Daddy." She choked on her words and then froze.

The doctor paused for a second, looking at Joanna, and then continued, "He wouldn't have felt a thing, Mrs. Busher. It was instantaneous. Your mother, fortunately, was at the bottom of her garden in a corrugated iron shed, apparently looking for her cat. The first words she whispered when she regained consciousness were, 'Where is my Tiddles?' Your mother evidently valued that cat, and well she should. It saved her life. It seems, according to our information, that your mother dragged herself over burning debris out to the road where she was found unconscious and lying on a heap of rubble."

The doctor paused, deciding upon what to say next.

"Your mother is now in a state of severe mental trauma and it may take a long time before we see any sign of recovery. Perhaps only days, maybe months, or even longer. It's difficult to say at this stage. It all depends on the extent of her injury."

The doctor smiled warmly, looking at Joanna's dazed and ashen face.

"However, I feel sure she will pull through. She's very strong for her age. A remarkable lady. If you would care to see your mother now then you may do so. But at the moment, she doesn't even know who she is. So be prepared, my dear."

Joanna stood up, a chill running through her spine.

She answered impassively, "Yes, thank you, doctor." Then she put her hand to her forehead. "Oh, but my little girl is still waiting for me in reception."

"Well, if you wish, I can send a nurse to bring her to your mother's ward?"

"Yes, I would like that. Thank you, doctor."

"She won't be allowed in of course," he said. "But on this occasion, I'm sure she will be permitted to wait just outside the ward. I'll ring for sister. She will take you to your mother's ward. Well, goodbye, Mrs. Busher, and if there is anything I can possible do to help, please do not hesitate in contacting me." He extended his hand.

Joanna stood calmly in front of him and shook his hand.

In a distant voice, far removed from everyone, she answered, "Thank you very much, doctor. I will remember that. Good day."

"Good morning, Mrs. Busher. I'm the ward sister. Would you follow me, please? I'm afraid you are only allowed ten minutes with your mother." She spoke in a hushed voice as they approached the ward. "Your mother is still very ill."

Joanna nodded and sat down by her mother's bedside. She scarcely recognized the woman lying on the bed to be her mother. She was covered in bandages. Joanna held onto her scared fingers and, for a brief moment, there seemed to be a glimmer of recognition in her mother's eyes, and then it was gone.

Joanna, dazed and bewildered, sat looking at her mother, unable to grasp the reality of the situation. The sister came and laid her hand on Joanna's shoulder.

"It's time to leave now, my dear, and your daughter is waiting."

Joanna looked at the sister. Her eyes swimming, she bravely contained her emotions, and whispered, "Yes, I'm just coming, sister."

"Hello, Mummy. The nurse said that's Nanny in that bed. What's wrong with her?"

Joanna felt ice cold. She was reluctant to speak. She took Mary's hand and hurried outside.

She whispered, "I'll tell you later, darling."

Once outside the hospital, Mary persisted. "What is wrong with Nanny? And why is she all bandaged up like that?"

"Nanny and Grandad had a bad accident last night."

Mary's razor-sharp brain was quick to answer. "What sought of accident? Were they bombed?"

"Yes, Mary. They were bombed."

"Is Nanny badly hurt?" In the same breath, Mary exclaimed, "Where is Grandad? Was he hurt too?"

Joanna whispered, "Yes, darling. He was terribly hurt."

"Is he in hospital too?"

"No, my sweetheart. He is not in hospital."

Mary screamed out, "Where is he? He's not dead, is he?"

Joanna nodded. Mary's lip dropped and the tears began to fall like rain.

Joanna knelt down in the middle of the busy street and gathered her sobbing daughter in her arms.

"Hush, hush, my sweet. It's all right. Grandad is in heaven now."

Chapter 25

Tucked away in a shelter at the back of his local pub, Josh was addressing his newfound band of crooks in a place he thought he would be able to operate freely and without suspicion.

"Well, chaps, that's it in a nutshell. We'll be laughing all the way to the bank when we've pulled this one off."

"Thank Gawd you've explained it. We all thought you weren't gonna turn up tonight," said one of the men.

"Now would I let yer down? When I say I'll do somefink, I keep to me word. I 'ad to show me face at the 'ospital otherwise they'll be wondering what's up. I was chatting to one of the young nurses. She kept going on about the rationing, just like every other bugger in the country. I tell yer, lads, we can't go wrong on this one. They'll do any bloody fing for a bit of extra grub. Know what I mean?" Josh laughed, arching his eyebrow knowingly, and the others nodded. "Now let's get down to business. My mate Fred will be supplying the transport." Josh paused and looked at one of the men. "What's up, Sol?" he questioned. "Why are yer looking so worried?"

"I'm not worried." Sol sat in the corner on his own looking somber.

"This is going to be a doddle," continued Josh. "Not a fing to worry about, Sol. My mate Fred is the driver. He's in the West Kents. All this stuff is nicked army grub, as yer all know. That's where you come in, Pete, with yer lock up garage."

"Well, I don't like the idea. Sounds too risky to me," said Sol.

"Now you listen to me," bellowed Josh. "You were quick enough to take the dough I gave yer last week. You're in it now, mate, up to yer eyeballs, whether yeh like it or not."

Josh then turned his back on Sol, ignoring him completely, and addressed the rest of the men.

"Jack and me 'ave the contacts to get rid of the stuff. Now, any more questions, chaps?"

There was a muffled echo among the team. "No. No, that's okay by us, Josh."

Meanwhile, Terry had been posted to a remote base outside the town of Aberystwyth in Wales. The men were on stringent military exercises and all leave had been canceled until further notice. Inevitably, he would be unable to attend the memorial service to be held for his father-in-law. However, he had been informed that he would be granted compassionate leave in due course.

Joanna would have to endure her sister and brother-in-law alone. They came down from Scotland for the memorial service with their two children, Elizabeth and Patrick. The difference between the two sisters was quite remarkable.

Annabelle, a tall, slim woman with a feigned type of beauty, had bleach-blonde hair and a heavily made-up face, which matched her personality. She wore a silver fox fur coat and coordinating hat to the memorial service. Even though it was early autumn.

Joanna stood in the pew next to Uncle Tom. She wore a simple, plain, black suit and a gray, Deanna Durban style hat framing her lovely face, which held her hidden grief. She glanced at her sister in the next pew, who was shedding enough crocodile tears to make her silver fox so wet she looked as if she'd been caught in a shower. Joanna couldn't help but feel pity for this very pretentious woman. Poor Annabelle. She had never been able to cope with a crisis.

In their childhood, her mother had conceded to her every whim. She paid for Annabelle's private tuition to enter secretarial college, in spite of the fact that she wasn't very bright at school. If Joanna had the same cosseting, she would have undoubtedly become an opera singer with her velveteen, soprano voice. Instead, she embarked on a nursing career until she met Terry.

When Annabelle finally left college, she worked only three months at the Mount Pleasant, GPO typing pool in London. That was where she met Mark, who was an adventurous social climber. Annabelle spied him to be a good catch. They were married within two months of meeting. Mark, now forty-five and balding, had been exempt from military service due to the fact he worked directly for the Ministry of Defence.

They once lived in a prestigious part of the London suburbs. When war broke out, Annabelle grew nervous and wanted to move. Fate kindly intervened and Mark was offered a position in Glasgow. Annabelle didn't hesitate. She insisted Mark must take it. They moved to the mid Highlands. Annabelle lived in a delightful house in the Trossachs. Mark, working long hours in the government, found it vital to be close to his work. Thus they had to rent a flat in Glasgow. "He is able to see his family on the weekends if he is lucky," Annabelle always said. Poor Mark consequently now suffered the blitz on Glasgow. Annabelle always expected nothing less than the very best that Mark could provide. They lived far beyond their means.

"Well, I'm pleased that's over with," said Annabelle dispassionately. "Went off quite well, I thought, at least as far as these things go."

She sat herself down comfortably in the armchair.

Uncle Tom stood up. "You really are a most overwhelming lady, my dear," he said mockingly. "It must be quite comforting for Joanna to have you here on such an occasion."

"Oh, we're not staying here any longer than we can help." She spoke with a patronizing voice. "Mark's work, you see. He has a very demanding, important job. We're leaving on the night train to Glasgow."

"Oh, I see." Tom paused. "Now, if you'll excuse me, I think I'll go and see where our hostess is."

"Why, of course," said Annabelle in a haughty tone. "Please don't worry about us."

Tom left the room in search of Joanna.

"Ah, there you are, Jo, in the kitchen already."

"Well, someone has to prepare the meal, Uncle."

"Yes, quite so, my dear. Can I be of any assistance?"

"No, thank you, Uncle. I'm ready to serve now."

"I've just been informed that your guests are on the point of leaving you."

Joanna sighed. "Yes. Thank God."

Tom coughed in a disgruntled fashion. "Yes, quite." He quickly changed the subject. "My word, that shepherd's pie looks appetizing. I don't know how you do it, Jo, on our measly ration. You're really quite an amazing young woman. Shall I take the dinner plates in, my dear?"

"Oh, thank you, Uncle."

Joanna smiled, but Tom noticed her eyes were like dark pools. He put a reassuring hand on her shoulder.

"I don't know if this is of any consolation to you, my dear, but I have been offered a practice in Gravesend."

"Oh, really? That's marvelous news, Uncle. When?"

"I'm not quite sure yet. There's a great deal of paper work to be done first."

"Terry will be pleased. We've both been terribly worried about you up there in the heart of it all."

"Well," said Tom. "I think I'm getting a little too old for London these days. I shall continue to do my bit down here, of course, perhaps in the local ARP." He looked directly into Joanna's eyes. "I think we can push our luck a little bit too far at times, Jo."

"How right you are, Uncle, dear. How right you are."

"That was a delightful meal, Jo," said Annabelle after dinner in her usual haughty voice. "It's really quite amazing how you do it. I wouldn't be able to manage if it wasn't for Mark's valued connections."

Tom looked stifled by her overpowering personality. "Well, some of us have to," he said. "After all, when you consider the lengths the Royal Navy and Merchant Navy have gone to protect our convoys, I think we should be grateful for whatever is served up on our plate. Furthermore, I think anyone who is caught black marketing should be severely prosecuted, or anyone else, for that matter, who is found buying black market goods. However, my dear lady, I do not hold any derogatory feeling towards you. After all, you are Joanna's sister. But when you consider a few months ago this country had only enough food supplies to last two weeks, it makes one realize how much we owe these brave seaman. However, I do not wish to jade this delicious meal by being so outspoken. I agree with you, Annabelle. Joanna is a splendid cook." He turned to Joanna and smiled. "Now, if you'll excuse me, my dear Jo, I'm afraid I will have to take my leave before our friends from across the channel pay us another visit."

"Oh, Uncle, I am sorry you're leaving so soon."

"I'm sorry too, my dear. But duty calls and I have a great deal of work to catch up on."

"We'll be joining you as soon as the children return from the park," interrupted Annabelle.

Tom turned and smiled. "If you don't mind me making a suggestion, wouldn't it be wise to stay another night with Jo? It may be hazardous travelling all the way to Scotland so late at night. Especially for the children."

"We'll be fine, thanks, Tom," said Mark in a kindly tone.

Annabelle interrupted abruptly, speaking through her nose in the same supercilious manner. "Oh, we'll be fine. We've reserved a first class sleeping compartment. I just couldn't possibly spend another night in that wretched tunnel. Anyway, we won't be putting up with all this for much longer. Mark has been offered a position in Canada."

Joanna turned from Tom and stared at her sister in surprise. "Canada?"

"Yes, that's right," said Annabelle in her dismissive, airy tone.

Tom smiled. "Well, whatever, I wish you both a safe journey home and wherever else you may journey. I bid you good day."

"Thank you, Tom. You're very kind," said Mark.

Joanna escorted Tom to the front door.

He smiled and whispered, "My word, that poor man. I'm pleased Terry chose the right sister."

Joanna gave him a warm smile. "She can't help it, Tom. She was born that way. But Canada, well, that's certainly news to me."

Tom took her hand in his. "Now it's all on your shoulders, my dear. But you know where I am if you should need me."

"Thank you, Uncle."

"Goodbye, my dear, and take care."

"You too, Uncle, and God bless you."

"Well, thank goodness he's gone," uttered Annabelle back at the table. "Self-righteous old bastard. He gave me the creeps. Not derogatory. The horrible man. He hates me."

"I can't understand you sometimes, Bella," replied Mark. "I think he's a lovely old chap. Anyway, he was speaking the truth, and you can't take it."

"Oh yes, that's just like you, isn't it? To be in favor of an old bastard like that."

"Well, Bella, he didn't have to come here today. He did so because he's a gentleman and knew it was the honorable thing to do in view of the fact that Terry was unable to be here."

"I know. I know. The wonderful, gallant Terry doing his bit for king and country. Well, he's a fool. He could have got out of it just like you. Anyone in their right mind would. Terry is just like his old man, honorably stupid. And *you* call that insufferable old goat a gentleman? He's a rude, old bastard."

"Why are you like this, Bella?" said Mark with tiredness in his tone.

"Like what?"

"So damned selfish."

"Who me? Selfish?"

"Yes, you, Bella. You've just lost your own father yet you can speak like that. And wanting to rush off tonight, God alone knows why. Old Tom was just trying to give you a little friendly advice."

"Well, I don't need his advice." Annabelle began to shout. "I have already told you, Mark. I'm not spending another night in that damned tunnel."

Joanna overheard raised voices as she was about to enter the lounge. She stood for a moment in the hall.

"I wonder where the hell Elizabeth and Patrick are. We're leaving as soon as they get back. But before we go, I'm having a word with Jo about mother."

"Now don't start that again, Bella. Have a little consideration, for God's sake."

"You stay out of this, Mark."

"Hello, am I interrupting something?" asked Joanna.

Annabelle began putting on her stuck-up voice again. "Oh no, Jo, dear. Just Mark being a little foolish."

"I see." Joanna paused, looking a little wary. "Shall we all have a nice cup of tea and some of my homemade rock cakes?"

"Oh, that will be lovely, Jo. No rock cakes for me. I never eat them."

Joanna smiled. "They're not rock hard, Bella, not when you know how to cook them."

"What do you mean by that?"

"Well, if you put extra water in the mixture and a little American dried egg, that causes them to rise, giving you something like a fairy cake."

"Jo, you're a genius."

"Yes," agreed Joanna in a cool tone. "You see, Bella, it's not what you have, it's what you can do with it."

Annabelle stood and followed Joanna into the kitchen.

"I wonder where the children are."

"I'm quite sure they're safe, Bella. They're probably waiting for Mary at the school gate. After all, they don't meet up very often. If you're worried, I'll pop down to the park and find them."

"Oh, I'm not worried. I just want to leave as soon as possible."

"Wouldn't it be nice to stay another night? If only for the children?"

"I thought I'd made it clear, Jo. I'm not spending another night in that dreadful tunnel."

"But supposing there's an air raid before you cross London?"

"Well, Mark knows some old friends at the Savoy. They'll take us down to their underground shelter, where we'll be much safer than stuck in that ghastly, old tunnel."

Joanna appeared cool. She looked directly at her sister. "I understand, Bella. I'll make some sandwiches for your journey. Elizabeth and Patrick will be hungry when they return."

"Thank you, Jo, dear. You're so understanding," said Annabelle.

She continued to wander around as Joanna sorted things in the kitchen.

"Would you care for anything else, Bella?"

"No, I don't think so, Jo."

Joanna began making the sandwiches and hadn't noticed her sister's scheming expression.

"There is just one thing I'd like to speak to you about, Jo."

"Oh, what's that?"

"The question of Mother."

"Yes, what about her?"

"Well, have you considered what is going to happen to her?"

"What do you mean?"

"When she comes out of hospital, of course."

"I really haven't given it much thought, Bella. Mother is still very ill."

"I'm aware of that, Jo. But you know as well as I do, she'll never be the same again."

"Whatever do you mean, Bella?"

"Well, surely, as a nurse yourself, you must realize that when she recovers her physical strength, they will want to release her as soon as possible. They need the beds, Jo."

"Yes, I understand that. What are you trying to say, Bella?"

"I'm trying to say, when she comes out, she'll be mentally handicapped." Annabelle slowly raised her voice. "She'll be totally helpless and won't be able to do anything for herself."

"You don't know that, Bella. With plenty of TLC, she may recover quicker than you think."

"Oh, be realistic, Jo. She's been there two weeks and she still doesn't know who she is."

"You're speaking as if Mother is a problem."

"And so she is. She has brought all this on herself."

"Well that sounds strange coming from you of all people, Bella. You hate air raid shelters."

"I'm not talking about that," said Annabelle. "If she'd married someone financially better off, she wouldn't be in this position. When she married Father, she married beneath her."

Joanna froze.

"If she'd taken Grandfather's advice," continued Anabelle, "she would be a wealthy woman now."

"I have no wish to continue this discussion, Bella. I have heard enough. If you'll bring the cakes, I'll take the tea tray into the lounge."

Annabelle was ready to explode. She grabbed the cakes and walked quickly with Joanna into the lounge.

"It's no good trying to avoid the issue, Jo. You'll have to face facts sooner or later."

"I have already told you, Bella, I have nothing further to say on the matter," Joanna said in a cold, flat voice.

"Don't be evasive, Jo. You know very well what I'm referring to."

Mark interceded, "Bella, for God's sake, not now."

"Shut up, Mark," snapped Annabelle. "If Mother is still in the same condition when they're ready to let her leave, then, my being the eldest in the family, I am going to suggest that she be put into an institution."

"What did you say?" exclaimed Joanna.

"Don't look so shocked, my sainted little sister. I thought I'd made myself clear. Unless, of course, you can suggest an alternative. Like giving her a home yourself? Because I certainly can't take her. And going to Canada is not the reason. I just don't think it's right. She needs proper mental treatment, and in an institution, she would receive that."

Joanna heard laughter coming from the kitchen and put the tray down on the coffee table. She ignored Annabelle and marched into the other room.

"Hello, children. Have you had a nice time?"

"Wonderful, Aunty Jo," said Patrick. "We found lots of shrapnel but Mary didn't want to look for any."

"Why, Mary?" said her mother.

"I have a headache. That's why."

"I'll give you something for it."

"No, I'll be all right, Mummy, when I've had a rest and something to eat."

"Well, I've made some nice sandwiches and cakes for you. I must ask you all to sit quietly and eat up your tea. Then maybe, if you're good, I'll give you all a nice piece of milk chocolate."

Joanna disappeared into the lounge again.

"Why did you go off like that?" raged Annabelle.

"I thought that was fairly obvious," said Joanna. "The children needed something to eat. Now where were we?"

"You know very well, Jo. We were discussing what to do with Mother."

"Oh yes, of course," said Joanna calmly. "You suggested an institution?"

"Yes. That's the only solution because I can't take her."

Joanna marched up to Annabelle and looked at her straight in the eyes. "Well, this is something you will take, Bella," said Joanna, and she struck her hard on each cheek. "That's what I think of your suggestion."

Annabelle flung the cakes she had been holding to one side, which landed on Mark's lap.

Joanna stormed, "Mother is my responsibility from now on. Never *ever* try and interfere again. Now get out of my house!"

Chapter 26

Josh and his gang were having a convivial evening in celebration of their achievements.

"Well, I told yer we could do it and we 'ave. That was a job well done, fellas," said Josh, raising his glass of brown ale. "A few more like this one and we'll be able to make good investments when the war's over. It'll be blokes like us with the money this country will need, not yer heroes."

"What makes yer so sure we're gonna win it, Josh?" Pete laughed.

Josh paused. "Well…Of course we're gonna win." Josh tried not to show the alarm he felt by Pete's innocuous remark. "Anyway, yer can't look on the black side, Pete." Josh quickly changed the subject to immediate issues. "I think we should only use this place twice a week in case the governor here gets suspicious. So I suggest we all meet twice a week at my place. Unless, of course, any of yer 'as a better idea?"

Sol was beginning to have his doubts about Josh and the whole business.

"What about your wife?" Sol inquired. "Surely she'll suspect something's going on."

"Yer, that's right," rang out the rest of the gang.

"Well, she can't say anything at the moment. She's in 'ospital."

"When she comes out, I mean," continued Sol.

"Oh, she'll be no problem. Not if she knows what's good for her."

"Why, you bastard," said Sol, eyeing Josh icily. "I may be a bit of a villain, but wife beating is not my style."

"What do yer mean by that?"

"Nothing. It's just I've heard rumors, that's all."

"I don't care what you've heard. It's none of your bloody business," bellowed Josh. "Don't try and play the bleeding nice guy with me because it won't wash. Now let's cut the crap and 'ave another bloody drink."

"That's right," said the gang, agreeing on the consensus to get drunk.

There was a sudden knock on the Anderson door. Josh opened it to find a man resembling that of an ape standing before him.

Josh smiled. "Come on in, Bill, me old mate. If yer can get in, that is."

The man had to crouch on all fours to get inside the Anderson shelter.

"This 'ere is Bill Thomson. Better known as BBB, Big Burly Bill! He's come to join us, lads," bellowed Josh. "What'll yer 'ave to drink, Bob, me old mate?" Josh took Bill aside and whispered, "Now you come 'round my place tomorrow night and I'll explain it too yer."

Bill nodded in agreement. Josh had his own devious reasons for having Bill as part of his team.

Pete grinned, looking at Sol. "Blimey. I wouldn't like to come across him in a dark alley. What the hell is he gonna do? Break someone's back?"

"I have no idea, Pete. But I don't like what's going on. It's all getting a little too hot to handle for my liking. I just want out."

Bill Thomson was a man in his mid-forties. He stood at six foot six inches, weighed nineteen stone, and had the brain of a seven year old. Bill, an ex-heavyweight boxer who once had a prison record, had become punch drunk before he was able to make it to the top. He had been used and abused all his life.

Now Josh would choose the right time to use Bill once again.

Chapter 27

Many women in the Red Cross had been posted abroad. This made Joanna's work more demanding. She found herself rushed off her feet. If she wasn't in the tunnel with Mary, she would be helping Dr. Stanley next door. Joanna could always count on her inner senses to sooth an aching heart. It was her philosophy at work. She had no time to feel melancholy over recent events. Even the thought of not seeing Terry didn't stop her from doing what she believed to be right.

Terry's leave had been postponed yet once again. It was obvious to Joanna that they were training him for some kind of mission. However, there was one beacon of light on the horizon. He would be home for Christmas on an extended compassionate leave.

Her mother had made a remarkable recovery. But her mental health had taken its toll. It was going to take time before she was completely better. Joanna felt confident in her belief that with tender love and care she would make a full recovery.

Joanna was pleased when Tom took up his new position in Gravesend. She hoped he would be able to throw some light on Nina's case. Up until now, Joanna could prove nothing about how Nina's husband had beaten her so many times. None of the hospital staff believed Joanna and Nina was too terrified to support her story. They didn't see how a husband so devoted to his wife as Mr. Franklin could do such a dreadful thing.

On a wet, dreary afternoon in late October when Joanna was picking up a delivery of medical supplies and piling them into her Red Cross van at the rear entrance of Gravesend hospital, two men approached her. One was wearing a white coat, who was obviously a doctor, and the other was a policeman.

"Mrs. Busher?"

"Yes," said Joanna, slightly taken back by the authoritative tone of the two men.

"The constable and I would like to have a word with you. It will only take a few minutes. If you'll kindly come to my office please."

Instinct told Joanna to be cautious. "Is this concerning my mother, doctor?"

"No. It's nothing to do with your mother."

"Well, I'm very busy. It's important?"

The doctor replied in a cold voice, "Yes. It's very important, Mrs. Busher."

"Very well," said Joanna, looking mystified.

In his office, the doctor drew up a chair. "Do take a seat, Mrs. Busher."

"Thank you. As I have already mentioned, I am very busy. So if you could tell me why I'm here."

"Very well. I'll come straight to the point," said the doctor in a curt voice. "Mr. Franklin has informed us that you have been making false allegations against him. And he can prove that you are in no way related to Mrs. Franklin. He states that, if you persist in these wild allegations, he'll have no alternative but to take you to court for defamation of character."

"What? It can't be true," exclaimed Joanna.

"Yes, I'm afraid it is, Mrs. Busher."

"Then am I right in assuming, doctor, that I will not be allowed to visit Mrs. Franklin?"

"Indeed you *may* visit Mrs. Franklin provided you drop these outrageous accusations. Mr. Franklin is an understanding man. He is aware that it would upset his wife if you didn't visit her."

Joanna realized that Josh had thought of everything. She had no alternative but to except the situation.

"Yes, of course, doctor. He'll never hear another word from me."

Joanna was enraged as she travelled back to the Red Cross base. She could not imagine how on earth that evil monster could get away with it. Her brain was now in turmoil. She would have to think of something.

If only she had pursued the matter when she had first returned home. She felt sure the ward sister who had been on duty the first day she came to see Nina would have believed her story. So much had happened since then. Precious time had been lost. Josh had gained enough time to enact his Machiavellian play. But Joanna was determined to do something about that terrible man.

Mary helped her mother a great deal during this difficult period in the house and running errands. In point of fact, she was an inspiration. Most of her friends had been evacuated or moved from the area. She felt sad when she learned that her new friend, Dora, had been taken ill with rheumatic fever. Dora recently moved down from London with her parents to escape the blitz.

Since her grandfather's death, Mary no longer found pleasure in searching for the largest piece of shrapnel. Instead, she would kick it away vigorously. Strolling into the school playground, deep in thought, as she so often did, she made her way to the river wall, which faced the Thames. It was there, on a warm, sunny afternoon only two weeks ago, that she had first met Dora.

"Poor Dora. I do wish she were here now instead of stuck in that horrible tunnel day and night in her bunk bed."

Mary gazed over the river and sighed. She felt all alone.

Then a young boy cried out from the other side of the playground, "Hey, Mary, what are you doing standing there like a lollipop? Are you deaf or daft? The siren has gone. Sister Patrick wants us all down in the crypt right now. So hurry up."

Mary turned her head slightly to look at the boy. "I'm just coming," she called. Then she turned her gaze back towards the river.

The sun peeped out through the clouds and cast a beam of light over her grandfather's boat, which was tied to a mooring. For a split second, Mary felt sure she had seen her grandfather sitting in his boat and waving to her, the same as usual.

But it can't be, thought Mary. He's in heaven.

Then she remembered the little matchstick girl, and a broad smile crossed her face.

Perhaps he's come to say goodbye to me.

The young boy shouted again, "Mary, Sister Patrick said hurry up. We're all down in the crypt now."

Mary looked up at the sky on hearing the heavy throb of bombers getting closer, and she ran like the wind to catch up with the others.

Chapter 28

Joanna continued to make her daily visits to see her mother and Nina. It was mid-November when the house doctor in charge of her mother's case asked to see her.

"How very nice to see you again, Mrs. Busher. Do take a seat." The doctor smiled.

Joanna looked straight at the man standing by the doctor's desk.

"Oh, allow me to introduce you. This is Dr. Heath. He is a psychiatrist. I took the liberty of inviting him here today on behalf of your mother."

"Oh, really?" said Joanna, looking surprised.

Dr. Heath was a tall, gaunt-looking man with piercing, gray eyes and iron-gray hair turning white at the sides. It was combed back from his temples, portraying harsh features. He was a fearsome-looking man to anyone in their right mind.

"Mrs. Busher, do you remember, some time ago, when we discussed your mother's condition? I explained to you it was going to take time."

"Yes, you did, doctor," agreed Joanna, looking anxious.

"Well, physically, she is quite fit for a lady of her age. She has made a remarkable recovery. Unfortunately, I wish I could say the same for her mental health." He sighed, shrugged his shoulders, and waved his hands in a nonchalant manner. "I'm afraid there is little else we can do to help your mother here."

"Are you saying that my mother is incurable?"

"No. No, she'll recover completely in time, but-"

Joanna interrupted him. "One moment, doctor. Do you not think that it was rather unethical to ask for the advice of a psychiatrist without asking for my permission?"

"Forgive me, dear lady, but surely, as a nurse yourself, you understand the situation and its urgency."

"Oh, yes, I do indeed," said Joanna. "Please continue speaking, doctor."

"I was about to say, it's going to take time, Mrs. Busher, precious time, and, indeed, a very long time. That is why I asked Dr. Heath to assist me. He thinks he'll be able to accommodate your mother in one of his institutions. It is out in the country, somewhere away from all these air raids, where she would be able to make a full recovery."

"What?" exclaimed Joanna. "If my mother went into one of those places, she would never recover."

Dr. Heath interrupted her, speaking for the first time in a churlish tone. "Are you implying that your mother would not receive satisfactory treatment?"

"I'm not implying anything, doctor. I am a nurse and I'm fully aware of the treatment my mother would receive in your institution or anywhere else."

"I do not think you quite understand, Mrs. Busher. You see, your mother will have to leave this hospital very soon."

"Very well. Let's cut to the chase," said Joanna in a calm, positive voice. "I am sure your intentions are perfectly sincere. However, putting my mother in an institution is out of the question. Furthermore, Dr. Heath, I'd appreciate it if you would leave the care of my mother to me. I will take full responsibility for her and find suitable accommodation in a nursing home for which she is accustomed."

"Well, you may find that rather difficult in these times, Mrs. Busher," stated Dr. Heath curtly.

Joanna didn't answer him. She turned to the house doctor. "How soon would you like my mother to leave here, doctor? This is the point in question, is it not?"

"Well, let me see now. Roughly a week or two, I suppose. You do understand, my dear, that we only want the best for your mother?" He smiled and extended his hand.

"Yes, of course," said Joanna. Making an effort to smile, she turned on her heel to leave.

The house doctor sprang to his feet and escorted her from the room. "Goodbye, Mrs. Busher. It's been a pleasure meeting you once again."

Dr. Heath looked on dejectedly without a word.

After visiting her mother, Joanna made her way to Nina's ward. She was no longer able to gain information on Nina's health. Since her confrontation with the law, and for posing as a close relative, various members of the nursing staff now ostracized her. However, providence prevailed, and Joanna became friendly with the ward sister, who believed her story totally. She didn't like or trust Josh. The ward sister had noticed that on particular occasions whilst Josh was visiting, Nina would invariably have a relapse. She had given Joanna vital information, which she needed. Nina, now almost recovered, had spent six months in hospital.

In 1938, Nina had her right kidney removed. It had been infected by tuberculosis. Since then, she had given birth to one child and had four miscarriages. That had consequently resulted in a rare blood disease. Nina had been totally unaware of this. Josh was the only person who had any knowledge of the disease, except, of course, for the medical staff. Josh had advised them to keep Nina's disease a closely guarded secret for fear of alarming his wife.

Joanna was determined to help Nina. But she had no idea how.

On entering the ward, Joanna was surprised to see Aunt Bertha sitting by Nina's bed. She had been aware of the bad feeling that existed between them, and she wondered what this embittered old woman was doing here. Joanna could not tolerate Bertha and was careful that their paths never crossed.

"Hello, Jo," said Nina, looking happy to see her. "I suppose you've been to see your mother?"

"Yes, I just left her."

Joanna had no wish to discuss her mother, or anyone else for that matter, in the presence of Bertha.

"How is she?"

"Oh, she's fine, Nina. How are you?"

"Well, you'll be pleased to learn I'm also doing fine. So much so that I'll be leaving here by the weekend."

"Oh, really? That is good news. I suppose you'll be going to a convalescent home to recuperate?" Joanna smiled.

Nina sighed. "Unfortunately, no. They couldn't possibly find a nursing home at such short notice." She looked up at Joanna with fear in her eyes, and whispered, "I will just have to go home."

Joanna stared blankly at her friend, unable to believe her ears.

"I'm afraid that's it, Jo. They need the beds for more urgent cases. After all, I'm almost better now."

"Are you?" questioned Joanna doubtfully.

"Of course she is. She can't stay in here forever," said Bertha in a brittle tone.

It was obvious that Joanna would not be able to speak to Nina with this old witch sitting next to her. She decided to leave.

"I've just remembered I can't stay long, Nina. I'm picking Mary up from school today. I had completely forgotten. I'm buying her new shoes."

"Oh, I am sorry, Jo. I always look forward to your visits. But I understand. I know how quickly kids wear their shoes out." She paused then smiled. "I know what mine were like. You know, Jo, it seems ages since I've seen their little faces. I wonder how they are. Bless their hearts."

"Och, away with yee, lass. You should be pleased they've been billeted with a good family," said Bertha.

Joanna, quick to answer, looked directly at Bertha. "Yes, I agree with you. But it's not quite like being with their mother, is it?" Joanna glanced at Nina, and then smiled. "I really must go now, dear. Take care. I'll see you again very soon. TTFN."

Joanna turned to leave. At the same time, she felt a sudden chill run through her spine. She looked up to find Josh standing in the doorway. For some reason, Joanna found herself walking back to Nina's bedside.

He had that same sinister smile.

"'Allo, me darling. 'Ow are yer ter day?" His loud, coarse mannerism didn't equal the phrase. "'Allo, Bertha, 'ow are yer?" Fake kindness invested in Josh's words.

"Och, not so bad, thank yee, Josh."

He was completely oblivious to Joanna and turned to Nina.

"My, yer looking well, darlin'. Ain't she, Bertha?"

"Aye. That's what I've just been saying."

Josh held a bunch of flowers behind his back, bent forward, and kissed Nina's hand in an obsequious manner as romantic as one would describe the actions of Beelzebub.

"Look wot I've got yer."

He held the flowers out in front of him as if acting out a magician's role.

"Oh, they're lovely," said Bertha. "Yee are that thoughtful, Josh. Isn't he, Nina?"

Nina didn't answer. She suddenly looked pale as if a shadow had been cast over her skin.

Joanna looked around the room.

"Josh, I think you're disturbing the patients. They will ask one of us to leave if you don't tone down your voice a little."

Josh glanced sideways with pursed lips and eyes that could pierce steel. "Okay then, yer bloody go," he growled. Turning to Nina, Josh lowered his voice and drew up closer to his wife. He spoke in a smarmy tone. "I'm looking forward to yer coming home, darling."

Joanna gave him a stony stare.

What came next shocked even Bertha.

"I do miss yer. Hurry up and get well. I need yer at home. I want to use yer."

Nina stared at him, speechless. She raised her head against the pillows.

"I think you'd better go now, Josh. I'm feeling rather tired."

"Why do yer want me to go? What about them? I notice yer ain't told them to go. I'm not leaving, Nina. I 'ave a right to be 'ere. I'm yer 'usband."

Bertha stood up and left immediately.

Nina looked deeply shaken. Her face was a deathly gray. She lay back against the pillows and closed her eyes.

Joanna stood up and quickly went to find the sister, who was standing at the end of the ward by the door.

"Excuse me. Can you come quickly, sister? I think Mrs. Franklin is having a relapse."

The sister took Nina's temperature then looked at Joanna, and then at Josh.

"I'm afraid I'll have to ask you both to leave. Mrs. Franklin's temperature has risen and that's not a good sign."

Joanna had put her shopping basket on the floor by Nina's bed. She bent down to kiss her goodbye, and then gently pushed the basket further under the bed with her foot.

Chapter 29

Josh led the way out through the main door, glaring at Joanna and muttering over his shoulder, "Bloody cheek. It's all your fault."

Joanna didn't say a word. She paused outside the lady's toilets, which were situated near the main entrance of the building. Josh glanced over his shoulder at Joanna entering the toilet, and then left. She waited a few minutes and then carefully opened the door. Seeing that Josh was nowhere in sight, she hurriedly made her way back to Nina's ward.

Fortunately Nina hadn't gone to sleep after her injection. She turned her head slowly.

"Why, hello, Jo. What are you doing here?"

"I rather stupidly left my shopping basket behind. I think I left it here somewhere."

"Yes, you did. Sister has it in her office." Nina smiled, looking a little brighter. "She's in there now."

"Actually, I came back to have a word with you. Nina, I want you to listen to me. We haven't much time. If I find a convalescent home for you, will you accept it? I have to find one for my mother, so I may as well try and find a place for you too."

"Well, I don't know what to say, Jo. It's all so sudden."

"You're drugged up to your eyes, Nina. You're not thinking clearly. If you go back to that monster, you'll get something sudden all right. A sudden death. Have you been in here so long that you've forgotten the reason why you were brought here in the first place? How did you acquire that scar on your skull, Nina? He smashed your head against the electric light switch and broke it. Remember? Not forgetting everything else that bastard has done."

"No, I haven't forgotten, Jo, and I haven't forgotten how you supported me. When the police threatened you, I, like a coward, sat quietly and did nothing. How on earth can I accept your offer? You mustn't get involved in this, Jo."

"The reason why you didn't speak, Nina, was because you were too ill and terrified. If you told them the truth now, they'd listen. I'll back you up. And I promise you, I'll find a nursing home."

"I can't tell them, Jo."

"Why not?"

"I can't say what he did, the things he did…and go through all the court procedures and so on. Suppose you can't find a nursing home. Then what?"

"Nina, I swear I will find you a place somewhere. However, if that is your main concern, then I'll tell you now, you will stay with me. But I promise you, Nina. I'll find a nursing home for you. Somewhere away from here where that monster cannot reach you. Quick, the sister's coming. You must decide now. You can't go back to that bastard. It'll be suicide."

"Yes, my dear, dear friend. I'll leave it to you. I really have no alternative, have I?"

Joanna smiled and shook her head. "No, not really." She held Nina's hand. "I promise you, Nina, it'll be okay."

During the week that followed, Joanna made endless inquires to find a suitable nursing home for both her mother and Nina. All had proved fruitless. Her anxiety grew by the day. Until Mary gave her an idea.

She came home early one afternoon and unexpectedly brought her friend, Dora.

"Hello, Mary. What are you doing home so early?"

"It's a holy day of obligation, Mummy, and Sister Patrick said we could leave early. All the rest of the class are in the choir. Sister Patrick said we make a terrible noise when we sing and put the others out of tune."

Joanna tried to refrain from laughing. "Really, Mary, the times I've tried to teach you."

"Oh, she didn't mind. She said I can't be good at everything. So she gave us homework to do. I've brought Dora home so that we can do our homework together before we have tea."

Joanna looked up from her writing bureau. "Tea? Oh, Mary, you should have asked me first."

"I did, Mummy. You invited Dora last week. Had you forgotten?"

"Oh, yes, I did. I'm sorry, Dora. Come in, dear. I've been so busy this week. It completely went out my head. Do you like spam fritters, Dora?"

"Yes, I love them, Mrs. Busher."

"Well then, Mary, you can either take your homework up to your room or bring it into the kitchen."

The two girls followed Joanna into the kitchen. They both sat down at the huge wooden table and began discussing their homework. They had to write an interesting story about places they had been and people they'd met.

Joanna, in the middle of cooking fritters, fried bread, and baked beans, had been deep in thought. She was totally unaware of the conversation between the two girls. But her ears pricked up at the mention of Derbyshire.

"Well, I know what I'm going to write about," said Mary.

"What?" asked Dora.

"When I went up to Derbyshire. There was an old lady in this old house who was completely mad."

"Oh, you're joking."

"No, I'm not. She even tried to kill Mummy."

Joanna stopped dead on hearing Mary's prattle. She had never heard her mention the incident before and assumed she had forgotten. She obviously hadn't. Joanna allowed her to continue with her childish chatter.

"I'm not going to write a story like that," said Dora. "It doesn't sound true. I'm going to write a real story about when we went down the underground during the blitz."

"That doesn't sound very interesting."

"But it's funny, Mary. You see, there was this old man and every night he would start sneezing around eight o'clock. He had a sister. She was very old too, and she also started sneezing and blowing her nose at exactly the same time. Everyone in the shelter would join in and say, 'Hello, they're off again, it's party time'. And we all started to sing, 'A tissue, a tissue, we all fall down'. Then everyone would pretend to sneeze."

Mary sat with a straight face. "Well, I don't think that's very funny."

"It's funnier than writing about your mum being murdered."

"She wasn't murdered. A handsome Prince Charming rescued her. He drove like the wind in his red sports car."

"All the princes I've read about, Mary, never had a red sports car."

"Well, this one did," said an indignant Mary.

Joanna laughed to herself. She realized that Mary had not been fully aware of what had actually happened and wasn't unduly worried. She had somehow mixed reality with make-believe. Nevertheless, the idea of a red sports car was correct. But the thought of David being a Prince Charming...The irony of it made her smile. Wouldn't he just love that? Charming, he may well be. But princely? Never.

"Mrs. Busher, those fritters smell delicious."

"Yes, they are nice, aren't they? Now, if you'd both like to put your books on the dresser, I'll dish up."

Mary looked up at her mother with her pencil under her chin. "Mummy, please tell Dora it's the truth."

"Well, Mary, sometimes things aren't quiet what we imagine them to be."

"But Mummy, what about that dreadful, old witch, Mrs. Cox? She did try to kill you, didn't she?"

"Mary you were at school at the time. How do you know this?"

"It's because I was at school that I remember it so well, Mummy. I thought maybe you'd forget to call for me and I was so scared of big Mazey and her gang. And I heard you talking to that man in the red sports car."

"Oh, I see." Joanna paused. "Well, you mustn't make a habit of listening to things that do not concern you. Mrs. Cox was a very nice lady, but I'm afraid she was very sick, Mary."

"You said *was*, Mummy. Is she dead?"

Joanna smiled. "No, she's not dead, Mary, and you never stop asking questions, do you? Now I'm going to leave you two rascals and continue with my letter writing."

Mary nudged Dora, and whispered. "See, I told you she was sick in the head."

Joanna sat down at her writing desk, put her hand to her head, and reflected for a moment.

I wonder. I just wonder…

Poor Betty Cox had told her about a rehabilitation hospital. When she had mentioned it to David Matthews, he told her that it was shortly to become a nursing home for severely disabled service men. But that would be of no use to her now. David would have joined his unit. Nevertheless, it was worth trying.

Now, what was the name of the hospital? I think it was something beginning with Bakewell. Was it Bakewell Lodge? Bakewell Manor? Bakewell House? Oh my God, I have no idea. This is a nightmare. What am I to do if I'm unable to find a suitable nursing home within the next week? If I write now, by the time I get a reply, it will be too late.

Her brain was in turmoil. Joanna stood up, walked into the hall, and picked up the telephone, not realizing it was still out of order since the bombing. She sighed and buried her head in her hands.

What am I going to do? Maybe I shouldn't have been so hasty.

She glanced wearily at her wristwatch and realized there was nothing she could do tonight. It would just have to wait until tomorrow.

Then she called out, "Mary and Dora, time to get ready for the tunnel, girls."

It was a clear, moonlit night, cold and frosty. They were able to see their way ahead down through the woodland cutting without the aid of a torch.

"Why, hello, Jo. You're early tonight," said Dora's mother, Margaret.

"Well, I knew you wanted to see Dora back safe and sound before Jerry arrives. I think they've enjoyed themselves this evening."

"Thank you, Jo, but you shouldn't have rushed."

"Don't mention it, Margaret. That's the least I can do. Heaven knows what I'd do without your help."

Margaret was a tall, slim, raven-haired beauty of forty-two. She wore her hair in a forties style swept up from her face portraying strong, high cheekbones. Dora was the youngest of her three children. She had two grown-up sons who were twins. One was in the Royal Navy and the other was now serving in the Merchant Navy in the north Atlantic.

On rare occasions, Bob would deliver urgent call out messages for Joanna. The deployment of Red Cross nurses abroad had left them short of staff and they needed all the help they could get. In those cases, Margaret would come to the rescue in caring for Mary.

Joanna put her hand to her head.

"What's the matter, Jo? Are you okay? You look awfully tired."

"Yes, it's just this dreadful headache. I can't seem to get rid of it."

"You work too hard."

"No, it's not work, Margaret. It's just that I've had so much on my mind lately."

"Why don't you take a walk outside and get a breath of fresh air before Jerry arrives? Mary will be okay with me."

"You know, I think you're right, Margaret. It may just do the trick. I won't be long. I'll be back to give Mary her supper."

"Oh, don't worry, Jo. Off you go before it gets dark, and enjoy your walk."

"Thank you so much, Margaret. I've no need to take my torch. It's a bomber's moon tonight. TTFN."

As Joanna went out through the small door at the end of the tunnel, a thought suddenly occurred to her. She took the short cut through the narrow woodland path that led to the avenue. She turned left when she reached the bottom of the hill and went into the park. Then she strolled along the promenade for a while and sat on the park bench.

The river was like a millpond. Gazing over the Thames, Joanna was able to see clearly the two sailing ships that were moored there permanently: the Worcester and the Cutty Sark. It was hard to believe there was a war on. If not for the Home Guard on their usual patrol guarding the ack ack guns at the rear end of the promenade, everything was very peaceful. She felt more relaxed now, gazing over the moonlit waters, and allowed her thoughts to wander.

Looking up at the starlit sky, Joanna whispered softly on the night air, "Oh, Dad, my darling Dad, where are you?" Her sigh was almost a sob. "What am I to do? Who will help me?"

She stood up and slowly made her way back up the avenue. Joanna was deeply wrapped up in her thoughts, so much so that when she approached the narrow woodland path, she didn't hear the rustling coming from the bushes behind her.

Yet, for some reason known only to her, she stopped dead in her tracks, turned around, and ran down the path and across the road at the bottom of the avenue into the village. She found the nearest telephone box and went inside. Then she realized she hadn't brought her torch.

Damn. Now what? Lucy at the Pier Inn, she will be able to help.

"Why, hello, Joanna. Surprised to see you in here," said the landlady in an auspicious tone. "What can I get you?"

"Nothing, thank you, Lucy. Actually I wonder if I may impose on you. Could I possibly use your phone? You see, mine has been out of order since we had the blasting and I have a very important call to make."

"You don't have to say another word. Of course you can, Jo. It's over there in the closet."

"Thank you so much, Lucy."

Joanna glanced around and noticed old Bob, the ARP warden, sitting in the corner enjoying a class of stout.

"Hello, Jo. We don't often see you in here. Like to join me in a drink?"

"Thank you, Bob. I'd love to, but I have to make an urgent phone call."

"Okay, when you come out maybe."

"Thanks, Bob. If we both have time."

Joanna turned and entered the telephone closet. She dialed the operator and asked to be put through to Matlock, Derbyshire. The operator there eventually put her through to the hospital in Darley-Dale. After the usual formalities, Joanna asked if the rehabilitation hospital had been converted to a nursing home.

The curt voice at the end of the line had not been helpful. "I would advise, madam, to go through the appropriate channels by making your inquires in writing. Now, if you'll excuse me, I'm very busy. Goodbye."

"Oh, one moment. Please could you possibly tell me if a relative of mine, a Dr. David Matthews, has returned to his squadron yet?"

"Oh, you're a relative of Dr. Matthews? Why ever didn't you say so? He only returned home on leave a couple of days ago. I wouldn't imagine he'll be going back just yet. Dr. Matthews is in his office. Would you care to speak to him?"

"Yes, of course," answered Joanna hastily.

"Oh, who shall I say is calling?"

Joanna's voice trembled a little. "I'm his cousin, Mrs. Joanna Busher."

It was amazing how the voice at the other end changed at the mention of Dr. Matthews.

"Very well, Mrs. Busher. I won't keep you long."

After half a minute came a man's voice. "Cousin Joanna, this is a wonderful surprise. I hadn't realized I had one! Lovely to hear your charming voice again, my dear. It's been a long time." David hadn't lost his debonair charm. "So to what do I owe this honor?"

Joanna told him everything. When she had finished, she breathed a sigh of relief. David reassured her that he knew of just the place, which would be suitable for both her mother and Nina.

She came out of the closet and noticed Bob getting ready to leave.

"Oh, I'm sorry, Bob. I do hope you haven't been waiting for me. My phone call took rather longer than I expected."

"That's okay, Jo. Don't worry. There's always another time. But I must push off now. I've got to be on duty in ten minutes. With a night like this, I'll be right in thinking they'll be over early."

Joanna quickly paid Lucy for the phone call, and then followed Bob outside.

"I suppose I'm an old worry pot," Bob continued.

He paused and they both looked up at the night sky.

"No, I quite agree," said Joanna, her eyes still looking upwards. "I think we could have a bad one tonight. I'm getting back as quickly as possible."

"That's it, Jo. You do that. I'm sorry I can't come with you. But I'm heading for the village tonight. Take care, Jo."

"And you too, Bob."

They both went their separate ways. Joanna crossed the road and entered the cutting.

Chapter 30

Joanna was half way down the narrow woodland path when she heard the sound of heavy breathing coming from behind her. She turned and saw the figure of a large man etched against the moonlight slowly making his way towards her. Joanna ran like the wind but was unable to see the deep-rooted branch lying across her pathway. She tripped and fell. The large figure came thundering towards her.

"Keep away from me," screamed Joanna.

She reached out to grab a large stone. But she was too late.

Big Bill's foot came crashing down on her hand. Joanna shrieked in pain.

"Who are you? What do you want?"

"You'll know it by the time I'm finished with you," came the coarse reply from deep within the zombie creature.

Joanna kicked out and screamed. Big Bill fell down on one knee and then closed her mouth with his massive hand. Leaning over her, he ran his other hand up her skirt and over her thighs. Joanna wriggled like a snake trying to fight back.

Bill had an inane grin on his face. In a rough, rumbling voice, he said, "Nice. I like a woman with spirit."

But, in his excitement, he didn't realize he had his face so close to Joanna's hand, which was lying flat on the ground. He loosened his grip slightly on her mouth. Joanna wasted no time. She bit into his fingers, causing him to jump back. She moved slowly sideways so she was able to see him clearly. Then Joanna opened her fingers wide and, in a flash, pierced him hard between the eyes.

The action took Bill off guard. He rose to his feet like a raging animal, dragging Joanna up by the hair of her head. Whilst Joanna fought, Bill had gone completely mad. He growled like an enraged beast. Holding Joanna up by her hair in one hand, he clenched the other in a fist ready to smash into her face.

Then, from behind Bill, came a familiar voice. "Okay, hands up."

The man thrust his torch hard into Bill's back.

"One move and you're a dead man. I've been after you for some time. I'm the chief inspector of police, Scotland Yard."

In the simple mind of big Bill Thomson, all he could think about at that moment was escape. The besieged creature threw Joanna to one side, turned, and fled into the woods.

"Blimey, he took off quick," said Bob.

Old Bob had been able to get a clear view of the man, even though it had only been a few seconds. Joanna rose slowly to her feet from the spot where Bill had thrown her. She looked a tiny figure, silhouetted against the moonlight with her hand pressed against a tree trunk for support.

"Are you okay, Jo?"

"Yes, thanks. I'm fine," she said breathlessly. "Apart from losing great chunks of my hair. Thanks to you, Bob, that's all I lost. What timing. I don't know why you came back Bob, but thank God you did."

"Luck really, Jo. Or should I say my stomach. I left my sandwiches behind. Just on my way back to pick them up."

Joanna had to see the humorous side of the situation.

"Well, thank you, Bob. Your sandwiches certainly saved my bacon." She sighed. "I wonder who that maniac was. And where on earth did he come from? I haven't seen him around these parts before."

"I have," said Bob, with a contemplating undertone. Then the siren sounded. "I'll explain on the way back. We'd better hurry." Bob's voice sounded somber.

"What is it, Bob? Tell me please. Where have you seen that lunatic?"

"Don't be alarmed, Jo, but…" Bob paused. "I've seen him entering your friend Nina's house."

"What?" cried Joanna. She stood perfectly still. "I don't understand."

"No, of course you wouldn't. I don't suppose Nina is aware of anything either. We must hurry. Jerry's getting closer."

"Never mind Jerry. I want to know."

"Well, you see, it's like this, Jo. The police, being busy and short staffed, have asked us to keep an eye on the Franklin house. Apparently Josh is up to some kind of shady business, but they don't know exactly what. I tell you, love, he's a dodgy character, that one. A really nasty piece of work. Most people around here know how he treats Nina. They aren't stupid. But what can anyone do? When it comes to husband and wife, he'll always come up with an answer. There's no saying what that so and so will do next." Bob spoke in a heart-warming voice. "Maggie and I admire how you're trying to help Nina. However, when the police are informed about all this, there is no telling where it could all lead."

"What do you mean, Bob?"

"My dear, I'm trying to say be careful. That bastard Josh is crafty. You could be the one getting imprisoned. Or worse."

Joanna nodded as she listened to Bob's sage words of wisdom.

"Thanks, Bob. I appreciate your advice, and for being here tonight. I shudder to think what may have happened had you not turned up. However, this only goes to prove that Nina needs my help now more than ever."

"Well, that's up to you, Jo. But for God's sake, take care."

"I'll be okay, Bob. Please don't worry about me."

"I must say, I admire your courage, Jo. You know, it's really quite amazing."

"What is?"

"How a little half-pint-size lady like yourself could possibly manage to put up such a good fight against a giant like that."

Joanna grinned and gave a slight cough. "It's all in the brain, Bob, remembering what you're taught. Whilst I was in Devon, Terry taught me a few tricks in unarmed hand to hand combat. Just for a laugh, of course."

Bob smiled. "Did he now? Well, it certainly came in useful tonight."

As they made their way to the tunnel entrance, Bob turned. "By the way, Jo. I think it would be a good idea not to mention this to the others. We don't want to cause alarm."

"I agree, Bob."

Joanna walked over to the tap on the wall and tried tidying up whilst Bob held his torch pointed downwards over her. The heavy drone of the Luftwaffe grew closer. Ack ack guns in the park opened fire.

"Are you sure you're okay, Jo?"

"Yes, I'm fine. It's strange though. I shouldn't be. I came out to get rid of a headache."

"And have you?" Bob laughed.

"Yes, I have. It would take more than a monstrous coward like that to scare me."

"My God, that's the spirit I like to hear. You know, it's strange, Jo, how a mere torch could fool a big chap like that. He must be as thick as two short planks."

"I agree with you entirely."

"I only wish someone could dream up a similar idea to scare off Adolf," said Bob.

Joanna smiled. "You know, Bob, you could be right. It's just possible that he would fall for an idea like that."

They both laughed and entered the tunnel.

Chapter 31

The annual Christmas party of 1941 would be held in the tunnel. This would be the second year in succession since the hostilities. Before the war, festivities were always held in the church hall and carol singers would gather in the park with their lighted lanterns whilst children watched, with eager delight, the firework display from the end of the pier.

Of course, everything had changed now.

Most of the villagers and all who inhabited the tunnel did their utmost to make sure everyone had a great time. They started preparing months in advance. All the decorations were handmade and the men would bring in a giant fir tree from the woods. On the night of the party, old Bob dressed up as Father Christmas, and every child would receive a present, whatever their age.

In the past, Joanna and her father would lay on a musical nativity concert. Joanna would play Mary, and her father, Joseph. This year, he would be sadly missed by all and sundry, not only for his singing duets with Joanna, but also for his artistic costume designs. This Christmas, Joanna chose the most talented members of the community to enable her to put on a good show. She chose an entire new cast.

Joanna herself only sang two arias from Madam Butterfly. 'Oh My Beloved Father' was one of them. No matter how many bombers Goring sent over that night, it didn't stop everyone from having a great time. It seemed they were all living just for that moment and were unconcerned if tomorrow never came.

Terry came home, at last, on his long awaited leave. Mary stood eagerly awaiting every train that pulled into the tiny station. When she had waited half an hour, and there was still no sign of her father, a sad and dejected Mary decided to go home. Kicking up small pieces of shrapnel in anger, Mary, in her child's mind, hated everything she knew about the war. Now she felt sure she wasn't going to see her father this Christmas.

She walked under the railway bridge and looked up to see the London train approaching. It stopped. Mary chased back to the station. She wanted so much to be waiting for her father when he arrived. Tears streamed down her cheeks as she ran up the slope to the station approach.

But he may not be even on it, she reflected morbidly.

Then, looking up, she saw him standing at the top of the slope.

"Daddy," she shouted, and ran into her father's arms. "Daddy, I didn't think you were coming home."

Terry smiled that slow smile and took her in his arms. "My darling child, did you really think I'd stay away from you at Christmas time?"

Christmas came and went all too quickly for Joanna. She looked somber, standing there in the kitchen, preparing sandwiches for Terry's return to base, carefully spreading their measly portion of butter over the bread.

She wondered just how long all this was going to last, especially now the Americans were with them. Her worst fears came to mind. What was once a European war had now emerged into a world war.

Oh, God. What is going to happen next? And where are they going to send Terry?

She prayed they wouldn't send him away on some secret mission. So far, Terry had disclosed nothing to her, even when she had asked him whether he'd applied for his officer's commission.

About one thing, she felt sure. Terry would never willingly volunteer for anything. He always said the war would never come between them.

Terry was upstairs packing his kit whilst Mary sat on a stool in the middle of the bedroom. She had newspapers strewn around her, busy polishing her father's brass buttons on his navy blue jacket.

"Daddy, why do you have to be ready four hours before you catch your train?"

Terry looked up and smiled. "Well, you see, Mary, in the Royal Marines, they are very particular on appearance. How one looks. You understand?"

"Yes, Daddy. I do understand. But four hours is a long time."

"Not really, Mary. Time goes very quickly when you're enjoying yourself. From now until I leave, anything could happen."

"Yes, but four hours, Daddy?" said a bewildered Mary.

"Well, look at it this way, my sweetheart, there could be an air raid, for example. It's always best to be prepared."

Terry stopped talking on hearing the doorbell ring. Joanna answered it. To her horror, she found Josh standing in the porch slouching awkwardly against the wall.

"'Allo, Joanna," he said, pursing his lips into a weird smile. "All alone now, are we? 'Ubby gone back, as 'e?"

Joanna nodded, realizing Terry would have heard the bell. She was curious to know what this scheming little serpent was up to.

"Yes. What do you want?" said Joanna curtly.

"I just thought I'd come 'round for a chat with yer."

"Really? I haven't anything to discuss with you."

"Oh, yeah yer bloody well 'ave," muttered Josh between his teeth.

He pushed Joanna to one side and entered the hall.

"Get out of my house," uttered Joanna.

"I'll go when I'm good and ready. It was yer who gave 'er the idea to go into 'hat bleeding nursing 'ome, weren't it?"

"I don't know what you're talking about," said Joanna, slowly moving back towards the stairs.

"Oh, yeah yer bloody well do. Yer bloody interfering bitch. She'd be 'ome now with me if yer 'adn't poked yer nose in. Yer've got no one to protect yer, not now yer old man's gone back, 'ave yer? So this is what I want yer to do. Yer gonna sit down and write 'er a letter telling 'er to come back 'ome to me."

"You must be joking," said Joanna cynically, and grinned. "Why would Nina want to come back to you? To take more beatings?"

"Shut up," shouted Josh.

"No, you shut up," yelled Joanna. "You can do your own dirty work. Now get out of my house this instant."

"I told yer I'll go when I'm ready. She finks the light shines outa yer arse. She'll believe anything yer say. Yer gonna tell 'er you can't afford to keep 'er there any longer. Now get in there, sit down, and get on with it. Otherwise yer'll get this. See." Josh came closer, holding up his fist.

Joanna stormed, "How dare you threaten me? Get out of my house."

She lifted her hand and indicated to the front door. Josh immediately raised his arm and threw Joanna to the floor.

Terry had been listening to every word. He leaped down the stairs at lightning speed and descended upon Josh with one fierce right-hand blow to the chin, taking him completely off guard. Then he brought up his left and delivered a mighty blow to his cheek, knocking Josh to the floor. Terry stood over him.

"Like it, Josh? Are you ready to stand up and fight like a man? Or are your fists only confined to women? If they are, then I'll finish you right now."

"No...No, Terry, I can explain."

Terry had no intention of giving into Josh's whimpering pleas. He allowed him to stagger to his feet.

"Please, Terry," said Josh, gasping for breath.

"Mr. Busher to you."

"Please, Mr. Busher, I just wanted to speak to your wife. But she wouldn't listen."

"And so you struck her?"

Terry grabbed Josh by the scruff of the neck and gave him the hammering of his life, his fists flinging left and right with trained precision into Josh.

Joanna screamed as she eased herself up from the floor, "Terry, for God's sake, stop it. You're going to kill him."

Terry grabbed Josh's scraggy neck and turned to his wife.

"This pathetic looking creature, Joanna, is this what Nina has been terrified of all these years. Makes you wonder, doesn't?" He threw him down on the floor. "You will stay down there where you belong until the police arrive."

Josh was terrified, and he slowly began crawling towards the front door.

"Don't even think of making a move," growled Terry. "Unless, of course, you'd like another lambasting?"

Terry picked up the phone, which was still out of order, giving the impression he was ringing the police.

"Okay. They're on the way. You'll be going down for this one, Josh."

Terry stood over him with clinched fists. He turned to Joanna.

"Are you all right, darling? That looks a nasty eye." He winked at her. "Go 'round to Dr. Stanley and ask him to have a look at it."

Joanna's astute brain knew exactly what her husband wanted her to do.

Josh continued muttering, "I wasn't gonna 'urt her. All I wanted was my wife back."

"What for, Josh? To use as a punch ball again?"

"She's my wife. I can do as I please. It's none of your bloody business."

"Watch your language," barked Terry. "Yes, you're quite right." Terry lowered his tone. "It's nothing to do with me. However, entering my house and assaulting my wife is."

"But I hardly touched her."

"I very much doubt if the police, or my solicitor, will look at it quite like that."

"Please, give us a chance, mate. I didn't do anything. Please."

Terry stood looking down at him with utter disgust. "You groveling, cowardice scum. You'll never ever trouble my wife and family again."

Joanna returned with a patch over her eye, and wearing a torn, old blouse. Her hair was wet and matted, which gave the impression that she'd put up a struggle and had been badly attacked. She looked terrible. She had definitely set to work on herself.

Within minutes, the police arrived and arrested Josh. One copper looked at Joanna.

"My goodness. He'll probably get three years for this. He must have scared the life out of you, love."

Joanna nodded.

Terry stated that when the incident occurred, he was in his greenhouse at the bottom of the garden taking a last look at his plants before returning to his base in Wales.

Mary had seen from where she sat curled up on the landing, peering excitedly through the banister rail. She was amazed at the scenario that had just taken place before her very eyes. Never before had she seen her gentle, quiet-tempered father so enraged. She watched the police drag Josh away, still protesting his innocence. When the commotion was over, she watched her father throw his arms around her mother. He hugged her tight.

"Darling, you were wonderful. We've nailed that bastard between us. I guarantee that from now on, Nina will have no more problems with him. I'll get Uncle Tom to act on her behalf."

Mary ran down the stairs. "Oh, Daddy, Daddy, you were absolutely marvelous thumping that horrible man like you did. He's so dreadful. I thought sometimes he was Hitler's brother."

Her parents gave a slight chuckle.

Joanna nodded. "Yes, there is a faint resemblance."

"Do you know what he said to Michael and John, Daddy?"

"No, what did he say, Mary?"

She looked straight at her father. "He told Michael and John not to play with me. He said I was a dumb idiot."

"I wouldn't think about that now, Mary."

"Very well, Daddy. But I'm so proud of you."

"Thank you, Mary, my darling. However, there is nothing to be proud of in hitting someone. I only wish it could have been avoided. Unfortunately, I had no other choice. Now, Mary, my darling, I want you to listen to me carefully." He spoke in a tender yet serious tone of voice. "I want you to promise me that you will not mention to anyone what you have seen and heard here today. Not even to your best friend."

"I understand, Daddy. I promise you."

"That's my girl."

"Daddy, when I go to school or anywhere else, I'm going to be like you."

"What do you mean, sweetheart?"

"Always be prepared."

Terry smiled, nodding his head in agreement.

Once again, the happy trio stood waiting on a train platform. Terry glanced up at the approaching train. He turned and gathered Mary and Joanna up in his arms in a tender embrace.

He gazed into Joanna's eyes. "Please don't wait until the train leaves. Go now."

Joanna sensed in that moment that Terry was going to see some kind of action in the war. But when and where, she had no idea.

"Oh, Daddy, why must we go?"

Terry smiled cheekily at Mary. "Now, young lady, you behave yourself. You're my best girl, remember?" He looked at Joanna with that slow smile, and whispered, "Look after each other. Off you go now."

Terry blew them both kisses in the cold winter air and watched them disappear into the mist.

Joanna's voice, soft and gentle, said, "Goodbye, my dearest love. Come back to me soon."

Chapter 32

Josh received a two year minimum sentence. The police were unable to obtain enough evidence to charge him with his more serious criminal activities. When word spread through the grapevine that Josh had been arrested, his entire gang disappeared into thin air.

The only lead the police had was that of big Bill Thomson, and he hadn't been sighted since the night he attacked Joanna. He'd vanished. He had no wish to face Josh for failing to carry out his orders. Curiously, a decomposed body of a large man had been washed ashore off the Thames Estuary. The police had not enough evidence to substantiate it being that of big Bill Thomson.

Joanna was now making frequent visits to Derbyshire. She would often take Mary to see her grandmother whenever the air raids had taken a respite.

Nina had made a remarkable recovery, owing to the care and good medical treatment she had received since her encounter with near death at the hands of Josh. However, her health was very much impeded by leukemia, a bone marrow disease affecting the blood cells, and the loss of her right kidney.

Joanna's mother had made excellent progress physically, though her mental health left much to be desired. One minute she would be placid, and the next, highly excitable. It was as if her whole character had taken on a complete metamorphosis. She was no longer the haughty lady from Ireland. At times, Joanna wondered whether she'd ever regain her mental stability.

It was on such a day, whilst they were having lunch, that Joanna recalled the bitter words her sister had once said to her. *She's shell shocked. Her brain has gone completely. She'll never be the same again.*

At lunch, her mother had been speaking quite rationally.

"It's Friday today, dear, so we're having fish and chips for lunch. Do you like fish and chips, Mary?"

"Yes, I love them, Nanny."

"Oh, Mary likes anything, Mum," said Joanna.

Joanna looked at the pot of jam sitting on the table and wondered why it was placed alongside the salt and vinegar. The fish and chips were placed in front of them. Joanna and Mary applied the usual salt and vinegar over their meal. Mary glanced at her grandmother and was surprised to see her tipping half a pot of plum jam over her fish.

"Oh, Nanny, why are you doing that?"

"It tastes lovely, Mary. Would you like some?"

"Yuck. No, thank you, Nanny."

"Yuck?" said the elderly woman in a low-pitched voice. "What is that?"

"Oh, it's a new American phrase Mary has picked up," explained Joanna.

"American?" said her mother, looking dazed.

"Yes, they're fighting the war with us now, Nanny. They're very nice. Do you know, Nanny, the other day, one Yankee soldier gave Dora and me some chewing gum and some chocolate. They call it candy. Mummy said the war will probably be over soon, now they're helping. That's correct, isn't it, Mummy?"

Mary's innocent chatter caused a chain reaction. Joanna's mother looked more confused than ever. At that moment, a young junior nurse accidentally dropped a steel tray. Joanna's mother stood up and ran to the dessert trolley, where raspberry jam pudding was waiting to be served. She gave the trolley an almighty push, causing it to collide with a nurse carrying a tray of hot coffee and tea. The nurse screamed, dropping the tea tray. The jam pudding landed on the floor.

Joanna's mother yelled, "Come on, everyone. What you sitting here waiting for? Let's all hurry up and get out of here. Quick! We haven't much time."

Joanna raced to her mother's assistance, followed by a nurse. Within a short while, the chaos was over. Mrs. Partridge was led back to her room, still protesting that everyone must leave the building before it blew up.

"I've sent for Dr. Matthews. He'll be here shortly," said the nurse. "I wonder what happened. She hasn't had a turn like this for quite a while."

Joanna held her mother's hand as she sat bemoaning and shaking in her chair. Mary continued with her meal. She had sat throughout the pandemonium trying to keep a straight face. She realized her grandmother was ill, but she still found the whole situation very amusing and wanted to laugh out loud. But Mary had been looking forward to jam pudding and looked po-faced at the jelly and custard when it was placed before her.

"Hello, Kathleen," said David in a calm voice. "Now, what have you been up to?"

Shaking her finger, Joanna's mother pointed to the door. "There's an unexploded bomb in the dining room, doctor."

"Not anymore, Kathleen. The bomb disposal squad have disconnected it."

"Oh, that's good. I was so frightened."

"Nothing to worry about now, Kathleen."

"What about my cat?"

David grinned. "Oh, he's fine. Tucked up nice and warm in his basket with a saucer of milk."

She sighed with relief. "Thank you, doctor."

"Think nothing of it, Kathleen. It's been a pleasure. Now, I would like you to take these two tablets with a nice warm cup of tea."

When Joanna's mother had settled down, David spoke to Joanna alone.

"There's no need to look so worried, Jo. This is quite a normal reaction."

"Reaction to what, David?"

"The nurse dropping a tray and her thinking it was a bomb."

"If that's so, she'll never get better."

"No, Joanna. She's seen or heard something from one of the residents, or maybe from you or Mary, even the radio. The nurse dropping the tray just amplified that which had been lying inactive in her brain and obviously triggered it off."

Joanna thought of Mary's innocent chatter with her mother.

"You know, David, I feel we've had this conversation before."

David came closer. "Joanna, there is no comparison between your mother and Betty Cox."

"I hope not, David. I sincerely hope not." She shuddered.

He took her hand in his. "I assure you, my dear. Your mother is going to be fine."

She looked up into his eyes. "But, David, out there in the dining room, she was completely oblivious to everything. She was reliving the air raid again."

David agreed, his voice a mere whisper. "I know."

He gazed into her beautiful, sad eyes. He just wanted to hold her in his arms and cast away all her doubts. That same feeling he had when they first met was still there. But logic dictated, once again, don't be a fool. You can only love this woman from afar.

He stood back a little and spoke in a more professional tone. "Joanna, I can assure you that your mother will make a full recovery. However, it's going to take time. Maybe longer than we thought. But with the right medical treatment and tender love and care, she will get there. And I stress, plenty of TLC, which is something she would never have received had you taken the advice of Dr. Crawford."

"The so-called great psychiatrist at Gravesend Hospital?"

"You made the right decision, Joanna, by not putting her into an institution."

She smiled. "I know that, David."

"You know, I'm due back at Biggin on Monday."

"Well, I'm lucky you were here then."

"No, I'm the lucky one," said David, grinning. "Incidentally, if something of this nature occurs when I'm not here, don't be alarmed. My colleague Dr. Baker will be here. He's our resident doctor. Getting on in years but an excellent man. Oh, and by the way, I'm trying to open another nursing home. Not just for our boys in the RAF but for other various regiments."

"Oh, really?" said Joanna.

"Yes. I'm sick and tired of seeing good men fighting for their country then return suffering from combat neurosis only to find themselves slung on the dung heap and left at the mercy of chaps like Crawford to be used as human guinea pigs."

Joanna was surprised. She had no idea David had such strong convictions.

Then he gave her a full update on Nina's health.

"I'm afraid she'll always be a sick woman. However, with care and a good, healthy lifestyle, I would give her another three years at the most, which is more than I was able to predict when she first came here."

Joanna's blood turned cold. "Three years," she said, looking blankly into space. Her face froze.

"Well, you're a nurse, Joanna. I'm sure you understand the implications."

"Oh, yes. I understand, David." She slowly raised her voice. "But what I cannot comprehend is how that monster will be out of jail in two years, beginning his life again while she…Oh God." She threw her fists in the air and shouted, "He's a bloody murderer. Can't you see that, David? I would like to kill him."

David stood and stared at her.

Joanna lowered her tone. "My God, that poor, dear soul. I'm sorry, David. You must excuse me."

"There is nothing to excuse, my dear Jo."

"David, surely something can be done?"

"Nothing short of a miracle will help her, I'm afraid."

Joanna looked at him pleadingly, and in a soft voice answered, "Then we must believe in that miracle, David. They do happen sometimes."

He came closer, looking straight into her dark, watery eyes. "My dear Joanna, you really do think a great deal of Nina, don't you?"

"Yes, I do. Even more than my own sister. You see, David, you've no idea how she has suffered."

"Oh, I think I have." He sighed then smiled at her. "I must try and make that miracle work for you." He turned and made his way to the door.

"David, I appreciate everything you are doing for me." She hesitated. "I have never asked you this before, but why are you doing so much for me?"

He smiled, looking down at his shoes, then opened the door to leave.

Joanna felt sure she heard him whisper in a voice barely audible, "Because I love you."

And then he left.

On Sunday morning, Joanna announced to Nina that she would be leaving in the afternoon.

"Oh, Jo, so soon. Why?"

"Because I'm working tomorrow, and also there's Mary's school to be considered."

"I do look forward to your visits, and it's been lovely seeing Mary again."

"Upon reflection, Nina, I'm not so sure it was a good idea to bring her along."

"Oh, why?"

"Well, Mary is inclined to put her foot in things at times."

"You mean what she said to your mother?"

"Quite." Joanna sighed. "I gave her strict instructions not to mention the war while in Nanny's presence. And what did she do? She sat through lunch trying her utmost to jolt Mother's memory."

Nina smiled. "Where is Mary now?"

"In the grounds out of harm's way, playing ball with a little girl she's just met."

Nina laughed heartily. "I'm sorry, Jo. I just can't help seeing the funny side of all this."

"I'm pleased you can because I can't."

Joanna was pleased to see her friend looking so well. David had provided

Nina and Joanna's mother with the two best rooms in the nursing home, which equaled that of a five star hotel.

It was obvious to Joanna that David was attracted to her. Yet he had never made any advances. She needed assurance that no strings were attached.

When she had packed and was ready to leave, David offered to run them to the station.

"You're wise to leave early, Jo, especially taking Mary through London."

Joanna smiled. "We'll be fine, David. Anyway, there haven't been any air raids lately. Rumor has it Goring is taking a brief holiday."

"Propaganda, Joanna. Don't be influenced by what you hear. Never take any chances. We have a long way to go before we see an end to this madness."

"I never take chances when I have Mary with me, David. However, I appreciate your sound advice."

David smiled. "Never take any chances with yourself either. Good girls are rare these days." His voice sounded soft and affectionate.

"Oh, before I forget, David, I didn't quite catch what you said yesterday when you left the room. Was it important?"

David paused for thought. "Oh, nothing really. I merely said because you're a very good friend."

Joanna looked relieved. She smiled. "You know, you really are a lovely person, David. I've said this once and I'm saying it again. I appreciate everything you've done to help. I have no idea what would have happened without you."

"Oh, I'm quite sure you would have managed somehow. You always do."

She smiled and added, "When my Terry…" She paused. "Returns home, we must have an evening get together."

David reverted to his usual debonair manner. He laughed. "My word, I'm going to look forward to that."

Joanna shook his hand before boarding the train. David looked into her eyes, which were full of uncertainty.

"Have no doubt, Joanna, my dear. Terry will be home when he has someone like you waiting for him. And remember what I said, Jo. Take care."

She smiled. "And you too, David. TTFN."

Their train to Kings Cross Station had been delayed over two hours owing to a derailment on the line. Consequently, they arrived in the middle of an air raid. The guard on the train told everyone to take cover in the nearest shelter.

The raid had been unpredicted and took everyone by surprise. People were running in all directions. The screeching roar of fire engines could be heard coupled with the ringing of ambulance bells.

Joanna headed towards the underground, holding Mary's hand in a tight grip. Suddenly, there came a loud explosion and heavy bursts of gunfire. Mary screamed. It was now dark. Joanna couldn't see very well through the haze of smoke. She took the wrong turning and raced down a side street. There came another explosion. Incendiary bombs were on fire in the street ahead of them. She turned and headed up the street from whence she had come, only to be blasted back.

They eventually took refuge in a boarded up shop doorway. Joanna took off her coat and threw it around Mary. Then she stood in front of her in an effort to protect her from any blasting.

Mary screamed, "Mummy, what are we going to do?"

Joanna, terrified, tried to calm her. "We'll be all right, Mary. Everything will be fine. We'll get out of it. You'll see."

She continued to stand in front of Mary. The streets appeared to be deserted.

Joanna yelled, "Is anyone there? Please, will someone help us?"

They could hear the heavy throb of the Luftwaffe dispatch their deadly weapons on London, ripping the buildings apart. The sky was now a red blaze as the ferocious turbulence intensified. Joanna shouted even louder as the ground under their feet seemed to vibrate under the intense heat.

Then a Red Cross van appeared. An ARP warden got out when he noticed Joanna waving her arms.

"Blimey. What the hell are you doing out here?"

They were taken safely to the nearest underground, where a member of the WVS gave them hot coco. Joanna sipped the drink with both hands wrapped around the mug. She hadn't time to think before. Now David's words echoed in her brain. *Don't take any chances.* He'd never before urged her to leave so promptly.

He was a squadron leader in the RAF. Perhaps he knew something she didn't?

Later, towards the end of April, Joanna understood the reason why. It had been a reprisal raid. It was one of the consecutive air raids that were now taking place throughout the major cathedral cities. The first of which had been Exeter.

Chapter 33

1944

Josh was released from prison in March 1944. Prison life did nothing to enrich his character. Quite the contrary, it had taught him how to become a professional racketeer. All he needed now was a camouflage to protect him from his sordid little activities.

The country was recruiting more ammunition workers. Josh, with a degree of cunning, was able to return to his old job. To his fellow workers, he appeared an honest citizen who had been wrongly convicted. It was the perfect cover for the time being. However, Josh had no intention of working hard all his life.

He had served his sentence and now it was time for retribution.

He found a room to rent above the sleazy Green Door Pub in Gravesend. He felt at home there. It seemed to match his character very well.

Josh had been astonished to learn that Nina had survived two years. He had never anticipated the divorce coming to a successful end. Josh had envisaged coming out of jail to a nice hefty sum of three thousand pounds left from Nina's insurance policy upon her death, which Josh had taken out when they were married. Nina had been completely unaware of the transaction.

Josh had no wish to resume any kind of relationship with Nina. The people who were now protecting her posed a threat to him. He found life without Nina and the children far more to his liking. He had planned to have the children adopted upon her death.

Josh reflected upon his wife's survival. *She should be long gone by now, with leukemia and only one bloody kidney. I can't understand it. I've spent Gawd knows wot on that bleeding policy. Some finks got ter be done.*

He sat for hours trying to work out a scheme. Finally, he had an idea.

There hadn't been any air raids for quite a while. People were able to move around more freely. Even the children who had been evacuated from London during the blitz were now returning to their homes. There seemed to be a growing air of complacency among the nation. Some believed the war was nearly over.

Terry still refused to take his commission in spite of pressure from Joanna and Uncle Tom, and even his commanding officer. He preferred to remain a corporal.

Uncle Tom was now established in his Gravesend practice, where he rented a large apartment above three adequately-sized offices.

Joanna continued with her work in the Red Cross. Work seemed a compulsion. She could never stop until the war was over and they had won.

"Uncle, are you quite sure Peggy will not be an inconvenience to you?"

"No, of course not, my dear. Peg's no problem. Anyway, she'll be company for Gracie. You need a rest, Jo. You've been working far too hard. You and Mary go and enjoy yourself."

Peggy and Gracie were two little Belgian terriers that Tom had rescued from a bombed-out house in London back in 1942. All the occupants had been killed. Tom gave Mary the younger of the two dogs, which he assumed was Peggy because she was the liveliest and more playful. Tom had been given their names by neighbors in the area. A great deal of amusement was to be had in trying to discover which dog was which. They were so alike.

Joanna looked at Tom anxiously with a little frown forming on her forehead. She was concerned for Tom's health. He had already suffered a minor heart attack, and now he ran the business almost single-handed with only a young office boy to assist him, since his partner and leading executive had been conscripted for military service. Joanna felt it her duty to help this brave, elderly gentleman, who had chosen to stay in London throughout the blitz when he could quite easily have left sooner. Even now, when approaching seventy-seven, he was choosing to work rather than retire.

"Please, my dear Joanna, take that worried look off your face. It doesn't become you. I've told you. I'll be quite all right. You and Mary go and have a wonderful time with Terry. It's only for the weekend for heaven sake."

"You are a dear," said Joanna affectionately, giving him a big hug.

"Yes, I know I am, and you're the world's best flatterer. By the way, where has Terry been posted? Somewhere in Hampshire, isn't it?"

"Yes, that's right. Apparently there aren't any hotels in the area. It sounds rather remote. I think Terry called the place Bursledon?"

"Where will you stay?" Tom chuckled. "With the marines?"

Joanna laughed. "No, you old silly Billy. Terry's found accommodation for us with an elderly lady and her daughter."

Around the same time, Josh had been busy wheeling and dealing. He became involved in some shady business with two dubious American rangers. He found the idea of teaming up with his ex-con inmates too risky, and he had no wish to find himself behind bars again.

Anyway, who needs them when you've got the yanks to do business with? It's hardly likely they're gonna give me any trouble. I don't expect they're gonna be in the country long enough. In a week or two, they could be anywhere. That's just the type I'm gonna do business with in future.

Josh had other things on his mind. He was determined to gain information on Nina. He couldn't believe how, with a complaint such as leukemia, she could possibly have survived. There must be a reason.

Maybe she's found a bloke. But who'd want her?

Puzzled, he set to work and found Tony Evens, a decrepit, old, ex-con private investigator. Josh did a deal with Evens. He paid him a little in advance, assuring him he would get the full sum if he could dig out as much dirt on Nina as he could possibly find.

Meanwhile, the spring sun never ceased to shine in Bursledon. Mrs. Fox gave her guests a warm welcome. She was a small-built, cheerful woman in her mid-sixties who always appeared to be smiling. Mrs. Fox lived in a large terraced house with her daughter, Mable. They had a sizeable garden with enough space to provide them with their own produce.

Mary instantly felt at home with the older woman. She loved her garden and was amused by the many baby rabbits living in it.

"Is this to your liking, darling?" said Terry, looking somber. "I realize it's not quite what we've been used to, and indeed, nothing like Ebford. However, under the circumstances, it's all I could possibly find."

Joanna stood by the bedroom window admiring the view over the bluebell wood. Smiling, she turned around slowly to face him.

"Terry, why do you worry so much? I think it's a wonderful place, darling. Anyway, we're together, and that's all that matters."

"Yes, you're right, sweetheart," Terry replied, taking her in his arms.

Joanna looked up into his eyes questioningly. "I can't help wondering though why they posted you to a place like this. You're virtually isolated in the middle of nowhere. You must get terribly fed up."

Terry had a pensive expression in his eyes as he gazed down into hers. "It doesn't bother me, darling. Especially now you're here. Anyway, I suppose they have their reasons."

"Oh, really? What kind of reasons?"

Terry didn't answer. Instead, he kissed her on the lips with deliberation in the hope that she may overlook the question. But with Joanna's tenacious character, she was not prepared to let the matter rest.

They were interrupted by a knock on the door. Joanna answered it to find Mable standing with a tray of tea and biscuits.

"Oh, thank you very much indeed." Joanna smiled. "That's awfully kind of you," she said, taking the tray from Mable, who left the room quietly. "Mrs. Fox is a very sweet woman," Joanna said to Terry. "I suppose she realizes there's nowhere else to go in these parts."

"Oh, there's a local pub on the other side of the village."

Joanna burst out laughing. "Did you say village? I wouldn't even call it a hamlet."

"It's not so bad, Jo, and the pub is actually a quaint little place. I think you'd like it. I usually go there with a few chaps from the base. But most of the younger lads stay in the mess."

Joanna laughed in a mocking manner. "Why? Don't they think it's worth the effort?"

"All right, Jo, you can tease as much as you like. But I think it's a delightful little place."

"So that's it? A pub, a few houses, plenty of fields, and cattle." She chuckled again.

"No," said Terry appearing slightly irritated. "There's a small post office that sells everything but the kitchen sink."

"Yes, it's beautiful, darling. I do apologize." She spoke on a more serious note. "However, you still haven't answered my question."

"Oh, what was that?"

"Why did they send you here?"

Terry, unsmiling, looked at her straight. "I don't know, Joanna. Why are you asking all these questions?"

"But surely you must know, Terry. A little while ago you said they have their reasons. What reasons, Terry?"

"Look, Jo, can we change the subject please?"

"Terry, why are you being so evasive?"

"I'm not being evasive. You're too inquisitive for your own good, Joanna."

"What? Terry, now you're being ridiculous. I simply asked you a civil question."

"And I've answered it, Joanna." He looked annoyed.

Joanna realized she had only been there a few hours and already they were having a heated argument.

"Now, please, Jo, I wish to change the subject."

Joanna knew it was useless to try and probe any further. But she was in a provocative mood and she asked him if he had applied for his commission. She had asked him this question a hundred times in the past, and always his answer had been the same. But she just needed to feel she had won her side of the battle once again.

"No, I haven't, Jo," came a curt reply.

"I'll never understand you, Terry. Most men would welcome the chance of promotion."

"Now, please, Joanna. I'm in this because I have to be. Not by choice. If I were to make it my career then it would be a different matter. Anyway, we've been through all this before. Why must you persist?"

"Because I think a man of your caliber deserves to be more than just a corporal. I'll never understand why you didn't accept a commission when you first joined the service. You would have held a high rank by now. Yet every time you've been offered a position, you've refused it."

"For heaven sake, Joanna, will you never stop?"

"No, I will not, Terry. You deserve better."

"Listen to me, will you, Jo? There are many good men who deserve better, but they just have to plod on and do as they're told. Some men are not officers and your self-styled gentlemen, Joanna. But they will win this bloody war for us."

"Yes," shouted Joanna. "But they all haven't your breeding and background. It's a question of status, Terry."

"What? I can't believe I'm hearing you properly, Joanna. You know, you're beginning to sound more like your mother every time I see you. Is that all that matters to you? Class? Status? You want me to be like Nina's fancy boyfriend, wing commander or something or other in the RAF? Is that it?" he flared.

Joanna stood looking at him, her eyes swimming. She realized she had said too much. It had all started as an innocent joke. She couldn't believe this was her beloved husband talking. Joanna was aware that war changed men slightly. But he sounded so hard and cruel. His transformation astounded her.

"If that's the way you feel, I'll pack my bags and leave immediately. You'd better call Mary and tell her." She spoke in a soft, clear voice. "It'll sound more fitting coming from you. We'll be on the next train home."

There was a brief silence between them. Terry stared at her, motionless. Joanna walked across the room, opened the wardrobe door, and began packing the few items of clothes she had brought with her.

Terry, shocked by her response, uttered, "Jo, please don't leave like this."

"It's too late for that now, Terry. I'm off."

"Jo, please. I'm sorry. I don't know what came over me." His voice sounded dry as he struggled for the right words. "Oh, Jo, my darling."

Joanna looked into his sad, blue eyes, and remembered her father's last words. *Never allow this terrible war to come between you and Terry.*

"We've both been through a great deal, Terry," she said softly. "But I always thought we would never allow this terrible war to come between us. It seems it has."

"No, it hasn't, my darling. I'm so sorry. Please forgive me." He came towards her, looking agonizingly into her eyes.

"There is nothing to forgive, Terry. I am just as much to blame. I provoked you, trying to win our little battles as always."

"You were right, my darling. We must never allow anything to come between us." He held her in his arms and whispered tenderly, caressing her hair, "You're so right, my darling. Dear God, you're so right."

Chapter 34

Tucked away in the foothills of Darley Dale lay the village pub, The King's Head, in which Nurse Jane Roland sat talking to her new sailor boyfriend.

"I hate my job at Bakewell Manor. The only reason I stay there is because I don't want to be called up. You know, Dick, it's strange. It's supposed to be a rest home for RAF service men and woman but, instead, Dr. Matthews sends all his friends there. Old Mrs. Partridge is a miserable old goat, and her hoity-toity friend Mrs. Franklin."

"Blimey," said Dick. "Can't you stop talking about your job for a second? And, if you don't mind, love, lower your voice a little. We don't want the whole bloody bar to hear what you're saying."

"I don't care," she replied. "I want everyone to know what poor wages they pay up there."

"Oh, come on," said Dick. "The money isn't so bad. I mean to say…" He grinned. "You could be in the services where all the action is. Now how would you like that?"

The bar was full. Nobody noticed the unassuming figure of an elderly man enter the pub. He managed to find a seat quite close to Jane and Dick, and overheard their entire conversation. When he stood up as if to leave, he held the remains of a glass of stout still in his hand, which he very conveniently spilled over Jane's skirt.

"Oh, I'm terribly sorry. Please forgive me. It's my fumbling old hands. Allow me to pay the price of the dry cleaners. I do hope the stain will come out."

"I'm quite sure it will," responded Jane. She was aware the man was in his dotage and acted accordingly. "Please don't worry. It was just an accident."

"Yes," agreed Dick, showing concern for the elderly man. "It's no wonder you spilled your drink. This place gets over crowded on a Saturday night. Here, take my chair. I'll go and get our drinks filled, Jane."

"Please, allow me," said the elderly man. "After all, it was my fault." He withdrew a white five-pound note from his wallet and handed it to Dick. "Please, have anything you wish to drink, and I'll have a scotch if they have any. Oh, and keep the change."

"What?" exclaimed Dick, looking surprised. "I couldn't possibly. I don't even know you, sir."

"Well, do you have to?" said the elderly man, nodding his head.

"Yes. This is a lot of money just for that."

Jane looked up and winked at her boyfriend. "The gentleman is just trying to be kind, dear."

"Well, if you're quite sure, sir?" said Dick.

"Of course I'm sure. It was me who ruined your young lady's skirt, wasn't it?"

"Yes. But..." Dick stood, opened mouthed. "Well, that's very generous of you, sir. Thank you."

Dick turned and made his way to the bar.

Jane extended her hand. "I'm Jane Roland. Very pleased to meet you, sir."

The stranger kissed her hand with a sly smile. "I'm Tony Evens, and the pleasure is all mine, my dear."

Evens regarded Jane and her boyfriend Dick. From experience Evens knew these people could be easily bought. As the evening progressed, Evens plied Jane and her beau with more drinks and a slap-up meal of pork chops, vegetables, and potatoes. Evens would put it all on Josh's tab. He'd pay dearly for the information Evens would serve up to him.

"It does seem this world is all about who you know," stated Evens subtly, gauging Jane's reaction, who was now more than a little tipsy.

She knocked against Evens' arm and slurred, "Too bloody right. Some people, no names mentioned, Dr. bloody snooty Matthews, use their power and influence to do anything they bloody well want!"

Dick looked at his girlfriend worriedly and tapped her hand. "Keep it down, Jane. I've told you before. I don't want the whole bar to hear about our business."

"And I told you I didn't bloody care. This man 'ere. What's yer name again?"

"Tony."

"Yeah, Tony. You know how it is. Despite the war and all the sayings of 'everyone is treated equally', I don't see it. We're still pandering to the hoity-toity set like Matthews. We ain't bloody equal. One rule for them, another for us."

Evens smiled with warm and encouraging affection. "You're very astute, my dear."

Janes nodded, her eyelids dropping in a dozy way, and she swung a look at her boyfriend.

"See, Dick? This bloke reckons I'm astute. Well, I knows one thing. That place is a racket."

"What place?" asked Evens.

"Bakewell bloody Manor."

"Why do you say that?"

"Leave it, Jane," said Dick.

But Jane shook her head somewhat too vigorously for the amount of alcohol she'd imbibed. Her face went a sallow green color and she swallowed down the bile that had been building in her throat.

"No, no. It has to be said. That chap Matthews, he stocks the place with his friends. He's even a bit sweet with one of them. A married woman, no less. Dirty sod."

"Is he really? With his patient, you say. Isn't that unethical?" slithered in Evens, raising an eyebrow.

"Could be. Dunno about that stuff. But he is taken with Mrs. Franklin."

"Jane, stop it. Loose tongues, remember? You don't know anything," snapped Dick, thoroughly uncomfortable with the whole discussion. He stood up abruptly. "Excuse me. Got to spend a penny."

In Dick's absence, Evens turned his full attention to Jane. He took advantage of the time he had with her one to one to get Jane's buy-in on a little job he had for her.

Evens took out his wallet and laid down two crisp ten-pound notes. Jane's eyes widened seeing the cash. She peered quickly around the bar, and then snatched up the money. She pocketed it, knocked back her drink, and winked slyly.

"It's a deal, Tony."

Chapter 35

The weekend was just a wonderful memory now, reflected Joanna, as she and Mary made their way up the stairs to Uncle Tom's apartment.

"My word," said Tom anxiously. "I'm so very pleased to see you, Jo."

"Why? What has happened?"

Tom looked at Mary, who was standing listening with all ears. "Mary, my dear child, would you like to take Peggy and Gracie out into the garden please? And get rid of that dreadful cat. He's pestering the chickens again."

"Yes, of course, Uncle."

Mary looked disappointed. She was old enough now to realize when grown-ups didn't want her around.

"I'm sorry about that, Jo. I must speak to you alone. Something dreadful has happened."

"It's not Mother, is it?"

"Well, yes and no," said Tom excitedly.

"Yes and no? What are you trying to say, Uncle?"

"I received a call from Nina just before you arrived. Apparently, your mother has been telling everyone that Nina and David are to be married. Naturally, Nina is very concerned. If news of her association with another man was ever disclosed, that so and so of a husband would do his utmost to impede her divorce proceedings by a couple of years at least. Maybe even completely."

Joanna looked troubled. "It's been quite a while since Mother had a bad turn. I wonder why she should say that. She is aware that Nina and David are friends, but that's all." She looked thoughtful. "I'll have to go up to Derbyshire tomorrow morning and get this problem sorted out. Uncle, would you mind if I left Mary here with you for a couple of days?"

"Of course you can, my dear. You need not ask. I'd be delighted to have her company. But you're going to be exhausted."

"I'll be fine, Uncle. Don't worry about me. We must get this problem sorted out, and then I'll return home on Wednesday. Tomorrow is a holy day of obligation. Mary will only be absent from school one day. I intend to sort this mess out once and for all. You just keep working on Nina's case, Uncle, dear."

"Bless you, Jo. Of course I will." He took her hand in his. "You're a wonderful person, Joanna."

She laughed. "Nonsense. I'm just doing what I have to do. And at the moment, we have to eat and prepare for tomorrow."

Joanna had plenty to muse upon whilst on her journey to Derbyshire. The romance between Nina and David had not been born overnight. It had taken two years to develop. She always remembered when Nina first disclosed her feelings for David. She had looked radiantly happy, just like any other woman in love. So much so that the pale shadows under her eyes could hardly be seen.

Initially, it had been difficult for Nina to accept her newfound happiness. She regarded it as one would a fairy story that only happens in romantic novels. She had often thought she was living a dream, where at any moment she would wake up and find Josh standing over her.

Moreover, somewhere in Nina's mind, it had been a matter of class. He was now a wing commander in the RAF and, in civilian life, a medical doctor, whilst she was a worthless nobody with an incurable illness.

She had been prepared to end the romantic interlude, until Joanna asked her, "Do you really love him, Nina?"

Her answer lay written in her eyes. "Of course I do."

"Then tell me, Nina. Would you still love him if it were not for his position?"

"Jo, my dear, I would love him if he were a tramp in the streets."

"Then what on earth are we talking about, Nina? You're going to turn him down and cause so much sorrow for both of you simply because you assume class is more important than love?"

Joanna closed her tired eyes and tried to sleep. Her thoughts returned to David, and how kind he'd been to Nina in the first six months when she had been admitted to the home. He had arranged for a medical research team to carry out tests on her. They tried every known cure possible with no success. Everyone thought it was the beginning of the end for Nina as she began a downward spiral.

When David came home on leave, he devoted most of his time to her, and, slowly, Nina found herself looking forward to his visits. David marveled at her recovery. She seemed to grow stronger every time he saw her. Slowly, there grew a great bond between them. No more could he see a sickly-looking woman before him, but a lady of elegance. The dreadful, gaunt features she once possessed now portrayed her delicate beauty. How she had acquired this, he had no idea. However, that miracle he had hoped for had happened.

And Joanna knew the reason why. Nina was in love for the very first time in her life, and she needed the love of this kind man in return. She'd moved out of Bakewell Manor nursing home when improvements to her health began. David was instrumental in finding her a small cottage close to the Manor, as she still had to be in close proximity. She was still attending the Manor for tests and treatment for her leukemia. Having her own home enabled Nina to bring back her children from Scotland.

Although Nina had her children back, there was still a gap in her life and, somehow, she felt the children weren't quite enough. She realized how quickly the two boys were growing up, and soon they would be making their own way in life. And with them, they would take the humiliating and disturbing memory of their father and how brutally he had treated their mother.

"I'm so I pleased to see you, Jo," said Nina, welcoming Joanna with open arms. "You're the last person I expected to see, especially when Tom told me you were away for the weekend."

"I came directly when I heard the news. Now what exactly has been happening, Nina?"

"Well, I'm not quite sure. It all started yesterday morning when one of the nurses congratulated me on my forthcoming marriage to David. You can imagine how I felt?"

"Yes, indeed," said Joanna.

"She came straight to see me after she had spoken with your mother," continued Nina. "Apparently she told her we were to wed in the near future. Of course, I denied it. However, when I asked your mother about what exactly she said to Nurse Roland, she said she couldn't remember. And I didn't like to probe any further. She was beginning to look mystified. David and I have spoken in the grounds on the odd occasion, but never about marriage. Just the casual chat, as one would with patient and doctor. That's all."

"That's nothing," said Joanna. "Most people do that. Now look, Nina. I don't want you to worry. Everything is going to be all right. I'm going over to see Mother now. She'll tell me."

"I'm so sorry to be such a nuisance, Jo."

Joanna laughed. "You've never really changed, have you, Nina? Still worrying. It's no problem. I'll get it all sorted out. I promise."

Joanna left the small cottage, where Nina was now living with little Marianne, and made her way up through the wooded lane to Bakewell Manor.

Nina and David had decided to get married when her divorce became final. Joanna had noticed a complete change in Nina's character. Gone were the days when she held her head low in shame. Nina now looked as if she had been designed for her new role in life. Joanna had never seen her friend look more healthy and lovelier than now. Her disease remained isolated for the time being. However, she knew Nina was living on borrowed time, and she had no intention of standing by and seeing her life crumble around her through idle gossip.

"Now, Mother, what exactly did you say to Nurse Roland?"

"Nothing, dear. She simply asked me if Nina was married." Her mother stared into space.

Joanna looked anxious. "Mother, please, you must try and remember, darling. This is very important."

"Now let me think," said the elderly woman. "Yes, it's coming to me now."

"Take your time, darling," said Joanna affectionately.

"She asked me how many children Nina had and where was her husband. I said I didn't know. And she said, 'Well, she must be married if she has children?'"

"And what did you say, Mother?"

"I said, 'Yes, she must be, or at least she should be for the sake of the children.'"

"And that's all?"

"Yes, that's all, dear." Joanna's mother paused. "No. One moment, Joanna. She said something else. Now let me think. What did she say?" She looked dazed. "Oh, yes, I remember now. She asked me if Nina had a gentleman friend."

"What did you say to her, Mother?"

"I said, 'I don't know. Why not ask her yourself?'"

"What else did she say?"

"Nothing. She gave me my medicine and left."

"Are you quite sure?"

"I am certain, Joanna. She isn't a very nice girl. I try to avoid talking to her whenever I can."

"Oh, thank you, darling. You've been marvelous." Joanna hugged her mother.

"That's good. I'm pleased I've made you happy. There aren't many happy people around here. Why didn't you bring Mary? She always makes me laugh."

"I will next time."

Joanna was pleased to hear her mother ask so many questions. It proved she was almost better. After Joanna had shared a meal with her mother, she felt an ache in her heart when saying goodbye.

"So there we are, Nina," said Joanna, back in the cottage. "You just have to sort out this meddling nurse. Find out what her game is and your worries are over."

"Thank you, Jo. I will never forget how good you have been."

"Nonsense. That's what friends are for."

Nina walked down the corridor in Bakewell Manor. She recalled Jo's instruction. Oh boy was she going to sort out this meddling nurse indeed.

Turning the corner, Nina came face to face with Nurse Roland.

"Oh, hello, Mrs. Franklin. How are you?" said Jane with a mock-caring inflection.

"Improving," clipped Nina.

"I can see that. You look positively rosy. Must be all that TLC you're getting."

"What do you mean?" retorted Nina sharply.

"Well, I'm not one to gossip, but it's plain to see Dr. Matthews is taken with you."

Nina's eyes widened and she pursed her lips, frowning hard. "Nurse Roland, I'm a married woman."

"I didn't know. I thought, well..." Jane's voice trailed off when she noticed Nina's sad eyes begin to water, and her face flushed up.

"It's none of your business. But if you must know, my husband is currently in a Japanese POW camp. I haven't told anyone as I find the whole situation distressing. We all know the horrors that happen in those camps, and I've blocked out talking about him. I've pushed him from my mind, as it is the only way I can cope with my life and not break down completely. I'm sure you understand, as a nurse, what I'm saying. How the mind can keep one whole just by sheer suggestion."

Jane's mouth dropped in shock, but Nina hadn't finished.

"So now you know the truth, I'd appreciate it if you could keep your sordid and unfounded innuendos to yourself. Dr. Matthews is just a good friend, in the same way as Mrs. Busher. Nothing more." Nina moved closer to Jane, eyeing her with a stony stare. "It does, however, make me wonder why you're so interested in my life."

Jane didn't answer and kept her focus on her feet.

"Nurse Roland, that wasn't a passing comment. That was a question. Why are you so interested in my life? You'd better tell me, otherwise I'll have no alternative but to inform Bakewell Manor management board of your inappropriate behavior and defamatory slurs against a patient in their care."

Jane flicked her eyes back up, amazed by the sudden forthright tenacity of Nina, who'd been so weak of spirit for so long. She thought Nina had finished, and tried to open her mouth, but there was still more Nina had to say.

"I'd hate to see you end up in one of those awful ammunition factories, but we all know how hard it is to get jobs these days. Of course, the matter won't go any further and your job will still be secure if…" Nina fixed a dark glare on Jane, and she watched her bottom lip tremble as she waited on Nina's next words. "You tell me exactly why you're so interested in my life."

Jane looked down and shame flooded her face.

"He was so persuasive, and he had lots of money. Dick and I are saving up to get married. We're saving our pennies. The money he put down was at least four months' wages. You've got to understand. I wouldn't have done it otherwise."

Nina continued her piercing stare and said nothing, but her head tipped to one side with curiosity.

Jane swallowed and gabbled on, "I didn't want to but it seemed to be all quite innocent. He just wanted to know if you had a gentleman friend up here. He told me to watch you and report back."

"I see," said Nina. "Go on."

Jane shuffled her feet and bit her lip. "So I've been watching you."

"Is that why you started those horrible rumors about me and Dr. Matthews?"

"Yes. Well, you know, no smoke without fire, and all that. I had to get people talking."

Nina held down her anger. "Who is the man who paid you?"

"He said his name was Tony Evens. He's definitely from the smoke."

"From London?"

Jane nodded. "Yeah. From that area."

"Have you seen him again?"

"No, but I'm due to see him tonight in the pub. I'm to tell him what I've found out so far. I won't go."

"No. No, you should still go."

Nina recounted the episode to Joanna an hour later back in the little lounge of her cottage.

"Good work, Nina. Evens doesn't know me, but I'm going to keep an eye on him tonight after Nurse Roland sees him."

"Be careful, Jo. You don't know who Evens is working for."

"Oh, I think I do. And so do you. Think about it, Nina. Who is the one person who wants to wreck your chance of happiness?"

"Josh."

"Exactly."

"Oh God, Jo. I thought that part of my life was over."

"With a man like Josh, it's never over."

Later, just after 8:00 p.m., Joanna sat in the saloon bar on a table with a clear view of Jane, who sat waiting for Evens. She was only there to observe and listen. The door to the saloon bar opened and Evens trundled in, glancing around with a furtive sweep. He noticed Jane at the bar and headed towards her. He took off his hat and laid it on the counter.

"Miss Roland, how nice to see you again. What's your tipple?"

Jane moved forward and Joanna watched her avidly, making sure she didn't blow her cover.

Jane smiled sweetly. "Just a port and lemon, Tony."

Evens turned his body around at an angle and stretched across to Jane. Joanna could hardly make out the nurse behind Evens' bulk. Slowly, Joanna slid herself along the leather seat to the next table, taking her drink with her. The new position gave her an unobstructed view of Jane and Evens again.

Joanna waited for Evens to speak, but from where she was, she couldn't hear everything that he was saying. She didn't want to risk getting closer as Josh may have given her description to Evens as a busybody he should be wary of. She could, however, discern that Evens' voice was gentle and somewhat cultured.

"So do you have something for me, my dear?"

"Well, I pressed that Busher woman's mother, but she didn't know much about whether Mrs. Franklin had a gentleman friend or not. I asked if she was married, as she has kids. The old girl thought her husband was in a Japanese

POW camp. I couldn't get any more information, Tony. It seems she's married but her bloke got caught by the Japs. Does that help?"

Evens rubbed his chin. Puzzlement crossed his face and he couldn't hide it. "Yes. Yes, it does," he muttered distractedly. "Excuse me."

"Hey, what about the rest of my money?" whispered Jane.

But her words weren't heard by Evens, who'd rushed for the telephone booth in the lobby outside the door. Joanna glanced at Jane who shrugged and sipped her drink. Joanna stood up quickly and walked around to the side of the wall, as if she was heading towards the toilets in the back. But she lingered, keeping close to the outside door where, beyond, was the telephone booth. The door was ajar. Joanna busied herself by looking at the pictures of Darley Dale on the wall. They were taken around the First World War, and Joanna appeared interested in the photographic work. But she was really listening in on Evens' conversation.

"Yeah. Yeah, Josh, I know. She's telling everyone you're in a Jap POW camp. Bloody cheek. Yeah, you must be. I understand, mate. I'd be the same."

Joanna could hear Evens' dialect slipping into cockney, a far call from his previous tone of a gentleman. Joanna stiffened when she heard Josh's name.

"So that's that then. I'll come back."

Joanna listened.

"Well, funny you say that. I saw your wife walking with another woman. She looked like that woman. What's her name? Joanna Busher."

Hearing her name, Joanna froze. But then she tried to edge in closer to hear what Evens was recounting to Josh.

"Yeah, laughing and joking they were with RAF pilots, pushing her battle-axe of a mother around the grounds. Yeah, she was like lady muck."

Joanna had a neck scarf draped around her shoulders. Quick as a flash, she brought it around her head and tied it back.

"Okay. Right you are. I'll see you when I'm back down in the smoke"

Joanna waited to hear if Evens was going to say any more.

Then he said gruffly, "See you, mate."

She turned abruptly away from inspecting the pictures on the wall and dove into the ladies restroom at the exact moment Evens emerged from the lobby, his jacket brushing just behind her.

Behind the door of the cubicle, Joanna breathed deeply. She knew that, although Nina was safe for now, Josh wouldn't let things rest.

Chapter 36

"My word, Jo," said Tom on Joanna's arrival home, "I am pleased. You must have worked a miracle in Derbyshire. I have just spoken to Nina on the phone. So that so and so, Josh, was paying a private investigator to dig out as much dirt on Nina as he could possibly find? I had a feeling he was in some way connected to all this."

"Yes, me too, Uncle."

"Well, I doubt if he will be able to do very much with the report he has now if Nina told Nurse Roland that her husband is a prisoner of war in a Japanese prison camp. You've done wonders, Jo, absolute wonders. I think this calls for a small class of cognac," said Tom, rubbing his hands together with satisfaction.

"Mummy, come over here and look at poor Gracie. Uncle Tom has been very worried about her while you've been away."

"Oh, please, Mary, dear," said Tom, "your mother is tired after her long journey."

"No, it's okay, Uncle." Joanna looked at the sad, little dog.

"What do you think is the matter with her, Mummy? She keeps being sick and she has a lump, look here, in her stomach, and she's not having a baby either."

Joanna smiled and looked at the little dog. "No, she's not," said Joanna, showing concern.

"I only wish it were simple, Mary," said Tom. "The problem is, I don't know exactly how old the dogs are. But I would say Gracie is at least fourteen years, maybe even older, judging from her behavior. She's always looked much older than Peggy. In fact, Peggy may even be her daughter, judging from her mannerisms. She hasn't moved from her side. She's been continually kissing and cuddling up to her ever since she became sick. I do hope it's nothing infectious."

"Oh, it's not serious, is it, Mummy?" pleaded Mary.

"I'm afraid it is," said Joanna, glancing at Tom. "I may be wrong, of course. I'm not a vet. But I'd say it's cancer."

"What's that, Mummy?"

"It's not a very nice decease, darling. I think you should get her to the vet as soon as possible, Uncle."

Mary sat cuddling both dogs.

"She's not going to die, is she, Mummy?"

"I don't think so, Mary. Not if we get her to the vet quickly."

Joanna turned her back to face Tom. She shook her head.

Tom loved the little dogs. He always remembered the first time he had seen them, frightened and bewildered after having been rescued from the bombed-out house where their owners lay dead beneath the rubble. If he had not taken them, they would undoubtedly have been put down. The ARP had too much to think about saving human lives. Animals were regarded as secondary.

Meanwhile, Josh had just agreed on a deal with his two American friends, Frank Garcia and Andy Romario. Both Americans were well-built, tall in stature, extremely good looking, and of Italian descent.

"Well, if we can pull this one off, lads, we're laughing all the way to the bloody bank. Don't worry 'bout a fing. I've got everyfing fixed. I know a few lads who 'ave good connections. They know just how ter get rid of the stuff," said Josh, rubbing his hands in a gleeful manner.

"Okay," said Frank. "Put it there, buddy. It's a deal." He shook Josh by the hand.

Andy was hesitant. He smelled a rat and didn't shake Josh's hand. He neither liked nor trusted the man.

Josh was pleased with himself.

But now he'd done the business with the yanks, he was eager to ascertain what information Tony Evens had found in Darley Dale. He took the long distance call from Derbyshire and was astonished to learn that Evens had no incriminating evidence whatsoever on Nina. On the contrary, she was said to be a happily married woman who was waiting every day on news of her husband's plight in the Japanese prisoner of war camp.

Josh grinned at the witticism of words.

Prisoner of war, eh? I wonder what that scheming cow will come up with next. I've got to do something.

However, Evens also noted in his verbal report the involvement of Nina's friend, Joanna Busher, and how they appeared to be so happy talking to RAF pilots and strolling around the grounds of the nursing home.

"That woman. That bloody woman," he said. "If it hadn't been for her, I'd have Nina where I wanted her."

And with all the vengeance of Beelzebub, Josh set to work.

In Kent, a mournful-looking Thomas sat in his armchair staring blankly into space.

Joanna entered the lounge carrying a tray with her homemade cakes and a pot of tea.

"Here we are, Uncle, a nice cup of tea. Do try some of my sponge cakes. You've hardly eaten anything."

"I'm quite sure they're delicious, my dear. But, frankly speaking, I'm not very hungry at the moment."

"Now, come along, Uncle. You must stop blaming yourself. You did everything possible for poor little Gracie. She was ill and in great pain. You had no other alternative. The vet told us the disease was terminable."

"I realize that, Jo. It was just so dreadful. I actually held her while the vet put the needle into her little side, and she looked up at me with her big, brown eyes, and then I felt her slump down in my arms. It was terrible, Jo. Really terrible. I can remember when I first rescued her and Peggy. She had the same frightened expression on her face. You see, Jo, it's when I close the office door and come up here in the evening, that's the time I miss the dear little soul."

"Maybe you'd like Peggy for a little while?"

"Oh, no. Good Lord, no. Peggy is Mary's dog. Anyway, when she's here, she's crying all the time, wondering where Gracie is. No, I'll be all right, my dear. I'm just a foolish, old man feeling sorry for myself."

"Rubbish," said Joanna. "I know what you need. You're coming home to Greenhithe with me. Have a few days' rest. I'll arrange a get together and you can invite some of your friends from London. It'll be lovely, Uncle. We'll be able to forget all our problems for a while."

"What about my work, Jo? I have so much to do."

"Uncle, you'll feel much better after you've had a rest and more interested in getting on with your work. Please, Uncle. I'll be very upset if you say no."

"Oh, very well," said the elderly man. His tired, old eyes gazed into hers, and he smiled. "You win as always, Jo. You know, you're a very persuasive young woman. Terry was a wise man when he chose you for his wife."

Joanna laughed. "No, I chose him. Incidentally, Uncle, have you heard from Terry recently?"

"Yes. I received a letter the other day."

Joanna looked surprised.

"Why, what's the matter, my dear?"

"Oh, nothing. It's just that I assumed he was on maneuvers of some kind. It's been five weeks since I've heard from him."

"Good Lord," said a surprised-looking Tom. "That's most unlike Terry. I wonder why. I can't recall you mentioning it, Jo."

"I knew you were upset about Gracie and had no wish to burden you, Uncle."

"That's very commendable of you, my dear. However, it still doesn't alter the fact. Why should he write to me and not to you?"

"I have no idea, Uncle," whispered Joanna.

"He must have a logical explanation," said Tom. "Maybe his letters to you have been censored for some reason?"

"No, it can't be that, surely, Uncle. May I read the letter he sent you?"

"Of course, my dear. It's in the study in the letter rack."

After reading the letter, Joanna realized it didn't sound like Terry. It was a rather dull letter, and there was no mention of her or Mary.

"Strange," she remarked, putting the letter back in the rack. *I just can't understand it.*

Chapter 37

"Well, he'd better have the dough tonight," said Andy. "We've given him enough time to cough up."

"Yeah," agreed Frank.

"I don't trust that guy. He'd better not have any lame excuses this time. Otherwise that two timing bastard will get what's coming to him."

"You don't suppose he's got an idea we're leaving soon and stalling for time?"

"If he is, Frank, I'll tear the son of a bitch apart."

"Hey, steady on, Andy. Don't get carried away."

"That sounds good coming from you, Frank. I noticed there was no holding you back on the deal."

"Look, what's got into you, Andy? I thought you were just as keen as I was. Anyway, it's no good keeping ranting on. We're in it now, and that's all there is to it."

"I know. I know," said Andy, annoyed. "I just get mad when I think about everything. Take you and me, for example, taking on the Nips at Pearl and the Pacific. We were both there. Remember what our boys went through? Now we're over here fighting for God damn bastards like him."

"Well, there's not much we can do about that, is there, pal?"

"No, you're right. But sure as hell, we're gonna get our money from that son of a bitch."

"You bet," agreed Frank.

The two men arranged to meet Josh in a nearby pub on the waterfront called the Brown Bear in one of the less salubrious areas of Gravesend. It was the type of pub that welcomed hookers, sailors, and swingers alike. At approximately 10 p.m., Andy and Frank walked in.

"What a dive," commented Frank.

"Well, where did you expect a creep like him to come? The Ritz?"

"He's nowhere around."

"Yeah, there he is," said Andy. "Over there in the corner leaning on the bar."

Josh looked up as they entered. "'Allo, lads," he echoed, and hurriedly went to meet them.

"Hi there, Josh," said the two men.

"Wot yer having ter drink?" asked Josh with a mocking smile.

Frank answered cautiously, "I'll have a whisky, if they have any. If not, a beer will do. Thanks, Josh."

"Wot about you, mate?"

"I'll have the same," said Andy.

Josh dropped his smile as he caught the look in Andy's eyes.

Whilst Josh was getting the drinks, Andy glanced uneasily at Frank. "Look, we can't do business in a joint like this, Frank. The God damn place is too overcrowded. When he comes back, you suggest we go for a walk."

"Yeah, okay. But why is it always me who makes the first move?"

"Because he seems to trust you more than me," replied Andy.

"Watch it. Here he comes," whispered Frank.

"You go, Frank, and assist the gentleman with the drinks." Andy grinned at his own words.

"Gentleman? That's a paradox if ever there was one," said Frank. Then he fought through the crowd to the bar. "Hi, Josh. Looks as though you could do with a hand."

"Oh, thanks, mate. I could only get beer. They've been cleaned out of whisky."

"I'm not surprised with this crowd."

"Bloody terribly, innit?" agreed Josh. "I should 'ave suggested somewhere else."

"Why don't we go find another place?"

"Good idea," said Josh. "Wot d'yer say, Andy?"

"What's that, bud?"

"Me and Frank finks we should go find a place less crowded."

"Yeah, okay. We'll go when we've drunk this down."

"Well," said Frank, "as you guys say here in England, asses up!"

"It's bottoms up," corrected Josh, laughing.

Once outside, the three men wandered along the waterfront towards the ferry jetty.

Josh began talking about the next consignment.

"When do you reckon that will be?" questioned Frank.

"Oh, in a couple of weeks, mate," said Josh nonchalantly.

"That's okay by me, pal."

"Well, it's not okay by me," said Andy. "Before you start talking about the next job, we'd like our moolah for the last one we did two weeks ago, *mate*," exclaimed Andy, his anger rising to the surface.

"Well now, boys, let's not get unfriendly about this. I've 'ad a few problems. Yer see, it's like this. I weren't able to get to the banks in time before they closed. I couldn't get away from work, and, as yer know, I've put the dough in more than one bank for security."

"Look, buster, you'd better cough up, otherwise things are gonna get a little nasty for you around here," said Andy, squaring up to Josh.

"Wot d'yer mean by that?"

"You'll find out, *mate*, soon enough if we don't get our moolah."

"I've already told yer," said Josh, looking anxious. "I'll get it fer yer tomorra when the bank's open."

Andy shoved Josh to the inside of the pavement, and then thrust his hand inside his jacket and pulled out a package wrapped in newspaper.

Josh bellowed, "Wot the bloody 'ell yer doing?"

Then he came up with his right fist straight into the lower part of Andy's stomach. Taking Andy off his guard, he fell backwards towards the sea wall. Frank stepped in, landing Josh a punch to his left jaw. Suddenly, an enraged Andy was back on his feet. A knife in his hand.

In a split second, before Josh could react, Andy plunged the blade deep into Josh's chest. He drew the blade upwards swiftly, as his training taught him, and there he found Josh's heart.

Josh slumped to the ground, and with eyes staring into the darkness, his last breath of life left his body.

"Why did you do that?" bellowed Frank. "You've gone and *killed* him."

"Shut up, Frank. It's gonna be okay," whispered Andy, trying to gain control of the situation.

"What'll we do, Andy?" said Frank, getting into a frenzy.

"Take it easy, pal. Have you got that package?"

"Yeah, it's here," answered Frank, bending down to retrieve the mysterious package.

"Open it," ordered Andy.

"Newspaper! There's no money in it."

"Yeah, just as I thought, Frank. He's put all the money in his bank. He never intended paying us. This guy was a Goddamn bastard. The worst you can get. The world will be a better place without him. Now let's get rid of him."

"But, Andy, how?" said a terrified looking Frank.

"We dump him in the drink of course."

"How can we? The tide's out."

"Do as I say, Frank," said Andy. "We're gonna carry him down to that narrow jetty and dump him in. That's as far as the tide goes out."

"How do you know there's a jetty?"

"I noticed it on the way here. Come on. Let's get on with it. It'll be high tide soon. Then he'll be washed downstream. With a bit of luck, no one will be any the wiser, and we'll be long gone. You've just got to keep your head, pal, and stay calm. Okay?"

With haste, both men carried the body to the end of the jetty where they dumped Josh into the water.

"Quick, Frank, duck down. Someone's shining their torch this way. They must have heard the splash."

"What do we do now?" whispered Frank, shaking with fear.

"It's okay. I think whoever it was has gone."

Frank stared down into the dark river.

"Don't worry, pal," whispered Andy. "By morning, the current will have taken him downstream. Now, when I say go, let's get the hell out of here."

Chapter 38

"Have you still not received any news from Terry, my dear?"

"I'm afraid not, Uncle. It'll be nine weeks on the first of June."

"Well, if it's any consolation to you, my dear, neither have I."

"I'm very concerned, Uncle. He hasn't answered any of my letters. I have this dreadful feeling something is terribly wrong."

"This time, my dear, I'm inclined to agree with you. I just cannot think what could have happened," whispered the elderly man, shaking his head.

"It's driving me crazy, Uncle." Joanna put her hands to her head. "I can't write to his CO. He'd look a fool if he were on maneuvers."

"Yes," agreed Tom, sighing and looking down at his toes. "It's all very puzzling. You must take the initiative, Jo, and do whatever you feel is right."

It hadn't escaped Tom's attention how thin and drawn Joanna had grown over the past few weeks.

"Yes, you're quite right, Uncle. I think if I haven't heard from him by the end of this week, I may just take a trip down to Hampshire."

During the week that followed, Joanna grew even more restless. She found herself waking in the night, coming downstairs, and making a pot of tea. Then she would sit in the armchair for hours on end trying to plan what she was going to do next. She would smoke one cigarette after another. Slowly, she was becoming a chain smoker and a nervous wreck.

Peggy sat beside her, looking up at her lovingly with her warm, friendly eyes.

Joanna patted her. "It's no good, old girl. Tomorrow you'll be staying with Uncle Tom."

Peggy lifted her paw and stroked the side of Joanna's dressing gown as a mark of approval.

On Sunday, June 4th 1944, Joanna rose early to prepare for the journey to Bursledon in Hampshire. She had decided to take Mary with her. She had no idea why she made the decision so promptly or what the outcome may be. The dominant factor in Joanna's brain now was to see Terry, and see him she would. Even if it meant moving heaven and earth, she intended to see Terry at whatever the cost.

Somehow, she had regained her old self-confidence. She appeared to know exactly what she was going to do next.

Joanna was just on the point of waking Mary when she saw her creeping down the stairs.

"Morning, Mummy. You're up early."

"Morning, darling. Yes. We're going down to Bursledon. Remember?"

"Oh, yes. I'd forgotten," said Mary, rubbing her eyes. "That's why poor old Peg's not here, isn't it?"

"She's not poor old Peg, Mary. She'll be quite okay with Uncle Tom."

"I know she will. I just miss her. I wish I was staying with Uncle Tom. I always have a nice time when I stay with him."

Mary glanced out the window while eating her breakfast of hot porridge.

"Oh, we're not going all the way down there in this terrible weather, are we?"

"Well, we're not walking, Mary. We'll be getting the train. The only walking we'll be doing is to the village station. Now hurry up and eat your porridge. The scrambled eggs and toast are ready."

"We're not staying with that elderly lady and her old-fashioned daughter again, are we?"

"Yes, I think so. Why?"

"Well, I wish we weren't staying with her."

"Why? For heaven sake, don't you want to see Daddy?"

"Of course I do, Mummy," said Mary. "It's not that."

"Well, what is it then?"

"It's just that Mrs. Fox's daughter is so miserable."

"Now, now, Mary. You mustn't talk like that."

"Well, you did! I heard you telling Daddy."

"Mary, you mustn't repeat everything you hear." Joanna sighed. "Look, darling, you're old enough to understand that I've been very worried about Daddy. It's been nine weeks since we've heard from him."

"Oh. I'm so sorry, Mummy. I didn't realize."

"Now, if you don't want to come, I won't force you, dear. You can stay with Uncle Tom."

"Of course I do, Mummy. It's just that you've looked so tired lately. I was worried about you going out in all this rain and getting ill."

Joanna warmed to her daughter's words. "I'll be all right, my sweetheart, once I've seen Daddy. We'll be together again for a little while. Just the three of us."

Waterloo Station was crowded. Military police were scattered everywhere. At the ticket barriers, they were checking ID cards. Joanna found herself waiting at the end of a long queue. She noticed that their train was standing at the platform and realized they would never get on it if they had to stand and wait.

She thought it strange. Waterloo Station was normally busy, but today there seemed to be a veil of scrutiny at the ticket barrier.

She whispered to Mary, "Now, listen, darling. We *must* get that train. So I want you to do exactly as I tell you. Do you understand?"

"Yes, I understand perfectly, Mummy." Mary sighed. "What do you want me to do?"

"Pretend to be sick. Start coughing. Right now."

Joanna had no idea what prompted her actions. She just knew she had to get to the front of the queue. She grabbed Mary's hand and hurriedly walked to the barrier. Mary fooled the officials with her excellent performance. They were soon allowed on the train without hesitation.

"Poor child. She shouldn't be traveling in that condition," said one of the MPs, as he helped Mary onto the train.

The train was full. Joanna had visions of standing all the way to Southampton until a helpful porter found them an empty compartment. As the train journeyed out of Waterloo Station, Mary looked at her mother. They both grinned and gave each other the thumbs up sign.

Unfortunately, once they arrived in Bursledon, the reception they received at the Fox's home wasn't quite so benevolent.

"What on earth are you doing here?" exclaimed an astonished Mrs. Fox, standing on the door step blocking Joanna's entry into her house.

Joanna had been taken off guard. "I'm dreadfully sorry to impose myself upon you. I have tried to contact you by phone with no reply."

"I'm not surprised," declared Mrs. Fox. "This whole area is off limits to the general public within a seven mile radius. I can't understand how you got by the security checks at Waterloo."

"What do you mean, Mrs. Fox?" said a surprised Joanna, recalling how she'd successfully conned the MPs with Mary's coughing antics at the station.

At that point, Mable came to the door peering over her mother's shoulder.

"You can't come in. Go away, Joanna. We've been given strict instructions from the MOD that no strangers are allowed on these premises."

"What?" gasped Joanna. "I'm afraid I don't know what you're talking about. And I'm not a stranger."

"You are to the MOD," continued Mable. "So you'll just have to go and put up somewhere else."

"Oh, what a little treasure you are, Mable. I think you frightened all the men away in your life with so much charm," said Joanna sarcastically. "Come, Mary. I'm not standing here to be insulted."

Mary suddenly began her well-practiced cough. She produced a handkerchief and displayed her fine art of sneezing.

"No. Wait a minute. That child doesn't look well, Joanna. What on earth possessed you to bring a sick child out in this terrible weather?"

"For your information, Mrs. Fox, Mary wasn't sick when we first set out on our journey. I'm not in the habit of neglecting my daughter. However, I don't think it's anything to do with you. Good day to you, Mrs. Fox." Joanna turned her back to leave.

"No. Wait a moment. My concern is for Mary. She's just a child," said the elderly woman. "Now, please, come in out of this terrible weather and take off those wet clothes."

"Mother, are you mad? She can't come in. We'll get into serious trouble."

Mrs. Fox glared at her daughter. "Will you shut up, Mable? And mind your own business. This is my house and I'll invite whoever I please."

Mrs. Fox gave them a hot drink and made sandwiches. She explained all about the MOD restrictions in the area.

"There is local gossip that something is going on down at the base. But no one has any knowledge of what it could be."

When Joanna explained she hadn't heard from Terry in two months, Mrs. Fox looked alarmed.

"I'm not surprised you've come down, Jo. I would have been the same if it were my dear Harry. God rest his soul."

"Mrs. Fox, I must go down to the base and see Terry. Then, when I return, we'll catch the first train home".

"What?" said the elderly woman in amazement. "You'll stay here. Anyway, they won't allow you anywhere near the place."

"Well, we'll just have to wait and see," said Joanna with determination. "However, I would like to thank you very much for your kindness. But I have no wish to impose on your generosity."

"No. You're staying here," said Mrs. Fox, and she finally let forth a reluctant smile.

Joanna took one look at the kind expression dancing in the elderly woman's eyes and threw her arms around her frail body. "Oh, thank you so much, Mrs. Fox."

Mable looked on enviously.

It had stopped raining when Joanna and Mary walked down the lane to a narrow dirt track leading to the Royal Marine Commando base. Joanna stood for a second staring down at the encampment. The entire area had an ominous feel that sent shivers down her spine. Before they reached the base, which lay at the bottom of the foothill amongst woodland and thick foliage, it started to rain. Before very long, a gusty wind blew up, turning their umbrellas inside out, and then it poured down in buckets.

Mary could feel the rain dripping from the fur around the hem of her pink, woolen coat and into her black Wellingtons. Her feet felt soggy and uncomfortable as she pressed her boots down into the mud. She glanced down at her mother's feet, who was up to her ankles in mud. It didn't seem to bother her in the least.

Joanna had only one thought in mind: Terry.

She was wearing a stylish, tan-colored coat draped in gray fur around the hem with smart, tan, high-heeled shoes. Underneath her coat she wore the red and white polka dot dress that Terry loved. Joanna was marvelous in making a decision on what to wear in town. Unfortunately, her taste for dressing for bad weather and muddy lanes left much to be desired.

As they approached, they saw the duty guard behind a high, barbed wired gate.

"Can I help you, madam?" he called.

"Yes. I would like to speak to your commanding officer or someone in authority," said Joanna, slowly moving a little closer.

He looked at them suspiciously with his rifle pointing outward at the ready. "Please don't come any further, madam."

Joanna stopped dead in her tracks. "Oh, please," said Joanna, smiling. "If you don't mind. I'd be awfully grateful. It's very important."

"One moment. I'll see what I can do," came the curt reply.

He went into his century box and spoke to another guard who picked up the phone.

Mary laughed. "I don't think he would have shot us, Mummy. He's English."

"I can't understand why he acted like that, Mary. He sounded really rude."

"Never mind, Mummy. Perhaps he's fed up with being stuck out here in all this bad weather."

Joanna smiled. "Yes. Maybe. Anyway, it's stopped raining now. Thank heavens." She bent down and tried to clean the mud from around her feet. "Help me clean this mess off, will you, dear?"

"Yes, of course, Mummy."

They were both bending down and didn't see the two officers approaching the gate. Mary rubbed her mother's ankles with the handkerchief she had used as a prop for her little performances. She burst out laughing.

"It looks as though you're wearing brown socks now, Mummy."

"Yes. You've rubbed the mud in, Mary. Oh, never mind, darling. You tried. It doesn't really matter. My only concern is getting through that gate and seeing Daddy."

Joanna glanced up to see two officers making their way towards her. One of them was a captain and the other, a major. They both saluted Joanna and then questioned her for fifteen minutes. Then they saluted her again and returned once more through the barbed wire gate.

The same procedure was to continue with higher ranking officials for another hour.

Anxiously, Joanna paced up and down, growing tenser by the minute. She was beginning to doubt whether she would ever see Terry.

Mary tried to occupy herself by playing hopscotch. After a while, she grew bored and looked for new adventures. She wondered over the field into a clearing at the edge of the wood. She noticed a few bluebells growing, which was unusual for the time of the year. She walked a little further into the wood and saw a high, barbed wire fence. But beyond the fence was something that made Mary gasp in wonder. Hidden from view lay bluebells, shimmering white and blue against the dew, where raindrops had kissed their petal tips, making a carpet of silvery blue.

Mary thought they looked beautiful. In her poetic mind, she drew a picture of bliss, a representation of how life should really be. Shining, with beauty in abundance.

Mary stood in awe. Her love for nature was such that she could not resist them.

She called out to her mother, "May I pick a few bluebells, Mummy?"

Joanna's thoughts were elsewhere, and she didn't hear her daughter's call.

Mary picked up a stone and began to dig a small hole under the fence, just wide enough to put her small hand through. She started to reach underneath, intending to pick the flowers. But just at that moment, the duty guard came to the gate and asked Joanna to follow him.

Joanna turned and called to Mary. It was then that she noticed her daughter picking the bluebells.

Joanna screamed out, "No! Mary. No. Come here immediately."

Mary dropped the flowers she had managed to skillfully pick and ran to her mother. She had never seen her mother quite so angry before.

"What in heavens name do you think you're doing, child?"

"I was just picking a few flowers."

"Flowers?" stormed Joanna. "That could be an electric fence. You stupid girl."

Mary stood up straight, holding back the tears, and answered in a quiet tone, "I'm very sorry, Mother. I had no idea I was doing anything wrong."

The guard led them both through the gate and showed them into the mess room, where they were given a hot mug of coco. Shortly after, an officer appeared. He asked Joanna to follow him.

Mary stayed in the mess room chatting with the marines, drinking her hot coco, and eating arrowroot biscuits by a warm stove. They were a happy bunch of men who were eager to entertain Mary by telling her jokes and making her laugh. Mary sat smiling on a high stool. She looked a little shy with her hands clasped around her mug of coco. Sadly, she told them of how she was unable to pick her favorite flowers from the woods.

A handsome young marine stood listening in the background, and then he disappeared without a word.

Joanna returned to the mess room accompanied by Terry. The men stood to attention and saluted him. Terry returned the salute.

"Daddy!" Mary shouted.

Terry looked up and waved to her. "Okay, men. At ease. Sorry for the disturbance here this afternoon."

"There hasn't been any disturbance, sir," said one of the marines. "More like home away from home, having your daughter around."

Terry smiled and thanked the men.

Mary was on the point of running to her father. Then she stopped when he returned back into the room from whence he came.

"Oh," said a very dejected Mary. "I haven't even had chance to speak to him yet."

At that moment, the young marine reappeared. "Here you are, love. Don't look so sad. You'll see your dad again." And he handed her a bunch of bluebells.

"Oh, thank you very much, sir," said Mary, overwhelmed by the surprise.

Joanna turned to look at the good-looking marine. She appeared even more amazed.

"Why, that's awfully kind of you. Thank you very much."

"Oh, that's okay," said the young marine. "It's just a bunch of bluebells. Strange, isn't it, how the little things in life seem to please some kids?"

"Yes," said Joanna. "But Mary is getting a little old for such things at her age."

"No, I don't think so. It's rather nice in times like these that kids can still appreciate the simple joys of life." He smiled, looking into Joanna's eyes. "Never had any kids of my own."

Joanna noticed a wistful expression in his eyes. She was deeply moved by the sentimental and intriguing young man. "Well, I'm quite sure you will one day."

She extended her hand, giving him one of her warmest smiles.

"Yes. Maybe," he said somewhat hesitantly, and shook her hand.

A voice called from the doorway of the adjoining room, "Mrs. Busher, would you and your daughter come this way please?"

Joanna quickly said goodbye and wished the marine well. Then she and Mary disappeared through the open door.

Chapter 39

Josh's body washed ashore off Gravesend creek two days after Andy had literally stuck the knife in their black market business arrangements. The police assumed, at first, that it was the remains of an enemy agent. With the mass invasion of Europe looming on the horizon, such a thought was entirely understandable.

A full-scale investigation was carried out after finding Josh's identity card tucked inside a leather wallet in his back trouser pocket, something Andy and Frank had forgotten in their haste to get away.

The police contacted Tom, as they so often did with difficult murder inquires. Tom was hardly able to recognize the body as Josh. He contacted Nina who came down from Derbyshire immediately and, as strange as it may seem, could still discern the bloated, eyeless lump as her husband. Nina gave the police a photo of Josh, which matched the description given to them by the landlady of the Green Door Pub where Josh had rented a room for his shady business dealings.

"Do you remember him mentioning any other place around here?" asked the detective inspector, looking intently at the Green Door's landlady.

She screwed up her worn but heavily made-up face and said, "Yeah, some dump near the waterfront. Black Bear or somefink like that."

Although not entirely accurate, the landlady's information led the police to the Brown Bear Pub on the waterfront.

"Yeah, I recognize him," said the Brown Bear's barmaid. "Rude bloke. Kept telling me to 'urry up."

"When did you last see this man?" said the detective inspector.

"Oh, about a week ago, I believe. Left 'ere wiv a couple of good-looking yanks. Funny, I ain't seen 'im or them since. Why? Wot's 'e dun wrong?"

The inspector ignored her question. "Thank you very much, miss. You've been most helpful. Good day to you."

Back at police headquarters, the detective inspector was going through details with his colleague.

"By the way, Higgins, did you check if there's been any deserters in the area recently?"

"Yes, indeed I have, sir. None whatsoever."

"Well then, Higgins, I think we now have enough evidence to make a final decision. Thanks to our good friend Tom."

The detective inspector smiled, folded the file, and then slipped it into the cabinet. Tom had assisted the police in digging out as much information on Josh as he could possibly find. What he discovered not only surprised the police enough to close the case, but also astounded Nina.

Tom escorted her to the mortuary. As she gazed down at the body lying on the slab, she brushed aside a tear. It had been a momentary reaction.

Tom looked at her pale face and led her by the elbow to the door.

Once outside, Nina stared at him. "Please excuse me, Tom. It's just the shock. Who could have done such a terrible thing?"

"Nina, I would like you to come back to my apartment. I have a great deal to discuss with you."

Back home, Tom led Nina into the lounge.

"Now," he said softly but with a firm inflection, "do take a seat."

Peggy came scampering up to them.

"Down, Peg," said Tom, trying to sound commanding. "Peggy is my charge this weekend," he explained to Nina, "while Jo is away. One word from me and she does as she pleases."

Nina smiled. "You're a very kind person, Tom. Now, what is it you wish to discuss with me?"

"Are you able to take a glass of cognac, my dear?"

"Yes. Just a small one. Thank you, Tom."

"Good, because I think you're going to need it with what I'm about to say."

Back in Bursledon, Terry had been welcomed by an astounded Mrs. Fox. She could hardly believe her eyes when she opened the front door to find the happy trio standing on her doorstep. Then she looked up to see four military guards hastily departing in their car.

"Good gracious. I didn't think Joanna would even be allowed to see you, let alone come back here with you."

"It's only for a few hours, Mrs. Fox. Not long, I can assure you," said Terry.

"Oh, I'm not worried. I'm only too pleased to see you, my boy. I'll be off and get you both something to eat and drink."

Mrs. Fox realized they needed to be on their own for a while, and she asked Mary if she would like to come with her and put her bluebells in some water.

Mary looked seriously at her parents, and answered, "Yes, I would. Thank you, Mrs. Fox."

She understood only too well that her parents wished to be alone. But she couldn't comprehend why everyone still treated her like a small child.

She looked over her shoulder at her father, and called, "Daddy, you won't go before I come back, will you?"

"No, of course not, sweetheart. I'll be staying nearly all night."

"Oh, that's wonderful, Daddy. Absolutely wonderful."

Terry had been granted a seven-hour stay overnight on compassionate grounds. The military guards would return to pick him up, at 2 a.m. in the morning to be in readiness for June 5th. Whatever yarn Joanna had spun to the high ranking officials at the base, it certainly paid dividends.

Joanna hadn't realized that Terry had received his commission. This, in turn, had at first led to even more confusion amongst the officials. Of course, Joanna didn't have any idea that the largest embarkation of troops the country had ever known was soon to leave Britain's shores. And her husband's platoon was to be the first, delivering vital reconnaissance information and carving a path for the brave fighters who followed.

"Mrs. Fox is really a marvelous woman," said Terry, as they made their way upstairs to their bedroom.

"Yes, she is," agreed Joanna nonchalantly.

Once inside the room, he turned to Joanna, looking straight into her eyes. "What brought you down here, Jo? What made you come here today of all days?" He spoke in a serious, virtually glacial tone.

"I should have thought that would have been obvious, Terry. It's been two and a half months since I've heard from you."

"I know, but why-" started Terry.

But Joanna cut through in her commanding voice. "No. You asked me why I came, and I'm asking you, why haven't you contacted me at all?"

"I..." Terry opened his mouth to speak but no more words came.

"You listen to me, Terrance Busher. Don't you realize I've been out of my mind these last couple of months? I had no idea what was going on down here. All this hush-hush business. Now I have a little clearer picture. But Terry, I had to see you. Surely you understand that? I felt something dreadful was going to happen and I would never see you again. I haven't been able to sleep at night. I'm chain smoking myself to an early grave. You just ignored me, and I was going out of my mind with worry. Why did you do that to me, Terry? What have I done to warrant such treatment?"

Terry gazed at her, speechless.

"I hope that answers your question, *Lieutenant* Busher," continued Joanna. "I didn't even know about that bloody commission and I made myself look a right fool asking persistently to see a Corporal Busher. I'm sorry if I've caused you any embarrassment, Terry. If I have then I'll leave right now. It's clear I'm no longer needed here."

He came in close, gazing into her eyes that swam like dark pools yet never shed a tear.

"Oh, my darling Jo."

He took her in his arms. Jo trembled. He bent his head and touched her lip that quivered under his fingers, and then he kissed her. Holding her close, he couldn't disguise the pain in his eyes.

He whispered, "Forgive me for ever having doubted you, my darling, darling, Jo. Thank God you're here now."

"What do you mean, Terry? Doubted me?" said Joanna, slowly pulling away.

"Nothing, Jo. I was speaking my thoughts aloud."

"You always say that when you're trying to be evasive." She walked away from him to the other side of the room. Then she turned around to face her husband. "Terry, tell me the truth," said Joanna in an adamant tone. "What are you hiding from me?"

"Forget it, darling. You're here now and that's all that matters."

"No, Terry. I want to know."

He sighed. "Very well. If you insist." He looked straight into her eyes. "I don't know quite how to put this, but I've been receiving anonymous letters that said you've been having an affair."

"What?" gasped Joanna. "I don't understand. Who is this person?"

"Supposed to be an RAF chap in Derbyshire. I knew it couldn't possibly be true, but you're so lovely, and I know what some chaps are like."

Joanna looked blankly into space, backing away from him. "How could you have thought such a thing of me?" Raising her voice, she echoed, "*How* could you think me so devious and despicable?"

Terry came closer, holding out his arms to her. "Joanna, please. Someone is obviously trying to tear us apart, and if you carry on like this, they will have succeeded."

"But why didn't you tell me, Terry?"

"Because your reaction would have been exactly the same as it is now and I wasn't able to see you to explain. Do try and understand how I felt, my darling. I just hoped that everything was still the same between us."

She paused, and then repeated his words. "*Still the same*? I've been out of my mind with worry. Don't you understand?"

"Of course I understand, Jo. I knew you couldn't do such a thing. You must believe that, my darling. You came all this way down here to see me. Only you could possibly be so perceptive as to realize that something was wrong. Only you, my darling. Only you."

She ran into his arms, sobbing. "Oh, Terry. Who could do such a terrible thing to us?"

"Hush now, darling. Whoever it was will get their comeuppance in some way or another." He held her tight. "Nothing in this wide world can ever part us now. We are bound together. You and I, we are one."

Joanna looked up into his sad, blue eyes as they stood locked in each other's embrace.

She whispered, choking back the tears, "Terry, please come back to me. Please. Please, come back."

He smiled. "I'm already back." He brushed his lips against hers, and then softly said, "I've told you before. Nothing can ever part us. Now and forever."

Chapter 40

Nina had been appalled when Tom gave her an account of his findings with PI Tony Evens.

"And the life insurance policy taken out by Josh," she said slowly, realizing its full impact. "He actually *wanted* me dead." She shook her head in horror. "You know, I never loved him. You know that, Tom?"

The elderly man nodded his head. "That's an understatement, my dear."

"It was a marriage of convenience right from the start, Tom. But even though he was a beast to me, I didn't hate him. Not until he began mistreating the children. And then he started on me again with a vengeance. I grew to despise him. I always assumed it was just his drunken rages which made him so violent and cruel. He had over me and the kids a power that I didn't dare cross. Knowing that everything he did wasn't because of his drunkenness, it was because he was consciously, deliberately trying to kill me, it's horrible, Tom. The times I could have died."

Nina shivered visibly and sipped her cognac.

"Yes, my dear. It would appear so." Tom spoke in a soft, positive tone. "When he found he couldn't accomplish killing you, he carried out his venomous plan on two innocent people in an effort to wreck their marriage completely, purely for his own satisfaction. I'm sorry, my dear, but you know as well as I do, that scoundrel deserved all he got."

Nina stood up from the armchair and walked over to the window. Her face was ashen. She looked near to collapse.

"Nina, my dear, do finish your cognac. It will make you feel better at this moment in time."

She gazed down into the street below at the passersby. Yet her eyes were blind to everything. Nina buried her head in her hands and sobbed.

"Oh my God, it's all my fault. Jo will never forgive me."

"My dear Nina, it is not your fault. You've been a victim as much as anyone in this sorry tale. Please don't get upset. Come, sit down and finish your drink. I'm sure, if it's humanly possible, Joanna will find a way of seeing Terry."

"Yes, but what if she can't? What then, Tom? If I'd never met Joanna, she'd not be in the position she's in now trying to sort out her marriage."

"Yes, my dear, and you would not be here today," whispered Tom in a sympathetic tone, underlining in Nina the true power of the friendship she had with Joanna.

Joanna arrived home on Wednesday June 7th. Mrs. Fox wisely advised her to stay an extra night until the activities had died down.

Tom was delighted by her good news.

"I knew you'd do it. I knew you'd find a way of seeing him. I tried to tell Nina, but she wouldn't listen. She blames herself entirely for what happened. I think that's why she returned to Derbyshire so quickly. You see, Jo, there is not going to be a funeral. She is leaving everything for the authorities to deal with. She made the excuse of having to be home for Marianne. I thought it odd when she has a very good nanny to help her. Then I realized the poor woman just couldn't stand the humiliation of facing you, had you brought bad news. Nina feels indebted to you. Indeed, very much so. And who knows, perhaps she's right. The hand of fate has definitely worked a miracle in her life."

"Yes," said Joanna. "Thank God it has, because one certainly worked for me."

Tom nodded his head in agreement. "That poor boy would have gone into battle with that on his mind had it not been for you, my dear."

She looked at Tom, reading his thoughts. "I'd rather not think of that at the moment, Uncle."

He lay a comforting hand on her shoulder and whispered, "We'll pray, my dear."

Mary came in from the garden with Peggy by her side. She entered through the French windows.

"Are you talking about Daddy?" she said perceptively.

"Really, Mary, you mustn't burst in and interrupt like that."

"I'm very sorry, Mummy. What I was going to say is, did you tell Uncle how I played the part of an actress?"

"No, not yet, Mary. I've had important matters to discuss with Uncle."

"Oh, I see," said Mary, and she ran off into the garden again with Peggy at her heels.

She sat on the garden seat.

"You're my very best friend, Peg. I can speak to you and you never tell me to shut up, keep quiet, or do as I'm told. You understand me."

Mary put her arms around Peggy, kissing and cuddling her.

"I wish Daddy were here now, Peg. He'd understand. Mummy doesn't realize that I miss him too, and if it hadn't been for me, she may not have seen him. She doesn't realize I can read the newspapers. I know he's in France fighting. Yet Mummy has never told me, Peg. She thinks I'm still a little child."

She buried her head into Peggy's coat and cried.

"I'll give Nina a ring right now, Uncle," said Joanna inside. "To put her mind at rest."

"Good. I rather hoped you'd say that."

Tom turned and walked out through the French windows into the garden.

"Now, come, come, Mary, my dear child. What's all this?"

When Mary had finished telling him why she was so fed up, Tom put his arm around her.

"My dear child, I'm quite sure your mother appreciates all you have done for her. And if she hasn't given you much attention lately, it's only because she's had a great deal on her mind."

Mary smiled at Tom's reassuring words.

"Now, come on, Mary. Let's see if Peg will fetch this ball for you, because she doesn't for me."

During the days that followed, Joanna scanned the newspapers and listened to news broadcasts. Her pulse rate quickened while reading an article written by a war correspondent describing the landing scenes from the Canadian ship, Prince David, stating the first casualties he saw were men of the Royal Marine Commandos.

She froze, holding the newspaper tight, and then her eyes focused on a passage that read: *The British and Canadian troops are continuing to make progress against Rommel, whose reserves are now in action along the whole front in Normandy.*

Joanna smiled, slightly relieved. So he's turning to his reserves now, is he?

She was about to put the paper down when she noticed an article that read: *Our fellows are striking fast and often catching the Germans by surprise. They all piled into a dugout where the Germans were about to have breakfast.*

They captured the place, and then polished off the eggs and milk laid out for the Germans.

Joanna suddenly found the story highly amusing and laughed so much it neared hysteria. Unconsciously, she spoke her thoughts aloud whilst reaching for a cigarette.

"Oh dear God, that is funny. That is really funny."

At that moment, Mary came in from the garden.

"Hello, Mummy. You look happy for a change. I thought you were celebrating something. What's happened?"

Joanna turned her head slowly to face Mary. She hadn't realized until this moment the dreadful effect the past few days had had on her daughter.

"No, darling, I'm not celebrating anything. However, you've given me a super idea. I think we'll have a party."

"What?" said Mary, totally mystified by her mother's sudden change of temperament. "Why?"

Joanna tilted her head to one side, looking thoughtful. "Well, I think it would be nice. A sort of get together."

"But, Mummy, there's nothing to celebrate, is there? You haven't heard from Daddy, have you?"

"No, I haven't. Nevertheless, we shall still have a party."

Joanna felt a calmness run through her body as if her faith in humanity had been restored once again. She realized that whatever the future held, she must be able to face it, for she had Mary to consider, and Mary was a part of Terry.

"Come over here, sweetheart. We're going to have a lovely party, and you can invite your friends. I would really like to invite everyone, just like Daddy and I used to do before the war. But the big question is food."

"Well, what about asking them to bring their own? Like we do at Christmas."

"You know, that's a very good idea, Mary. You are excellent at coming up with these ideas, sweetheart. That way, they can choose what they would like to eat. I'll ask Mrs. Stanley next door and Mrs. Hayes if they'd like to contribute. I'm sure if they're willing, everyone else will follow suit. Yes. That's just what we need, Mary, a jolly good get together."

Mary threw her arms around her mother's neck. "Oh, Mummy. It's going to be a wonderful party. I'll run up to Dora's house and tell her."

Chapter 41

Once again, Tom had the unfavorable task of conveying information to Nina. This time, it was that her Aunt Bertha had died suddenly of a heart attack. Her solicitors, Penman & Penman, contacted Tom promptly. They gave him full details of Nina's true background, which flabbergasted him. In shock, he asked for Joanna's advice.

"I just don't know how she will react to this, Jo, in her state of health."

"Well, I would have thought she'd be happy. It's not every day you find out you've come into an inheritance."

"To you and I, yes. But don't you see, Jo? If her divorce had gone through, she would not be entitled to any of this. It's laid down clearly in the contract. Look."

"I don't quite follow, Uncle. Josh is dead. What's the problem?"

"The problem is that villainous creature apparently became friendly with the old lady Bertha, and although she may not have realized it at the time, she was slowly becoming his accomplice to murder, had he succeeded in doing so. I assume it all began when she told Nina to get out. She knew poor Nina had nowhere else to go. She couldn't have cared less, and you, the only friend Nina had, were in Devon at the time. With Nina out of the way, Bertha stood to gain everything. The legacy would automatically go to her. Josh wanted the three thousand pounds life insurance he'd taken out when they were wed. That's why he hired Tony Evens, and when that proved fruitless…" Tom paused. "Well, the rest you know, my dear."

"Yes, quite. The rest I know, Uncle." Joanna looked somber. "I just can't believe it. How could she do such a dreadful thing? Bertha actually wanted her dead."

"Think about it, Jo. A lonely, embittered, middle-aged woman who'd spent her youth working hard under extreme conditions. In her desperation, she grasped at whatever straw was available at the time, and that happened to be a little girl who we now know as Nina. It was her way of acquiring everything she never had in life. Bertha, in her acrimonious state of mind, left the inheritance to Josh, though he was obviously unaware of it. Nina, now being his widow and next of kin, will automatically stand to inherit a vast fortune. A fortune that was always supposed to be hers, and one she'd been cheated out of by cruel circumstances. I'm not entirely sure of the sum. However, I've been told it's quite a hefty one."

"Dear God. Poor Nina. It's unthinkable, Uncle. I knew Bertha was a bit of a battle-axe, but this..." Joanna shook her head, putting her hand to her mouth. "How could she be so evil? She hated Nina so much that she would actually go to such length. It's quite unbelievable, Uncle."

Tom was quick to change the subject. "Nina will be attending the funeral. It will be a small affair with just a few of Bertha's friends from the church. Penman & Penman are aware of the matter concerned. They are dealing with the transaction and are keeping me informed."

Tom noted Joanna's saddened face and made an effort to heighten her spirits.

"Apart from them, only you and I know about this, Jo, and you're a very good friend of Nina's, are you not?"

Joanna laughed. "Well, of course I am. You're a silly old thing at times, Uncle. You know very well I am. Why do you ask?"

"Oh, I'm a stupid, old fool. Please forgive me, Jo. I was speaking in my official capacity. I'm getting old and forgetful."

Joanna laughed heartily. "Well, for a minute, Uncle, I thought I was standing in the dock. You know, you're working much too hard. You should be retired. Why not come and spend a few days with me before we have our party? You'll feel much fitter and ready to enjoy yourself."

Tom smiled. "I'm quite sure I would, my dear. However, what I'm trying to say is you know and understand her better than anyone. How do you think she's going to react to all of this?"

"Well, Uncle, as you say, knowing Nina as I do, I think she would naturally assume that the police would think that she had something to do with his murder, even though they've closed the case. Nina has been through so much. It's left her believing a cloud of darkness hangs over her constantly, and she doesn't feel she has any right to any kind of happiness. It may be due to her upbringing. I don't know. However, she may very well go in a dilemma, postpone her marriage, and consequently become very ill. That's just my opinion, Uncle. You're her solicitor. What do you think?"

"I agree with you entirely, my dear. I just needed to be certain. That's why I asked you."

Joanna paused before speaking. "It's amazing. As if the war wasn't bad enough, then we have people like Josh and Bertha."

"Quite," said Tom, nodding his head. "However, whatever she may consider in that mind of hers, she has nothing to worry about now."

Later that day, Joanna sat at the kitchen table organizing the party with Mary.

"Well, I think we have enough guests coming now, Mary."

"Yes, but I hope they don't forget to bring food. Otherwise we'll starve for the next week."

Joanna smiled. "Mary, you're always thinking of your stomach."

"Is Aunty Nina coming?"

"No. Unfortunately, she's going straight home after her aunt's funeral. Her birthday is this Tuesday. That's why I particularly chose June 13th."

"Oh, what a shame. I'd love to have seen Marianne. Why isn't she coming?"

"Well, apparently Marianne is starting a new school or something or other."

Mary looked thoughtful. "Strange, isn't it, Mummy? You didn't see her last time she came down. I wonder why."

"I really don't know, Mary, and I'm very busy and very tired. I do wish you'd stop asking questions and help me."

"What would you like me to do?" said Mary abruptly, feeling her mother's obvious brush off.

"Take these tablecloths upstairs and put them in the linen cupboard."

Mary glanced at her mother as she handed her the tablecloths.

"I'm very sorry, Mummy. I didn't realize I'd said anything wrong. I promise I won't ask you anymore questions. I'll wait until Daddy comes home."

Joanna, surprised by her daughter's remark, followed her upstairs. "Mary, what's the matter, dear?"

Mary turned around on reaching the linen cupboard and looked her mother straight in the eyes.

"If I'd been grown up, I would have asked you the same question. But I can't because I'm only a child and you'd tell me not to be rude. I thought we were having this party to cheer us up? I have tried to help you, but all you keep saying is stop asking questions, or be quiet, children should be seen and not heard." Mary's eyes grew glassy by trying to hold back the tears. "I'm not a tiny girl anymore, Mother. I'm nearly eleven years old. It's because you haven't heard from Daddy fighting in France, isn't it? Well, I'm worried about him too. Mother, I must ask you this one question. It's been on my mind. And then I will never ask you another. Will we ever see or hear from Daddy again?"

Joanna's face was full of pain as she stared, dumbfounded, listening to Mary's little speech. She wrapped her arms around her daughter.

"Oh, Mary, my love, you're so grown up for your years, and I had no wish to make you any older than you already are. Of course we'll hear from Daddy again. We must have faith in God."

"Yes, I have faith in God. But God took Grandad."

"Mary, my sweetheart, we must never stop believing in all that is good. We must believe that we will see Daddy again."

Mary agreed with her mother, though she did not look totally convinced. "Yes. You're right, Mummy, and I do believe."

Nina wrote apologizing for not accepting Joanna's invitation. She stated that she had found the news of the two deaths so close together quite disturbing. She felt the need to return home to the peace and tranquility of her much loved Peak District in Derbyshire.

Joanna understood how much the place meant to her, as well as being with her David whenever possible, which, at the moment, wasn't very often. David, like Terry, was occupied with the invasion. His squadron were on early morning missions bombing the coastal defenses of Normandy.

Nina gave Joanna an update on her mother's condition. She had made great progress and was indeed looking forward to coming home to Kent and living with Joanna.

The night of the party went with a swing. Nearly all the guests brought various types of food. What one didn't bring, someone else did.

Audrey Stanley and Ann Hayes from next door, as well as Margaret, Dora's mother, were all an enormous help. The landlady of the Pier Inn made a wonderful contribution by bringing beer for the men and port and lemon for the ladies. Dr. Stanley came with two bottles of medicinal brandy. Tom brought his usual cognac. Even Pete the postman managed to acquire a bottle of whisky.

Margaret's husband, Alfred, played the piano, while Joanna accompanied him by singing nearly every well-known song of the era. She sang her heart out. Everyone had a great time.

Mary sat at the top of the stairs looking down through the banisters at everyone enjoying themselves. She couldn't help but admire how beautiful the house looked that night with its impressive marble arch surrounding the staircase. Both she and her mother had worked hard in preparation for all this. Mary thought it had been well worth it just to see so many happy faces.

"Oh, there you are," a voice called. "What are you doing tucked away up here?"

Mary looked around to see Dora making her way from the bathroom. "Not much really, Dora. I was just thinking, wouldn't it be lovely if every night was like this?"

Dora looked puzzled. "With all this food and drink, you mean?"

"No, silly. Seeing everyone enjoying themselves."

"Yes, it would," said Dora thoughtfully. "Shall we go down and join in the fun?"

"You go if you like, Dora. I can't move at the moment. I've eaten too much."

Dora laughed. "You know, Mary, you'll soon have to start watching your figure."

"That's what grown-ups say to each other."

"Well, I'm nearly grown up," said Dora. "Oh, come on, Mary. Let's go down and have some fun. I rather fancy your Pete the postman."

Mary looked straight ahead. "No. I'm staying here for a while."

"Come on, Mary. Don't be a spoil sport. You don't want to be sitting here all night."

"Dora, did you know Peter is seventeen?"

"Well, I'm nearly fourteen." Dora grinned. "Oh, I forgot you're still a child yet." She ran down the stairs laughing her head off, and added, "You'll be sitting there when you're an old maid, Mary."

"Well, that doesn't matter," said Mary, looking smug. "You'll be drawing your old age pension before me."

After a while, Mary peeped through the banisters to see Dora sitting on her own and went down to join her.

"So where's Pete?"

"He had to leave early because he's in the stupid Home Guard."

Mary burst out laughing. "Well, he's got to do his duty."

"Yes, I know that, Mary. But there hasn't been any air raids for ages."

"I shouldn't worry, Dora. Look. Dr. Stanley is over there. I think I heard him say he'll be leaving soon. Why don't you ask him for a dance before he goes?"

"Well, I don't want to dance with him, stupid. He's an old man."

Mary laughed with a twinkle in her eye. "Never mind, Dora. Dance with me instead?"

"Okay. I might as well," said Dora, dejected, and she reluctantly took Mary's hand. "Anyway, I think most of them are leaving now."

"Dora, haven't you enjoyed it?"

"Yes, of course I have. It's been wonderful. And your mum has a lovely voice."

"Thank you," said Mary proudly. "And your mum is a marvelous cook."

"There you go again," giggled Dora. "Always thinking about your stomach."

Both girls danced away the rest of the evening, jitterbugging to the sound of Glen Miller music.

The next morning, Peter delivered the long awaited field card Joanna had been expecting, stating that Terry was alive and well. Closing her eyes, she sighed with relief.

"Thank you, Pete."

"Good news?" he inquired.

"Yes. Very good news," said Joanna.

"Blimey. You look as if you've come into a fortune."

"Believe me, I feel as if I have, Pete. My husband is still on this mortal coil."

"Oh, that's wonderful news, Mrs. B. I'm very pleased for you, and I'd like to say thank you for last night. I don't know when I last enjoyed myself so much. It was a wonderful turn out, especially the cabaret."

"Thank you, Pete, but I really think your gratitude should go to all those who contributed in making it special."

"Yes, but you sparkled last night, Mrs. B, with that beautiful bird-like voice of yours."

"Why, thank you, Pete. That's a lovely complement."

"Well, I mustn't stand here gassing all day. Got to get finished. The Home Guard wants us on duty early."

"Do they? Strange. I wonder why. Perhaps you're needed on exercises."

"Maybe. But I doubt it. The message that came through sounded urgent. I can't understand it. There haven't been any air raids for ages. Anyway, if something is up, I'll let you know. TTFN."

Joanna smiled. "Thank you, Pete. Bye for now."

"See, I told you, Mummy, that everything would be okay if we had a party and enjoyed ourselves."

"You're quite right, Mary. Very wise of you. Now hurry up and get ready for school. I'm doing a little shopping in Gravesend today. They have a fresh delivery of fish on Tuesdays. I must be there early before they sell out. Then I'm dropping in on Uncle Tom. He consumed a great deal of cognac last night. I'd like to see how he is."

Mary burst out laughing. "Wasn't he funny when he started singing that song Daddy is always singing? Now what were the words?"

Joanna laughed. "Uncle can be very funny at times. But I'm afraid I can't remember the words either, Mary, at the moment."

"It's coming to me now, Mummy. Isn't it something like this? 'I've been fishing with the boys today. I fished like so, and so you know, I caught a little tiddler with a nice soft roe. Now I've been a-fishing with the boys today, in a little pond that's down our way, I stood like so, and soon, you know, I caught a little tiddler with a nice soft roe'. Then something about…'With a cotton and a pin…'" Mary wrinkled her face, concentrating. "'Oh how I laughed when I dragged him in, but coming home oh dear-o, that rude boy dickey diddler, he poked his finger in my galley pot and he pinched my tiddler…' Oh, what a shame. I've forgotten the rest."

Joanna laughed. "Thank heavens for that. It was a good try, Mary. But it didn't sound quite the same when Uncle Tom sang it."

Mary uttered indignantly, "No, because he was half drunk."

Joanna laughed. "You were fine, sweetheart."

"Oh, Mummy, don't forget to buy some shrimps and winkles."

"I'll try," said Joanna, still laughing. "But we can't always get everything we want at the same time."

"Surely the war will be over soon, won't it, Mummy?"

"Yes, of course, darling."

Mary smacked her lips at the last morsel of porridge. "Then we'll have plenty of food to choose from. You know, Mummy, some silly children at school say the war is already over. I suppose it's because we haven't had any air raids. Strange, isn't it, Mummy?"

"Yes. Very strange," said Joanna reflectively.

"I'm looking forward to school this morning. Dora will have lots to say for herself. Do you know, I think she'd like Peter to be her boyfriend?"

Joanna laughed. "Well, providing you don't follow her example, it's really nothing to do with us. I'm sure her mother can deal with that, and you have a lot of studying to do, my girl. So I wouldn't worry about boyfriends at the moment, dear."

Mary pulled a long face. "Oh, not me, Mummy. Anyway I think they're silly."

Joanna grinned, talking cheekily to herself, "Yes, but one day, you won't."

Joanna stood in the fish queue waiting to be served the cod, shrimps, and winkles that had just arrived. She decided to cook Tom a nice piece of cod for his lunch before returning home to prepare dinner for her and Mary.

The fishmonger seemed unusually quick in serving. He appeared anxious when handing Joanna her purchases, and looked up. The rest of the queue behind Joanna followed suit. Joanna picked up her fish and walked out. She raised her eyes upwards to see a curious object flying low over their heads at a tremendous speed, its tail on fire.

Chapter 42

The siren sounded for the first time in months. There was confusion and panic in the queue.

Woman and children shouted, "What's that? What's happening? What's going on?"

The fishmonger called out, "I didn't want to alarm anyone. I heard on the wireless a little while ago that Hitler was going to unleash his secret weapon on London. It's a flying bomb called the V-1."

At that moment, a loud explosion could be heard in the distance.

Joanna, petrified, put her hand to her mouth, staring wide-eyed into the heavens.

The fishmonger yelled as he closed up shop, "There's a shelter out the back if anyone wants it."

Joanna realized that she wasn't far from Tom's office. She fled up the road, turned the corner, and ran like the wind up Harmer Street. She heard the sound of another flying bomb rapidly approaching overhead. Looking up, she saw it was the same as the last one with the tail on fire making a fearful noise. Someone from behind called out take cover. But Joanna didn't stop. She just continued running until she reached Tom's office, where she burst in to find Tom sitting under the stairs with a client.

"Joanna," gasped Tom. "You've obviously heard the news."

"Briefly, from the fishmonger."

"Oh, this is Mrs. Adams by the way," said Tom, nodding to the woman next to him.

"How do you do?" said Joanna hurriedly. "Uncle, I'd like to ring St Joseph's School."

"Certainly, my dear. You know where it is." Tom anxiously pointed to his office.

"Oh, Uncle, you'll be relieved to know Terry's alive and well."

"Thank God," whispered Tom. He turned to his client. "I do not think it's much use us sitting here, Mrs. Adams. If you'd care to accompany my niece and I up to my apartment then we can listen to the wireless and have a nice cup of tea."

Mrs. Adams, a tall, thin woman in her early sixties, slowly emerged from the cubbyhole shaking with fear. Then she followed Tom upstairs. He switched on the wireless immediately and put on the kettle.

Joanna quickly made her call and then hastened upstairs.

Gasping for breath, she echoed, "It's okay, Uncle. They've taken Mary with the rest of the children into the crypt. They're keeping her there until I pick her up in the Red Cross van when I report for duty. Now, Uncle, shall we sit down and hear what the hell's happening? Oh, please excuse my language, Mrs. Adams."

"That's quite all right, my dear. I think we all feel the same."

Tom brought in a tray of tea and biscuits while they heard the strange sound of the V-1 flying bomb roar above them. They sat and listened to the latest news bulletin.

The news reader announced, "The public have been warned to take cover if they hear the curious engine noise stop or if the flame disappears. It can take up to fifteen seconds for the V-1 to explode. The popular belief is that as long as you can hear the rocket engine, you're still safe. The 'buzz bomb' or 'doodlebug', as Britons are already calling it, flies at low altitudes, powered by petrol and compressed air. It is steered by gyroscope and designed to stall when it runs out of fuel, exploding on impact. That is the end of the news bulletin."

"The problem is," said Tom. "I didn't hear him mention what I heard on the earlier bulletin. They're sending them from Pas-de-Calais."

What?" said Joanna, panic-stricken. "That's just across the channel. That means this raid could go on all day. I must get home somehow."

At that minute, the all clear sounded.

"There you are, Jo," said Tom, trying to look cheerful.

"I'm off. I must hurry and get to the unit and then home." Joanna looked from Mrs. Adams to Tom. "You both take care."

"But, Jo, for heaven sake, finish your tea."

"No time, Uncle."

"If I'm right, I believe he mentioned on the bulletin that they are capable of flying at a speed of four hundred miles per hour."

"And you're sure you heard him say Pas-de-Calais, Uncle?"

"I'm perfectly sure, my dear."

"Then flying at such a speed, the siren could be going on and off all day."

"I'm afraid so, my dear," said Tom, nodding his head gravely.

"I must leave right now, Uncle."

Tom followed her downstairs.

Joanna turned and looked at him. "I'll ring you when I get home. Do take care, Uncle."

"And you, my dear. Don't take any chances."

She paused before leaving. "I often wonder sometimes, Uncle, whether we wouldn't be safer on the battlefield."

His sad, old eyes looked into hers. "My darling Jo, we're on the battlefield now."

Joanna used the Red Cross van, whenever it was available, to take Mary and the children next door to school. Their mother, Ann, would join them, followed by Peggy. In some strange way, they seemed to feel safer in numbers. At night, they would shelter under the stairs. It was as safe as anywhere could be. The tunnel and Anderson were inadequate protection from the VI flying bombs, which could strike anytime, anywhere, mainly over London and the southeast of England, day or night.

"I don't know whether I'll be able to have the van on Monday. We're getting busier by the minute," said Joanna, as she dropped Ann off on the way home.

"I'm not surprised. It's like the blitz all over again," said Ann. "Only this time, they come without any warning."

"Yes," sighed Joanna. "The mad little corporal has really done his homework well this time. Trouble is, he doesn't realize when he's beaten."

Ann was hesitant in her response. "Well, I'm not so sure about that, Jo. You never know what he has up his sleeve."

Joanna understood why her neighbor made such a pessimistic comment, but she ignored it by changing the subject.

"What are you doing this Saturday and Sunday?"

"Well, buzz bombs or no, we're having a picnic on Gravesend promenade tomorrow. I promised the girls I'd take them, and I am."

Joanna smiled. "Well said, Ann. I agree with you entirely." Smiling, she raised her thumb. "We have to carry on with our normal lives, and not allow that wretched little Hitler to change anything."

Ann nodded in agreement. "Oh, I wonder, would Mary like to come with us? She can bring Peggy too if she wishes."

"Thanks awfully, Ann. But tomorrow I'm taking her to Dartford to buy a pair of shoes for school. Mary grows out of them so quickly these days. She has awkward feet to fit. There's a very good little shoe shop just off the high street that specializes in children's growing feet. But I'd be awfully grateful if you'd take Peggy. She loves the river, and I have no wish to take her shopping, especially on Saturday. And she hates being left alone in the house."

"Jo, say no more. I'd be delighted. The girls love Peggy. They're always asking me to get them a pet like her. But with conditions being the way they are, it wouldn't be advisable. Never knowing what's going to happen from one day to the next."

"Yes, I agree. We only took Peggy to give her a home, and Tom is too old now. He has enough to do with his work and looking after himself." Joanna laughed. "And not forgetting his chickens. Oh, by the way, I nearly forgot to ask you. How is Charles? Have you heard from him recently?"

"Yes. He's just come out of solitary again for trying to escape. You would have thought he'd learned his lesson by now."

Joanna noted her doleful expression, recalling that Charles, a captain in the British expeditionary force, had been captured at Dunkirk, and he'd been a prisoner ever since.

"Never mind, Ann dear. It'll be over soon and we'll have them home with us. Chin up. See you tonight. I must dash off or I'll be late. TTFN."

"Oh, why do we have to go shopping, Mummy?" asked Mary the following morning. "I'd rather have gone down the prom with Peg and the girls."

"Because, Mary, you need new shoes for school."

"I know that, Mummy. I wouldn't mind if it were for nice, smart shoes like you wear. I'm almost grown up now, Mother. I don't know why I have to wear those plain old things."

Joanna grinned. "Why is it, Mary, that you always call me Mother when you're trying to appear older?"

"No, I don't," said Mary, standing on her tiptoes and trying to look even more grown up. "If wore high heels, I'd look as tall as you."

Joanna smiled. "The reason why I get you strong, sturdy shoes with plenty of room in them is because they last longer. It'll be different when the war is over and we don't have to stretch our points."

"Oh, when the war is over. The times I've heard that. Mummy, it doesn't seem as if it's ever going to be over."

"It will be soon. I promise you," said Joanna, looking agitated.

Mary stared at her mother. "Yes. When all these terrible doodlebugs have flattened everywhere."

Joanna saw fear reflected in her daughter's eyes. "Mary, my darling, I think I should take you up to Aunty Nina's for a little while. It'll be lovely for you up there. You'd have great fun with Marianne and the boys, and you'll be able to see Nanny every day."

Mary looked at her mother questioningly. "Will you be coming too?"

"I'd love to, Mary. But I can't. I have to stay here for many reasons."

Mary sat and thought about it, and then, in a resolute tone, replied, "No. I don't want to go. I hate Derbyshire."

"I know you do, sweetheart. This time, I assure you, it will be different. We have Aunty Nina and Nanny there."

"No. That isn't the reason why I don't want to go."

"What is it then?"

"You, Mummy. I'd be thinking of you all the time, down here on your own, working hard and without Daddy, and maybe getting yourself killed. No, Mother. If you're brave enough to stay here, then so am I."

Joanna, deeply touched, sighed. She looked at her daughter admiringly and smiled. They both hugged each other.

Joanna whispered, "Very well, my darling. I'm not going to force you."

The shoe shop was tucked away off the main high street. They had gone through numerous pairs of shoes before deciding on a pair. Mary fell in love with a dark, navy blue pair of stylish buckle straps.

"These are lovely, Mummy. Can I have them?"

Joanna smiled, pondering. "Well…I suppose so. They are rather expensive."

"Yes, but they do suit your daughter, madam," said the assistant.

At that moment, the siren sounded.

"Yes. I'll take them," said Joanna hastily.

"I have an Anderson shelter out the back. If anyone would like to take cover there, you'd be most welcome," said the assistant.

Before she had finished speaking, the sound of the dreaded V-1 flying bomb could be heard rapidly approaching. It was too late, of course, to think of any kind of shelter. The few people who were in the shop stopped what they were doing and looked up in terror.

Holding Mary's hand, Joanna rolled her eyes upward as the roar of the V-1 grew louder. It sounded as if it was just above the shop. Then the engine stopped. Those fifteen seconds of silence before impact were terrifying.

All the windows in the shop came crashing in when it finally exploded further up the street. There was a collective sigh of relief among the customers. It had been complete mayhem for a while. When the all clear sounded, no one seemed interested in buying shoes anymore.

The amount of carnage from one V-1 had been incredible. Joanna and Mary got up from sheltering behind the counter. They made their way out of the shop and over the rubble, Mary still clutching her treasured shoes. Joanna had one thought in mind: getting to some kind of safety before Hitler unleashed more of his deadly weapons.

Outside was filled with the echo of bells ringing from ambulances and fire engines chasing around all over the place and trying to save lives. ARP men hastily blew their whistles, directing traffic and comforting the people who were walking around in a daze close to where the V-1 had dropped.

Joanna realized traffic would be diverted. She asked a warden where they could catch a bus to Greenhithe. He told her where to go.

"Be careful where you walk," he called. "There's a lot of burning debris lying around."

"Yes, thank you. I will," replied Joanna.

Once on the bus, she felt more relaxed. They were on their way home, out in the open countryside. The driver had to slow down when they approached Horns Cross. He eventually stopped, jumped down from his cabin, and came around into the bus. He spoke to the conductress first, and then announced that a couple of flying bombs had dropped nearby. He stated it would be impossible to try and get through at the moment.

"I'm very sorry, folks. But unfortunately there isn't much I can do about it until they clear the road. So anyone who lives close by, you'd be quicker making your own way home. All those for Gravesend, stay on the bus. I shouldn't think it'll take them long to clear the way."

Joanna and Mary, followed by a few others, alighted the bus and began the rest of their journey on foot. The debris grew worse as they approached the corner of the lane. Joanna had a dreadful feeling of foreboding.

They walked further along and found a massive accumulation of rubble and burning debris. The ARP and fire brigade were running around franticly.

Joanna heard someone shout, "We can't find anyone. It looks as if there was nobody in the house."

"It doesn't matter. For God's sake, carry on digging," came the hurried reply.

Joanna recognized old Bob's voice as they turned the corner. Bushes had been ripped from their roots and torn apart.

One of the firemen called out, "I wouldn't go up there, lady. One of those flying bombs has just landed."

Joanna saw old Bob's face appear from behind a broken tree. He stared at her and paused. Then he looked straight into her eyes. He didn't speak.

Joanna called, "It's my place?"

Bob nodded.

She stood on a mound of earth looking down at the big, black hole where her house should be without saying a word.

Someone from behind her echoed, "I wouldn't go too close, lady."

Bob laid a kindly hand on her shoulder. He spoke softly. "Jo, my dear, I'm terribly sorry. I just don't know what to say. I have informed the others that you're the owner. They wondered if you had any idea where your neighbors are."

Joanna appeared not to have heard him. Then she answered in a dazed, almost disassociated voice, "What? Oh, yes. The prom. The prom in Gravesend." She repeated the words as if she'd just regained consciousness. "They have Peggy, our dog."

"Blimey. What a lucky dog," said one of the men.

"What about the other side?" questioned Bob.

Joanna held her hand to her head, and whispered as if in a dream, "Oh, I have no idea where Dr. Stanley and his wife are."

"Better check on that," said Bob, addressing one of the firemen.

Joanna looked as if she couldn't quite comprehend the entirety of the situation.

Bob shook his head, looking into the big, black hole. "The bastards," he muttered.

Mary sat sobbing on a large piece of stone. "Oh, Mummy, why did it have to be our house? Our beautiful house. We have no home now. I hate those terrible Nazis. I really hate them," she screamed. "I hate them. I wish they were all dead."

Joanna turned around and knelt down beside her daughter amongst the rubble.

She held her in her arms, and whispered, "Hush now, sweetheart. That's enough." Holding her daughter in her arms seemed to give her solace. "There are many people in this war with far greater reasons to hate them than we have. You must not speak in such a way. But you're quite right when you say we have no home. We have less than that, Mary. All we have now are the clothes we stand in." Her voice sounded flat and hollow. "However, what we do have is our life, our love for each other, and Daddy, who is alive and well. With that alone, we must be thankful. We can build a new future when the war is over. This is something more precious than money can buy. It's a heavenly gift. Remember that, Mary, my darling."

Mary stopped sobbing. She put her hand in her pocket and produced a sixpence.

"Look, Mummy, what I've just found."

Joanna looked at the coin and endeavored to smile.

Bob looked at Joanna. "Thank Gawd they were detached houses. Otherwise there would have been worse tragedies."

At that moment, one of the wardens shouted out, "Bob, I've found someone. I don't know whether he's still alive. He looks in a bad way. He was over there at the back of that old oak tree."

Joanna turned her head towards her neighbor's house, her eyes full of pain, as they carried Dr. Stanley out to a waiting vehicle. As she looked, her throat constricted, and she felt choked. He'd helped her so much. Why did it seem like so many good people were dying in this dreadful war?

"Sad about the poor old chap," said one of the men. "He was a very good doctor."

Joanna heard and she called out, wanting Dr. Stanley to be truly remembered, "He was more than that. He was an angel of a man. A wonderful angel." With tears pricking her eyes, Joanna looked down at the sixpence in the palm of Mary's hand.

"Keep that sixpence safe, sweetheart, and pray that it will bring us luck. Always keep it with you."

As Joanna spoke, they heard Peggy barking in the distance.

Chapter 43

David arrived home. He had been given a short forty-eight-hour leave after heavy air attacks over the French coast. He was eager to marry Nina without delay by special license. She, however, felt differently.

"No, we can't do that, darling. We're not prepared, and I would like to have the boys down from Scotland."

"Why is it, Nina, that whenever I mention marriage, you make some excuse?"

She put her hand to his thin, drawn face. He looked totally exhausted.

"I'm not making excuses, David. You know I love you. It's just that I would like everything to be right. And you, my love, must get some rest before you return to base."

He bent his head forward and kissed the palm of her hand.

"You're quite right, my dearest. I understand. We'll make it on my next long leave."

Nina appeared more relaxed. "That would be better, David. It will give me time to get everything arranged, and, with a bit of luck, the war may even be over by then."

"How right you are, darling. But we're going to need a great deal of luck before it's over."

"Indeed."

"I doubt very much whether it'll be over by my next leave. That madman will fight to the bitter end."

Marianne came running in from the garden. "Look, Uncle David. I've just found these two baby frogs in the stream."

Already, Marianne was treating him like the father she had never known.

David immediately responded to her charm. "They look delightful little things, Marianne, my sweet. But I think we should pop them back in the stream."

"Oh, why?" said Marianne in a disappointed tone.

"Because their mother will be wondering where they are. She'll be thinking something has happened to them."

"Oh, I didn't think of that."

David laughed. "Come on. We'll pop them back." He winked at Nina as he walked off into the garden.

"Well, while you two are playing, I'll make a pot of tea," she said.

Nina usually had a housekeeper but today was her day off. David made absolutely sure that Nina usually didn't lift a finger.

Nina paused in the doorway when returning into the lounge carrying the tea tray.

"Well," said David, laughing as he entered through the French windows, "we've restored the frog family back to their former glory again. I think you'll have to explain a little animal biology to your young daughter before she's much older. She's sitting out there watching the frogs with goggle eyes. She asked me why they keep giving each other piggyback rides." He laughed heartily then glanced at Nina. "Why, what's the matter, darling?"

She suddenly looked ashen. He hastily took the tea tray.

"Sit down. I'll pour."

"Oh, it's nothing. Please don't fuss, David. I'm all right. Really. I was thinking about what you said."

"What was that, my love?"

"The fact that bloody little Hitler is going to carry on to the bitter end. I just thought about poor Jo and Mary being down there amongst it all. It must be dreadful for them."

"Yes, I'm sure it is," said David, with thoughtful reflection.

"It must be strange for her having to share rooms with old Tom after her lovely home was destroyed. She was even thinking of having her mother home."

"Well, she can't now," clipped David, his voice sounding cold and hard. "And I don't want to see you getting upset by worrying and making yourself ill again. You've asked her to come up with Mary, and she flatly refused you. It's her choice, darling, and there's nothing we can do to make her change her mind. Anyway, what's wrong with sharing rooms in Tom's luxurious apartment? I could think of worse suffering, and so can you, my love, if you care to speak the truth."

Nina paused. She looked straight into his eyes. "Precisely, David. That's the reason why I feel I must help her. You know what it's like down there. It must be terrible for poor Mary."

"You're absolutely right, darling. It's utter hell. However, what can we do if she prefers to stay where she is and continue to act the heroine? She's probably enjoying every minute of it. You know what she's like, darling. It's people like Jo who'll get very bored when it's all over."

"Oh, how can you say such a terrible thing, David, when you know very well she's the dearest friend I've ever had?" Nina had tears in her eyes. "If it wasn't for her, I would not be here now."

"I know sweetheart." He put his arms around her, and whispered, "She's a wonderful person. But you mustn't make yourself ill over her. She wouldn't wish that either."

Tom, anxious to help Joanna, had given her his two largest rooms on the second floor with an adjoining bathroom and connecting kitchen leading from the lounge.

"Uncle, please. I insist on taking the two upper rooms. You're a darling. You've given us so much. But you cannot go up and down all these stairs. Especially during the night raids. You've already had one heart attack."

With eyes twinkling, he smiled. "Now, look here, young lady. Whose house is this?"

"Oh, don't be silly, Uncle. You're the big, white chief. However, I'll not stand by and watch you kill yourself. I simply will not allow it. You've been an angel in disguise. I really have no idea what we would do without you."

He looked at her tenderly. "My dear Jo, this is your home, and it's been a pleasure to have you here. I'm an old man, and you have Mary to consider. She must be your main concern. I can make my own way down at my leisure." Tom laughed. "I'll enjoy putting you in charge of the kitchen."

"Oh, Uncle, you are a dear."

"Yes, I know I am," he said, smiling.

In the weeks that followed for many who lived in the southeast, it was the blitz all over again. Joanna continued working part time for the Red Cross, which had naturally grown busier. She also helped Tom with his work whenever possible. He had been terribly busy and was now working solo, having lost his one and only member of staff during an air raid, a young junior clerk of only seventeen. Joanna felt it imperative that she help this lovely man, who had given so much of himself to the war effort, as well as his love and care for her and Terry.

When the night raids intensified, Joanna's loyalties were once again divided. Nina had begged her to allow Mary to stay with her in the north. But Joanna had mixed feelings. She had considered taking Mary to Derbyshire. Logic dictated that Nina was right. Yet taking her posed an even greater threat: traveling across London, maybe during an air raid.

Joanna always believed that in some odd way, they would be safe if they stayed together.

She often cast her memory back to London and the blitz of 1940 and 1941. She remembered seeing all the children lined up on the platform like cattle. Some were little more than toddlers. They had labels pinned on their coats and were carrying their gas masks around their little necks, totally unaware of where they were going or who with. Joanna had looked down at her child, who couldn't speak a word, and vowed she would never send her away. Never in a million years.

She realized now it would be different, of course. Mary would be with Nina and her mother. However, Joanna was never going to send Mary away against her will. At least here, she was always with her.

Joanna never allowed her daughter out of her sight. She used the Red Cross van to take her to and from school. Mary was well cared for by the nuns who would take her, and the other children, down to the crypt during raids, which was as safe as anywhere in the region. But then, upon reflection, who knows? Oh God, how she wished this bloody war was over.

For Mary, the V-1 flying bombs would be something she would remember for the rest of her life. Some nights were worse than others. She would sit under the stairs in the hall beside Tom, holding onto Peggy with all her strength. Her mother would be upstairs making a pot of tea to cheer them all up. The roar of the V-1 could be heard growing louder, and then, when it cut out, the engine stopped. On many occasions, it sounded as if it was right above the building.

Mary would look up, wide-eyed in terror, at the ceiling. In her child's mind, it sounded like a wild beast roaring before devouring its victim alive. The fifteen seconds of silence before impact would denote whether she would be in this life or the next. Mary prayed out loud. It helped her overcome her fear of death, knowing she would enter the next world praying to God.

Then came the explosion somewhere nearby. Mary would stare at her mother, who most probably would be standing at the foot of the stairs holding a tea tray with cups and saucers rattling.

Expressing her thoughts aloud, Mary would often hear her mother say, "I wonder which one of the poor souls received that one." Mary always remembered that her mother's calm voice would then announce, "Nice cup of tea, my darlings." And once again, Mary would realize that she must be the luckiest girl in the whole wide world to be alive and have such a wonderful mother.

Occasionally, Joanna came home early. This gave her the opportunity to help Tom with his work. She had grown concerned for his health since his last heart attack. On one such afternoon, when entering the hall, she overheard voices coming from his office. She naturally assumed Tom had a client with him until she heard laughter and immediately recognized David's voice. She paused for a second, curious.

It was unusual for him to stop off here on route unless he had urgent news.

"Why, hello, David. What a lovely surprise. To what do we owe this visit?"

Joanna didn't fail to notice how thin and tired David had grown since his last visit. She knew he had been on endless missions since being transferred to bomber command. The war had definitely taken its effect on him.

"I do hope Mother and Nina are keeping well?" she inquired anxiously.

"Have no fear. They're both fine."

"Yes, worry pot, they're both well," mirrored Tom in a comic, jocular fashion, beaming from cheek to cheek. "Nina and David are getting married on his next long leave. He just popped in to give us the good news."

"Oh, I'm delighted. That's wonderful news," said Joanna with a broad smile.

"My words exactly," said Tom. "Now if you would take David upstairs, my dear, and give him a little refreshment, I'll join you as soon as I'm finished here."

"Oh, please, sir, don't let me put you to any inconvenience. I can't stay long anyway. Got to get back to base as soon as possible. They've got a flap on."

"Nonsense, my boy. It's a while since we've had anything to celebrate, and your base is quite near here, isn't it?"

"Okay," said David, smiling. "You win. But I promise you, I can't stay long."

Joanna led the way upstairs and showed David into the lounge.

"Please do take a seat, David."

Taking off her Red Cross hat, she loosened her hair, which had been tied up in a bun.

"Now, what would you like to eat? I'm afraid there isn't much of a choice.

Spam and cress sandwiches. Cheese and cress sandwiches. Or maybe you'd like something hot? Oh yes, and I have some fairy cakes I baked at the weekend."

"Please, Jo, I…"

Joanna continued to describe the contents of the larder whilst making her way into the kitchen.

"Please, Jo. Thank you. I really don't feel that hungry."

"Oh, but I insist, David. You must have something to keep your strength up. Especially now," she said cheekily, her eyes twinkling. She began making the sandwiches. "I'm so pleased you've named the happy day. It's wonderful news. When did you say it's going to be?"

"Well, we haven't exactly chosen the day yet. God knows when I'll get my next long leave."

"Why not make it on your next long weekend?"

"I'd like that, Jo. But Nina would like to have the boys down from Aberdeen. She's quite right, of course. That's why I'm leaving all the arrangements to her."

"Oh, I understand," said Joanna in a quiet, reflective tone. She placed the sandwiches deftly on the plate. "With us women, our maternal instincts preside over everything else."

Joanna picked up the tea tray and carried it into the lounge. David followed with the plate of sandwiches.

"Yes," continued David. "But some mothers' instincts seem to have the capacity to preside over their children so much, even to the extent of undermining their safety."

Joanna, in the process of pouring the tea, paused. She raised her eyes and gave David a long, hard stare. She didn't respond. Joanna couldn't quite understand why he made the remark, and she chose to ignore it by speaking of her mother and the food shortages.

"Your mother is fine," said David. "Practically her normal self. The staff see that she has plenty of good food to eat, and living in the heart of the Derbyshire Dales helps too. She misses you, of course."

"Yes, I know. Poor darling. Do give her my love when you see her again, David."

"Yes, I will when I see her again. But I think it would be better coming from you personally."

"Well, I do write and ring her regularly."

David looked slightly irritated that she hadn't touched upon his remark, and sighed. "You know, Jo, Nina's worried out of her life about you and Mary."

"Worried? Why?"

"Being down here amongst all this, and I must say, I agree with her when you could very well be safely out of harm's way."

"I appreciate Nina's concern. You must tell her not to worry, David. There really is no need."

Her words kindled David's reaction. "No need? How on earth can you sit there and calmly say that? No need indeed! People are getting killed every day by these damned flying bombs, and you say no need."

"Okay, David, will you please come straight to the point? What's bothering you?"

"Very well. Nina is worrying herself sick over you and Mary down here. So much so that it's making her ill again."

"One moment, David. I thought I heard you say Nina's keeping well?"

"She is. But you know as well as me that she's living on borrowed time. What I'm trying to say, Jo, is won't you please come up and stay with her? If not for yourself, for Mary."

"No. I'm sorry, David. I can't. I've told Nina a dozen times that I cannot leave here. And Mary certainly wouldn't wish to go without me, not after what happened last time."

"Then why in heaven's name will you not come with her?"

"I have already explained, and quite frankly, David, it has nothing to do with you."

"Oh yes it has when it involves Nina's health. I tried to tell her what your reaction would be from the very start. But she wouldn't listen. I can't understand you, Jo. What kind of mother are you to allow your child to live in fear like this?"

Joanna, with fury in her eyes, stood up and walked over to him, her long, blonde hair dancing on her shoulders. She looked up at him. "No one has ever spoken to me like that before."

"Well, they have now, Joanna."

"How dare you speak to me in such a way? You have no idea how I've suffered."

She raised her hand to strike him across the cheek. But he was quicker and, in a split second, he grabbed her by the wrist and pulled her to him. Suddenly, his lips were on hers.

"I've always wanted to do this."

Then, realizing what had happened, he released her immediately.

She backed away, staring at David in astonishment. "You bastard. Get out of here."

"Joanna, please. I don't know what came over me. I'm sorry. I swear it will never happen again. It's just that you…" He paused.

"I remind you of Ann," said Joanna in an icy voice. "Please go, David. Get out of here."

David lowered his head, nodded, and then turned and walked out the door. He put one foot on the top stair, looked down, and found Tom lying in a heap at the foot of the stairs.

"Joanna," he called. "Come quick. It's Tom." David swiftly descended the stairs and loosened Tom's collar. "He's okay. He's still breathing. It's his heart."

Tom had his head turned to one side. He looked a ghastly gray color.

Joanna smoothed his face tenderly between the palms of her hands.

She said softly, "Uncle? Uncle, darling? Wake up, Uncle."

Tom turned his head slowly and stared into Joanna's eyes. He babbled, "Where am I?"

"You're at home with Joanna, my darling," she replied.

David stood back looking from one to the other. He'd seen some miracles in his lifetime, but none performed with such sanctity as this. It was as if she had called him back from beyond the grave.

David whispered, "Jo, have you any cognac?"

"Yes. Upstairs in the kitchen cabinet."

Slowly, Tom began to recover enough to allow David to carry him up to Joanna's bedroom.

"He'll be okay now," said David. "He's almost back to his normal color. Better to let him rest now."

"Yes, and I've just called his doctor, though he won't thank me for it," said Joanna. "Dr. Morgan has tried desperately to make him retire. Tom just refuses to listen. He has severe angina since he had his last heart attack. I suppose you knew that, David?"

"Yes, I gathered that." David looked ill at ease. "Well, I should really be shooting off. But under the circumstances, I think I'll wait until his doctor arrives. I'll ring up the base and tell them I'll be a little late."

"No. You can't do that. You must go. I can manage now. Thank you, David. I appreciate your kind help. The last time he had one of these attacks, I stayed with him downstairs until he recovered. That's why we put the soft armchair in his office. Just in case."

"We? Who's we, Jo? Don't tell me you and Mary moved that heavy armchair."

Joanna smiled. "No. It was a few of weeks ago when poor Alan the office boy worked here."

"Where is he now?"

"Killed by a doodlebug."

David lowered his head. "Oh, I see." Suddenly everything became clearer to him.

"You see, David, someone has to stay and do their bit. Otherwise there would be nothing left worth fighting for. And I intend to do mine until it's all over, and Terry walks through that door. But thank you, once again, for your kind help."

"May I presume that we're still friends?"

"We will always be friends, David."

"Thank you, Jo."

Joanna paused. "David, there is something I'd like to ask you."

"Go ahead."

"Do you really love Nina?"

He answered in the words he knew she wished to hear. "Of course I love her. More than anything in this world. And once again, Jo, I'm terribly sorry for what happened here today. I was just carried away. Quite a few of us are behaving strange these days. They call it battle fatigue."

She smiled. "I understand, David, and nothing did happen here today. Now go and win the war for us. Then come home and do that which you love most."

"Oh, what's that?"

"Flying. Playing golf. Curing the sick."

He smiled. "Well, you know, you're quite good at the latter yourself. In fact, you're amazing." He gazed into her eyes. "Take care, Jo."

"Yes. I'll try, and you too."

David smiled, and then quietly left.

Chapter 44

"Mummy, can I invite Anna for tea tonight?"

"No, I'm afraid not, Mary. Uncle is still unwell."

"Yes, I know, Mummy. But if he had a bad heart attack then why is he still working?"

"Well, he shouldn't be, Mary."

Tom appeared in the doorway. "Of course I should, and you can bring your friend to tea, Mary."

"Oh, hello, Uncle," said Joanna, looking surprised. "I thought you were having your afternoon nap."

"I was, until Peggy decided it was time for me to get up by washing my face all over with her tongue. Take her for a run in the garden, would you, Mary? And see that she doesn't make a nuisance of herself with the chickens again."

"Very well, Uncle, and thank you so much."

She beamed from cheek to cheek and ran down the stairs with Peggy close on her heels.

"Really, Uncle, you spoil her," said Joanna.

"And why not? The poor child has little enough as it is with this damn war dragging on so long. I sincerely hope that, in generations to come, this nation will remember the tremendous sacrifice this country has made for the price of freedom. I pray that we are never inadequate enough, or imbecilic enough, to ever sell it cheap, and never allow any country, creed, or sect try and dictate to us in any aspect of the word."

Joanna smiled. "You sound like Winston Churchill, Uncle."

"Good Lord, I hope not. The man is overweight. He eats and drinks far too much. Damn fine leader though."

Joanna smiled. "Yes. I agree with you, Uncle. However, some people have short memories, and I very much doubt if anyone would want to remember this era."

"I only hope you're wrong, Jo. However, it's up to people like you, Terry, and Mary. She will remember what we are going through every day of our lives, and with a bit of luck, if we survive, Mary will hand these facts down to her generation and her children."

"Anyway, Uncle, it's time for afternoon tea. Like a cup?"

"What? Oh, yes. Yes, of course, my dear."

Joanna went into the kitchen and put the kettle on.

Tom continued to mutter to himself, "I hope you're wrong, Jo. I only hope you're wrong."

She realized this was something about which he felt very deeply.

"Mummy, Mummy," cried Mary, running up the stairs with Peggy in quick pursuit. "I managed to put my hand inside the chicken run behind the trap door. And look! Nancy's laid two eggs."

"Oh, that's wonderful, Mary. How did you manage to do that?"

"Peg barked then Nancy clacked and flapped her wings. She is silly. She didn't realize I was taking her eggs. I did it once before. You'd think she'd realize by now, wouldn't you?"

Joanna laughed. "You be careful she doesn't snap your hand off. Nancy can give a nasty bite."

"Why can't we let them all out into the garden?"

"No, I don't think so, Mary. The last time we did that, the very next day, a doodlebug dropped. Uncle and I had to run around all the gardens searching for them. When we did find them, they had half their feathers shot off."

Mary burst out laughing. "I wondered why they looked moth-eaten. I thought they had all began to molt like dogs."

Tom chuckled. "Well, at least you have something for your breakfast. Now, Mary, my child, you can invite your friend any time you wish."

Joanna sighed, looking at Tom with a whimsical smile. "Very well. How about Sunday? What would Anna like to eat? Not that there is much of a choice. Winkles, shrimps, and watercress, they're fresh in on Sunday."

"Oh, that would be wonderful, Mummy. I'll tell her when I see her tomorrow."

"Yes, Mary, and tell mother superior I'll pick Anna up about mid-afternoon when I've finished work, and I'll take her back in the evening."

"Well, I'm glad that's settled. I've had my nap. Now I'm going to start work again," said Tom, winking at Mary.

"Don't overdo it, Uncle," called Joanna.

Tom whispered to Mary, "That's my orders. Your mother is becoming more like a sergeant major every day."

Mary nodded and laughed.

Mary's friend, Anna, had recently become orphaned and sent down from London to seek accommodation in the convent until suitable foster parents could be found. Failing this, she would inevitably be placed in a convent orphanage. Anna was an extremely beautiful girl with long, jet-black hair and dark, flashing eyes. Mary felt terribly sorry for her, and the two girls had become very close rapidly.

Mary threw her arms around her mother. "I'm so pleased you've invited Anna. I like her very much. I'll help you in preparing the tea, Mummy." Mary looked sad. "I wish we could do something to help her. I think I'd die if anything happened to you and Daddy."

"You mustn't say such things, Mary. Nothing is going to happen."

"No, of course it's not. I'm sorry."

Mary quickly changed the subject. "You know, Mummy, Anna really is a funny girl. Or maybe I'm just stupid? But…" Mary sat and thought, looking blankly into space.

"But what, Mary?"

"Well, do you remember the other Saturday when you took me to confession, and then you left to do some shopping?"

"Yes. I remember. What's funny about that?"

"Well, we confess our sins so that we can take Holy Communion. That's right, isn't it?"

"Yes," said Joanna, wondering what her daughter was going to say next.

"Well, I did something very silly." Mary began to struggle with her words again.

Joanna looked amused. "Yes? I'm waiting, Mary. Whatever you did couldn't have been all that bad if it was in church."

"You see. You're getting ready to laugh at me, and I haven't said anything yet."

"What is the matter with you, Mary? One minute you're telling me how funny Anna is, and the next you're saying how silly you are. Now, what is it, Mary?"

"Promise you won't laugh."

"I promise."

"Well, I was in the confessional, and it was the old priest in there, the one who gives me lots of penances. Well, you know, Mummy, I'd only missed mass four times, and he gave me four Lord's Prayers and six Hail Marys and the Stations of the Cross. Well, I couldn't concentrate on the prayers knowing I had the Stations of the Cross to do. I felt ashamed. I thought people in church would think I'd committed a very bad crime. So I went back into the confessional and told him..."

"Well? What did you tell him, Mary?"

"That I'd made a big mistake and only missed mass twice. He said, 'God bless you, child. Say three Hail Marys and three of the Lord's Prayer."

Joanna gave a slight cough trying to refrain from laughing. "Yes, well, darling, I'm sure God will forgive you for that little lie."

"No, Mummy, it's not God I'm thinking about. It's Anna. She was standing at the back of the church laughing like mad. She said I didn't have to do that. I wish I could be more like Anna. She's so grown up and yet we're nearly the same age."

"Mary, darling, poor little Anna has had to grow up fast. You enjoy what little time you have left of your childhood. For you never get it back."

Mary looked long-faced and not at all convinced.

"Anyway," said Joanna. "That's enough of this silly talk. I believe there are some sweets in the jar. Have a look, Mary."

"No. We haven't. I had the last two this morning. I'm sorry, Mummy."

"Well, I'm sorry too, Mary, because that's all our points used up until next week."

Mary walked over to the kitchen drawer where her mother kept the ration books.

"No Mummy, you've still got points," exclaimed Mary. "Two ounces on mine and four ounces on yours."

"Really? I had no idea. We'll have a picnic, Mary."

"Can I go to the corner shop and get some?"

"Yes. I'll just put this pie in the oven and we'll both go."

"Oh, let me go on my own. Please, Mummy. I'm fed up with being cooped up here. There haven't been any doodlebugs for three days now, and it's just around the corner."

Joanna knew she couldn't keep Mary a prisoner forever. She felt apprehensive. Nevertheless, she agreed.

"Very well. You may go. But do take care."

"Can I take Peg with me?"

"Yes. Put her lead on. I don't want her roaming all over the place."

"Very well, Mummy. Did you hear that, Peg? I'm taking you for a run."

Peggy jumped up, scampered to the corner, pulled down her lead, and then sat upright in a begging position with the lead in her mouth. Joanna smiled, glancing at the little dog. But every fiber of her body trembled as she wrestled with her conscience. She realized that she must be more confident and trusting of her daughter's abilities to handle her own life. She had, after all, seen many children playing around down the prom and elsewhere.

"Now, you're to be a good girl," said an excited Mary, clipping the lead to Peggy's collar. "TTFN, Mummy. I won't be long" She ran down the stairs.

Joanna tried to relax and continued with what she was doing.

Four minutes later, the siren sounded.

Within seconds, the dreaded sound of the V-1 flying bomb was to be heard yet once again. Joanna ran down the stairs like the wind. She threw open the front door, calling out to Tom at the same time, "Uncle, take cover. I'm off to get Mary."

She fled down the street.

Somewhere in the background, an ARP warden yelled, "The bastard is right above us. For God's sake, take cover."

Joanna didn't heed the warning. She just kept on running and looking up at the flying bomb. She turned the corner, and within a few yards of Philpot's Sweet Shop, she screamed, "Mary! Mary, are you there?"

Mary heard her mother's voice. "Mummy," she screamed out.

The flying bomb flew straight ahead and exploded near the riverfront. It was too late. The blast threw Joanna across the road, her head crashing into a telephone pole.

The ARP warden had taken cover in a shop doorway. After the explosion, he went in search of the screaming woman. Mr. Philpot opened his door to find the warden holding Joanna in his arms. He carried her inside and laid her on the floor.

Mr. Philpot asked, "Is she alive?"

The warden shook his head. "I doubt if anyone could survive that."

Mr. Philpot knelt down amongst the rubble beside Joanna and took her pulse. Both men shook their heads.

"I'm afraid she's gone."

Mary screamed out, "No! No, Mummy. Mummy. No."

Mrs. Philpot tried to restrain her, but she broke free and dashed to her mother's side.

"Mummy! Mummy," she sobbed. "Don't leave me. Please, please, don't leave me. Dear God, please don't take my mummy." Then Mary spoke in a calmer voice and held her mother's hand tight. "Mummy. Mummy, don't go. Don't leave me alone. Please stay here with me, Mummy. I love you so much, Mummy. Mummy..."

Mrs. Philpot held Joanna's other hand and felt her pulse.

Astonished, she said, smiling, "She's still breathing. Her pulse rate is low, but she's still with us."

Mary kept talking to her mother, telling her to stay with her. Then the all clear sounded and the ambulance arrived. They put Joanna on a stretcher. The driver announced that no children were allowed.

Mary stood up, raised her shoulders squarely, held her head up high, and declared with a voice of authority, "I am not a child. I'm staying with my mother."

Mr. Philpot explained to the driver that this was an exceptional case, and Mary should stay with her mother.

Mary looked at Mr. Philpot, and in an adult tone of command, she stated, "I wonder whether you'd mind informing my Uncle Tom of what had just occurred, and also, if you wouldn't mind taking care of Peggy for me."

"Of course I will, darling. You leave it all to me." Looking at her tight, worried, little face, he said, "Your mum's going to pull through. Don't you worry, my love. She's a fighter."

During the week that followed, Tom and Mary were constantly visiting Joanna. Mary rarely left her mother's bedside.

One afternoon before Joanna had been taken off the critical list, Mary looked up from dozing against her mother to see David standing at the bottom of her bed. He put his index finger to his lips. He kissed Mary gently on the cheek and whispered, "Don't say a word, Mary, my dear child." Then he patted her lovingly on the shoulder and left quickly.

When Joanna had recovered enough to receive visitors and friends from the Red Cross, the mother superior and Sister Patrick showered her with gifts. She had been overwhelmed by their kindness. The day before she was due to leave the hospital, the duty doctor asked to see Tom.

"Do take a seat, Mr. Busher."

Poor old Tom looked anxious as he sat down on the edge of the chair.

"Please relax, Mr. Busher. Don't be alarmed. I haven't bad news."

"Thank God for that," said Tom, sighing with relief.

"Your niece, Mrs. Busher, has made a remarkable recovery. In fact, it's really quite amazing. We're very pleased with her, and, as you know, she can go home tomorrow." The doctor smiled. "She'll have to take it easy for quite a while, of course. But Mrs. Busher is a very strong lady. Anyone who can survive a blast like that and a crack on the head..." He paused. "Well, it's really incredible."

Tom interrupted him, looking puzzled. "If my niece is well enough to leave tomorrow, then what is it that you wish to discuss with me, my dear young sir?"

"Well, I'm baffled, Mr. Busher. Two men, Mr. Philpot and the ARP warden, took her pulse and both initially pronounced Mrs. Busher dead."

"Well," said Tom, "I think we were all a little stunned by the bomb landing so close."

"Yes, I agree," said the doctor. "But all the ARP wardens have taken courses in first aid. Yet when her daughter began speaking to her, and then Mrs. Philpot took her pulse, her heart was beating."

"Well, perhaps Mrs. Philpot is a little better at first aid. Or maybe, it just wasn't Joanna's time to go," said Tom in a confused voice. He really didn't know what to believe.

"Yes. I thought that at first, until we allowed her daughter, Mary, into the ward. We were breaking the rules having a child by her bedside for such a long period. So, the next day, we didn't allow her to visit. That night, your niece took a sharp decline. That's when I suggested, against a great deal of opposition, I might add, that her daughter be allowed into the ward every day from then on. Now, Mr. Busher, I'm just a junior doctor, you understand, and we're very busy here. So whatever proposals I may put forward are hardly likely to be accepted. However, I have noticed that, in some cases, having a relative or loved one by the patient's bedside is of great help. It's to do with that connection. Somehow, the patient draws energy from their loved one."

"Oh, I agree with you entirely, my dear fellow."

"You do?" said the doctor, appearing somewhat surprised.

"Yes, I do indeed. However, I find it advisable to remain a little closed these days. People are so cynical, what with the war and death being all around us. But I still have my own personal feelings on such matters." Tom looked a bit embarrassed. He coughed and straightened. "I would like to say, however, that I cannot thank you enough, young man, for all your good help."

"Then I take it that I can rely upon your support in putting this proposal forward to the hospital board?"

"Why, of course you can, my dear fellow, if it's going to save lives." Tom smiled. "Well, if that is all you need of me, doctor," continued Tom, leaving the consulting room, "I really must get back to my two young women."

The doctor smiled warmly. "Yes, of course, and I have the rest of this block to get through."

Tom nodded.

The doctor walked with Tom out into the corridor.

"Good news about Paris, isn't it?" said Tom. "I left my niece, Mary, giving her mother a running commentary on it. Her father, my nephew, is over there. He's alive and well. Thank God. He was one of the first to land, you know."

"Was he really?" said the young doctor, smiling. "You must be very proud of him."

"Yes, I am indeed." Tom sighed, looking down at his toes. "However, I'll feel more relaxed when I see him again."

"Yes, of course," agreed the doctor. "I sometimes wish I were over there with them in the medical core."

"Nonsense. We need more good men like yourself. You're doing a worthwhile job here. And thank you, once again, my dear fellow, for saving my niece's life."

"You keep thanking me, Mr. Busher. But you seem to forget your young niece, Mary, had a great deal to do with it."

Tom nodded. He had a faraway look in his eyes. "Yes. Indeed. She's a wonderful child. Just like her mother."

On Saturday 26th August, Joanna came home after a four-week stay in hospital.

Mary and Tom saved their meat ration for two weeks in preparation of her return to give her a scrumptious dinner of roast beef, roast potatoes, and vegetables with the help of Mary's friend, Anna. Nobody seemed capable of cooking a Yorkshire pudding. But Mrs. Philpot came to their rescue. She brought chocolates for Joanna and mixed sweets for all and sundry.

Anna had now been given a home with a good family in Claraden Road, which was just around the corner from Tom's apartment. Since there hadn't been many air raids in the past week, the two girls would meet up by the clock tower before going to school. Anna gave Mary great support during the difficult period while her mother was ill.

"Is Mrs. Lang giving you a birthday party on Saturday, Anna?"

"No."

"Why ever not?"

"Well, she was going to, but then she found out she had to work this

Saturday, and she's usually tired when she gets home."

"Well, what about some other time?"

"No. It wouldn't be worthwhile, Mary. Mr. Lang works nights at Tilbury docks. We'd have to be as quite as mice."

"We never did have that tea we promised you, did we?" said Mary. "Why not come around to our place for your birthday tea?"

"Thank you, Mary. I'd love to. But I'm afraid I'll have to ask Mrs. Lang first. She may need me to help her in the house."

Mary looked surprised. "What? On your birthday?"

Anna appeared a little sad.

"I thought you told me you liked it there?" continued Mary.

"I do, but..." Anna paused. "You know how it is, Mary. They're very nice, but nothing like your mum and Uncle Tom."

"I'm sorry, Anna. I'm sure if we had our own home, Mother would suggest that you live with us."

"I know she would. She's a lovely lady. You're lucky, Mary."

Mary smiled. "Yes. I know I am."

Joanna, with the help of Mary and Tom, prepared a delightful tea for Anna's birthday. She made fairy cakes, jelly, and blancmange.

"Well now, the table looks very inviting," said Tom.

"Yes," agreed Joanna. "Though I very much doubt if you've made enough sandwiches, Uncle. I'll just make a few more."

"Well, they're not going to stuff themselves just on spam and cucumber sandwiches, are they?" said Tom, grinning. "Anyway, lucky to get cucumber at this time of year. I thought they were nearly all finished?"

"They are, really. I just smiled sweetly at the greengrocer and offered him my marrow in exchange for the cucumber. And the cheeky old thing said, 'No, I'd rather have you than your marrow.' But then he did say, 'It's okay. I'm only joking.'"

"And did he take the marrow?"

"Yes. If he hadn't, I think I would have flattened him with it."

Tom laughed with gusto.

Joanna looked at her wristwatch. "Anna will be arriving soon. I must hurry up, Tom. I think I'd better put those shrimps and winkles in the fridge."

"Very well, my dear. I'll let you get on with it. I'm going into the other room to sit down. I'd rather like to hear the news before they arrive."

Joanna looked at her wristwatch again. She appeared agitated as she tried to push what little food they had into Tom's small fridge. She remembered her own large fridge, which sat in the corner of her delightful kitchen. Joanna didn't dare overload this one for fear of alarming Tom. He was so scared it would break and he wouldn't be able to get another. Since the war, they were in short supply and only produced when necessary.

In her haste, Joanna dropped a plate.

Tom called out, "Are you all right, Jo?"

"Yes…Yes, Uncle. I'm not overloading it."

Tom stood in the doorway. She turned to look at him and dropped the shrimps and winkles on the floor.

"Oh, I'm sorry, Uncle. Now look what I've done."

"I'm not bothered about the floor or the stupid fridge," said Tom. "I was about to give you the news I've just heard."

"What is it?" said Joanna, looking anxious.

"Oh, that can wait. What is going on here? Feel like smashing plates, Jo? I thought only the Greeks did that at parties."

"I'm so sorry, Uncle."

"I think you should rest. You've done enough for one day, Jo. I'll do the extra sandwiches. You seem a bundle of nerves, my dear. Just a little while ago, you were happy and laughing. Come and sit down."

"No. No, Uncle. I'll be fine." Joanna, looking down at the floor, held her hand to her head. "I must get back to normal. I've got to pick these up and wash them before Mary returns from the garden with Peg. It's all we have."

Old Tom knelt down beside her. "Oh, dear me," he said. "Now I'm down here, how on earth am I going to get up?"

Joanna smiled. "Don't worry, Uncle. You can lean on me."

They began picking up the shrimps and winkles together.

Tom grinned. "I'll wash these, and no one will know the difference." He looked at her straight in the eyes. "Joanna, my dear, this place is your home to do as you please. However, I promised the doctor you were going to take it easy."

"Well, I have, haven't I?"

"No, you haven't, Jo. You're beginning to race ahead. Four weeks ago, you were at death's door. You've made a remarkable recovery. Keep it that way. Take one day at a time, my dear."

Joanna smiled. "Oh, Uncle, you are so like Terry."

His eyes gleamed. "Do you really think so?"

Joanna nodded.

"That's the nicest complement you could pay me, Jo. Now I think that's enough of the melodrama."

"Yes, and so do I, Uncle. I'll put on the wireless. I believe Itma is on, Mary's favorite program. It'll cheer us up."

To Joanna's surprise, instead of hearing the humorous sound of Tommy Handley, an urgent news bulletin was being issued. It was giving details of a new and terrible weapon known as the V-2s. They were long-range rockets being launched on London and the southeast from Holland and Germany. People had been warned to quickly take cover when they heard the siren.

They both looked at each other.

Tom shook his head. "Dear God, will this madness ever be over?"

Joanna stared at him, and whispered, "But you knew. That's what you were going to say to me." Her glassy eyes and drawn face said it all. "Of course it will be over, Uncle. Of course it will. We must have faith."

Anna's birthday went ahead as planned. Joanna was determined nothing was going to change their way of life, not now or ever. They had all been through far too much.

After tea, all three walked home with Anna, along with Peggy. Before Anna reached for the doorbell, she turned around.

"Thank you all so much for a wonderful birthday. It's the best time I've had since..." She paused. "Well, for years."

She rushed forward and kissed Joanna and Mary then turned to go inside.

Tom shouted, "What about me? Don't I get a kiss?"

Anna giggled and ran up to him.

"I'm so sorry. It's the convent, you know. They say kissing men is dangerous."

Tom and Joanna howled with laughter.

As time passed, Joanna grew restless seeing the devastation the V-2 rockets had caused, adding to the chaos left from the doodlebugs. Just sitting around doing nothing and wondering when the next rocket would drop was driving her mad. She realized that she must get back to normality as soon possible. And that meant work.

Chapter 45

Margaret, Joanna's old friend from Greenhithe, came to visit her and explained that she had recently been transferred from the Red Cross unit in Greenhithe to be made head of the Gravesend branch. She happened to mention how short staffed and busy they had been. A delighted Joanna grasped the opportunity.

"Are you really sure you want to do this, Jo? After all, you've only been out of hospital a short time."

"Of course I'm sure. I'll go crazy if I have to sit around here all day thinking about things. It wouldn't be quite so dreadful if Tom needed me. But since I've been ill, he's found a seventeen-year-old boy to help him with the books. Just lounging around here all day isn't doing me any good. It's just not me, Margaret."

"Okay, Jo. An hour in the morning only."

"No," said Joanna in an adamant tone. "One hour in the morning and two in the afternoon. Also use of the van. That way, I kill two birds with one stone and pick Mary up from school."

Margaret smiled. "You drive a hard bargain, Jo. I've never heard of such shear audacity. If you weren't such a damn good nurse, I'd flatly refuse." Margaret looked at her and sighed. "Okay. You win."

Joanna beamed. "Thank you, Margaret. I assure you, you won't regret it."

Margaret looked at her doubtfully. "Please be careful, my dear."

"I understand what you're trying to say, Margaret. But, quite frankly, is there such a thing as being careful in these times?"

"Mummy, I thought you said you weren't going back for a long time?" asked Mary when Joanna told her she was returning to work.

"Yes, I know what I said, Mary. But I'm so much better now, and at least

I'll have use of the van. I'll be able to run you and Anna to and from school."

Mary sat and thought, tenderly looking at her mother. She smiled and mumbled in a somber voice, "Well, I don't suppose it's so bad."

Joanna stared at Mary, thinking how she had grown up in the past few weeks since her recovery. She marveled at her daughter's amazing courage and how she had brought her back from the edge of death. Joanna always believed that whilst they were together they would always be safe. However, this was a question she never wished to put to the test again.

Mary had become almost over protective of her mother's wellbeing and always felt the need to be near her. Joanna read her mind and laid her arms around Mary's shoulders.

"Don't worry, my darling. I'll be fine. Everything is going to be all right."

"I know it will, Mummy. It's just..." Mary paused. "Well, we haven't heard from Daddy since you were in hospital, have we?"

"No, we haven't, but..." Then Joanna paused. "It takes a long time to receive a delivery these days. But we will. You'll see."

"You seem so sure, Mummy. Why are you always so sure?"

Joanna sighed. She realized that she could not delude Mary any more. Her daughter wasn't stupid. She was able to read the newspapers better than most children her age. Her character and understanding had developed beyond all recognition.

"I'll not pretend to you, Mary. I can only put it this way, which is according to news reports. Daddy, along with many more men, are gaining ground in France. One almighty push is what we need to bring this terrible war to an end. One push to finish it all. However, we must never lose faith that all will be right in the end, and I believe it will be. That's all I can say."

Mary could not help but notice the tension in her mother's eyes as she spoke. She remained silent, and then changed the subject.

"I'll take Peg down and feed the chickens," Mary said, not realizing her mother was currently mixing their food.

"Very well, darling. You take Peggy and I'll bring their food when it's ready."

Once on her own in the kitchen, Joanna pulled out a chair from beneath the table and sat down. She buried her head between her hands, and whispered, "Oh God, when will I ever see my Terry again?"

The V-2 rockets that fell in and around Gravesend caused a blast that could be heard for miles. They were known to drop from a height of fifty miles faster than the speed of sound. Yet Mary didn't feel as afraid of these monstrous weapons as she had with the V-1 doodlebugs. Maybe it was because, so far, none had dropped within the immediate vicinity of Harmer Street. Or perhaps it was due to the fact that you were unable to hear them coming. It was said that on approaching impact, they made a sound similar to that of a train letting off a gust of steam.

Starting work boosted Joanna's confidence. She began to look and feel better. Yet within her subconscious lurked a terror she was desperately trying to overcome since her confrontation with the V-1 doodlebug.

"Oh, Jo, am I pleased to see you this morning. Dartford unit suffered a terrible blasting last night. They're setting up a new unit outside of town. Westhill are helping the best they can, but they're inundated too. Honestly, what a mess. Anyway, since we've had two deliveries this week, I said we'd help. So would you be a dear and take this consignment up to Westhill as soon as possible?" Margaret noted the expression on Joanna's face change. "I know it's a bit of a nerve asking you to drive so far at such short notice. However, they are in great need, Jo. The casualties they've suffered have been catastrophic."

Joanna stared blankly into space and then replied, "Yes, of course I'll go. But as much as I'd like to help, Margaret, wouldn't it be wise to keep the supplies? I mean, who knows, we may be in the same position ourselves."

"No. We're expecting another delivery tomorrow morning, and Bath Street have enough. I wouldn't ask you, Jo, but..." Margaret paused. "Our two regular drivers are sick, Betty has the flue, Bert's still recovering from the accident he had with his leg last week, and I can't drive."

"Margaret, don't say another word. I'd love to go."

Together, they finished loading the van.

Then Joanna said casually, "Well, that's it. I'd better be off."

"Oh, do have a cup of tea before you go, Jo."

"No, thank you, Margaret. I'd rather like to make an early start. You never know what's in front of you these days."

She climbed into the driving seat and looked down at Margaret.

"It's quite all right, Margaret. Please don't look so worried."

"I feel dreadful asking you to do this when you've only just recovered yourself. I really wouldn't ask you, Jo, if I had someone else. I hope you understand that."

Joanna smiled as she started up the engine. Laughing, she called out, "Have a nice cup of tea and some of your soft rock cakes waiting for me when I return. TTFN."

Margaret, though concerned, could not help but admire her tenacity and courage.

Joanna put her foot down on the accelerator and soon gathered momentum. As she approached Dartford Hill, the siren sounded. She had no intention of stopping. No one else on the road had stopped. It would have been pointless. There was no where she could run anyway. Her hands sweating on the wheel, all she thought of now was making the delivery and returning home as soon as possible.

Just before she turned at the crossroads to go down Dartford Hill, she noticed a young man in naval uniform waving his arms and indicating for her to stop. He had dashed out of one of the nearby houses.

Joanna shouted, "Go away. Are you mad?"

There was something about the urgency in his face that made her stop. She pulled into a turning.

"Please come quick," he said. "My wife's about to give birth."

"All right. Calm down," said Joanna. "Go and bring your wife out. I'll make a place for her at the back of the van. We'll get her to Westhill Hospital in no time."

"But you don't understand. She won't leave the house. She's terrified of these rockets. Please come. It's our first child."

"How far gone is she?"

"She's ready to give birth."

"Where do you live?"

"Over there. Number 10."

"Very well," said Joanna. "I must find a safe place to park. Then I'll be straight with you."

"Please hurry. She's in great pain," said the young man, clasping his hands in anguish.

Joanna drove the van up a driveway between two houses and straight into a private garage. She was trespassing, but she didn't care. Her main concern was to keep the supplies safe.

Back at number 10, on examining the woman, Joanna whispered to the young man, "How long has she been like this?"

"She's had pains on and off all morning. Then, when the siren sounded, they got worse. Oh, what's going to happen, nurse?"

"You're going to be a father, and I need your support," said Joanna calmly. "I can't imagine why you haven't tried to get her doctor before now."

"He lives the other side of Dartford. Oakfield House off Highfield Road. It was difficult, the state she was in."

"Oh, well. Never mind." Joanna sighed. "Do you have any hot running water?"

"No," exclaimed the terrified sailor.

"Then boil as much hot water as you can and hurry."

Meanwhile, the woman continued to scream.

Joanna turned around. "All right, my dear, I'm with you now." She threw off her jacket and rolled up her sleeves. "Right. Let's get started then."

Fifteen minutes later, Rose Thomson was still pushing and screaming her head off.

"You're doing fine, Mrs. Thomson. Another push and we're nearly there. I can see the head clearly. The baby is coming normally. You're nearly there, my dear." Joanna called out, "John, will you please come in here and hold your wife's hand."

He shouted, "I can't watch. I'm scared."

"Come in here now," demanded Joanna harshly.

It wasn't only Rose Thomson who had beads of perspiration rolling down her face, but also Joanna, especially when she heard an explosion in the near vicinity. She kept her mind on the positive thought of new life, not a V-2 taking their lives.

Rose Thomson gave an almighty scream, and the baby's head was out.

"Oh, that's wonderful. You're nearly there, my dear. Baby is nearly born." Joanna, working from one end and trying to comfort Rose from the other, yelled out, "John, will you *please* come in here and be with your wife."

He eventually walked in like a dog with his tail between his legs.

"There," said Joanna. "That's the first sight of your new baby. It won't be long now. Your wife is a brave lady."

Rose Thomson started to scream again, gripping her husband's hand.

"Speak to your wife, for heaven sake. Don't just stand there like a dummy. John, please, I'm telling you, whatever happens next, your main concern is Rose, not what is happening outside. Now say something to her."

Joanna worked meticulously with every contraction. Rose gave a most horrendous scream, and the baby was born. Simultaneously, as Joanna cut the umbilical cord with some scissors, a tremendous explosion erupted. Glass crashed in around them and the whole house shook with the vibrations. Joanna was thrown to the other side of the room whilst John managed to hold down his screaming wife and newly born child.

Joanna had only one thought in mind: to save mother and baby.

Within ten minutes, the all clear sounded and Joanna was laying a baby girl in Rose Thomson's arms.

"Thank you so much for everything, nurse," said Rose Thomson. "We don't even know your name."

"I'm Joanna Busher, and think nothing of it. It's been a pleasure. It was just lucky I brought my little black case." Joanna looked at Rose. "You'll be fine now, but you'll need medical attention. I'll make contact with your doctor. What's his number?"

"Dartford 242," said Rose.

"I'll also try and get someone from Westhill to look in. Depends on how busy they are with this little lot." Joanna smiled. "I must go now. I've left my ambulance in someone's garage."

"Nurse Busher," called Rose in a weak voice. "I've decided what we're going to name our daughter."

"Oh, really?" said Joanna, anxious to get away.

"Yes. I'm calling her Joanna."

Joanna smiled warmly. Her eyes lit up. "Why, thank you. That's the nicest compliment anyone could pay me."

John Thomson escorted Joanna to what was left of their front door.

"Look after her, John. Haven't you any relatives?"

"Well, yes…" He paused. "Both our parents live in Erith. Rose's parents don't approve of me. You see, we had to get married. We intended to marry anyway, but not quite so soon. I was lucky enough to get a spot of leave to be with Rose. I'm due back in a few days in Belfast."

"Well, you contact both your parents and tell them they have a beautiful baby granddaughter. I really must go now. Goodbye and take care of yourself. You're a family man now."

"Goodbye, Mrs. Busher, and thank you once again."

Joanna found the garage door wide open and hanging on its hinges. Yet she was surprised to find the van still intact. Two women were looking over at the vehicle shaking their heads and shrugging their shoulders.

One of the women looked at Joanna. "I suppose this belongs to you?"

"Yes, I'm afraid so. Is this your garage?"

"Yes, it is," replied the older woman.

"I do apologize," said Joanna, and she began to explain.

"Oh, don't bother with all that, love. When we saw it was a Red Cross van, we knew whoever parked it there had a good reason."

"Yes, indeed I had." Joanna smiled. "Thank you very much. You're very kind. By the way, have you any idea where that thing came down?"

"Yes. Three streets away, love," said the younger woman in a cockney accent. "Bloody terrible things. As if we ain't 'ad enough. Hitler needs a bleeding rocket shoved up his arse."

Joanna, scarcely able to refrain from laughing, gave the two women a broad smile.

"Yes. Quite. Well, anyway, thank you very much. Goodbye."

Margaret awaited Joanna's return nervously.

"Oh, thank heavens you've arrived. We thought something had happened to you until we received news from Westhill. My word, Jo. Everything happens to you."

"Yes," said Joanna, laughing. "I have an arrangement with the man upstairs."

They both laughed.

"Seriously though, Jo, the midwife from Westhill has just visited the Thomsons. Apparently they cannot speak highly enough of you. They would also like you to attend their baby's christening."

"Oh, that's very sweet of them. However, I doubt very much if I'll be able to." Joanna stood reflecting for a second. "You know, Margaret, I do so dislike being regarded as a wonder woman, because I'm very far from that. If you hadn't sent me to Dartford, I doubt very much if I'd ever have regained my self-confidence again."

"Oh, I'm sure you would."

Joanna shook her head. "No. Allow me to finish, my dear. I've often thought, if faced with the same adversity as before, just what would I do? Now I don't have to think or wonder anymore. I know. And it's you I have to thank for that. You're a damn fine leader, Margaret."

"Thank you, Jo. I appreciate what you say. It has been rather worrying running a town branch. I only took a first aid course in Greenhithe. However, when I heard you were very ill and they urgently needed someone, I thought I'd like to give it a try. So here I am."

"You're doing incredibly well, Margaret. You've achieved so much since you've been here."

"Thank you, Jo. However, if you'll allow me to finish speaking."

Joanna smiled. "Yes. Go ahead, Margaret."

"The Thomsons also described you to the midwife. They said not only were they aware of your efficiency, but also of your kind love and consideration. John Thomson admitted he was terrified when the rocket dropped. He thought you were knocked out. But then when you got up and continued with mother and baby, he was astounded. The word love is rarely described times in of crises, especially in times such as these. It's all very well to have science and technology on our side. However, when the two go hand in hand with love and compassion, as in your case, Jo, it can only be described as a gift."

"Well, thank you, Margaret. However, who wouldn't try and do their very best? The poor woman was scared enough of these damn rockets, let alone having a baby. Look here, Margaret, I had better go now. It's getting late, and my halo is slipping off."

Margaret just smiled. "All right. I know you can't take praise."

"No, it's not that, Margaret. But when I think of all the brave people taking part in this war, what I do is just a drop in the ocean. Now I really must go, Margaret, and pick up the girls from school."

"Do have that cup of tea I promised you, Jo?"

"I wondered when you were going to suggest that."

They both laughed.

"I can only stay ten minutes, Margaret, and then I really must go. Oh, and by the way, how is your family these days? I nearly forgot to ask you."

"Well, Alf's still working harder than ever." She chuckled. "And getting fatter than ever, in spite of the rationing. My two boys have survived. Thank God. They'll be coming home on leave soon. And Dora is fine. She's nearly fourteen now."

"Is she really? My, how time flies. Talking of which, I must fly myself. Your tea and rock cake were delicious. When this is all over, Margaret, we must have a fabulous get together."

"Yes. We must, my dear. Bye for now, and do take care."

"You too, Margaret. TTFN."

"Hello, Uncle," said Joanna, back home later that day. "You look exhausted."

"Yes, I am, Jo. I've had all these files to get through."

"Well, that's Andy's job, isn't it? Where is he, by the way?"

"It's his day off."

"Couldn't you leave it until he returns tomorrow?"

"No. Some of these are urgent cases, Jo. I've been in court all morning."

"Surely he hasn't left you in a muddle, Uncle?"

"Jo, my dear, that young man is doing his best. However, at the moment, he is not quite au fait with the work system yet."

"Uncle, please put all this away. I'll come down and help you later."

"I appreciate your thoughtfulness, Jo. However, you're looking rather tired yourself."

"I'll tell you about my day when we've had dinner, Uncle."

She held his elbow and led him up the stairs.

Chapter 46

That night when the siren sounded, Mary walked sleepily into her mothers' room.

"I'm so tired, Mummy. Do we have to go downstairs tonight?"

"Well, I suppose we should," whispered Joanna, unable to open her eyes. "I feel very tired too, Mary. Here, jump in beside me, sweetheart."

Within two seconds, they were both sound asleep.

Suddenly, the bed shot up with a tremendous force, hitting the high ceiling and then landing back in the same position on the floor. They both held onto each other.

Mary screamed, "What was that?"

"The V-2 rocket, that's what it was, darling."

Within a few minutes, the door opened, and there stood Tom in his pajamas holding a garden shovel in his hand. In parallel, Peggy rushed in, barking and howling. She jumped up onto the bed, scratching at the covers, and then ran around in a circle chasing her tail. Then she jumped down again and peed in a corner of the room.

"The breakfast you laid in the kitchen, Jo, has been blown away with the windows, I'm afraid."

"Oh, not my breakfast," yelled Mary, and she jumped down from the bed.

Tom breathlessly said, "No. Stay where you are, Mary, until we've had time to investigate. There is glass everywhere and heaven knows what else in the kitchen."

"Uncle, what are you doing with the shovel?" said Joanna.

"Well, Jo, it sounded as if it came from that direction." He pointed towards the riverfront gardens. "If that is so," he puffed, "I shall go and help dig the poor souls out."

Tom looked very funny standing there in his pajamas with a shovel in hand.

Mary laughed. "Are you going in your pajamas, Uncle?"

Tom looked down at his toes. "Oh my goodness. How stupid of me. I'll have to get dressed first."

Suddenly, the whole situation presented itself to Joanna as being extremely comic. Both she and Mary laughed. At one point, the laughing turned hysterical and Joanna realized this, and quickly regained herself.

"I'm sorry, Uncle, darling. You're not going anywhere. They'll have enough help. Listen. Do you hear the noise out there? Ambulances and fire engines. I know your intentions are admirable, darling, but really, Uncle, I must be honest. If you had a bad turn out there, you wouldn't be of much help now, would you?"

"No. I suppose you're right," said Tom despondently.

"You sit down, and I'll see if I can make us a nice cup of tea," said Joanna.

"I doubt it. Wait until you've seen the kitchen."

"Oh, there goes the all clear," said Mary. "I'll help you, Mummy."

"No, sweetheart. I'd better check everything first. You can help by trying to stop Peggy from howling and whining, and we'll have to do something about her wee in the corner."

"I'll clear it up, Mummy."

"No. Not until I find something to clear it up with."

"She couldn't help that, Mummy. She was scared."

Joanna smiled. "I know that, Mary."

She made her way into the lounge, which seemed all right, and then she walked across the landing to the kitchen, which, surprisingly, wasn't as bad as she had imagined. The blast seemed to have affected mainly the back part of the house, where most of the windows had been blasted in.

She called out, "There's not a great deal of damage, Uncle. I don't think there's much to worry about."

"It may not be advisable to use the gas, Jo."

"I'll find out, Uncle."

Joanna ran down the stairs and out into the busy street, where all the action was taking place.

She called out to a local bobby, "Where did that one come down?"

"At the back of Fort Gardens," came the hurried reply. "Demolished nearly a row of houses."

"Is it safe to put on the gas?"

"Yes. Too far away to affect these houses. They're in a terrible state over there."

"I'm a Red Cross nurse. When I've attended to my family, I'll come down and try to be of some assistance."

"Thanks, love. They need all the help they can get."

When most of the mess had been cleaned up in the kitchen, they sat down to a nice cup of tea.

"That powdered milk tasted nice, Mummy," said Mary, her eyes closing.

"Yes. I enjoyed it, darling."

"Very nice indeed," agreed Tom. "In fact, the whole evening could have been a darn sight worse."

Joanna nodded in agreement, and then glanced at Mary. "I think you should go back to bed, sweetheart, and get what little sleep you can."

"Are you coming back to bed, Mummy?"

"I'd like to, darling. However, I should really go over there and try to be of some help."

"Very well, Mummy. But please be careful." Mary's voice trembled.

"I will, sweetheart. Don't worry. You have a good sleep."

"I'll pray for you, Mummy."

Tom looked up abruptly. "You're never going over there, Jo. You look exhausted."

Joanna yawned. "Well, look who is talking."

"Yes. I admit I was wrong, and you were quite right to stop me, especially in my pajamas."

"We're all tired, Uncle. However, I do have the van and it's my duty to help. Margaret will find it difficult coming from Greenhithe. I'll be as quick as I can. Will you be okay, Uncle?"

"Of course I will, my dear child. But you are so terribly tired."

"Yes, I am. However, I must go. See you later, Uncle."

Joanna found the casualties and deaths alarming. It was a horrifying scene of just how much devastation one single V-2 rocket could cause. After working throughout the night, Joanna lent against a brick wall, near to collapse.

Betty, a fellow colleague, came up to her. "I think we should go home now, Jo. There isn't anything more we can do here, my dear. We should leave the rest to the others."

"Yes," agreed Joanna in a distant tone. "You're absolutely right. I'll drive you home."

"No. It's okay, Jo. Dick will give me a lift."

"All right, Betty. If you're sure. See you tomorrow."

Joanna made her way wearily to the van.

Betty called out, "Jo, are you okay?"

Joanna waved her hand with the thumbs up gesture without turning around.

She mumbled to herself, "I'm fine. Just need to sleep."

In the morning, Mary crept out of bed, leaving her mother to sleep, and made her way to the kitchen. Tom was putting the kettle on.

"Ah, there you are, Mary. Is your mother still sleeping?"

"Good morning, Uncle. Yes, she is."

"Then we must be very careful not to wake her. I'm afraid we've all overslept this morning."

"Why? What time is it?"

"9:45, to be exact."

"Oh my goodness. I'll be late for school."

"I wouldn't bother going this morning, Mary, after the night we've had. And if your teacher gives you a reprimand, blame it on me. I waited up for your poor mother until 4:30." He sighed. "And then, I must confess, I ashamedly went to bed."

"Well, why shouldn't you, Uncle?"

"Well, I feel I ought to have done something to help your poor mother. But tiredness overcame me, and I just had to go to sleep."

"Mummy will understand, and anyway, you do help. Mummy is always saying she doesn't know what she would do without you."

Tom shrugged his shoulders then glanced at Mary and smiled. "Now, what shall we have for breakfast, my dear child?"

Mary laughed. "Is there a choice, Uncle?"

"I'm afraid not, Mary. Porridge."

"Porridge will be fine, Uncle. Though I prefer cornflakes."

"Yes, well, they were blasted away with the windows." He sighed again. "Which reminds me, I'll have to do something about that."

"One moment, Uncle. Isn't that the doorbell?"

"Yes. You're right, Mary. That'll be Andy."

"I'll go down and let him in for you, Uncle."

"Thank you, Mary, but I think I had better go. I have to show him what to do, and also collect the mail, if we have any."

"I'll finish cooking the porridge, Uncle."

"Thank you, Mary. It's in the pot. It has to be stirred continuously."

"I do know how to cook porridge, Uncle. In fact, I can cook a great number of things. We managed quite well when Mummy was in hospital. Remember?"

"Yes. I do indeed, my dear child."

"Good morning, Mr. Busher," said Andy. "Sorry I'm late. It was the air raid last night."

"Yes, I understand, Andy. We're all a little late this morning. Are your family all right?"

"Yes, they're fine, thank you, Mr. Busher. It didn't affect us very much. It's just my mother. She gets so frightened."

"She's not alone, Andy."

"Well, I think we had better get started. I'll show you what I'd like you to do while I check the post."

Among Tom's mail, there had been one letter that hadn't been type written. He left it until last, thinking it was unimportant. When he eventually came to it, he muttered, "Good Lord." He immediately recognized Terry's hand writing. It had been posted in this country.

"Andy, I'm just going upstairs for a few minutes."

Andy replied, "Okay, Mr. Busher."

"It's very strange, Mary. It's been posted in this country."

"Oh, come on, Uncle. Let's open it."

"No. We can't do that. It's addressed to your mother. Mary, take this letter and give it to your mother. But only if she's awake."

"Yes, Uncle," replied Mary, as if butter wouldn't melt in her mouth.

"I'll dish out the porridge," said Tom, "and then I must return to my work."

Mary had actually tried not to think of her father's homecoming in the past five months since D-Day for fear of something happening to him, of him being killed or badly injured. So much had happened in this war. Her darling grandad had been taken from them, and even her mother had nearly died. She tried to think of all the good things in life instead. She realized there were people who had suffered much more than she had. But, nevertheless, now was the time to know what was happening.

Mary carefully put her head around the door. Her mother was still sleeping. She quietly closed it again, and then stood looking at the envelope she was holding. Her brain was a turbine engine. She quickly ripped it open.

Her father's handwriting was difficult to understand. It sometimes faded away into nothing. However, she was able to understand that her father was now in Portsmouth, in this country. He would be home on leave in two weeks. Mary put her hand to her mouth and beamed from cheek to cheek.

She swept into the kitchen. "Uncle! Uncle, Daddy's coming home on leave."

"Now, now, Mary. You'll break a blood vessel getting so excited." He glanced at the letter in her hand. "Where is your mother?"

Mary looked down at her toes. "She's still sleeping."

Tom grinned. "I thought so," he said, giving her a disparaging look. "Oh, dear Mary, what are we going to do with you? You knew that was wrong."

"Yes. I know it was, Uncle."

"Whatever is your mother going to say? She may think we both opened it. Or even worse, she may think I opened it."

"Oh, Uncle. Daddy's coming home. Aren't you pleased?"

Their voices were slowly getting louder.

"Of course I'm pleased, Mary. But it was very naughty of you."

"Yes, I know it was. But isn't it wonderful?"

Tom was having little success in his reprimanding.

"Oh, Uncle, you are an old worry pot. I'll tell Mummy it was my fault."

They both turned their heads to find Joanna standing in the doorway.

"Morning. Am I interrupting something?"

"Ah, there you are, Jo," said Tom in a sheepish tone. "Did you sleep well?"

"It would appear so, judging from the time. Now what have you two been up to?"

She glanced at the letter in Mary's hand.

"Well, you see, my dear," said Tom, "I mistakenly opened your letter. It was among my business mail. I do apologize."

Mary shouted, "No, it was me, Mummy. You were sound asleep, and I didn't want to disturb you."

Joanna gave a slight smile. "I've been listening to every word you've both been saying. You're very naughty, Mary, and you're a big fibber, Uncle. Now, can I have my letter please, Mary?"

Tom sighed. "Yes. I'm a big fibber. I must admit. However, I think this calls for a celebration. I wonder if that bottle of cognac I hid away is still safe." He smiled. "It should be. I wrapped it up in a thick blanket. Now, let me think. Where did I put it? Ah, yes. I remember now." Tom made his way into the lounge and opened a small cupboard. He chuckled. "Found it."

Joanna grinned. "I very much doubt if porridge and cognac will go well together, Uncle."

Mary handed the letter to her mother.

"Thank you, Mary. I won't be long." She turned and disappeared into her bedroom, where she could savor every word in peace.

"Why did she go in there to read it?"

Tom looked at Mary with a slight smile. "You'll understand when you get a little older, my dear child."

Mary thought for a few seconds. Then a lovely smile crossed her face. "Oh, I understand, Uncle. They are still very much in love."

Tom, holding a spoonful of porridge to his mouth, raised his eyes above his glasses and nodded.

Joanna read the letter and laid her fingers upon the lettering. A tear trickled down her cheeks. "Oh, thank God. He's actually home."

In the week that followed, Joanna received quite a few calls from Terry. Happiness was in the air again. He rang in the evening, which enabled him to speak to all three of them at the same time by using Tom's office phone. He usually rang while they were having dinner.

On one such evening, the phone rang. Joanna jumped up.

"That's Terry. I'll get it."

"He times it right." Tom laughed. "Just when we're in the middle of our fish and chips."

"Why, hello, Nina," said Joanna. "How lovely to hear from you. How are you?"

"I'm fine," said Nina excitedly. "I'm ringing to tell you David and I are getting married in two weeks' time."

"Two weeks," said Joanna.

"Yes. When he has his first long leave. I wanted you to be the first to know."

"Oh, that's wonderful news." Joanna paused. "Well, I'd love to come, naturally, Nina. However, I'm not quite sure."

"Not sure? Why?"

"I've heard from Terry. He'll be home next week. He's also on an extended leave."

"Well, that's marvelous news, isn't it? Now you'll all be able to come."

"Nina, my love, it's been so long since I've seen Terry. You understand, I'd love to come, of course, but I'm not sure if Terry would wish to."

Nina's voice sounded deflated. "Oh, I'm sorry, Jo. I naturally assumed." She paused. "I somehow thought…Oh, well, it doesn't matter. How is Terry?"

"Well, he managed to escape the campaign virtually unscathed, except for a few minor injuries, a fractured elbow and so forth. Anyway, my darling Nina, I'm so pleased for you." Joanna realized her friend was hurt. "I'll be able to tell you more when I see Terry."

"I understand," said Nina. "You've been through so much, Jo. It's just that we were all looking forward to seeing you again, your mother included. I suppose I'm a bit selfish. But apart from David and the children, you're all I have."

"Look, darling, I'll try my very best to come. I promise. That's all I can say."

They both said goodbye and Joanna returned to the dinner table to finish her meal.

"I've just put it in the oven to keep it hot," said Tom. "I didn't know how long you were going to be. How are they all in Derbyshire?"

Joanna gave him an update.

"My dear, you'll have to go. You're part of her life now. Why, she's like a member of your own family. If it hadn't been for you, they may never have met."

"I know that, Uncle. I've heard it a hundred times. But you seem to forget that David has been able to nip back and forth at short intervals, whereas I haven't seen Terry since the beginning of June."

"I understand that, my dear. But Terry will be home next week. When did you say they're getting married?"

"October twenty-eighth."

Tom smiled. "Well, there you are then. Terry will be home one whole week before we go, and knowing Terry as I do, Jo, I'm sure he'd like to go."

Joanna looked troubled.

"What's the matter, my dear? Are you concerned about the rockets? Because they're becoming fewer now."

"No. No, it isn't that," said Joanna.

"Then what is it, my dear? I know the war isn't over yet," said Tom. "However, you've always given every indication that we're safer in numbers, and we'd all be together. We can even take Peg."

"No, it's not that at all. You see, Uncle, it's been a long time since I've seen Terry. I don't know what to expect."

"Whatever do you mean, my dear?"

"Well, I have heard, in some cases, and I know it to be true, that war sometimes changes a man."

Tom looked at her tenderly. "I understand what you're trying to say, Jo. But believe me, not your Terry. He has a strong character. He'll be fine."

Tom had noticed Joanna's tendency to worry unduly since her misfortune with the flying bomb.

He changed the subject. "By the way, where is Mary?"

"In the garden doing her homework. She'll be up in a minute."

"In the garden?" repeated Tom.

"Yes. She likes it out there. It seems to give her inspiration with Peg and the chickens."

"That poor child. She never goes anywhere."

Joanna looked at him. A slight smile crossed her face.

Tom glanced at her over his glasses. "She would have enjoyed the wedding. However, I suppose it will be held in a registry office."

"No. They're tying the knot in a cathedral in the small country village of Tideswell. Wherever that is."

"Oh dear, oh dear. Mary will be disappointed if you don't go."

"Uncle, dear, let us just wait and see."

Chapter 47

On a sunny afternoon in mid-autumn, when the leaves began to fall, Mary and Anna strolled through the park on their way to the fish shop. The gold and crimson colors of autumn spread around their feet and the sun shone through the trees like a colorful mist against the dew. Mary felt a warm glow within her. She turned around and could not help but admire the scene.

Anna said, "Why are you standing there like that? Come on, Mary. Hurry up. We want to get the fish while the shop is open."

"I'm coming," answered Mary in a lingering voice.

"What were you looking at, Mary?"

"Oh, nothing really."

"Yes, you were" continued Anna. "You were miles away then."

"Well, doesn't it look beautiful over there?"

"What? That row of bombed-out houses where the rocket dropped? I don't think that's very beautiful."

Mary laughed. "No, silly. Come on. I'll race you to the fish shop."

Mary was aware that Anna may be getting tired of her romantic view of life.

"Let's get to the fish shop fast, and we mustn't forget the watercress."

"Are you sure your mother has invited me, Mary?"

"Yes, of course she has. Anyway, even if she hasn't, it doesn't matter."

After they had purchased their precious shrimps and winkles, they made their way home.

On entering the hall, Mary said, "What is that smell?"

Anna replied, "I don't know. Smells like pipe tobacco to me. Maybe it's your uncle's."

"No, it's not him. He doesn't smoke."

Mary flew up the stairs. She rang the doorbell. The door was slightly open. She pushed it, and her mother came to the door.

Mary looked at her, and whispered, "Daddy's home, isn't he?"

Her mother nodded. Mary walked into the small hall between the kitchen and lounge, and there stood her father.

She quietly but confidently said, "Hello, Daddy. I knew you were coming. That's why I bought some shrimps and winkles." She paused. Then she walked into the lounge and exclaimed, "I've forgotten the watercress. What are we going to do? I know you like watercress with your shellfish, Daddy."

Her eyes were glassy as if she did not know whether to laugh or cry. Her father looked at her with that slow, magnificent smile. His presence seemed to dominate the entire room.

"Mary, my love, it doesn't matter," he whispered.

Anna's voice echoed from the kitchen, "Mrs. Busher, would you like me to get the watercress?"

Joanna had been unaware of Anna standing out on the landing.

"Oh, Anna, dear, come in."

"No, no, Mrs. Busher. But I would like to get the watercress for you."

She glanced up at Mary and her father. Mary turned around suddenly as if she had been awoken from a dream.

"Oh, Daddy, this is my friend Anna. We met at secondary school."

"Hello, Anna. Come in, dear."

"Thank you very much, Mr. Busher. But I'll get the watercress first."

Anna discreetly disappeared down the stairs to get the much needed watercress. She was aware that Mary needed to be alone with her father.

Joanna thought Mary's reaction to her father's homecoming was rather curious. She was unlike most children, who ran straight into their father's arms, especially girls. But then, on reflection, Mary was unique. Just like Terry.

Mary just stared at her father, and smiled. "Oh, Daddy, I don't know what to say. I thought sometimes that I would never see..."

Terry came over and sat in the armchair beside her. "Don't say any more, my sweetheart."

She sat on the arm of his chair and gently cupped his face in her small hands, and kissed him on the forehead. "Oh, Daddy, this is the moment we've all been waiting for."

A broad smile crossed his face. "Yes, it is, my sweetheart. But how you've grown in such a short time. You'll soon be as tall as your mother."

"I am now if I stand on my toes. Look. I'll show you. Come over here, Mummy, and let's make our usual circle. It's just the three of us again."

Joanna smiled, looking at Tom drowsing in his chair. "Well, not quite, Mary. Four, to be exact."

"Oh, don't worry about me," said Tom, in a sleepy voice. "I'm only the lodger." He laughed. "I'll pop on the kettle for a nice cup of tea."

When the siren sounded that night, no one seemed bothered. They were all together again and that's all that mattered.

On the eve of her wedding, Nina had misgivings. Joanna was busy making last minute preparations to Mary's dress. It was to match Marianne's, which was made of pale pink wool. Nina had bought a lovely, pale turquoise suit.

"It's a beautiful suit, Nina. But are you sure you've bought the right size? It seems a little large for you. Or maybe you've lost weight?"

"Well, it fitted me fine when I bought it. Your mother was with me. She bought a soft woolen scarf the same color." Nina sounded anxious. "Oh dear, it'll be too late now to take it back."

"Yes, I'm afraid so," agreed Joanna. "What a pity. It's such a lovely suit. Beautiful color. One moment, did you say Mother bought a scarf at the same place?"

"Yes. Exactly the same. They were meant to match."

"I have an idea," said Joanna. "Has David left his car?"

"Yes, I think so. He usually leaves it when he goes to his club."

Joanna glanced out the window to see the red sports car still in the driveway.

"Yes, he has." She grinned. "That means the jolly boys are on their stag night out. I hope Terry doesn't have too much to drink. I'd like to see him standing up when he hands the ring over to David."

She looked over her shoulder at Nina's troubled face.

"Now you're not to worry, darling. Everything will be fine. I'm just popping over to Mother's. I'll only be a few minutes. TTFN."

Joanna zoomed off in the red sports.

Meanwhile, the jolly boys, as Joanna so brilliantly described them, were having a convivial evening at the club. Most of its members were similar to David and Terry. Some were long-term service men who had served with distinction in both first and second world wars.

"Well, Terry, what does it feel like to be home again?"

"Home? I haven't a home as such. But if you're referring to my being with my family again, well, words cannot describe it, David."

"I'm not surprised, old boy. You have a remarkable family. Especially your wife."

Terry looked at David straight in the eyes. He didn't fail to pick up on the remark, and noted something in his voice. Terry opened his mouth to speak. David quickly changed the subject, realizing that he'd never be a contender for Joanna's affections.

"I see they've promoted you again."

"Just acting captain temporary," replied Terry. "I happened to be there when they needed someone, that's all."

"I don't suppose you'll be seeing much more action?"

"I hope not. I must confess, I never wanted to go in the first place. I'm not one of these types who willingly volunteer to go. However, this war has been different from the others, where politicians sit around on their fat arses playing with toy soldiers and expecting men to die for king and empire. We all had to fight in this one, as well you know, David. But of course I'll be ready if they should need me again. What about you?"

"Well, Jerry can't give us any flack if they haven't any, can they? Rumor has it Harris has a great deal in store for us yet."

"So you're on bomber command now, David?"

"Yes." David paused. "That's why I wanted to get the wedding over as soon as possible, and then Nina will be well provided for, whatever happens. You see, Terry, Nina is a very sick woman."

"I know she is, and I think it's very commendable of you," said Terry, looking serious. "However, I wouldn't worry unduly. I'm quite sure Nina will be fine. Believe me."

"How do you mean?"

Terry smiled. "Oh, nothing really. It's not important. Just take care of yourself. By the way, what exactly did you mean, David, when you referred to my wife and family being remarkable? I think most people in this country have all put their shoulders to the wheel. Wouldn't you agree?"

"Yes, of course. However, when you consider that all three of them escaped death by a narrow squeeze, it is remarkable. Your Uncle Tom had three heart attacks. Your daughter, Mary, nearly blown to pieces on her way to school. And your good lady, who is like a cat with nine lives. And not forgetting your mother-in-law. I've been fed so much information by that old lady, you'd be surprised, and, of course, by Nina. If I had never met Joanna during that tragic time with poor Mrs. Cox, I may never have laid eyes on Nina. Not forgetting you, Terry. If you had never given that bastard, Josh, the pasting he deserved, we may never have been sitting here drinking."

Terry paused. He looked at David with that slow, cautious smile of his. "I see," he said in his usual quiet manner. "Yes. You're quite right, David, in all that you say. However, that was an incident which I found most distasteful at the time. Yet I have no compunction in what I did. The man was evil through and through. At the time, I felt like killing him. Or anyone else who dared lay a finger on my wife."

"Well, who can blame you, Terry? It's strange though how the police never found the killer. I wonder who did it. Have you any ideas?"

Terry grinned. "Well, this may come as a surprise to you." He paused, looking straight into David's eyes. "I know who did it."

"What?" gasped David. "You must be joking. Who?"

"I'll tell you one day. However, this is neither the time nor place."

"One moment, Terry. How on earth could you have possibly known when you were preparing for the invasion at the time? For heaven sake, man, put me out of my misery and tell me. You're killing me with suspense."

Terry looked at him and slowly smiled. He laid his hand on David's shoulder. "Come on, pal, let's have another whisky and go rolling home."

Within no time at all, Joanna was back with her mother's scarf. To her surprise, she found Nina sitting and holding her head in her hands.

"Why, whatever is the matter, Nina? Are you all right?"

"Yes. I'm fine. I've just been thinking, that's all."

Nina had no wish to express her doubts to Joanna. After all, she had begged her to come to the wedding.

"Well, you need worry no more, darling. Mother didn't mind lending you her scarf. She said you could keep it. Then she decided to loan it to you instead as something borrowed. Not that she's bothered what she wears. She's too busy talking to Tom. I think she'll take his advice and wear her gray suit." Joanna laughed. "It's amazing how well they get on together. Here, slip it on, darling. There. Just as I thought. Tied around the waist, it accentuates your lovely, slim figure."

Joanna clapped her hands with an air of contented bliss in her eyes. Nina looked at her face in the mirror. It was then that Joanna noticed the sad reflection looking back at her.

"Whatever is it, darling? Tell me what's troubling you."

Nina stared into Joanna eyes as if searching for the truth. "Jo, do you think I'm doing the right thing?"

"What do you mean, Nina?"

"Well, this may sound stupid, but sometimes I wonder if he's marrying me out of sheer pity."

"I'm sorry, Nina. I don't quite understand. I thought we'd been through all this before?"

"Yes. That was when Josh was alive. I thought he may be trying to help me get rid of that monster."

"Nina, I've asked you this before. Do you really love David?"

"You know I do, Jo. He's the only man I'll ever love."

"And he loves you very much, Nina."

"Yes. I know he's very fond of me. But is that enough, Jo?"

"Fond? He loves you. Why do you say that, dear?"

"Well, he still has a photo of Ann. The other day, I saw him looking at it. The door was half open. I could see him clearly through a crack in the hinges. He couldn't see me. The expression in his eyes…" She paused, on the verge of tears. "He still loves her. I'm sure of it."

Joanna's mind flashed back to the incident that had occurred a few months ago. She realized that Nina could possibly be speaking the truth. Yet she had seen David look at Nina with so much devotion. She also realized that to lose his love now could very well break Nina.

After the wedding, Tom would inform Nina of her inheritance. However, rich or poor, this would not alter the situation. Nina loved David, and that's all that mattered to her. If she broke up with David now, without him to protect her, she may very well run straight into the arms of some get-rich-quick philanderer.

"Nina, my darling, when we're young, we fall head over heels in love very quickly. In your case, you never had that opportunity. David and Ann met and fell in love quickly and were married just as quick. They had only known each other a short while when she was unfortunately killed. So who can tell whether they would have stayed together? You and David, however, have been together nearly two years. I think that speaks for itself. Falling in love is wonderful, Nina. But actually loving a person is totally different. Terry and I fell in love. Now we just love each other for what we are, ignoring each other's little indiscretions. We have grown together as one, and this is how I see you and David."

"I understand what you're trying to say, Jo. But is that enough? You see, I have nothing to offer him. Why, I can't even give him a child."

Joann smiled. "I shouldn't let that bother you. I don't think it matters to him. After all, he has a ready-made family. It's nothing to do with me, Nina, but there are few men around like David."

Nina smiled. "Yes. You're right, Jo. He adores the children."

"Well then, what are you worried about?"

"Nothing, I suppose. I just have cold feet."

Joanna smiled. "Exactly. After Josh, who wouldn't have second thoughts? Well, now that's settled, let's get down to business. What shall we have to drink?"

"I'll have a small port and lemon, please, Jo."

"Well, I'm having a large cognac. Now, I'd like you to tell me how my new red suit looks on me. I've been saving up my coupons for this occasion."

Joanna slipped on the suit complete with accessories: a red hat, royal-blue gloves, and a white cravat.

Nina laughed. "Jo, only you could get away with wearing something like that."

"Why, don't you like it? Mary thinks it's lovely. She'd like one the same. I haven't shown it to Terry yet."

"Well, he's going to look twice when he sets eyes on you in that. You look gorgeous, Jo. Like some film star. Really."

Nina looked at her friend flouncing around with her new clothes in one hand and a drink in the other.

Joanna laughed excitedly. "Oh, I'm so looking forward to all this."

"Jo, you're so dynamic. You're like a child at times."

"Well, why not? It's good to live once in a while."

Nina beamed. "Jo, my dear, I'm so very pleased you came."

Nina couldn't help but notice how life had taken on a whole new meaning for Joanna since her near miss with death. She seemed to live life to the full now with no doubts.

The small wedding reception was held at the Rutland Hotel. When it was all over, David and Nina were all set to spend a few days holiday in Inverness in the Highlands of Scotland, an idyllic spot.

Before they returned home to Gravesend, Tom had the task of giving the newlyweds the good news. He knocked on their bedroom door.

"Hello, Tom," said David. "Do come in and take a seat."

"No. I'd rather stand, if you don't mind."

"You look troubled. Is anything wrong?"

"No. Good Lord, no. I would rather like to speak to you both in private before you leave. If I may?"

"Yes, by all means," said David.

When Tom had finished, he handed the legal documents to Nina. The news had taken them both by surprise.

"My God, Tom," said Nina. "How long have you known about this?"

"Since the death of your Aunt Bertha," said Tom, looking slightly reserved.

"Five hundred thousand pounds. Surely it can't be true?" exclaimed Nina.

"Oh, it is, my dear. Believe me. You see, if your Aunt Bertha had survived you, she would have stood to gain the whole sum. She was fully aware of this, of course. However, frankly speaking, it's a small amount compared with the legacy and title of the Lady Christina, heiress to probably at least a million, land, and property deeds, which would have been yours, of course, had your aristocratic, narrow-minded family thought otherwise and not cut you off from the full inheritance. Josh, however, was totally unaware of this. All he wanted was the three thousand pounds he'd taken out on your life policy. He'd bribed Bertha into believing that she would receive one thousand pounds if she went along with his plans, which I have already explained to you, Nina, some time ago."

Nina nodded.

Tom was about to continue when David exclaimed, "One moment. There must be some sort of conspiracy going on here. You all knew about this?"

"Oh, yes, indeed, my dear boy. But, as I have just mentioned, only since the miserly Aunt Bertha died. We all thought it better to wait, under the circumstances, until after your wedding before you were told officially."

"Why?" said David, looking mystified.

Tom didn't answer.

At that moment came a knock on the door, and in walked Joanna and Terry.

"Have you told them yet, Uncle?" said Terry, grinning.

"Yes, indeed. Everything."

"Wonderful," shouted Joanna, beaming from cheek to cheek. "Congratulations to both of you."

Looking at Tom and then Terry, David asked, "Are you all quite sure there is nothing else we should know?"

"Absolutely, my dear fellow. Nothing whatsoever," said Tom, smiling.

Terry patted David on the shoulder. "There you are, Dave." With a whimsical smile, he whispered, "Now, I'd like to have a word before you leave."

David nodded with relief. "Okay, Terry."

Chapter 48

1945

The next celebration was to come on 8th May, VE Day, Victory in Europe. It had been a day never to be forgotten. The end of the war in Europe brought much jollification and hilarity. Tom invited everyone, friends and family, to celebrate at his apartment.

Nina and David came with the children and Joanna's mother for a brief stay in a nearby hotel. Quite a number of people gathered outside in the street, singing and dancing, and making their way up Harmer Street towards the clock tower. The atmosphere had been euphoric with the crowds shouting and cheering. It was as if everyone had stopped what they were doing for that brief moment in time.

Mary and her friends stood out on the balcony singing and dancing to the rhythm of the crowds. Tom relentlessly advised them to come in, stating that the old balcony was highly unsafe, especially to jump up and down on. Poor Tom. No one gave any attention to him.

"It's absolutely futile trying to speak to them. They just will not listen."

"What's the matter, Uncle?" said Joanna on entering the lounge.

"It's the children. I may as well talk to myself. They're going to have a dreadful accident. That balcony is unsafe. I was told when I took the apartment to be very careful. Only one or two people should stand out there at one time."

Joanna stared at Tom's straight face, and then bust out laughing.

"I'd like you to tell me just what you find so funny, Joanna."

"Well, you, Uncle." She tenderly took his elbow and led him to the window. "Look here, Uncle, darling, these old Georgian buildings are very strong. They have withstood the rockets and doodlebugs, and heaven knows what else in past years very well, I would say. So I'm willing to give them a try. Don't worry. I'll tell the children to be careful."

Then she stepped out onto the balcony to join the youngsters.

Tom sighed and followed her. "Well, if you're going to risk your lives then I may as well join you." He lumbered out onto the balcony and took a breath. "My word. What a marvelous sight to behold. You know, Jo, at times I never thought I'd live to see this day. Everyone enjoying themselves like this. I only wish Terry were here."

"Yes, I do too, Uncle. Never mind. He'll be here next week, and that's when everything will start to happen."

"Yes. It feels good, Jo," said Tom. "However, we still have Japan to contend with."

"Yes. I'm aware of that, Uncle. However, we have waited nearly six long years for this day. I think we should all enjoy it."

"Why, of course, my dear." On realizing he was becoming an old bore, Tom changed the subject. "By the way, what time are Nina and family coming around, and, of course, your dear mother?"

"I think about four o'clock."

"Well, in that case, I'd better sit down and wait for them…" He turned and stepped back into the lounge, mumbling to himself, "Out of harm's way."

Joanna peered through the window. "What did you say, Uncle?"

"I said, I'm going to do just as you say and enjoy myself by sitting in my armchair with a small class of cognac, and await your dear mother. She's a fine woman."

Joanna turned around, glancing in through the open window to give him a cheeky look. Since the wedding, her mother and Tom had struck up quite a friendship.

The girls crossed their arms and began to hum to the sound of Auld Lang Syne, which had been wafting up from singers in the street below. Joanna wrapped her arms around Mary and Anna, and began singing along with them. Once she'd started, she couldn't stop. She sang all the old war time songs: 'There'll always be an England', 'There'll be blue birds over the white cliffs of Dover', and 'When the lights go on again'. Raising her arms to the heavens as if she were holding the whole world in her hands, Joanna sang with passion. Then they heard clapping from the lounge behind them. Not realizing that they had an audience, Joanna and the girls turned around to find that their guests had arrived.

"That was wonderful, Jo," said Nina, clapping.

"Well, Joanna has always had a lovely voice. She inherits it from her father," said her mother proudly.

"Oh, now, that's unfair, Mother. Give a little credit to my splendid chorus." Joanna laughed, indicating with her hands to the youngsters.

When everyone had thoroughly enjoyed themselves, people began to depart, including Tom's old friends from the Bar. They looked quite comic figures, trying to hide their unfinished bottles of whisky, which they'd brought with them by tucking the bottles inside their jackets. They were obviously aware that rationing would continue for quite a while. How right they were.

David found the opportunity to whisper in Tom's ear, "I'd rather like to speak to you in private, Tom."

"Why, of course, my dear fellow," said Tom, looking puzzled. "We'll go into my office. I doubt if we'll be disturbed there."

"Please, don't look so surprised, Tom. I haven't any bad news."

"Thank heavens for that."

"Nina will see you later," said David. "At the moment, she's keeping Joanna occupied."

"Joanna occupied?" said Tom, mystified.

"Yes, Tom. I'll explain later."

David continued to speak in Tom's office.

"Now I thought I heard Terry mention that he was going to resume his commission. It's strange, don't you think, Tom? I mean, a man like Terry, I'd assumed he'd want to be home with his family."

Tom sighed. "Oh, he does. Believe me, David. However, it's a question of work and money. You see, they won't be requiring any more men for his MOD-funded engineering work, and he didn't finish his university degree in law. Great pity, that. He'd have made a damn good lawyer. He knows more about the law than some of us older chaps. He only had another twelve months. Strange thing is, he'd like to join me now, and I'd love to have him as a partner." Tom looked far away. "Never mind. That's life, David. Anyway, young man, I have no idea what I'm doing rambling on like this, telling you my family's private affairs. I must be going soft in the head. Or perhaps I've had too much to drink. Now, would you mind telling me what you have to say?"

David smiled. He couldn't help but admire the old man's pride and respect for his family.

"Oh, didn't I tell you?" said David. "How stupid of me. I nearly forgot. This is from Nina." He produced a check for one hundred thousand pounds. "She has entrusted it to you to deposit into Joanna and Terry's bank. She has an idea of what their reaction would be, had she given it to them herself. They are a very proud couple in spite of having lost their home and everything they have. Oh, I suppose they have a sizeable bank balance. But it would take them years to build up this kind of money. They need this, Tom, to rebuild their future, and you'd have your partner."

Old Tom spluttered and swallowed, feeling almost choked with emotion. "What...what can I say, my dear boy?"

"Nothing. Just put it into their bank as soon as possible. And remember, Tom, not a whisper to anyone."

Tom nodded his head in agreement. "Of course, my dear boy." Then he repeated softly, "Of course."

There was a knock on the door.

Tom called, "Who is that?"

"It's okay, Tom. It's me, Nina."

David quickly asked her, "Where have you left Jo?"

"It's okay, David. She was disappointed that she couldn't find you two, so she's taken all the kids and Marianne to her friend's apartment across the road. Apparently she has a piano and they're all having a sing song. She said she wouldn't be long. Oh, yes, and her mother is sitting waiting for Tom in the lounge."

Nina noticed Tom's face. He looked overwhelmed.

"Are you all right, Tom?"

"Yes...Yes, quite all right. It's just that I don't quite know what to say when they ask me."

"Oh, bless you, Tom. Please don't look so worried. This is a day to be happy."

"You must try to look at it this way," said Nina. "David has given me more than enough happiness in every way. If you do not take this, I will be very upset. And I want you to know that if there is anything I can do for you, Tom, it would give me the greatest pleasure. It's because of Jo and Terry that I am still here, and, of course, you, my dear old friend. You're all my family. Not the family who left the legacy. They didn't care if I lived or died. So therefore, we are all entitled to share in the pleasure that the legacy brings."

"I understand, my dear," said Tom in a whispered voice, nodding his head once again.

"Good. Well, now that's settled," said David, "I think we should go over and join in the fun with Jo and our children." He beamed, looking at Nina.

"Good idea, darling," responded Nina, looking happier than she had in years.

Chapter 49

By the time Terry came home, the celebrations were well and truly underway. Mary had been invited to a number of parties, but declined the offers on account of not knowing exactly what day and time her father would be home. To Mary, personally, the street parties didn't bother her. However, waiting to greet her father at the station on his arrival mattered a great deal. Mary was slowly developing an unassuming character yet still had the ability to mix with others. She enjoyed the company of her friends, and whilst her brain remained alert and active, she also liked to be alone at times, reading or just playing with Peggy.

Her father's train was late. Mary sat and waited two hours at Gravesend Station reading her book until, finally, she saw her father's head leaning out of the window as the train slowly approached the platform. For a split second, her mind flashed back to the spring of 1941 when she stood waving her father goodbye and saw his head disappear out of sight around the bend of the tiny railway station.

Now the war was over, she would have her father all to herself once again.

Terry spotted her immediately and beamed, radiant with joy. Mary ran alongside the train before it finally came to a halt.

"Daddy, Daddy, isn't it marvelous? The war is actually over."

"Yes. It's marvelous, my darling," said Terry, as he alighted the train and swept her up in his arms. "Well, now, what have you been doing with yourself?"

"Oh, such a lot has been happening, Daddy." Mary updated him on everything. Before they finally approached Harmer Street, she asked, "When will you be leaving the Royal Marines, Daddy? I suppose you will be home for good very soon now."

Terry whispered, "Yes, I hope so, sweetheart."

He had battled with his conscience. He knew he may have to stay in the armed services longer for the purpose of achieving their financial and life goals.

Joanna, busy in the kitchen, was preparing for the weekend that lay ahead. She had been pleased that Mary wanted her father to herself for a while, and knew there would be plenty of time for them to be together. However, all the unrest in the world concerned her greatly. And there was still Japan.

She prayed that Terry would not extend his commission, despite the attractive salary being offered now as a full captain. She wanted him home with her. They had waited so long to be together. Even if he only started off as a banker's assistant, they would be able to manage. She would continue nursing, and between them, they could save enough for a deposit on a small house. Her thoughts were only of Terry and having him back again.

Tom came up from his office early. Joanna didn't hear him enter as she took a tray of sponge cakes out the oven. She looked up, suddenly burning her hand on the oven door and causing the cakes to fly everywhere.

She held her hand. "Damn that. Oh, hello, Uncle, my dear."

"I'm so sorry. I didn't mean to startle you. I just thought Terry may have arrived by now. Mary must be still waiting for him."

"Yes. She's still waiting," said Joanna forlornly, pulling out a chair from under the kitchen table. She sat down, leaving the cakes where they had fallen on the floor, and put her hand to her head. "Oh, Uncle," she sobbed. "What is going to happen?"

"Why? Did you hurt yourself, my dear?"

"Oh, don't be stupid, Uncle. Not this, silly."

"Then whatever do you mean, my dear?" said Tom, looking confused and a little hurt.

"I'm sorry, Uncle, barking at you like that. You see, I do not want Terry to take this commission."

Tom held her hand in his and looked her straight in the eyes. "Joanna, I want you to believe me and trust me when I tell you that you have nothing to worry your pretty head about."

"Why? Are you going to wave a magic wand or something?"

"I don't have to. Terry loves you and Mary far too much. Besides, he has no reason now. Even if he wanted to."

"Why? What do you mean? I don't understand."

"Never mind. I'll explain later. Meanwhile, I think we should pick these cakes up before Mary returns with Peggy, and hopefully Terry."

The day after Terry's return home, all the celebrations began to commence with an enthusiasm that had never been seen before. Mary sat outside on the balcony reading, and waited for her two friends, Anna and Dora, to arrive. They had made arrangements with the rest of their friends to carry lighted torches through the streets and up to Woodlands Park, where a huge bonfire was to be lit. It was a party that had been arranged especially for the youngsters.

When her parents returned home from walking Peggy on the promenade, they had no idea Mary was sitting out on the balcony. She thought she would sit a little longer, and then jump out and surprise them.

"Where is Mary?" said Terry, sitting himself down comfortably on the sofa.

"Oh, she was waiting for her friends, Dora and Anna," said Joanna. "I assume she's gone out with them."

"Oh, yes. That's right. I remember. However, she should really leave a note telling you exactly where she is."

"Yes, I agree. But I suppose she's excited with everything going on."

"Yes. You're probably right."

"I think we'll have a nice cup of tea now, Terry, before the others arrive."

"Good idea, darling."

As she laid the tea tray down on the coffee table, she said, "You know, Terry, this is the first time we've been alone together since you arrived yesterday."

"I know it is, my darling. But what can we do?"

"Absolutely nothing at the moment, Terry. Tom loves to entertain his old friends, especially at a time like this. And, after all, why shouldn't he? It is his home, and a time to celebrate. However, it'll be better once all the festivities are over and everyone settles down. Old Tom is a dear, and we do have a roof over our head."

Terry sighed. "Yes. I only wish it were our own."

"Oh, we have more than most people in our situation, Terry. I've been eager to ask you something since you arrived." She hesitated.

"Well, don't look so worried, sweetheart. What is it?"

Joanna looked at him pleadingly. "Terry, please do not take that commission for another five years. I don't think I could stand it. We'll manage. I'm taking a post full-time nursing at Westhill in Dartford. For you, there are positions in the banking sector and insurance business."

"Jo, I'll be forty next year. I'll have to start at the bottom again. Young chaps who are leaving college now will have a head start on me."

"Terry, listen to me. I would rather have you home here with us than climbing the ranks in the Marines and maybe, in the process, getting yourself killed. You know deep down in your heart that you hate it. Why try and pretend? Terry, listen to me, darling. You say you'd be starting from the bottom again. Well, I would rather start as a pauper with nothing and have you by my side than go through the torment of losing you again. We've both had enough of that."

Terry gazed into her eyes and held her tenderly in his arms. "It would be a tremendous struggle, Jo. You've been through so much. You deserve more."

Joanna shook her head. "No. We'll have to work hard, yes. But being together and loving the way we do, I know in my heart that we'll make it through, my darling. I told Mary on the day that wretched doodlebug dropped, I stared into that huge black hole in the ground, and I said to her that nothing else mattered in the world. Only the fact that we loved each other and were still alive. And through our love, we would build a new future. And we will, my darling. Other people have suffered more than us. We must be grateful for what we have. Everything is going to be fine, Terry. I feel it deep down inside. You know the feelings I get."

Terry smiled and nodded. His gray-blue eyes stared into hers as if he were looking into her very soul. "If that's what you wish, Jo."

"I do, Terry. I really do. You're everything to me."

He put his arms around her and closed his eyes, savoring the moment. He whispered, "Then so be it, my darling."

Meanwhile, Mary, still outside on the balcony, discretely made herself small by crouching down close to the wall. She didn't want to be seen now, for she realized that the moment was for her parents only. She grew anxious when Peggy began sniffing around the window, and she wished Dora and Anna would hurry up.

"Shall we have our tea now, sweetheart?"

"Yes. We'd better, before they all arrive. Peggy, come and lie down. What is she doing sniffing around over there?"

"Perhaps she wants to go out again, Terry. We've only just brought her in. You know, since you've come home, she's been acting very strange."

He grinned. "Well, I'd better pack my bags and go."

"No, be serious. What is she doing?"

"I have no idea, sweetheart. Perhaps she's looking for her boyfriend, the little dachshund."

Joanna laughed.

"Oh, you can laugh," said Terry. "But the way she dashed in the water after him makes me think."

Joanna burst out laughing. "Yes. Maybe if she'd known he was a German sausage, she would have thought twice."

He looked at Joanna, his eyes gleaming. "I'll pop her in the kitchen. Come on, old girl. You're getting too old for that sort of thing."

Joanna, pouring the tea, appeared suddenly mindful. "That reminds me, Terry. You were in the middle of telling me something about Josh earlier when Peggy ran off and interrupted us. Perhaps I was mistaken. In fact, I'm sure I must have been. This may sound ridiculous, but I thought I heard you say you knew who killed Josh."

"No, darling, you are not being ridiculous. I was speaking in a quiet tone so as not to be overheard. But you evidently heard me loud and clear. It all seems a long time ago now. But can you possibly cast your mind back to June fifth last year?"

"Yes, darling. Vividly."

"Do you remember the young, handsome marine who gave Mary a bunch of bluebells?"

"How could I ever forget? Why, of course I remember."

"Well, he was the one who told me."

Joanna looked mystified. "What? But how? I don't understand, Terry."

"Jo, I want you to promise me that you will not breathe a word of this to anyone."

"Of course not, darling. You know me."

"There are only two others I've told, and that's Tom, of course, and David."

"Oh, really? Are you quite sure that you can trust me?"

"Now, don't look at me like that, Jo. I thought he had a right to know, being married to Nina, and Tom dealt with the case." Terry paused.

Joanna smiled, looking anxious. "Well, aren't you going to tell me what happened, darling?"

"It's all rather difficult to explain. It happened so quickly. Gibson, the young marine, was hit and badly wounded. We lost touch with him, and he was reported missing, possibly dead. I found him later. Apparently, he had staggered from the border of Gold onto Omaha Beach. How it all happened, God alone knows. He met this American chap. For some unknown reason, the American thought Gibson was a priest. The poor chap was in a terrible state. According to Gibson, he had half his stomach shot to pieces." Terry paused again, staring at Joanna's shocked face. "Well, darling, I won't go into the gory details. The American wanted to confess his sins, and he managed to tell Gibson his name. He said, 'I've murdered'. Gibson was a bit confused and told him, 'Well, we've all been killing chaps, mate'. On his dying breath, the American just managed to whisper, 'Gravesend. Josh'. He was dead before he could say another word."

Joanna looked stunned. "What was his name?"

"Andy Romario."

"Dear God. It sounds unbelievable."

"Yes, it does. Except for the fact that it's true. I checked with Tom. The details given to him by the police fit that of Andy Romario's description. Apparently there was another chap involved. I don't know what happened to him, and I'm not bothered. The police have closed the case on Josh. We all knew he was a bastard, my darling. On the other hand, Andy Romario died fighting for his country."

"Yes," said Joanna, nodding her head in agreement. "Where is that lovely, young marine now, Terry?"

"I'm afraid he died later of sustained injuries."

Joanna put her hand to her mouth. She remembered his wistful look when she'd spoken to him about the future and children. "Oh my God." She faltered, trying to find her words. "How dreadful it all is."

"Yes, my darling. Gibson was truly an unsung hero. Just like Andy Romario and many more good men. But not only were they heroes to Britain, America, and the rest of the world, but moreover, Romario was Nina's true hero."

Joanna agreed. Holding her hands to her face, she paused. "That sweet marine. I shall always remember his words when he spoke to me. He said, 'They're only kids once. It's nice, at a time like this, for children to remember the simple things in life, and, after all, it's just a bunch of bluebells'. I remember his words made me feel quite ashamed for being so strict with Mary." There was a brief silence. Joanna murmured, "All those poor, young boys gone."

Terry looked down and nodded his head. He looked pained. Then he changed his expression, looking lovingly into her eyes.

"You've been in the front line too, my brave, little soldier."

She looked up at him. "Oh, Terry, war is so terrible. I thank God we still have one another. We haven't much money, but-"

He intercepted her and laid his index finger on her lips. "No. You were right the first time. We have each other, my darling."

Terry held Joanna lovingly in his arms. Kissing the top of her forehead, he closed his eyes as if in reverie.

Holding her close, he whispered, "And thank God you had Mary."

Mary, hiding on the balcony, had been eavesdropping every word that had been said. At that moment, she looked down into the street to watch Anna and Dora turn the corner carrying lighted torches.

They shouted up to her, "Hey, Mary, are you going to join us?"

Mary waved and nodded her head without saying a word. Then she gazed over her shoulder at her parents in each other's arms. And, once again, she thought she must be the luckiest girl in the whole wide world.

THE END

Epilogue

June 2009

By the time Mary had finished telling Bill of her experiences during the war, it was the morning. Neither had slept. The cognac bottle was empty. And two full plates of sandwiches had been whoofed down.

"My word. That's an extraordinary story, Mary. How on earth a child as young as you could possibly remember so much, it's incredible."

"Yes, isn't it a truly extraordinary story? Perhaps I should write it down," said Mary reflectively, and she gave him one of her mother's long, slow, signature smiles.

ENJOY THIS BOOK?
POP UP A REVIEW – FOR MUM'S SAKE!

I know Mum, the author of this book isn't around but as her daughter, I would love to see your thoughts on what you made of Mum's musings on her past in Wartime England.

Hopefully, the more reviews 'Bluebells' gets, the more sales it will secure, and most importantly, the more donations Dementia UK and Alzheimer's Society will receive from me as a result.

Please join me - make this book a bestseller and help to rid the world of dementia forever.

You can jump straight to the Review page on Amazon by visiting the link below.

https://geni.us/zEBBG6w

Printed in Great Britain
by Amazon

61209943R00163